A Deadly Sisterhood

A Murder Mystery

A Deadly Sisterhood

A Murder Mystery

B.K. De Paolis

MERANO WRITERS PRESS

LOS ANGELES

Cover design by Chris Askew

ISBN 13: 978-0692313435
ISBN 10: 069-2313435

Printed in the United States of America

Acknowledgements

The author would like to thank the following for their assistance with research and editing of this mystery.

Lt. Reginald L. Wright, Jr. *Los Angeles County Sheriff's Department, Retired*

Denise Bertone, *Los Angeles County Department of Coroner*

Det. Arthur Castro, *Los Angeles Police Department*

Jane Hallinger, *Pasadena City College, Professor of Creative Writing, Retired*

Sisters in Crime International, *Los Angeles Chapter*

Merano Writers Group *at Zephyrs, Pasadena*

Mary Walsten *Retired English Instructor*

Linda Burns, *Professor of Reading and Writing, Citrus College*

Mike Curran, *Professor of Writing, Citrus College*

Beverly Daniel, *MSN, NP, RN*

ONE

Night revealed LA at its grittiest: no sweet scent of night blooming jasmine, no soft, velvety grass, no breeze to stir the palm fronds. Here were only flat, hard-packed earth and stacks of lumber resting in beds of moldering wood chips giving off a scent of rancid resin. And the rain, when it fell, unobstructed from the heavens, left a damp, smoky residue on whatever uncovered wood it touched. A blaring siren crossing the 4th Street Bridge overwhelmed the other night sounds that went unheard or unheeded by those beneath its spans.

Manny Torres looked at his cell phone when he unlocked the heavy Master lock and unwound the length of chain on the gate of the new construction site. He couldn't believe the company had razed a perfectly good warehouse to build some shoddy lofts for the Anglos moving back into the city. Lofts were in, suburbs were out. As he struggled with the heavy chain link gate, he saw from the stream of his headlights that the workers had made little progress since he had been off work.

He parked his old Toyota pickup next to the foreman's trailer, got out, and turned on the overhead light attached to a white four-by-four makeshift pole that someone had haphazardly nailed to the side of the trailer. He limped over to the gate, relocking it with a key attached to a leather ring that he jammed back into his jean's pocket.

Manny clocked-in and took a few seconds to study his time card. Four days plus two hours were missing on this pay period. More beans and tortillas. He slipped the card back into the

1

rack, stepping over papers, and unrolled blue prints littering most of the floor of the dusty office.

Working as a security guard was a piece of cake. The nightly routine rarely changed: coffee and a sweet, then make the rounds. He kept an eye out for the homeless. They would drop over the fence to steal whatever wasn't nailed down: lumber, rusty nails, ripped tarps, any kind of building material to construct their makeshift hovels. Still, Manny understood. He'd been homeless a while back. Living beneath underpasses was no joke, but things were different now; he had a job to protect, and he had a paper in his shirt pocket that he'd memorized. The doctor wrote in an almost illegible script that Manny Torres had "incurred an injury to his left knee and needed to stay off his leg for a week." The note did not say that Manny, after drinking several six-packs with his homies, had stumbled and busted his knee playing soccer. Even with an excuse that no one would ask for, he knew he couldn't miss any more work.

A cheap plastic sports bag yawned open against the leg of his chair. Manny poured from a thermos and took out a large *pan dulce*, broke it in half, and dunked it into the hot coffee, watching large bits of crude sugar pieces float on top as he slowly raised the plastic cup to his lips and blew into the rising steam before sipping.

When he finished, Manny took a pack of Camels from his jacket pocket and lit one, then carefully reared his chair back against the metal wall of the trailer. He took longer enjoying his nightly ritual because of the pain in his knee. Inhaling deeply, he released a cloud of willowy circles that floated into nothingness overhead. The solitude was a blessing. He would take his time, maybe even make the circuit around the perimeter of the construction site twice instead of four times. If things stayed quiet, he would put his leg up and grab a nap.

Several blocks away Dixie, her mouth hanging open, a string of drool dripping to the ground, inched forward in excited anticipation.   As she waited, her tail beat a heavy cadence, anxious to be leashed and off. Dixie was impatient. She had things to see, to smell, to mark.

"Let's go!" The gruff command came after the heavy leash had been hooked into her choke chain.

They walked slowly, allowing Dixie to sniff the already malodorous sidewalk. She stopped to pee over a patch of yellowish-green grass, a rarity in this area. Dixie took her time, enjoying her few moments of freedom. She peed again at a light standard just to say "Dixie's been here."

They stood in the chilly darkness and peered through the heavy chain link fence, looking toward the trailer. Dixie's companion stared past the man and scanned the shadows. Feeling impatient, Dixie pulled until her choke chain cut through her brown fur and pressed painfully into her flesh. She growled but resisted pulling again.

"Stay!" Her companion jerked on the leash bringing her to attention.

Dixie let her disapproval rumble deep in her throat, then sniffed, barked, and fell silent. Finally, a door slammed and a narrow river of light slowly flowed away from the trailer.

A loosened chain allowed Dixie to edge closer to the fence and visually follow the movement away from the well-lit site. She whined and sat, realizing their adventure wasn't going any further.

Manny heard a dog bark followed by a pitiful whine as if someone had hurt the dog's feelings with a reprimand. Ignoring the outside intrusion, he flashed his light around the site, realizing that progress on the construction was almost at a standstill. He had heard there had been disagreements, and money was now tight. Jimmy Tran, the guy who usually worked in Manny's place when he was off, called and told him he had found another condo construction job over on First

Street. Maybe the rumors were true. This time, no one had been hired to replace him for the four nights he'd been out.

Well, not my fault if they rip the place off when I'm gone.

He kept his eyes on the hard-packed drive as he approached the dumpster but   stopped when he thought he heard something coming from that direction. There was only silence.

"*Chingada!*" The temporary light by the dumpster was out. He edged closer, directing his flashlight's beam around the base of the container and caught an odor so repulsive it stopped him in his tracks. *Ah, la chingada, Esta muerto.*

Finally, he took a few steps forward, then froze as the sickening stench gripped his stomach muscles, the contractions pushing the pan dulce back up into his throat. Manny caught his breath and swallowed hard, forcing the half-digested bread back down. Maybe someone had fallen in the dumpster and died. Maybe someone homeless, dead for days, rotting away amidst scraps of lumber and other debris.

El bastardo agarro lo como merecia.

Manny backed away from the dumpster to his sports bag and retrieved his cell phone. He started to dial 911, then picked up the bag, and walked to the truck. He put the key in the ignition, turning over the engine. He would call from a pay phone on the way home. That way no one would know who called. He thought he saw some movement in the street, then looked back at the dying fire he had made earlier. Shit! He forgot: no fires. He got out of the cab and emptied the remaining coffee from the thermos on it. Now he would have to take the can home.

The dog barked again. Manny jumped, remembering he had clocked in. Maybe whoever was walking the dog would know that someone was at the site. He took out his phone again and dialed 911.

"What's your emergency?" A tired voice asked.

"I think somebody in the dumpster."

"Is the person injured?"

"I didn't look." Pain shot through his knee and up his thigh. "Can you send somebody?"

"Could it be a dead animal?"

"No, it's different, the smell." The hairs on Manny's neck bristled.

"We're sending a unit. What's your address?"

"675 Croaker Street—it's a construction place."

Manny clicked off his phone and, now more aware of the pain, limped to open the gate.

Dixie panted and pulled on the slack leash. She wanted in.

"No, girl. Let's go!"

Dixie barked loudly when her companion jerked the chain as they moved away from the fence and trotted briskly in the direction from which they had come. As they melted into the gray night, a black-and-white with flashing lights and screaming siren pulled into the graveled parking lot.

Officer Todd Riley dragged his long legs from under the steering column and stretched to his full height. He adjusted his Sam Brown on his narrow hips, patting his gun to reassure its presence.

Riley's partner, Bob Carter, took his time following. Things had been slow on their shift.

Manny was surprised at the cruiser. He had asked for an ambulance and now he had to deal with a couple of cops. He limped over to close the gate.

"Are you okay?" Carter asked.

"I think maybe somebody fall in the dumpster." Manny pointed.

"Sure it's not an animal?" Riley asked.

Manny shook his head.

Carter hooked his hand in his belt. "You mean it's dead?"

5

"I can't climb up." Manny patted his left knee, grateful for an excuse.

With Maglites in hand, Carter and Riley followed the limping watchman toward the dumpster.

"Phew!" Carter turned his head away, taking shallow breaths through his mouth. "When did he fall in?"

Again, Manny shook his head. "I don't know."

Both cops moved closer to the dumpster. The stench, smelling like rotten pig, pushed them back a few steps. Something was indeed in the early stages of decay.

"Whoever fell in there smells like he's been there a while or hasn't bathed this century." Riley tried to mask his dread with humor, then looked around for something to climb on. His roving light settled on an empty nail keg that he pulled to the side of the dumpster. He stepped on it, careful to balance his weight before he lifted the metal lid.

Riley's flashlight bounced off the rim and fell in, sending an arc of light skyward. "Shit! Ohhhh, shit."

"What?" Carter demanded.

"Whoever it is, ain't going nowhere. We need to call the coroner's," Riley said.

"Is he dead?" Manny grabbed his throat.

"Looks like a woman." Riley put a hand to his nose.

"What's that noise?" Manny asked.

Riley stepped off the keg. "Rats! I think you got rats."

"Shit! My God, I hate rats!" Carter edged back from the dumpster.

Even clutching his throat, Manny could not still his churning abdomen. No amount of pressure could push down what was rumbling to the surface. He turned and stopped as he bent forward, placing his hands on his knees for balance. He gagged, then brought up his coffee, *pan dulce,* and hard little pieces of sugar.

TWO

Dina Goode stood in the outer office of the Hansen Modeling Agency, pocketed a ring of keys, and picked up several pieces of junk mail. She and her associates had recently debated changing the agency's name since Sybil's death. After all, they had a reputation to uphold, and they didn't advertise. Dina and several others voted against any name change.

There was no one behind the high walnut and chrome counter. Sindy, who ran the front office, was late as usual. Well, an unattended receptionist's desk didn't really matter. They had few walk-ins, maybe a naive young woman seeking an agent. She would be told that the agency was not taking on any new clients. Well, that was a lie. The Hansen Modeling Agency always welcomed new business: male, well-established, and well-heeled. With no one at the desk, the answering service would take any phone calls, directing most clients to desired or available escorts.

Still, Dina was in favor of replacing the metal on the counter that left the reception area looking cold and uninviting. It needed warm colors and flowers, but for whom? For me, Dina thought. If she was going to have to take care of the day to day operation of the business then she wanted a pleasant atmosphere. She leaned over the counter and found a clean slip of paper for a note but balled it up and tossed it in the trash. She would order the flowers before she left.

Dina looked around the two walls of head shots, glamour photos of some of the women they represented. She laughed at the idea and the display. These young beauties would never grace the cover of a legitimate magazine. If they had the body, one or two might make it in a spread of some adult magazine or pant and scream in fake ecstasy on someone's 50-inch plasma TV. There were also the few who used the easy cash to pay for college, then quickly got out of the business, hoping their clients remembered their bodies and their bedroom antics and not their faces.

Her picture in its gilded frame had hung among the head shots once when she was younger and stupid enough to think that someone would come in and select her for a photo shoot. Yet even with her good-looks, at five-seven she was too short to grace a serious runway.

She glanced at her image in the mirror that covered a side wall. Her curly auburn hair was smoothed back into a pony tail. Her flawless olive complexion was brightened by gold hoop earrings that barely touched the top of her green turtle-neck sweater. She brushed a fleck of brown mascara from her cheek. Out of habit she checked the rest of her eye make-up that enhanced her hazel eyes.

Dina had been described as exotic rather than beautiful by the few men who had seen her image smiling from her photo on the wall or who had called back to request her again. Now Dina's head shot was stored in the back closet, replaced by younger and even more enticing women, whose beauty or desirability had not been marred by a keloid scar across the throat, compliments of a deranged client.

Agonizing memories swept over her: a flash of cold steel, the pain, the blood, the deep, calming voice, those cold gray eyes, the warm, wet hand on hers. She shook her head. She still could not blot out the face of Detective Stas Nowak.

The assault and then the murder of her boss, Sybil, should have made her get out of the life. Instead, Dina was about to take over the management of The Hansen Agency, one of the most expensive and exclusive escort services in Hollywood. Their enterprise catered exclusively to men seeking the varied services of the world's oldest profession performed by some of the world's most beautiful and talented women. She nervously bit her lip. *It could all be good, if....*

Dina hesitated as she turned the knob and entered the inner office. She found Raven resplendent in brown leather pants, leopard-print top, and leopard four-inch pumps that brought her height to six feet three. Raven hadn't made it on the runway either. She wasn't black enough, or her features weren't African enough. So Raven with her "fuck you" attitude took her height, beauty, and talents down another road.

Since Sybil's death, Raven had taken on their European operation, and it was rumored that an agency in Asia, barring any local competition, was in the works. No doubt Dar Ling, if she got her act together, and if the deal went through, would go to Hong Kong to run it.

A half-full bottle of Merlot with three wine glasses set on a tray to Raven's left. She poured a glass and offered it to Dina before refilling hers again. An array of multicolored fabric swatches and small squares of carpet samples were arrayed on the mahogany conference table.

Dina pulled up one of the Queen Anne chairs and fingered the nubby texture of an African-inspired print. She raised one of the brown and black carpet squares to her nose. "Smells funny."

"We're going to be walking on it not screwing on it."

"Whatever." Dina looked around as she returned the swatch to the pile. "I didn't know you were planning to redecorate. I thought you were going back to Paris?" She ignored the wine.

"Aren't these old colors starting to get to you? Too many memories." Before Dina could respond, Raven pushed everything aside and looked intently at her. "Are you okay? You look tired."

"I'm fine. I just need a good night's sleep and maybe a massage. One always relaxes me, makes me sleep like a baby." She flexed her shoulders, cracking her neck in the process.

"Well, a good lay will do the same thing, if it's with the right man. I heard he can work wonders for your hormones."

Dina toyed with a couple of the samples.

"What's happening?" Raven asked.

"Nothing."

Raven gave her a questioning look.

"Nothing, really." Dina responded.

"I saw the discs in the vault. Where'd they came from?"

"They're our clients."

Raven frowned. "I know what they are. I want to know where they came from."

"Sybil's computer."

"I figured as much. How did you get them?"

"Stas gave them to me."

"What else?"

"What do you mean?" Dina reached for the wine and took a sip.

"Why did he take such an interest in Sybil?"

"It's a long, complicated story."

Raven sipped her wine. "I've got nothing but time."

"Well, for one, Sybil didn't commit suicide." Dina drained her glass. "She was murdered."

"Did they find her killer?"

"Stas figured it out, but...."

"What?"

"There wasn't enough evidence to use in court. Most of the stuff he found was too personal." Dina paused. "He found out Sybil was his half-sister."

They sat in silence for several minutes.

Finally, Raven spoke. "That's really some deep shit. What happened to her killer?"

"He met with an accident," another long pause, "like Matt."

Raven poured more wine. "Did your detective have anything to do with the accidents?"

Dina slowly shook her head. "I don't think so."

"But you're not sure?"

Dina didn't respond.

Raven reached for her wine, started to sip but changed her mind and swirled the liquid around in the bowl of the glass. "I'm curious. How did he react?"

"To what?"

"Finding out about Sybil."

"He was angry. Not mad. He held it in, the real anger, but I could see it in his face, especially his eyes, his jaw, like set really hard. If he'd gotten his hands on Tony, or whatever his name was, I think he would have killed him, but somebody beat him to it."

"Who's Tony?"

"The guy who shot Sybil, tried to made it look like suicide."

"Did Stas say anything afterwards?"

"Not much. He left, went to Chicago. It was the end of his vacation. I haven't seen him since."

"And you really think he's coming around after that?" Raven drained her wine, refilled her glass, then stacked paint chips. "If you're having second thoughts, I can get someone else, maybe Dar Ling."

"Are you serious? She couldn't run pantyhose! No, no, I'm doing it. Send her to Hong Kong. Keep her out of my hair." Dina straightened. " I need to do this. I need a change."

"Is this what you want or is it what he wants?"

"I...it doesn't matter. He's not in the picture...."

"Don't say I didn't warn you. They don't hang around."

"Yeah, I know. I should have listened."

"You miss him?" Raven dug into her oversized handbag for her silver cigarette case. "I guess I should rephrase that. Do you still lust after him?" She offered the open case to Dina who waved it away. "So what's the attraction, you find a man who gives better than he gets?" She smiled, hesitating a second before lighting up. She took a long drag and blew smoke toward the ceiling.

"I never heard him complain."

"He wouldn't." Raven took another deep drag, inhaling smoke into her lungs before exhaling. "He's not the type. He'd just move on."

"You knew him before."

Raven half-nodded. "It was a while back. We all knew who he was, but no one really knew him even though he worked Vice. He had other connections." She paused. "You've heard of Honey Malone?"

Dina nodded.

"Well, she's not supposed to be in the business any more, but she is, top drawer, low key. They're all beautiful young women, some of them working their way through grad school. You know the drill. Get in, make the quick bucks, get out. Honey was run out of Nashville, then Memphis, but not because of pandering. Seems she was involved with a cop, high up, deputy chief. They came here together after he retired from the Nashville PD. So she's turned her business into a boutique operation, catering to rich men from the South: oil, tobacco, and North Carolina finance."

"How do you know all this?"

"Gossip, plus Sybil talked about her as competition."

"So you're saying Stas was one of Honey's connections?" Dina asked.

"I've heard he knows her and her chief."

"But how could he afford being her client."

"A client? No, from what I heard, he helped her out of a jam. She just shows her gratitude. So if you didn't run into him, personally, you heard about him. The good old rumor mill."

"Was that about the time he busted Sybil?" Dina fanned smoke.

"Yeah! He was a little more needy then, hadn't learned so much self-control. Didn't know at the time who she was." Raven stubbed out her cigarette. "If he'd stayed in Vice, he could have been legend. But then, you know that."

Dina bit her lip. The question gnawed at her like a bad toothache. "Did you sleep with him?"

"No. He could've been sleeping around with some of our girls, but I doubt it. You know, boys will be boys. They always find a way and a woman with or without Honey Malone. Maybe it's time to give it up."

Dina looked puzzled. "Give what up?"

"Your fantasy, him, whatever you think is going to happen. He's not coming back. His vacation's over. He's back out there catching the bad guys. Speaking of that, did you see the news? They found a young woman in a dumpster the other night. No I.D. Paper said she was pretty and white. They're probably trying to find out who she was. She made the news again tonight with an artist's sketch."

"You don't think...." Dina shrugged her shoulders. "I can't believe she was on the street."

"What? You don't think one of ours could end up in a dumpster? If they find out she was an escort for any of us, you know the boys in blue will be all over us like white on rice." Raven paused. "Suppose they find out about you and your detective?"

"There's nothing to find out. It wasn't like that."

"No, then how was it? You want to explain that to some unsympathetic cop investigating the murder of a beautiful woman while he imagines you romping with one of his brother detectives in some sleazy motel."

"Stas is different."

"Isn't that always our excuse? Do you think the cops give a shit? He got what he wanted. Case closed. It never works anyway. We're always in denial." The bitterness was evident in her tone. "I know."

"What?"

"It's a long story. I'll tell you one night when I've had too much to drink, and I don't mind being reminded of the pain." Raven turned back to her fabrics. "So, are you still sure you want to take over this end of the operation? You know, you could find some rich old fart, be his trophy."

"Like I said, I'm ready for a change, but not with some grandfather." Dina shoved the mail to the center of the table.

"Besides, there's been a change. We're not going to Hong Kong. The Chinese kicked us out. But one official helped ease us into Thailand."

"What did you have to do for that, sleep with him?"

"Not that simple." Raven smiled. "He wanted an off-shore account in the Grand Caymans.... Plus..."

"What was that like?"

"Like trying to get off using a Vienna sausage." Raven laughed and wiggled her pinkie. "But if you change your mind, you can go to Bangkok."

Dina shook her head.

Raven continued. "Aren't you part Thai?"

"Who told you that?"

"Sybil."

Dina played with some of the fabric samples. "I don't consider myself Thai. My grandmother was. My opa married her when he was in the Merchant Marines. He met her over there, married her, and brought her to Milwaukee. But she didn't like it over here, and his family didn't like her, so after she had my mother, she went back."

"Without her baby?"

"She left her here since she didn't look Asian. I think they paid her off. I was told she came from a poor family. It's like she went back rich."

"You think she was in the business?" Raven asked.

"No one ever said. I wondered. Opa was good looking: blonde, blue-grey eyes, very German. My mother identified with all things German. Learned to cook all the dishes, but she was a little unhappy with me 'cause I was a little too tan. She blamed it on her mother, until she learned my father was passing, had been when she married him."

Raven nodded. "Well, if you decide to go, maybe you can look up your grandmother."

"I have no idea where she is, and I have no desire to go to Asia. The only connection I have with anything Thai is the food."

THREE

Lupe, a pretty young Salvadorian, pushed her dark hair out of her face and busied herself at the off-white marble counters of the spotless cream and stainless steel kitchen. She looked up when her employer, Mona Talbott, dragged in, wiping sweat from her face with a dish towel before taking a fresh bottle of water from the pantry. She stood in the doorway and watched Lupe work, then drank most of the bottle without taking a breath.

"You can get the girls up now. Did you make their lunches?" Mona asked. She was in her mid-thirties, blonde, about five-feet six, with a perfect body that she worked at keeping that way. Mona was not beautiful, but attractive, and she used every trick in the beauty book and then some to enhance her looks. She had done well as a trophy wife. Her husband, Ryan Talbott, Jr., was the only child and heir of Ryan Talbott, Sr., the late owner of Talbott Ice and Cold Storage. The company had been in the family for decades, and old man Talbott had made a fortune. Before he died, he had established a healthy trust fund for Mona, her reward for continuing the Talbott line with two almost copycat off-springs. Plus, the trust money hadn't been tied to Ryan's pre-nuptial agreement.

She stood by the sink after finishing her water and tossed the empty bottle onto the counter.

"Lupe, we have to change your day off. I need you to stay with the girls tonight."

Lupe frowned as she wiped a water spot off the marble counter before going up the back stairs to get Heather and Susan ready for school.

16

"I'm sorry for the short notice, but I'll make it up to you." Mona called after Lupe.

The Talbott mansion was located in one of those old gated estates in the Hollywood Hills. The younger Talbotts had lived there for three years, moving in after the death of the senior Talbott and the completion of extensive renovations on his house. The children had outgrown or intimidated their last two nannies, so nine months ago Lupe came to take care of them and the house, with occasional relief from a local cleaning service.

They attended the Spenser Country Day School in Sherman Oaks. Usually, when Ryan was home, he took the girls to school, then doubled back to his office in LA. Now Lupe, who had recently gotten her driver's license, was entrusted with chauffeuring the girls to and from school or dropping them off for various after school activities when the parents were busy.

Ryan Talbott entered the kitchen, set his briefcase on the counter, and poured a cup of coffee from a stainless steel carafe before picking up the *LA Times* and turning to the Sports Section. His lean frame sported the latest men's fashions. Some women liked his pale good looks, his platinum blonde hair thinning slightly in the center, and his cornflower blue eyes that seemed darker under his tinted contacts.

Mona watched him in silence as he drank his coffee and read. They had everything, and more was promised with the sale of some prime LA real estate when the market picked-up. Ryan was patient. He had enough money to wait out most financial storms.

"Don't be surprised if the police come calling." He spoke without looking up.

"About the girl they found in the dumpster?" Mona asked.

Ryan nodded. "Paul's in Cabo, and I'll be gone for three or four days finalizing the sale of some land we've got to unload. So if they can't reach us, they might want to talk to you."

She smiled. "Well, that might be fun for a change. I've never been interviewed by a detective. They would send a detective, wouldn't they?" She took several sips from a new bottle of water before dropping it into the sink. "Someone like those handsome ones on *Law and Order*, not some uniformed cops."

"Don't get cute with the police. Just tell them I'll be back if they call. Otherwise, Molly can talk to them."

"How can Paul manage anything if he's not here. Why is he in Cabo, anyway?"

"He was supposed to sign some papers today. If everything went well, he's gone fishing."

"He should be here. We can't sell lofts if they aren't built, and we can't make any money if we have nothing to sell."

Ryan folded his paper. "You're right, but I'm trying to hold off on the sale of the final piece."

"Why? That's just wasting time and losing money."

"I've been thinking about a micro-brewery. We could make a lot more money and not have to worry about the real estate market."

She frowned. "You'd still have to sell the beer."

"Everybody loves beer, and it would be a lot more fun. I'm going to do some checking while I'm in Phoenix. See if they can light a fire under the investors to hurry with their end of the cash." He fingered his keys and grabbed his briefcase. "I hope that girl's death doesn't dampen their interest."

"Why can't Frank handle the police?"

"He's got a lot on his plate, especially monitoring demolition. We don't need to drag him into this. I have some calls to make before I leave. Send the girls in when they're ready." He gave her an indifferent peck on the cheek. "I'll see you in a couple of days."

Mona stared after him, glad she didn't have to play the loving little wife, glad she now had financial independence, with the prospect of more to come. She picked up the front section of the paper, scanning it. "Do they know who she is yet?" she asked the paper.

Mona changed into black and white designer pants and top before coming back to the kitchen. She laid a list on the counter.

Lupe turned from the sink and looked, unsmiling, at the paper before drying her hands and picking it up. "Miss Mona, Mr. Frank called while you were out running."

"Why didn't you tell me before?"

"You in the shower." Her soft voice almost a whisper.

Mona frowned as she looked at the counter under the wall phone. "Where is the message?"

"He say 'no message.' He call back later."

"I told you to always take a message. Are you sure you understood him?"

"He say...."

Mona threw up her hands. "Damn it! Just forget...." She jumped when the doorbell began its loud and lengthy chime. "I'll get it."

Before she could reach the front entrance, a man knocked on the French door off the patio. "Frank!" Mona turned abruptly.

She smiled and opened one of the doors to Frank Seno, a muscular five foot ten with receding light blonde hair, intelligent green eyes, and a ready smile. Frank had worked for Talbott Storage since he'd come from the Midwest twelve years before. Now he worked for B & T Construction although his job description was somewhat dubious.

He moved with familiar ease into the house. "Have Ryan do something about that front gate. Anybody can get in. You could use a dog. Nothing like loud barks to let you know you got company." He brushed Mona's lips with a warm kiss. "How about making me some coffee?"

Mona looked at Lupe. "Will you get Frank coffee? He likes it strong. If there's none left, make some but don't use decaf." She turned back to Frank. "I don't see how anyone drinks that stuff."

Lupe stopped what she was doing at the sink and poured from the fancy carafe. Mona grabbed two bottles of water and held one out to Frank who waved it off. Lupe gave him a steaming mug. He took it, letting his fingers linger on hers ever so briefly.

"Thanks, Lupe." He winked before turning his attention back to his hostess.

"I've told Ryan several times about the catch on the front gate. He couldn't care less. He thinks I should call the men who did the renovations and have them fix it." She put one hand on her hip and downed the bottle of water. "I'm not sure about a dog, unless you have one that doesn't shit." She laughed. "I'm not into pooper-scooping." She looked toward Lupe. "She already has enough to keep her busy."

"We'll talk about it later. I'll work on the gate the next time I come over." He looked Mona over. "Where you off to?"

"The gym and some shopping."

"Don't you have enough stuff?"

"I can never have enough of anything. You should know that."

Frank moved to sit on a stool at the island counter. "You want me to pick up the girls?"

"Would you? Take them some place fun and don't forget to feed them."

"Where's Ryan?"

"He says he has to go to Phoenix on business. I'll be glad when this is all over. I want him to buy me a condo in Hawaii."

"Why? He'll never go. He loves the LA scene too much."

"I said 'buy me.' If he doesn't want to go, then I'll take you."

"What about the girls?"

"Oh, I'll take them too, but I'll need a nanny." She sighed. "So much for my wish list." She sat on a stool next to Frank and ran her fingers up his arm, massaging under his rolled up shirt sleeve, revealing part of an elaborate tat, a woman's long, shapely legs entangled in leafy vines trailing down his arm. "Lupe's staying over while Ryan's gone."

"So you're free tonight?"

"For you, any night."

"One of these days you're going to get caught up in your intrigues."

"Yeah, but not tonight!"

Early the next morning, Frank's black Escalade was parked in the drive near the front entrance of the Talbott home. He had been working on the gate for over an hour. Although the air had a slight chill to it, small beads of perspiration dotted his brow. Parts of the electronic mechanism that opened and closed the gates and supposedly secured entrance to the estate were spread out on newspapers on the ground. Raw wires protruded from an opening in one of the columns that flanked the driveway.

He looked at his watch as Mona, wearing all black sweats, stopped on the lawn by the SUV and began her stretches.

"You're getting started a little late." He returned to his work, squatting over an assortment of parts.

"So I slept in. Don't you think I deserve to indulge myself?" She jogged in place. "I had a good time. Will you still be here when I get back?"

"Why, did I forget to finish something last night?" He looked up from his work.

Mona wasn't smiling. "I don't know. Did you?"

Frank wiped his hands on a greasy rag but didn't respond. "I'm supposed to stop by the office and get the paperwork on the demolition. Paul wants me to set it up, but I promised the girls I'd take them to Griffith Park after school. I don't get to sleep in, even when the boss is away."

"Yes, but just think of all the fun you've been having."

He started toward Mona, when two girls, five and seven, in Barbie night gowns and bare feet, bolted out of the house, leaving Lupe standing in the front doorway, a look of disapproval on her face.

"Heather, Susan, come back, please." Lupe called after them. "You got to get ready for school."

The girls ignored her and tried to climb up into Frank's arms. He was caught off balance but managed to hold himself upright by releasing Heather, the older of the two.

Mona shouted back to Lupe who had not moved from her vigilant post. "They're all right. They can stay out here while you fix breakfast."

Frank played with Heather's unruly curls while Susan clung to his neck. When his hand was free, Heather grabbed it in a sisterly duel for his attention.

"Frank, smell my hair."

He buried his nose in her blonde head and inhaled. "It smells sweet like strawberry shortcake. Did you rub strawberries in your hair?"

She drew back to look at him and giggle. "No, silly. It's strawberry shampoo."

Ten minutes later Lupe reappeared at the front door and shouted, "Come eat!"

Frank escorted the girls to the entrance and tried to transfer Heather's hand to Lupe's.

"Fra-nk, Fra-nk!"

Lupe grabbed Susan and put her down, and Frank finally managed to hand the other sister over.

"Breakfast is ready." Lupe looked at her watch. "It's late."

The usual tug-of-war was avoided as Frank gave Heather a pat on her bottom. The distraction allowed Lupe to jerk the child into the foyer and slam the door.

"She's such a bitch." Frank turned back to his repair work.

Mona looked away from the house. "She doesn't like you, but then, she doesn't know you like I do."

"I'm going to bring some chain-link for the dog run tomorrow."

"You're serious about this dog?"

"Yep."

"You still haven't told me who's going to clean up after him, feed him. Remember, I don't do dog."

"It's a she. Anyway, that's why you have Lupe."

"I think you're using this dog thing as an excuse." She started to do some leg stretches.

"An excuse for what?"

"To come over, hang out with me and the girls." She headed through the opened gates.

"I didn't think I needed an excuse. Have a good run." He shouted after her.

She waved as she jogged into the narrow street.

Frank was putting his toolbox away when the girls, wearing their navy and black-watch plaid uniforms, walked out of the house still munching their frosted Pop-Tarts.

Heather held hers derisively with two fingers. "Breakfast. You want some?"

He smiled, waving off the offer.

"Are you taking us to school?" Susan asked.

Lupe stood in the doorway, waiting for his answer.

FOUR

Chris Marlowe stood by the door of the captain's office waiting for Stas Nowak, fellow detective with the Robbery/Homicide Division at Parker Center. The forty-four year old Marlowe cut an imposing figure in his highly polished, hand-tooled cowboy boots that added another inch or so to his six-foot-three frame.

The detective's love of all things Western was not a mere affectation; they had, in fact, become his trademark which was the more puzzling since Marlowe was black with smooth, milk chocolate coloring and flecks of white in his close-cropped black hair. Marlowe had, since his youth, followed the rodeo circuit from Robbins, Illinois, where as a teen, he participated in his first bull riding event. After a stint with the Navy and before joining the LAPD, he did a few shows with the Bill Picket Rodeo in Southern California.

Lieutenant Boyer usually conducted most routine briefing, but Captain Moore decided to take this one and sent Detective Nowak to find Boyer, not always an easy task since he was often summoned to the sixth floor where he was being groomed as an articulate and empathetic spokesman for the LAPD. He could often be seen on local TV putting a favorable spin on the Chief's point of view. And the fact that he was one of the department's golden boys who looked and dressed the part was not lost on rank and file police officers.

While waiting, Marlowe glanced at his partner, Ben Jonson, who busied himself with a new murder book. He had been married for over a month but still looked like a newlywed, nervously toying with his unfamiliar gold wedding band. Marlowe wondered how long the euphoria of matrimonial bliss would last. After-all, this was Jonson's third trip to the altar. Marlowe would miss hanging out with his partner. They certainly were opposites: black and white, six-three and five-ten, plus, Jonson eagerly acknowledged that he had no great love for anything equine. He would rather bet on a horse than ride one, and now he was married. Well, Marlowe had no intention of traveling down that road again.

Jonson looked over to his partner. "Why's the Captain giving the briefing?"

"I guess we'll find out soon enough."

Captain Moore stepped to the door of the squad room. "Marlowe, get in here. Nowak just called. He's on his way down."

The detective reluctantly headed into the office, dreading being trapped there, trying to breathe through the pall of gray smoke that hung like a barrier that miraculously never escaped into the squad room. What seemed like an act of sorcery was, in reality, the Captain's air purifier, a gift from his overworked secretary, who often threatened to report him for blatantly disobeying department rules on not smoking. When she threatened, help magically appeared until her workload diminished, then the threat was withheld until another day.

"Pull up a chair." Moore waved a lit Cuban cigar, confiscated by an old buddy at LAX's Customs Office. No one knew how these premium smokes turned up in the humidor in his closet, and no one ever investigated.

Marlowe eyed the pair of hard chairs in front of the captain's desk. Moore was famous for his hard-ass chairs and loved to watch his detectives squirm trying to get comfortable.

Within minutes Nowak entered, quietly closed the door, and took a seat next to Marlowe. "The Lieutenant's not coming."

"Don't worry 'bout it." Moore looked toward Marlowe. "One of you can bring him up to speed later."

Stas Nowak had recently returned from a long overdue, take-it-or-lose-it vacation. He had planned to do some of the things he had never found time for while working, but the time off had not been restful or productive as vacations go. Most importantly he had needed to come to grips with turning forty. It had been a strange several weeks, when the discovery of family secrets had shaken him to his previously unshakable core.

"Nice suit, Stas." Moore laughed than coughed. "Did you see Boyer's new threads? I think he had on navy too. You two, I don't get it."

But Marlowe knew that Stas got it. He wore an impeccably tailored suit, a meticulously laundered snow white Egyptian cotton shirt, and an Italian silk tie in silver and blue stripes. He hadn't forgotten the sartorial image that he felt, more than ever, had to be maintained.

With his years on the LAPD, he had never been saddled with a nickname. Since people tended to murder his Polish surname, Nowak, trying to pronounce the "W" as a W and not a V, he was just Stas, charming but distant. His rakish good-looks came with an unspoken warning that kept many from delving too deeply into his business. He could beguile witnesses, especially females, with a hint of old world magnetism, but his beguiling nature had failed with his ex-wife. His divorce, early in his law enforcement career, left him with extra time to develop into an outstanding police officer, pursue a few women, drive his sports car, and practice on his sax.

The two detectives looked at each other and waited for the Captain to begin.

Moore hacked. Nothing came up, but they could hear the phlegm rattling like a loose cannon in his chest. "We ID'd the woman found in the dumpster. Disappeared on a modeling gig to Vegas. This is a very cold case that needs closing. She's Cyn ..." He cleared his throat. "Cynthia Lenox, the daughter of the late Judge Harold Lenox."

"Didn't he shoot himself, what five, six years ago?" Marlowe asked.

"More like seven years next month, a year after his daughter went missing," Moore added.

"Then where's she been all this time?" Stas asked.

"That's what we'd like to know, and that's what you ladies are going to find out. The Chief's made this a top priority and said to put my best on it." He looked back at the file, then up again. "You are my best, right?"

As if by magic, Moore produced a pack of Marlboros, shook one out, and took a kitchen match from his top desk drawer, striking it with his thumbnail. He flinched when the flame erupted singeing an already badly stained finger. The smoking match left a strong smell of sulfur in the air. He took a deep drag, then tried to fan the small vapor trail towards the air purifier.

There was an awkward silence as the captain smoked the cigarette down half way, leaving a gray tube of ash that refused to fall.

"Is there something else?" Marlowe asked.

"Yes, dammit!" Moore scowled. "There's Crum."

"Crum? You mean Judge Crum?" Now it was Stas's turn to feel discomfort as he shifted his weight in the hard seat.

Marlowe looked anxious. "How did Judge Crum get involved?"

Moore stubbed out his butt in a small paper plate on his desk and hacked into his fist. "He and Lenox attended the same law school. They clerked together. Crum was Cynthia's godfather. The families were about to announce her engagement to his son, Robert, before she disappeared."

"If she was getting engaged, then why was she running off to Vegas? Doesn't seem like she was planning to marry or settle down any time soon," Marlowe interjected.

"Is this the source of the heat from downtown?" Stas asked.

Moore nodded as he contemplated another cigarette but seemed to think better of lighting up. Everyone in the department knew the captain didn't like taking heat. It galled him, and he took it out on those around him.

"Crum wants to be kept up-to-date on the investigation, and he doesn't want you talking to his son. Any questions that might involve his family need to be directed to my lieutenant, me, or his office."

Now it was Marlowe who sounded annoyed. "You mean any question about Junior? He can't compromise our investigation."

"That's why you're on the case. Give Crum a wide berth. If you dig up anything too sensitive, run it by me first. Then we'll..." Moore put the pack of cigarettes back in the desk drawer, "see what we have." He passed a file to Marlowe. "Give this to Jonson for the book and get back to me ASAP."

Both detectives rose instinctively.

"Keep a close rein on your partners, especially yours, Stas. I don't need any loose cannons. Keep'em away from the press. No interviews, no comments. Boyer will conduct any media briefings."

Marlowe whispered as he closed the door behind him. "Somebody's got to turn him in before he burns the place down."

Stas looked at the ceiling. "I doubt that. We're outta here soon. Anyway, they got enough sprinklers around."

Stas and Marlowe returned to their desks in the squad room.

"So what was that all about?" Jonson asked.

"Don't worry about it for now." Marlowe handed his partner several copies of information on Judge Lenox and his daughter, plus a grainy DMV photo of the vic. "Stas, you and Edwards..." He looked over to an empty desk. "Where is your partner?"

"He had to go to school about one of the kids."

"Hmmmm. Well, you guys need to check on the grandmother. She's in some upscale nursing home. Jonson and I'll visit the cousin and B & T Construction."

Stas quickly glanced over the sheet. "Yeah, while you're there ask'em how the body got through the locked gate and into the dumpster."

Marlowe watched Nowak, always the loner, always looking for clues, for reasons, yet never revealing his hidden desires or deeply embedded secrets. Maybe these were some of the traits that made him one of the best detectives in the squad. "I'm going out." He picked up his gray Stetson, brushed off the brim, and headed for the door.

"Where to, Texas?" Jonson asked, with a broad smile.

The detectives broke for lunch early. Marlowe and Jonson headed for beef dips at Philippe's. Stas went to Little Tokyo for sushi and got back to his desk just as his partner came in. They acknowledged each other with a nod but said nothing. Stas would have to brief his partner sooner or later, but it was taking time for him to fall back into the rhythm of things ever since he returned from his three week vacation. He had spent Christmas in the office and New Years with a new bottle of Chopin for company. He felt distracted, sleeping too little, drinking too much.

He looked at Jonson, talking to the others about his honeymoon in Mexico. Then Stas glanced at his own partner. He wouldn't call Edwards happy, more like content with his lot. He might as well be. It wasn't going to get any better. At least he hadn't strayed. He was still with wife number one. Stas even doubted if Edwards had ever been tempted, or if he would know a seductive ploy if some hot chick dropped a bra and thong in his lap and invited him to life's old dance. Then images of Dina standing in a pool of silky undies made him wonder if he would ever have what Jonson and Edwards had: wife, family, a mainstream existence. Well, if nothing else, a complicated murder would certainly bring him back to reality.

Stas sat at his desk and began carefully reading his section of the file. The first pages gave a brief family history. The

Judge's wife had died from cancer when Cynthia was five, and Lenox had raised his only child, alone, except for help from a string of nannies and maids until she was in her late teens. He never remarried but devoted his life and career to his daughter. She attended college in Claremont and returned to LA after graduation where she took a job with an advertising agency.

When she turned twenty-five, she got the acting bug but decided to give modeling a try first on the advice of one of the Judge's close friends. Cynthia could have been in demand with her wholesome all-American good looks, long blonde hair, blue eyes, pale skin, but she was too short for any serious modeling. Cynthia Alexandra Lenox would have to settle for print. Stas stared at what had once been a lovely face and wished he could talk to her over a cup of coffee, have her tell him her side of the gruesome tale, her journey from fashion runway to dumpster.

Instead, he had to settle for the cold, impersonal file in front of him. Cynthia disappeared on her way to a modeling workshop in Las Vegas. The trail went cold somewhere between LA and Baker.

Her Toyota Celica with keys still in the ignition was found abandoned in the desert off the shoulder of the road to Death Valley. The car was clean. The police found nothing, no luggage, no prints, no tire tracks of another car, nothing. There was no sign of foul play. Cynthia had just vanished into the warm desert air, all traces of her existence swept clean by desert wind. Now her body turns up eight years later in a dumpster near the train yards. Where had she been all these years? Had she returned to the LA area? Was she abducted in the desert? All of these questions would have to be answered.

Jonson was the first to read the preliminary coroner's report which indicated that Cynthia Lenox had died from an overdose of heroin, yet there was no evidence that she had been a user. The coroner found no needle tracks anywhere on her body, only the one needle puncture behind her ear. There was also evidence that she had given birth by C-section, and they had found traces of milk in her mammary glands. So what had happened to the infant?

"Where's the rest of the report?" Jonson fanned through the file.

There was a note written in pencil above the "cause of death."

Stas stood and moved to look over Jonson's shoulder. "What's wrong?"

Jonson lifted off a yellow post-it. "Smith, who in hell is this Howard Smith? Says 'full report forthcoming pending results of tests on tissue samples.' How long is that going to take?"

Stas shook his head. "Must be another new ME. Don't hold your breath. They'll get it to us when they're ready. They don't give a damn about our investigation."

Edwards listened and read but did not contribute to the discussion, trying to get up to speed as soon as possible.

Earlier, before settling in at his desk, Stas had dropped his jacket over the back of his chair and rolled up his sleeves. Now, before leaving for their first interview, Edwards jingled the keys of the department's Crown Victoria in anticipation.

"You ready?" It was then that he noticed the new Tag Heuer on Stas's wrist. "That's not a fake!"

Stas grabbed his jacket, fixed his shirt sleeves, depriving his partner of a chance to scrutinize the watch further.

Edwards would not be put off. "How much did that set you back?"

Stas didn't answer, but straightened his jacket and cuffs as they walked to the elevator.

"I don't understand how you do it. I wonder how I'm going to pay for high school sports let alone, college. You always got something new: car, clothes, and now that watch. I've seen them in magazines. I know how much they cost."

"Your problem, Sid, is you've got a wife and kids to support. That's where your money goes. What would you say if I told you it was a gift?"

Edwards stopped for a second. "Shit, you're lying. Who would give you something like that?"

They got in the crowded elevator.

But Edwards would not be put off. "What did you have to do for it? You know any kinds of favors are against police policy?"

"I know that, Sid." Stas just smiled as they reached the car and got in.

FIVE

Because of heavy traffic, the trip from downtown LA to San Marino took forty minutes. During the ride Stas tried to block out the litany of Sid's problems: gophers eating flower bulbs, the kids' crooked teeth needing costly braces, his wife harping about going to work.

"What can she do?" Stas finally asked.

"What?"

"What kind of work can Jill do? Does she have any skills?" Stas asked again.

The question seemed to break a spell, bringing Edwards back to reality. "For God's sake, she's a housewife. She takes care of me and the children. That's what she's trained to do."

"How does she feel about that?"

"I don't care. I finally told her so. Sometimes I just have to put my foot down."

"Did that shut her up?" Stas asked.

"Not really. She just changed her tune. Now she wants to go back to school."

"That sounds promising."

"Yeah, but she wants me to help more, with the kids, with the house. I don't have time for that!" Edwards frowned and made a quick lane change almost cutting off a pick-up.

"What did she say?"

"'Tough', said if I wasn't there, she'd get a sitter. Why do you think I made the move?"

Stas looked over at his partner. "What move was that?"

"From a desk to detective. Did you know that I had the highest score on the detective exam?" Edwards smiled broadly. "I kick butt on tests."

"You got me there. So what about Jill going to work or school?"

"I told you. I put my foot down."

They exited the 10 Freeway and drove through a section of Alhambra that looked as if they'd been transplanted to Hong Kong.

"I don't know. If she finds something, it's more money going out. We'll need child care," Edwards continued.

"I'm sorry I asked." Stas turned his attention to the passing scenery as they moved into San Marino: lush green lawns, yards with roses in profusion, stately old oaks with tops stretching across the wide streets to embrace in a full canopy of intertwining foliage.

They continued through a residential area before pulling into a wide drive blocked by a tall wrought iron double gate. The Belvedere Senior Retirement Home was located on a carpet of greenery and blooms that made it look more like a luxury hotel than a repository for the elderly and infirm.

"I hate these places. My grandmother died in one."

"Looks okay to me." Stas got out of the car, walked around to the intercom set into a brick wall, and pushed the buzzer.

When a voice came through, he identified himself and briefly stated their business. Slowly the iron gates swung inward. They drove up a short, curved driveway and parked. At the entrance Stas rang another bell. The door was answered by a matronly redhead who was in need of a good touch-up. Her brassy permed hair drained her already sallow complexion, but her smile was infectious.

Both detectives produced IDs. Her plastic name tag read "C. Miller."

"How may I help you, detectives?"

Edwards read from a slip of paper. "We'd like to see Mrs. Judith Rathbone."

The smile faded as Ms. Miller rolled her eyes up to the ceiling. "She's upstairs."

Edwards and Stas also looked upward as if Judith Rathbone were suspended from the sparkling crystal chandelier.

"Is she dead?" Edwards asked.

Stas wanted to kick him but smiled weakly at Ms. Miller.

"You'll have to see Mrs. Cox. She's the only one who can authorize you going upstairs."

They fell in behind her as she marched them to Mrs. Cox's office. The sign on the door read DIRECTOR. Ms. Miller tapped lightly.

"Come in." The voice on the other side was deep and warm.

"These detectives are here from the Los Angeles Police to see Mrs. Rathbone."

She held the door for Edwards and Stas to enter an elegantly appointed office in earth tones and oak trim, then closed the door behind them.

Stas had expected, from the voice, another middle-aged woman with hair pulled back into a tight bun, wearing a severely cut mannish suit and old-lady oxfords, someone from an Agatha Christie novel. The Director was a far cry from Miss Marple as she came from behind her desk wearing a navy skirt that stopped just above the knees. He noticed the swell of full breasts, then looked into a pleasant face framed by a stylish shoulder-length hair cut. Stas took a quick glance at shapely legs in smart navy pumps. So much for the stodgy British matron stereotype.

"What can I do for you?" she asked.

"We'd like to see Mrs. Rathbone," Edwards requested.

The Director looked both men over. "What's your business with her?"

"We were told we had an appointment" Stas looked at his watch, "at one."

"No one cleared anything with me." She frowned. "We are very careful about our guests on the second floor."

"We're investigating the death of her granddaughter." Stas smiled and looked for a wedding ring on her finger.

"Which granddaughter?"

Stas caught a flicker of warmth or maybe sympathy. "Judge Lenox's daughter, Cynthia."

"The one who's been missing? I've heard about her."

"Yes." He relaxed his stance and looked directly into large brown eyes.

"I thought she had gone away." Her smile was ever so slight. "There were post cards." She shook her head. "Where did they find her?"

"In a dumpster." Edwards blurted out.

Mrs. Cox recoiled at Edwards' bluntness.

Stas stepped closer to the young director. "How long has Mrs. Rathbone been here?"

"I'm not certain, about twelve years. Before I came."

The trio moved toward the office door.

"How long have your been here, Ms. Cox?" Stas paused for a second to see if she reacted to the change in his address.

"I've been director here for two years."

"And before that?"

"I worked at a facility in Claremont." She grabbed her suit jacket from a coat tree by the door, but before she could struggle into it, Stas took it and held it for her. "Thanks." Her smile widened. "Come with me."

As she passed ahead, to escort them, Stas caught a faint scent of roses. It was light and fresh, a welcome change from his partner's Old Spice that was always overdone. Something about Ms. Cox's perfume triggered a sensuous memory.

"Which way?" Edwards asked.

"The door on your left. Wait here." She walked to a door on her right and returned with a tall, buxom woman in a blue print nurse's smock and white pants. "Pat will take you up." She stepped back and addressed the attendant. "Bring them back to my office when they finish. I need their cards." She turned and walked into a large open dining room.

Pat unlocked a heavy grated security door that opened onto a flight of stairs. "We house our Alzheimer patients on the second floor."

Edwards followed closely behind. "You lock'em in twenty-four/seven?"

Pat turned on the stair. "If you don't, they're outside, running around, stripped down to their Depends."

"Depends?"

"Adult diapers, it's not a pretty sight."

There was another door at the top of the stairs. Pat pushed a button on the wall. They heard a bell sound on the other side. In seconds, the door was opened by a tall, muscular male attendant. "This is Joe. These detectives want to see Mrs. Rathbone."

The upstairs facility, while orderly and clean, was more Spartan in its furnishings and decorations than the area they had left downstairs. Here they were bombarded with layers of smells: disinfectant, room fresheners, colognes and perfumes, food scents both fresh and stale.

The detectives were led into a large day room with tables, chairs, and a big screen TV suspended from one wall. Several patients sat around a table talking, but on closer observation, they were not holding a conversation with each other but just talking to themselves. Two men slept in their wheelchairs in front of the TV where a cook on the Food Channel droned on about making a quick meal using chicken. Stas was suddenly aware that no one was watching, yet the voice on the screen seemed to have some pacifying effect on those in the room. He realized that television was forever being used to baby-sit or calm even the elderly and demented. Joe's voice interrupted Stas's thoughts. He turned.

"She's over by the window." He pointed to an elderly woman sitting in a straight-back chair, one hand poised on the walker next to her, the other hand fingering mother-of-pearl rosary beads as she stared vacantly out the window.

Stas stood behind her to see her frame of reference in the tranquil garden below.

"You're in luck. She's having a good day." Joe leaned down speaking slowly and softly. "Judy, you have company. Let me turn you around." With little effort, he repositioned her chair.

Even in old age, Judith Rathbone was still a beautiful woman. Her hair was cut short, its wispy whiteness framing a lovely face that had, somehow, escaped the ravages of declining years. Her complexion was fairly smooth; her eyes, when she looked up, were a slate gray that seemed to delight in some internal dialogue rather than in her surroundings. However, the hands that fingered the rosary had not fared as well as her face. They were gnarled with arthritis and discolored with brown age spots. Stas wondered if the aging process, even the dementia, had settled in the weak, vulnerable, and internal parts of the body and left the outer shell to grapple with existing as best it could. She wore gray sweats and a pair of knitted pink house slippers and smiled when Stas stooped to be on her level.

He spoke slowly. "Judy, I'm Stas. How are you?" He took her hand from the walker and held it in his, surprised at how cold the fingers were that gripped his.

"I'm fine. How are you, young man?" Then she looked around and saw Edwards. Her smile broadened. "There's another one to see me? Are they friends of Hal?"

"Her late son," Joe turned from Stas then back to Judy. "These gentlemen want to ask you about your niece."

"Sara?"

Joe looked over to Edwards.

"No, Cindy, Hal's daughter." Stas replied.

"I had a postcard from her." Judy tried to lift herself from her chair, then fell back against the square pillow at her back.

Both detectives looked at each other.

"Do you still have the postcard, Judy?" Stas asked.

"Of course, I have everything."

Joe released the brake on Judy's chair and led the little procession to her room. Edwards walked on the other side.

Pat followed behind with Stas. "See how she just lit up?"

"You sure it's not the drugs?" Stas took another look around the room at the other patients.

"She likes men. All the old ladies do. I work up here sometimes as relief. They don't give me the time of day, but they love Joe. He gets a lot more out of them than I ever can."

"And the men?" Stas asked.

"They'll rub up against the female attendants, try to grab a breast, or fondle your butt if they think you're distracted. I had one guy drop his sweat pants once but couldn't undo the tabs on his diaper." Pat laughed.

Mrs. Rathbone shared a room with another elderly woman who followed Pat to the room. The roommate shyly watched from the side of her bed and applied lipstick she pulled from her sweater pocket. She edged closer, lightly rubbing Edwards's sleeve. Surprised at this hint of intimacy, he turned to stare into a blankly smiling face.

Judy opened a battered leather jewelry case from her night stand and handed Stas a stack of cards held together with a thick rubber band that had broken and was now tied into a knot. He took a moment to look at the colorful scenes of each card then turned them over to read the brief messages on the back. There were several cards of greeting: birthdays, Easter, Christmas from other people. He handed those back to Judy.

"Do you have any pictures of your granddaughter?" he asked.

Confused, Judy looked over to Joe. "Pictures?"

"Do you have any photographs of your family?"

"Yes," Edwards affirmed. "Do you have one of Cynthia?"

Judy opened the top drawer of the night stand and fumbled. Confused, she turned to Joe. "There's nothing here."

Joe gently guided her hand to the bottom drawer. "Maybe you put them down here to keep them safe."

Judy bent slowly and looked in the drawer. A broad grin lit her face as she took out a small photo album marked "Grandmother." She gave it to Joe who handed it to Stas.

He flipped through pictures, some labeled with names and dates. There was a formal graduation portrait of Cynthia in cap and gown signed in the corner, "Cindi". On the next page was a snapshot of a young woman posing with a distinguished gentleman whom Stas presumed was Judge Lenox.

"Judy, may I borrow these for a few days?" He gently touched her arm. "I'll take good care of them."

Judy frowned.

"He'll bring them back." Joe added.

Stas smiled. "I promise."

Judy nodded and brushed her fingers lightly over Stas's right cheek.

"You just made her day. She'll dream about you tonight."

"She won't be the first." Edwards added with a frown..

Before leaving, Stas stopped in the Director's Office.

"Will we see you again?" Ms. Cox didn't rise but read his business card. "Detective Nowak." She pronounced the W like a W.

"Nowak." Stas corrected. "The W is pronounced V."

"Oh, I'm sorry." She looked at the receipt.

"I took some postcards and two photos. I'll return them as soon as we finish the investigation."

"How long might that take?"

"We never know. But if anything new comes up, just give me a call."

She smiled. "I'll be sure to do that." She started to rise.

"You don't have to show me out."

"Don't you think I get tired? Don't you ever want to drive?" Edwards asked as he settled behind the wheel.

"Not really! It's not the driving that gets to me but what we drive. Do you know anyone besides the police who buys Crown Vics? God, they see us coming a mile away."

"They're good cars. By the way, my sister-in-law is coming down. You remember Barbara, a real cutie, cuter than Jill and a whole lot thinner?" Edwards sighed as if he carried the weight of the criminal world or his wife's on his sloping shoulders. "I think she wants to move down. Just another mouth...."

His words droned on and faded as Stas thought about the woman he'd met a couple of weeks ago on his flight back to LA from Chicago. She too was cute and thin. The thought of their chance meeting warmed him and also gave him reason to pause. Would he find her interesting, and would he discover that she had long, strong legs? He wanted to find out.

Stas put on his sunglasses and pushed his seat back so that he could stretch out. This was his signal to his partner, don't ask questions, don't comment on the case, just leave me alone. We're through being cops for the rest of the drive back to RHD. He closed his eyes and conjured up the flight and the woman who had sat next to him.

The flight attendant's voice, sharp and merciless over the intercom, came across like an old army drill sergeant. "Hurry up and take your seats. We have a full flight, and we cannot pull away from the gate until everyone is seated and all bags are stowed in the overhead compartment or under your seat. Any bags that don't fit in the overhead or under your seat must be checked. If you need assistance with that, press your call button, and we'll check the bag for you."

From his seat, Stas peered down the aisle. There were a few stray passengers still struggling with bags and trying to find nonexistent space in the overheads. Sergeant Major Flight Attendant was making her way towards the back, slamming the doors to the overheads as she passed. Stas noticed the two flight attendants in the front of the cabin. They had to be anticipating retirement. Whatever happened to those perky stewardesses in their trim, form fitting uniforms, or even better, pink hot pants and vinyl white boots that he'd seen once in an old magazine?

Lots had changed in the friendly skies. Gone were pillows, mediocre meals, metal utensils, and any semblance of personal attention. Stas looked up, undid his seat belt, and stood to help a smartly dressed young woman who had just stopped at his seat. She was struggling to fit her stuffed roller bag in the already full overhead. In the process, her all-weather coat fell to the floor.

"Here, let me help." He did some rearranging, grabbed her bag, and squeezed it into the corner of the bin, after removing his top coat, and dropping it in his seat. He stepped back and raised the middle arm rest, to allow her to slip easily into the middle seat.

He retrieved her coat. "I think I can fit it in." Stas neatly folded it and placed it over his carryon. He looked down the empty aisle, took his coat out of his seat, and handed her his blanket. "If this isn't warm enough, you can have my coat."

She reached for it. "Maybe I should have kept mine." Her smile was warm, revealing beautiful teeth. "Thanks."

"Please take your seats and fasten your seat belts." The Sergeant Major Flight Attendant marched down the aisle checking for unbuckled belts.

She was about to say something when Stas leaned over to his seat companion. "We need to fasten up." He found the part of the belt closest to him and helped her before lowering the arm rest.

"Amanda Brighten."

"Stas Nowak."

"Save the getting acquainted for when we're in the air. Just fasten that seat belt." The Flight Attendant looked them over.

Finally, the door was secured, the plane pulled away from the gate, and moved on to the runway. Amanda clutched the armrests with such intensity that her knuckles turned white.

Stas noticed her flawless pale complexion. That was a good sign. She took care of her skin. He looked at her wrists. They were so thin and delicate that they reminded him of his mother's good dishes, a fine porcelain that she brought back from some place in Europe on a trip to Poland. He wondered about women like Amanda. Is that what he wanted, a "Sunday only" wife, like fragile Sunday china? Hadn't he had one of those? One with whom he needed an appointment to get laid, where even the suggestion of anything intimate turned her off?

Amanda turned to Stas after the plane was airborne. "I hate flying."

"It's not at the top of my list either, especially now."

She tried to look out, but the passenger at the window had pulled the shade down and gone to sleep using his coat as a pillow against the window.

So she turned back to Stas to make in-flight small talk. "What do you like to do?" A warm smile accompanied her question. "What is your great passion?"

The question took Stas by surprise. Usually women wanted to know what he did for a living, see if he was worth the effort. He hesitated. "I never gave it much thought."

"You strike me as a man who could be passionately committed to something: a cause, a hobby, a job... a woman."

Damn, she was quick. "I... I don't know." Was she fishing?

"I'm sorry. I didn't mean to put you on the spot. I teach a writing class at Glendale College." She reached down to a large handbag under the seat in front of her and took out a business card from a side pocket. Amanda had everything on the card: titles of her two books, address, phone number, e-mail. "Do you live in Southern California?"

"Yes."

"Then you should take my class. I'm always recruiting. Got to keep my numbers up. Come join us. Let me show you how to find your passion, unlock your inner being." When she spoke, her excitement lit up her face.

"And have you found your passion?"

She blushed. "I think I have."

Stas wondered how many men she had snared with that line, "What is your passion?". He had four hours to find out. He loosened his seat belt and turned to hear Amanda's sales pitch.

She talked easily about herself. Amanda was twenty-nine, a native of Cleveland, Ohio. She'd come to LA to teach but found it difficult to get a full time position at any of the local colleges even though she had a Master's degree from Case Western Reserve University. So she had self-published two books that she had written and gave self-discovery seminars. Finally Glendale College hired her as an adjunct to teach a writing class at night.

Amanda was easy to listen to. Stas took it all in, the cornflower blue eyes behind contacts that made her blink when she had to focus, her short brown hair, highlighted as if she spent lots of time in the sun. He tried to isolate her fragrance, but the spicy scent of her deodorant clashed with her sweet smelling hair spray and a weak cologne that had started to fade. Stop being the detective and enjoy her company. He looked at his watch and felt a pang of guilt.

"Flight Attendants, cross check and prepare the cabin for landing."

More instructions followed: turn off electronic devices, don't turn on cell phones, fasten seat belts, be careful opening overhead bins, stay in your seats until....

Stas blocked out the words flooding from the intercom and filed away details on Amanda in his mental notebook. He planned to check-out this pretty college professor. He told her he would like to visit her Tuesday evening class as soon as he got settled.

Edwards's forceful braking brought Stas out of his reverie. He sat up and removed his sunglasses.

"What's up?"

"That big-ass semi cut me off!"

"Where did you learn to curse?" Stas looked out the window and checked the side view mirror. "Get over! We need to exit! I have somewhere to go tonight!"

Edwards barked at his partner. "You didn't lose any time. I get sick of you doing this."

"What the fuck are you talking about?"

"That woman."

"What woman?"

"The Director, Mrs. Cox."

"What about her?"

"That's why you're in such a hurry. You made a date with her when you went back to her office."

"You must be losing it. No wonder your wife needs to get away from you."

"Well, are you going out with her?"

"Hell, no!"

SIX

Stas felt an unusual rush of anticipation about seeing Amanda again. He went down to the local coffee shop, Sam's Java. When he didn't order a coffee, Sam, the owner, waved him to the back. He had known Stas for years and knew the drill. Sometimes a cop needed a phone without caller I.D. So Sam let him use the old phone in the back and never asked questions. Stas called Amanda several times from the cafe's land line. He wasn't so excited about this new prospect that he would give her access to his cell number. His first call was to tell her that he'd enjoyed their meeting. The second was to ask her if he could check out her class.

That evening he showered, shaved, and dressed in gray slacks and a heather gray Polo sweater. It took less than ten minutes to get to Glendale College campus from his place but nearly thirty minutes to find a parking space.

After locating the room, he stood in the corridor for a minute and observed Amanda through the open front door. She moved from podium to whiteboard with confidence and ease but stopped in mid-sentence when she saw him in the hallway.

"Come in." She beckoned from the doorway.

Stas felt awkward as he took a desk near the back and fumbled with his gold Cross pen and small spiral notebook. Over the course of an hour, the class turned out to be amusing. It had been almost twenty years since he'd been in a college setting. There was a youthful exuberance that kept the dialogue between instructor and students light and sometimes silly. There was no way that he could imagine the informal banter and laid-back attitude at the Police Academy.

46

In the last half hour the class was assigned two writing exercises. Students were to explore their passions, their dreams. Before starting Stas looked around. Most of the students were bent to the task, but the young woman to his left held her phone to her side and awkwardly punched in a text message. Stas glanced over the shoulder of the young man in front of him who was busy sketching Amanda sitting at her desk.

Shaking off the distractions, Stas turned to the brief exercise. He touched his gold pen to his lip in thought, then paused. He didn't have a clue what he wanted in a long-term mate. Plus, if he had, he sure as hell wasn't about to share it with a room of post-adolescent students.

With pen poised over paper, he thought about his ex-wife, Joy. Did he really want to go there again? Well, this was only hypothetical. He started a list: new fishing rod, a new gray suit, some black Kenneth Coles. He stopped writing as his mind wandered. He imagined a woman who was warm, passionate, fun. Someone who laughed at his jokes. If he described her in the exercise, he would add long, shapely legs that caressed his back as they....

The retracting point of the pen clicked. Stas put it back in his pocket. Going back to school seemed like more busy work, as if he didn't have enough paperwork to keep him occupied at RHD. *Well, I'll see what happens.*

When the time was up, Amanda rose and stood behind the podium. Several students read from their lists. He strained looking over the bent head of the young man in front of him and tried to read her face and the reactions of the students as she took questions and emphasized various points. He looked at his watch, wanting to leave, but waited until the class was empty before approaching her.

Stas stood by the podium. "I guess I survived all this passionate youth."

She didn't comment but finished neatly packing her briefcase. "I need a really big favor." Her blue eyes widened in caressing appeal. She didn't wait for his response. "Could you give me a ride home?"

Even though it was late, he was game. "No problem. I'm in student parking."

They walked to the lot, talking about the class. Amanda continued expounding on the importance of journaling. Stas started to tune out, wanted to ask her about her car, and how she would have gotten home if he hadn't been available, but he let it go, mentally reminding himself not to fall into detective mode every time he met a woman.

"Your ideal woman doesn't have to be a superwoman, does she?" Amanda asked.

"No, I imagine she's kinda mainstream, but I never gave it much thought."

"What about her passions? Must you both care about the same causes?"

Before he could respond, they had reached his car. He imagined he heard a short intake of air when he stopped by the Mercedes. Stas laughed as he opened the car door for her and helped her get in. "That's not the kind of passion I want. We need to be compatible," he ran his hand through his hair, "... in bed."

"Oh?"

"I'm sorry. I didn't mean to embarrass you. There are other levels, but that's important, very important." He had to remember that he wasn't talking to a bunch of cops. He pulled out of the parking lot into light traffic and headed for the 2 Freeway.

She settled into the leather seat and turned to continue the one-sided discussion of her philosophy, more causes, and passions. The words started to merge together in his mind much like the traffic merging as he made the transition to the 210 Freeway. Amanda gave a running commentary on La Canada. Her detailed descriptions of the unique beauty of the profuse flora of Descanso Gardens got lost in the wake of an eighteen wheeler who drifted over into the third lane. *Where are the damn CHP when you need them?*

"I just love the camellias. We'll have to go there some time."

Stas stifled a groan.

She started to give directions as they neared downtown Pasadena and exited the freeway. Amanda lived in a complex of one-bedroom cottages on Euclid. Stas managed to squeeze into a narrow parking space at the entrance of the courtyard. He grabbed her briefcase, took her arm, and walked with her along a brick path lit by low wattage garden lights.

"Would you like to come in for a drink?" she asked fumbling with her keys.

He reached to help, but she pushed the door open and turned on a lamp next to a plush white sofa. As he followed her in, she busied herself straightening some magazines on the coffee table.

At first, Stas was a little hesitant. "What's on the menu?"

"Coffee, tea, or…?"

There was a sweet naiveté to her offer that made him wonder just how innocent she was and if the seduction ploy that had begun on the plane was moving into another phase. He inwardly wished for a stronger drink.

She smiled and took her briefcase, placing it on a desk in a combo office/dining room. "So what is it going to be?" she called from the entrance to the kitchen.

"Coffee, black."

Amanda closed the door when she went into the kitchen, but he could still hear noises that indicated she was doing more than just brewing coffee. He was tempted to join her.

"You need any help?" he shouted through the closed door.

"No, no, I'm fine. Just had to start the dishwasher."

Puzzled, he moved away from the kitchen and draped his leather jacket on the back of a chair by the front door. He looked around the living room, making mental notes, trying to get a read on Amanda. He noticed that everything had its place, yet there was the absence of those little homey touches:

photos, fresh flowers, incense, candles, dust-catchers. He realized they both had one thing in common, order. Well, Stas liked that.

He sat on the sofa, picked up one of the three Cosmopolitans, and paged through, looking at several articles. "How to Please Your Man in Bed and Have Him Beg for More" caught his eye. He read the lead then turned a few more pages. Although the titles were sensually provocative, the male models looked like they were still in high school. He couldn't imagine any sexually mature woman taking any of them seriously. He frowned and looked at his watch. Be patient. It was another five minutes before Amanda returned to the living room with the coffee.

"I'm going to change into something comfortable."

She handed him a mug and went to the bedroom closing the door behind her. Stas hoped whatever she slipped into would be more revealing. He sipped the coffee and frowned again. It was instant, weak, and tasteless. He put it down on the coffee table and took another look around the room. This time noticing several nondescript prints, the kind bought at a local craft store, hanging on snowy white walls. The bland art did nothing to reveal Amanda's passion. So what was it? Teaching about passion? He hoped not. What did she know about passion? He yawned. It had been a long day, and he needed something to help him unwind, but was she it?

Amanda reappeared wearing a beige mid-calf duster. She dimmed the light and turned on soft music, something by Yanni that flowed from speakers hidden in the room. Stas angled himself next to the arm of the sofa when Amanda joined him. He closed his eyes and breathed deeply, anticipating that warm surge that would signal his body's reaction to her closeness.

She touched her fingers to his face and snuggled up to him. As he bent to kiss her, her lips parted but their contact lacked that fire, that desire. His hand ran through her hair, pulling her closer. He needed to feel that connection, feel her passion, feel some urgency.

Stas was distracted briefly when she pulled away and her hands raised his sweater to touch his chest. He opened his eyes, the thin, cool fingers brought him back to reality. Her motions were awkward, even hesitant as she slid them to his belt and stroked his crotch. As she unzipped his fly, he felt a cold sensation spreading outward from his groin. His hand covered hers, stopping her from going any further.

Although Stas wasn't one to panic, something was definitely wrong. What was happening? There was no warm rush, no beginning of arousal, no tension in his breathing. Nothing! God, he had just turned forty and felt nothing. He knew he couldn't perform even if Amanda continued touching, fondling.

He took her fingers in his, feigning a caress, as he pulled her away from her task. She looked up, flush with anticipation, then her eyes clouded in disappointment. Stas held her, felt her rapid heartbeat, finally releasing her as her racing heart slowed. He knew she sensed something was wrong. She finally looked up, staring into his cold, gray eyes, searching for an answer.

He coughed, still holding her hand like a child he'd caught trying to touch an expensive doll in a fine toy store. "I'm sorry. I guess I'm just too tired." He looked at his watch and needed a drink. "Amanda, it's late." He released her, making no further effort to comfort her, to help her understand that nothing was going to happen. "I've been working long hours. I guess it's taken its toll." His smile was weak.

Amanda rose awkwardly, almost losing her balance as she stepped away from the sofa. Stas straightened his sweater and zipped his trousers. He fastened his belt when he stood and moved to the chair to get his jacket, slipping it on as he opened the door. "I'll call you. We'll get together again." His voice was cool, indifferent, the tone he used sometimes at an interrogation. He inhaled deeply, wishing he could suck the words back.

She forced a smile. "Don't forget to do your homework." She seemed cemented to the spot in front of the sofa.

Before closing the door, he looked back at the legs, shapeless and thin. Was it really legs that turned him on?

When Stas got home, he threw his jacket on his desk chair, pulled off his sweater, tossed it on top, and with some effort, kicked off his still tied shoes. He could feel the funk slowly creeping into his psyche. He knew of two remedies. In the kitchen he grabbed one of the cures from the freezer and returned to the living room with a glass and a chilled bottle of Chopin.

The message indicator on his phone blinked red, catching his attention before he could sit and have his drink. He punched the button, hopeful that the second remedy was a thirty minute drive away, one that he could make in twenty. The voice, though warm and husky, was the wrong one. "Hey, Stas, this is Livia. Call me. I got a leg of lamb in the fridge. I need to cook it ASAP. You game for dinner, or have you forgotten?"

Yeah, he had. He poured four fingers of vodka and turned on the TV before flopping in his leather recliner. He thought, with disappointment and brief pangs of guilt, about Amanda, that what had happened at her place wasn't her fault. So much for his pursuit of the all-American girl. He leaned back, slowly sipping his drink, and let the repressed memories of Dina seep into his consciousness. She certainly had a way of making him feel alive, and she made him laugh. Hell, even Livia made him laugh, and those legs.

He finished his drink and returned his bottle of vodka to the freezer. In the darkened bedroom, he shed the rest of his clothes, foregoing his usual ritual of putting everything away, and dropped them on the chair. When he slipped into bed, the cool sheets did little to assuage an urge that warmed him as he punched his pillow releasing an essence, a mixture of his after shave and an exotic perfume. Sleep eluded him.

He tossed, kicked the comforter off strong, muscular legs. His thoughts drifted to Dina, her warm sensuality, her exotic look, marred only by the long, raised scar running several inches across her throat. Had it been less than a month since she'd gone back to her place after being, what had she called it, "under house arrest" at his?

He had tried to be professional, maintain his cool, but outside events had driven him into her arms. He remembered the few times they had made love, remembered her scent, her caressing touch, her cries of release, and afterwards, her soft snores.

Stas turned on the light. He felt worse, willing his arousal to abate and realizing his encounter with Amanda just a few hours earlier had been an aberration. There was nothing wrong with his libido. He went to the bathroom, got in the shower, and brought himself off, a release that culminated with the utterance of Dina's name. He returned to bed. Since he'd expelled one demon, he made a decision before drifting off to sleep not to succumb to it again.

SEVEN

The team gathered the next day around a small table in the squad room where Stas had spread, in chronological order by postmarks, the ten postcards. The first one in the queue was a bright green aerial image of the MGM in Las Vegas. Jonson picked it up to read the back, while Stas began filling the detectives in on a possible eight-year odyssey of Cynthia Lenox who supposedly had been offered a modeling job and who had won seven hundred dollars playing the slots at the Luxor. She briefly mentioned meeting other models but gave no names or other details, nor when she would return to LA.

The second card, postmarked Phoenix two months later where she supposedly did some print work, indicated that she would visit when she returned. The third was postmarked Boston a year after the first two, then there was a two-year lapse between the third and the fourth which was sent from New York. She said nothing about work there or returning to LA.

Jonson handed the card back to Stas. "What do you make of all this?"

"Well, the greetings get shorter, just 'Wish you were here', 'Great food', 'Lovely sights'. If you had disappeared, left your car in the desert, why would you send a bunch of damn postcards, especially wishing your senile grandmother was there? Why not call your father and tell him where you were? Or that you're okay?" Stas looked puzzled. "If they were so close, wouldn't you know your old man would be worried? How come she didn't know about his death? These cards are bull shit."

Jonson shook his head. "Remember that woman in Georgia, the runaway bride? She just took off without a word."

"Yeah, but she was crazy." Marlowe waved the idea away. "You remember that look on her face? Reminded me of a scared colt."

Edwards picked up two cards. "Maybe since she knew her grandmother had Alzheimer's, she didn't need to say much." He turned one over in his hand. "The old lady wouldn't know the difference anyway. The postcard is just another pretty picture."

"But that's not the point. Why send anything to her? Why wouldn't you want to let your old man know you were okay? Doesn't make much sense." Stas handed Jonson two more cards. "Like the dates on these, the sixth and eighth cards."

"Had he already swallowed his gun?" Marlowe asked.

The detectives fell silent for a few moments.

Jonson finally spoke. "Man, we don't need to think about that." He turned the cards over to look at the pictures, one of the Eiffel Tower and the other of the Paris Opera House, then shook his head. "Say, what am I looking for?"

"Number six is postmarked Paris. Look at the stamp. The one of the Paris Opera House is postmarked New York. We need to check if she had a passport, and if she used it for any trips to Europe. I bet there's no record of her leaving the country, especially after she disappeared. Someone else sent these cards. When I went to Poland, I bought extra postcards just to have the pictures. I could just as easily have mailed the cards from here, saved my money on foreign postage. If no one paid attention to the postmark, no one would know when I was there. It's the thought that matters."

"When did you go to Poland?" Edwards asked.

Stas cut his partner a cold look.

"We need to have the handwriting checked," Marlowe said, "Where did the last two come from?"

"Las Vegas and Phoenix. We can contact IRS and Franchise Tax Board to see if she filed tax returns for the gigs in Vegas and

Phoenix or if she filed at all for those missing years." Stas returned the cards to their original order, banded them together, and set them next to the blue binder.

"This is all very confusing." Edwards grabbed the tox report from the murder book. "Cause of death was an overdose of heroin, injected in the neck, under the hair line."

"Was there any evidence of other injections, any tracks on other parts of the body?" Stas asked.

"She was clean, just the incision for the C-section and that one injection. She took good care of herself."

"Or her captors did...."

Marlowe's deep baritone spoke from the coffee maker. "If she's been held captive all this time, what was she doing?"

"I have a theory." All eyes turned to Edwards. "She was a white slave."

Marlowe boomed. "A what?"

"A white slave, you know, held captive in a brothel. Where do you think all those missing women disappear to? I heard on the news that some woman went on a cruise, and her daughter was kidnapped when they got off the ship on one of those third world islands. Later some sailor was in a whore house in Columbia, and an American woman whispered to him that she was being held against her will."

"So did we rescue her?" Marlowe glared over his steaming coffee.

"No, 'cause he didn't tell the mother 'til later."

"How much later?" Marlowe asked.

"Years later, when he got out of the Navy."

"Sid, why is it we only hear of young white women becoming sex slaves? Can't they do anything else but fuck? Why don't we hear of them picking coca leaves or cleaning house for some cartel family?" Marlowe nursed his cup.

Edwards shook his head. "I don't know."

"So much for getting a handle on white slavery." Marlowe frowned. "Don't you think other women get kidnapped and forced into prostitution? You know what it is? Nobody gives a damn about them."

"Well, that's not relevant. We need to figure out the pregnancy." Stas looked at the Coroner's report. "Where's the baby?"

"You think it's dead or sold on the black market?" Edwards asked.

"Where the hell do you get these off-the-wall, pee-brained theories, Sid?" Marlowe shook his head.

"It's better than all the 9/11 theories. There are plenty of black market babies, just check out the surrogate mothers, you know, rent-a-womb." Edwards laughed.

Jonson snorted. "Yeah, that's a good one, but sadly, it's true."

"What did you get from the cousin?" Edwards turned to Jonson.

"Not much. She still does things for the grandmother. And she hasn't seen Cynthia for eight, nine years. She wasn't sure about the timeline. They weren't close. She seemed to resent the way her cousin just took off to get into the movies."

Stas picked up the postcards and fanned them before returning them to the murder book. "It's hard to believe that an attractive young woman goes missing without a trace and turns up eight years later in a dumpster at a construction site wearing cotton panties and a faded housedress, and all we have are a bunch of frigging postcards that were mailed at yearly intervals, plus, evidence that she had a baby that we can't locate or that we know nothing about."

"Well, there's always white slavery." Edwards tried his theory again.

Again Marlowe's voice boomed like thunder across the room. "Where do you come up with this shit? Other women get abducted, especially Asian women. They bring'em in containers, shut-up for weeks on the ocean. Where do you think they get some of those girls working massage parlors? And they're not white. Ask your partner."

All eyes turned towards Stas as if he'd just busted a seafaring container in San Pedro smuggling in dozens of Asian beauties.

"He worked Vice." Marlowe added.

Edwards bristled. "So what's your point?"

"Man, you always stuck on stupid? You need to learn the ways of the world. Have you ever had a hooker?" Marlowe stared in disbelief, flecks of saliva collecting like tiny white webs in the corners of his mouth. "Get a life, experiment a little. Lily might appreciate it."

"Jill. My wife's name is Jill."

EIGHT

On the way home Stas stopped at Glendale's Whole Foods. He still hadn't taken the time to seriously grocery shop after returning from Chicago. Since his vacation, he hadn't gotten back into the habit of shopping, cooking, and eating alone. The thought of Dina at his coffee table when she was under "house arrest" at his place brought a chuckle when he remembered her love for hot fudge sundaes topped with globs of whipped cream.

Stas scanned the array of fresh fish spread on mounds of shaved ice then selected a filet of salmon, took the wrapped fish from the high counter, all the while totally oblivious to the movement on his right. He missed Amanda as she moved out of his line of vision to take refuge amidst the tall shelves of juices and sodas that concealed her while she observed him checkout and exit the store.

Even with the makings of a good supper, the cold apartment offered no refuse. He knew if he stayed home, he would polish off the Chopin and maybe make that call. He opened the fridge and stared at the frosty bottle in the freezer, then put the fish next to it, tossed a packaged salad into the crisper, and left.

Stas stopped at Ming's Palace and got Chinese take-out. When he arrived at the apartment complex in Hollywood, he retrieved the plastic key card from the glove compartment and inserted it into the slot. As the garage gate slowly churned upward, he wondered if there had been some subconscious reason why he hadn't returned it to Livia, the building's manager. The opener was one thing that still kept him connected to Dina, gave him an easy excuse to drop by. He parked in an empty parking space in a corner and took the stairs to the first floor.

Spying new greenery in the entrance, Stas envisioned Livia with her spray bottle feeding the new plants with super Miracle Grow and smiled trying to picture what else she had in her arsenal of tricks to make things grow.

Approaching her door, he thought about her dancer's stance: strong shapely legs slightly parted, hands on hips, maybe even an unfiltered Camel dangling from red lips that bled beyond the lip line, or flakes of black mascara that had escaped from artificial lashes to dot her overly rouged cheeks. Whatever the state of her make-up, she would be unfazed.

Her apartment door was ajar. Stas could hear the 7 O'clock News blaring through the slight opening. His knock moved the door enough to get a view of Livia in one of her brightly colored muumuus and three inch furry mules, lounging on the oversized sectional that crowded the apartment.

"Give me a minute to get to the door, will ya?" Her raspy voice was always serious and sexy. You knew when you heard it that Livia didn't play, no matter the game. She was forever ready for any visitor, whether apartment applicant, intruder, or prospective lover. The dancer's legs uncrossed. She stepped to the floor in a fluid dance step and smiled when she saw who it was. "Stas, come in." She glanced at the Ming carry-out bag. "For me?"

Every lamp in the apartment was on, highlighting a variety of Livia's photos that chronicled her dancing career. She struck a pose showing off her beautiful legs that seemed to go on forever under the short muumuu.

He sat the bag just inside the door. "I thought I'd see what Dina's up to. It's been a while."

"You still got my opener?" Livia asked knowingly.

He nodded, "Yeah, I'll give it back later after I see if the welcome mat's out."

"If hers ain't, mine always is, especially for one of LA's finest." est."

"So when's dinner?" he asked.

"When you didn't call back yesterday, I figured you were busy, so I promised my cousin I'd come out tomorrow and take the lamb."

"Sounds good. How about a rain check?"

She nodded.

He moved into the hallway grabbing his bag. "Then I'll call in a couple of weeks."

"Stas," Livia followed him and stood on tip-toes to plant a kiss on his cheek, "it's good to see you."

Dina wrapped her wet hair in a towel and applied the Fango, careful not to get any of the mud near her eyes. When she heard the loud knock, she angrily wiped her gray fingers on several tissues, then tightened the large towel around her torso. She moved through the living room, lit only by several large candles that cast wavy shadows on the walls. She turned the dead bolt, then the knob, opening the door a crack.

There he stood, still dressed to the nines, even with his red and white striped shirt opened at the collar, his gold and red tie neatly folded but partially visible in his jacket pocket. She wanted to rush into his arms but laughed instead. He hadn't taken time to change. That was a good sign.

Her breath caught in her throat as she whispered his name. "Stas."

"Hey, babe." A broad smile brightened his usually serious demeanor.

Dina let him stand in the doorway for a second. He dropped the take-out bag just missing her bare toes.

"Well, can I come in?"

"You could've called."

"I was in the neighborhood."

She looked at the bag that had just missed her foot. "What's that?"

"Dinner, have you eaten?"

"No." She moved to the living room and flipped on a table lamp.

"It's Chinese. Most of your favorites." He picked up the bag and followed her.

Dina left him standing by the TV. "Let me change." She took the bag to the kitchen before going to her bedroom. "Have a seat," she shouted through the open doorway. She was glad to have burned fresh incense, lemon grass. Its subtle aroma seemed to envelop the entire room.

Dropping the towel by the shower, she went to work removing the hardened mud from her face. She felt flushed which added to the after effects of the facial. Dina stood still for a second, trying to control her excitement. Stas seemed to have a knack for catching her off guard. She slipped into a silk caftan and fussed a second with damp hair. *Forget the makeup. Forget the food.* But her stomach growled.

She glanced at Stas as she moved to the kitchen. He had taken off his jacket and was bent to untie his shoes.

It took ten minutes to get the food from carton, to microwave, to bowls. Dina nervously filled the tea kettle, put it on to boil, and fixed a tray, popping a garlic shrimp into her mouth from the first container of food. "Hot, hot!" She fanned her mouth.

In the living room, she set the tray down on the coffee table, pushing aside several sputtering candles.

"I'm starved." Stas reached for chopsticks. "Smells good." He gave her an anxious look while he filled his bowl.

"Tastes good, too." Dina mumbled and looked up, her chop sticks poised to grab another shrimp. "I didn't realize how hungry I was."

They ate in awkward silence, picking and tasting, exchanging glances between bites. Dina took the last egg roll from the saucer and dipped it into plum sauce. Biting it in two, she quickly licked the sauce as it dripped down the side of the wonton crust, just catching the drops before they fell on her caftan.

Stas looked on, his steel gray eyes softening as she consumed the egg roll. There was always this sensuous relationship between Dina and the things she ate. Before pouring tea, she slowly licked the last of the rosy residue from her fingers. While he sipped his tea, she got up and took his jacket from the sofa to the hall closet.

He cleared his throat. "How are things?"

"Okay."

"I wasn't sure you'd be home."

"I do have a phone, two, as a matter of fact."

"I know, but I needed to see Livia."

"For dinner?"

"Later, in a couple of weeks." Stas put down his half empty mug. "Still working?"

"Yes." She looked into his eyes. "I'm running the business now."

"What does that mean?" His tone was icy, his eyes cold.

Dina felt the chill like a draft had blown in on some Arctic wind. She busied herself with clearing up, avoiding his gaze. "So what are you doing?"

"What I always do. This time it's a young woman they found in a dumpster."

She bit her lip. "I saw it on the news. Did you find out who she was?"

"A judge's daughter. Been missing a while. It's dangerous out there, babe."

Dina nodded, her voice almost a whisper. "I know."

He watched her put empty bowls on the tray, noted the silky fabric cling to her slim body, imagined her naked beneath the caftan. "You want to tell me what 'running the business' means?" His voice was dry. The muscles tensed in his neck.

"Raven came back from Paris and reorganized. I'm taking over here. She'll go back and run Europe, then there's the Asian operation. I don't know...." Her voice was lost as she disappeared into the kitchen with her tray.

This time Stas followed her. She took a frosty bottle of Chopin from the freezer and poured a half glass of icy vodka. He set it on the counter .

"Are you turning tricks?"

Anger flared in her tone. "What do you care?"

"I'm a cop." He brushed a finger lightly over Dina's cheek. "It's my business to care." He picked up the glass and sipped. "So are you?"

"Does it matter?"

"I don't want you getting in any trouble,... and I do care."

She touched his sleeve. "I don't,... I haven't since Sybil died. I don't want to,...not anymore. I want a different life."

"I'm glad." Stas took his drink and returned to the sofa and started to relax, leaning back into the downy softness of the sofa.

She returned with the frosty bottle of Chopin and set it next to his glass. He sipped, set the drink down, and reached for her. She moved easily into his arms and playfully popped his braces.

"Why are you wearing these silly things?"

"They're braces. What every well-dressed detective should wear, a gift from my tailor. I thought they'd make a fashion statement." He laughed.

Dina slid them off his shoulders, letting them fall to his waist. "They're ugly, and they just get in the way."

He didn't move as she slowly unbuttoned his shirt, undid the cuff buttons, and tugged the sleeves from his arms. He leaned forward so she could remove the shirt, dropping it unceremoniously to the floor. Stas ran two fingers across the scar at her neck, then raised her face to his open mouth. He tasted ginger, garlic, and red pepper. The kiss was long, deep, and hot from a chili flake that he passed from his tongue to hers. Shifting his position, he worked the zipper down on her caftan without fully releasing her. With some maneuvering the garment awkwardly slid from her body. She rose to step out of it and let it join his shirt.

Dina pulled away, trying to catch her breath. "Not here." She could feel the urgency building in her body, and sensed, then reached and felt his.

He shed the rest of his clothes in the dimly lit bedroom. There were no preliminaries as they fell to the bed, ready to devour each other after a long fast. She closed her eyes and whispered his name as he took her, losing herself in the heat building in her thighs, her pelvis. Her pounding heart raced to catch his. She caressed his back, captured his hips with her thighs, then clutched his shoulders, urging him, her body warm and damp from his movements. She abandoned herself entirely to his forcefulness, his need. But it came too soon. Stas emitted a low groan, as if control was slipping away. Slowly as she felt that sensation welling up in her inner core, it was over. She felt his dead weight and cried out, hanging on the edge, needing to feel completion.

"Babe, babe, I'm sorry." He choked into her ear as he eased off her body.

But it wasn't over. Dina saw to that, and Stas didn't disappoint the second time. His renewed passion rocked her to an intense climax. No one had ever had her so completely.

Afterwards she slept, curled like a newborn kitten in the curve of Stas's warm body, content that he was back, and it was all good. No, dammit, it was the best.

Later, Dina disentangled herself from his embrace and padded across the thick carpet to the living room. Two candles had burned down to nothing; the other sputtered as she bent to blow it out. She picked up Stas's shirt from the chair, slipped it on, and headed for the kitchen. The ceiling light shone brightly, and the back burner on the stove was still on, although the tea kettle was on the counter. She turned everything off and returned to bed. *Damn, guess I know where my mind was.*

Carroll Wilson left the club early, at least earlier than he would have, had there not been the promise of some new threads. The meth he'd had earlier was making him anxious to keep moving.

Out in the street, he'd been warm then cold. He couldn't remember where he'd left his jacket. Maybe it was at the club or in his car. Whatever! He flipped his yellow suspenders and vigorously rubbed his hands on his light blue shirt. The chilly night air was getting to him as he quickened his pace. He felt confused. *Where is my fucking car?* He finally gave up after two hours of wandering around the mid-Wilshire district and headed towards Blackwood's.

A friend at the club had told him there would be something new, something hot in the dumpster behind the elegant men's shop. *That little narrow-assed, switch-tail, wanna-be queen had better not be lying or...;* he rubbed his arms more briskly, anything to ward off the cold.

Now he remembered. How stupid to have left his jacket in the car just because he felt overdressed going to the club. He should have gone home and changed after meeting with his last client, but he had been in a hurry to get away from the design studio.

As he stepped off the curb to turn into the service drive, a big SUV roared out propelling him backwards into the wall of the opposite building. Carroll only managed a weak "Bastard!" as he tried to regain his balance. He gave a quick glance after the vehicle, then moved away from the brick wall and peered down the stretch of narrow pavement leading to the rear of the buildings.

Even with his goal in sight, he still felt cold, shaken. He walked slowly towards the dim light that hung over the service entrance of Blackwood's. A few feet away, shrouded in shadows, stood the black dumpster. A stack of small boxes littered the ground at its base. Stepping on the pile of discarded cardboard, Carroll grabbed a garish, multicolored tie topping the heap of trash in the dumpster. *Dammit, if those bastards beat me to the good stuff....* He picked through papers and other debris, throwing the tie aside. There was nothing else except a green and black t-shirt that was equally as ugly as the tie. Carroll rubbed his face, trying to clear his mind, then clumsily stepped onto the bottom rung of the metal refuse container. Since the lid was up, he was able to hoist himself over the edge, only to be thrown off balance, a surging stench slammed into him like a wave of vile decay clutching at his entrails. He fell forward, reaching for the edge to break his fall as he stepped on something solid yet soft and slippery under foot. "Shit! Shit!" He gagged, then spewed forth the contents of his guts.

Stas tossed into wakefulness as cold air hit his naked torso when Dina rose. He reached for her but touched empty space cooling in her absence. He pulled the comforter over his shoulders and tried to regain the euphoria of sleep but couldn't. His mind drifted to Amanda. Whatever had happened that night at her place had to have been some sort of sexual distraction. Yet the thought of that failure and his earlier performance with Dina brought a surge of warm desire that slowly coursed through his body.

He listened as the shower ran for what seemed like an eternity, then he felt Dina's cool body slip under the covers. He pulled her closer, arching his hips as he took her again. She gasped through half-closed lips and repeatedly called his name as the heat of their passion intensified. He was vaguely aware of his name giving way to mournful cries and sensual instructions. He could feel her quivering thighs, her legs repositioning to give him greater leverage, her hands caressing his back, again urging when he needed none. He was aware of her ragged breath, her racing heartbeat, her tightened embrace. They were both holding on for that frenzied moment, those agonizing yet exquisite final movements that took them over the edge together. Neither wanted it to end.

Stas fell to her side and pulled her to him; his mind fought to comprehend the feelings, but he let it go and drifted into a deep, restful sleep.

The repeated buzz came through a hazy dream of entangled limbs and raw emotions ready to blaze again. Stas barely opened his eyes as he reached for his phone on the nightstand, then realized he was at Dina's. Easing out of bed, he found his cell where it had fallen to the floor. It was Edwards. Stas gathered up his discarded boxer briefs and pants and headed for Dina's kitchen to dial his partner on her wall phone. "Sid, what's up?"

"Stas?"

He knew Edwards would be puzzled by the displayed "private caller".

"Where are you?"

"Are you calling," he looked at the time on the stove's clock, "just to find out where I am? Man, it's 4:37 a.m."

"I know, but they found another body. They want us at the scene as soon as you can make it."

"Just what did they find?"

"Another young woman, in another dumpster."

"Where?"

"In Hollywood."

"Why us?"

"Orders from the Captain."

"Okay, I'm leaving now."

Dina stood in the doorway of the kitchen wearing Stas's shirt and holding his shoes and socks.

"I'll call you from the car for the address." He put the receiver back in its cradle and reached for the rest of his clothes.

Dina moved into the kitchen. "You want some coffee?"

"No, I'm fine." He splashed cold water over his face at the sink and ran his wet fingers through his disheveled hair trying to rake it into some semblance of order. "But I think I'll need my shirt."

"You're leaving, now?"

Dina moved within arm's reach but made no effort to unbutton the one that held the shirt together just below her breast.

Stas slid both hands under the shirt tails and pulled her to his midsection.

"I got a call, babe." He unbuttoned his shirt and caught it as it slid from her shoulders. "Smells delicious." He held it to his nose for a brief second before putting it on.

"Then stay, go in later."

"I can't. We got another body."

"Is it always like this?" she frowned.

"Sometimes, I warned you."

Stas looked at Dina standing nude before him. He bent to kiss her but patted her on the head instead. "Don't tempt me, babe."

She bit her lip. "Well, I guess I can get used to it."

NINE

After getting the address from Edwards, Stas drove through light early morning traffic from Dina's to the crime scene. He ran his tongue over his teeth; they needed brushing. The faint taste of ginger, garlic, and Dina still lingered. He felt stubble on his cheeks and looked at the dashboard clock. There wasn't time to go home, shower, shave, and change. *Let's get this over with.*

It took less than ten minutes to reach the scene. He spotted the Coroner's van before he saw Edwards. When Stas reached the cordoned off area, techs were about to load the gurney with its victim for its ride to Mission Street. They stopped when they recognized the detective.

"I guess you want a look?" the tech, Paul Givens, asked.

"Yeah." Stas approached and waited for the body bag to be unzipped down to the victim's midsection. He recoiled and held his breath as the waft of decaying flesh rose to slam into his face. It was a young woman, dressed in a floral print that had been opened in the front. She looked as if she'd been dead two or three days from the discoloration of her flesh, but it was the hair that caused Stas to look closer. Blonde curls framed her face. He was struck by how the corpse's hair resembled that of the first victim. Here was another young woman cut down in the prime of life.

The tech re-zipped the body bag when Stas stepped back. It took a few seconds before his breathing normalized.

Edwards joined his partner as the van moved from the service drive into the street. "You see her? Similar M.O. as the other one. Same kind of dress, another blonde."

Stas nodded as he walked toward the SID team working the crime scene. "Who found the body?"

Edwards pointed to the curb as they walked. "Some, some," he tried to find the right word, "guy, found her, said he was shopping."

"At four in the morning?" Stas asked. He moved to the curb.

The young man sitting there was dressed in tight black pants and a tight green and black long-sleeved t-shirt. The shirt was wrinkled but fairly clean but the pants were filthy and stained with flecks of dried vomit down the front where the previous shirt hadn't reached. He was shoeless and dazed as if unaware that he had nothing on his feet.

Stas bent to the curb. "I'm Detective Nowak."

"Carroll."

Stas turned to Edwards for confirmation. "Carroll?"

Edwards read from his notebook. "Carroll Wilson."

"What happened, Mr. Wilson?" Stas asked.

"Ms. Wilson."

Stas wasn't ready to deal with a sexual ambiguous witness this early in the morning, especially when Carroll turned and batted what seemed like several pounds of heavy mascaraed eyelashes at Edwards who inched back on the curb.

"May I just call you Carroll?" Stas took out his own notebook and pen.

"Like I told the other officer, my friend mentioned to me that there were some new things my size out back."

"Then what were you doing in the dumpster?" Stas asked.

Carroll nodded and smiled. "The stuff was supposed to be in the dumpster."

"Is that a new way to shop?" Stas looked Carroll over.

"Not really. You just need the right connection."

"And you had one at Blackwood's." It was a statement rather than a question.

Carroll batted eyelashes and straightened his head and neck. "Well, not after tonight."

"Can you tell me what happened when you got here?" Stas asked.

"I told the other cops." More fluttering and posturing.

"Well, we're a new set of cops, like a change in shift. I'd like to hear it from you. Get your slant on things." As Stas moved closer, he smiled as he noticed stained white suspenders hanging from Carroll's waist.

"I climbed over, then lost my balance and fell in the rest of the way. She must have been under the paper. I didn't see her at first. Things shifted. Damn! I couldn't get out! I couldn't breathe!" He shook his head and almost gagged. "That smell, then I must have moved the paper. I saw her, staring at me. For one second I thought she was a mannequin, but the stink, then my foot slipped, like her skin was moving." He retched, then sucked in air. "I'd been drinking. I tried to hold it down, but everything just came up. I don't know how I got out. I called 911."

"What happened next?" Stas asked.

"I don't remember. I guess I fainted."

"They found him stretched out on the sidewalk." Edwards added. "Thought he was drunk, then he started screaming about a woman in the dumpster."

Stas turned from Edwards, back to Carroll. "Did you see anyone around here when you arrived?"

"The shit I did." The query seemed to animate him. "He almost killed me."

"Where?" Stas tried to follow Carroll's line of vision, as if he too could see the errant attacker.

"It wasn't a car. It was a fuckin' red SUV comin' out the alley. I thought, that bitch's stealing my clothes."

Edwards interjected. "What are these clothes you're talking about?"

Carroll looked up, then off. "You know, I rarely buy clothes. You see these pants?" He slowly ran his slender, manicured fingers down his legs and stared at Edwards. "I got these in a dumpster and this shirt." He snatched up the dress shirt covered with vomit from the pavement. "Shit, this is my good shirt. It's ruined." He patted the t-shirt he was wearing. "This was hanging on the dumpster."

Stas tried to bring everybody back. "Carroll, what time did you get here?"

"About three, we left the club. I told my friend, Eddie, I was coming down here. He didn't want to come, 'cause he wasn't getting anything." He used his arms to indicate his friend's size. "He's too damn big, like some Amazon. So he went to his car, and I walked over here."

"Where do you live?" Edwards finally drew closer.

"South Pasadena. Where do you live?"

Edwards backed away.

"How were you going to get home, since your friend left you?" Stas took notes.

"I got my car."

"Where is it?" Stas asked.

"I don't know, but I'll find it, or they'll call me from im-pound to come get it."

"Isn't that kind of expensive?" Edwards asked.

Carroll jammed his hand in his pocket and pulled out a wad of bills. "I got money."

"If you have money, why are you diving in dumpsters for discarded clothes?" Stas looked down the service drive.

"It's a little game we play." Carroll collected himself and rose from the curb.

"How do you plan to get home?" Edwards asked.

"If I don't find my car, I'll walk."

"Hollywood to South Pas, that's a long walk," Edwards said.

"I've done it before, unless you want to help me find my car." Carroll batted lashes again. "Or that other nice detective." He nodded toward Stas.

"Detective Nowak doesn't give rides in his personal wheels."

Carroll shook his head. "Then the other one."

73

"I don't think so. The city's not paying for you to be chauffeured around Hollywood by the department either."

Stas watched Edwards finish the field interview. They would have another talk with him as the investigation progressed. As they were winding down, a television van with its early morning skeleton crew had gathered at the corner, held back by a couple of officers and yellow tape. Ralph Townsend emerged standing in a cloud of smoke between the officers and the TV crew. He was the *Times* reporter who covered the LA crime scene. Stas acknowledged him with a slight nod but wasn't hanging around for any of Townsend's questions.

Edwards stood next to his partner sniffing. "What're you wearing?"

"What?"

"Cologne? Were you with that Cox woman?"

Stas took a deep breath. "Don't worry about it." He realized it was his shirt that still held a faint residue of Dina's scent.

"So where were you this morning when I called?"

Stas seemed agitated. "Sid, back off, I'm going home. See you later."

Edwards followed, trying to keep up with his partner's long, deliberate strides. "You still wearing what you had on yesterday. Is she the one who gave you the watch?"

Stas spoke to his partner's reflection in the window as he unlocked his car. "Go get some coffee, go to work, or go home. There are certain things that shouldn't concern you."

"So did you make it with that teacher woman?" The question faded as Stas got in, closed the door, and started the Mercedes. "But I'm your partner. I should know these things." The words were lost in the chill and the noise of the early morning traffic. Edwards turned and slowly walked back to his car.

By 9:38 a.m. Stas, looking like he had just stepped out of the pages of *GQ*, had gone home showered, shaved, changed, and found Edwards in the squad room nursing his coffee.

He tossed an evidence bag onto Edwards' s desk. "We're going to Blackwood's. They open at ten. Bring the shirt."

Edwards brushed the permanent wrinkles in the front of his permanent pressed jacket and grabbed the Crown Vic's keys. "You think they may have seen something?"

"I doubt it. They closed at six, and we didn't see a security cam out back, but I'm curious about the clothes in the dumpster."

"Do you believe the wit?" Edwards asked.

"I don't know. He said he found the shirt hanging there."

"And the rest of his clothes? Why not just buy them instead of dumpster diving?"

"Dumpster diving?" Stas asked. "Who told you that?"

"The uniform told me. He said some do it for food, but some do it for clothes."

"There's no explaining what people do, even those with money." Stas settled into the passenger side of the car, took out his shades, and pushed back in his seat.

They rode in silence, maneuvering through late morning traffic that never seemed to lighten, no matter the time of day. Edwards huffed his annoyance when they slowly cruised by Blackwood's, on the Hollywood side of Wilshire before approaching Beverly Hills. He continued to drive around the area for ten minutes looking for a parking space.

Stas pocketed his glasses and pointed to the curb. "Hey, just park in that loading zone." He took the police placard out of the glove compartment and placed it on the dash, "Cops see this, they know it's police business."

Once out of the car, he took a minute before entering to scrutinize the sartorial offerings displayed in the window. He turned to his partner. "You take the lead." When they entered, Stas quickly surveyed the well-appointed but low-key interior, feeling an adrenaline rush like a kid turned loose in a toy store. He paused, slyly fingering the leg of a pair of heather gray slacks, then admired the fine fabrics of the suits and jackets hanging strategically near the entrance. Before joining his partner, he was drawn to a display table laid with shimmering silk ties next to an array of beautifully crafted shirts. He hung back while Edwards made the introductions and showed his ID. Stas's senses were being bombarded as he slowly inhaled the aroma of colognes displayed on a highly polished glass counter.

Edwards accompanied a distinguished-looking gentleman to where Stas stood. "This is Mr. Holcomb, the manager."

"I'm Detective Nowak."

Holcomb held out a well-manicured hand. There was nothing out of place on this walking mannequin from his imported Italian toupee to his highly polished black Bruno Maglis. The detective took a second look at the shoes, committing the style to memory before turning his attention to the purpose of their visit.

"We found several officers here this morning. They let me open but not for clients. They said we had to wait for the detectives."

"As the officers told you earlier, we're investigating an apparent homicide. A body was found last night in the dumpster out back. The person who discovered the victim says he was dumpster diving. Can you enlighten us?" Stas asked.

Before Holcomb could respond, Edwards took out his notebook. "Do you normally just throw good clothes in the trash?"

The manager stiffened. "Sometimes our associates get a little careless with our inventory. If there is a return or some imperfection in a garment, it usually ends up in the dumpster, and sometimes things that are not damaged go the same route. We've fired several young men for that very reason." He turned to Stas. The officers said a dead woman was found in the dumpster."

"The body of a scantily dressed woman was found in the dumpster out back. We're assuming by its location near your rear door that it's yours," Stas said.

"Yes, it *is* ours."

"How often is it emptied," Stas asked.

"Once a week."

"When?"

"Tuesdays."

"So anyone familiar with the trash pick-up could dump a body there and be fairly certain that it wouldn't be discovered until Tuesday at the earliest."

Holcomb nodded but said nothing.

Stas took out a small envelope from his jacket pocket and removed two photos and passed them to Holcomb. "Have you ever seen these women?"

Holcomb's only reaction was a frown. "Which one is the victim?"

Stas indicated by holding up the photo. "This other young woman was found in similar circumstances. There may be a connection."

Holcomb just shook his head.

"Who closed last night?" Edwards asked.

"One of our new hires, Andre Fouche." He turned up his nose. "It's fake French. I don't like these young men, but for some reason the owner is impressed by their sartorial savor faire and Andre's fake accent. I must admit they are usually well put together, and they bring in a young crowd that has the money,..." he paused as if trying to find the right word, "good taste, and can afford us." Holcomb nodded at Stas. "I'm happy to see the police dressing better."

Edwards put the evidence bag with Carroll's shirt on the counter. "So are you missing any clothes?"

"Sorry." Seemingly distracted or bored, Holcomb picked an imaginary piece of lint off his jacket sleeve, then opened the plastic bag and looked at the shirt. "We would never carry something so, so.... well..." He looked at both men. "You understand."

Edwards stared at the shirt. "No, I don't understand. What's wrong with it?"

Holcomb took out his black and gold Mont Blanc pen and used the tip to lift the front of the shirt. "Here, see this. This is a poly-blend. Our t-shirts are Egyptian cotton. The hand is rough to the touch. Do you want something like that touching your body? Observe the shirt, Detective...." He looked to Stas.

"Nowak."

"Detective Nowak is wearing. His dress shirt is made of fine Egyptian cotton."

"How can you see that?" Edwards asked.

"That's my business." He pointed to Carroll's shirt on the counter. "This shirt is not one of ours."

"We would like for you to let us know if any of your stock is missing. Also, we're going to need to speak with Mr. Fouche." Stas handed Mr. Holcomb his card. "Have him give me a call when he comes in. By the way does he or any of your salesmen drive red SUVs?"

"No! They're into sport's cars, usually on their last legs."

On their way out, Stas stopped to look at a well-cut sports jacket on display. "Do you keep a customer file, the names, addresses, and measurements of your clients?"

"Of course, we let them know when we have sales, special events." He picked up a card from the counter and handed it to Stas. "Would you like to be on our mailing list?"

Stas filled out the card and handed it back. Edwards pocketed his notebook and headed towards the exit, murmuring, "Thank you."

"Wait!" Stas held back, fingering the fabric of several shirts on the counter. Unable to resist, he bought a white on white Egyptian cotton shirt with a diamond pattern and a navy, white and silver silk tie.

Edwards had waited at the cologne counter, spraying several scents on his hands while his partner paid for his purchases. "I can't believe you spent that kind of money on a white shirt and tie." He grunted as he pulled out into traffic.

"Egyptian cotton. Navy and white with flecks of silver. Always pay attention to the little details. And never splash on more than one aftershave. They can clash, and you end up smelling like a five dollar whore or much worse, her pimp." He reached for his shades. "We need to find out where that t-shirt came from and who put it in the dumpster."

TEN

Stas closed the murder book, put his clean mug in the top drawer of his desk, then took out a small yellow cloth to dust the surface of the computer monitor. Edwards entered the squad room as his partner finished cleaning and picked up the blue book.

"Put it on Jonson's desk. I'm through with it," Stas said.

Edwards hovered. "I'm barbecuing tomorrow. Barbara's in town, interviewing for some jobs."

Marlowe turned off his computer and looked at Stas's desk. "How come we all bust our butts, and Stas is the only one gets invited to one of your cookouts? What's that all about?" He stood and grabbed his jacket.

Color rose in Edward's neck. "It's just that the weather's been nice. I thought...."

"I didn't ask about the weather. What? The rest of us not good enough?" Marlowe wasn't smiling.

"It's not that. I thought you'd be bored. It's for my sister-in-law." He looked towards Stas. "He knows Barbara."

"You playing matchmaker? Maybe I'd like to meet Barbara." Marlowe reached for his hat. "Anyway, he's got a new squeeze. Don't you, Stas?"

All eyes turned to the detective.

He wasn't going to be sucked into that one. "Tell you what, we'll all come."

Jonson walked in and stood by the door. "We'll all come where?"

Marlowe put his hand on his partner's shoulder. "Edwards invited us for a cookout."

"Great! This is Luz's ex's weekend with the boys. She's been dying to meet you guys. What time?"

"About three or four," Edwards stammered.

Marlowe could have shot himself getting talked into going to Edwards's cookout? And then to tell Stas to pick him up? Male pride, racial pride. Hell, he didn't know anybody who even wanted to go to one of Edwards's barbecues except his partner, and he probably went out of some displaced loyalty. Marlowe didn't even like Edwards, and here he was putting a spit shine on his new hand tooled black boots and brushing off his best hat. Come to think of it, he didn't feel any great bond with Stas once they left work.

At first, he had liked the idea of riding in Stas's fancy wheels, and he was anxious to meet Edwards's sister-in-law, see what kind of woman Stas turned down.

He heard the horn in the driveway and looked out of the living room window. The black Mercedes was a bitch. With the car and his clothes, he bet Stas was into the man up to his jockey shorts. Well, if he hadn't had to pay spousal and child support to his lazy second wife, he could cruise around in something like that 500 SL and have the babes salivating for him, especially that new hire working in Records.

He grabbed his keys and his Stetson and went out to the driveway where he opened the passenger door and stuck his head inside. "I think I'll take my own ride. If I get bored, I can bail."

Jonson's white SUV was already parked in the driveway of Edward's beige stucco and stone ranch when Stas pulled up and parked on the street. He grabbed his leather jacket and a brown paper bag from the passenger seat as Marlowe pulled in behind him.

Marlowe reached for a twelve-pack of Samuel Adams, then followed Stas to the front door. "What's she like?" Marlowe asked.

The question surprised Stas. "Who?"

"The sister-in-law."

"Nice, I guess."

"Then why ain't you balling her."

"Not my type." Stas shook his head.

"See, I knew it. You got something else going on. It's been what, a couple of months. Is it the same chick?"

"I think Jill's pressuring Sid to get her sister a man."

"You on the list?" Marlowe asked.

Before Stas could answer, one of Edwards's boys broke through the front door in a burst of energy as Marlowe reached for the bell.

"Sorry!" The kid took three steps in one long leap, landed on the lawn, and never looked back.

"What was that?" Marlowe looked after the kid who ran into the street and headed down the block.

"David, I think. He's the oldest."

"How many does Sid have?"

"Three boys, but I'm not sure. I think there's a girl in the mix somewhere." Stas held the door waiting for another offspring to make his escape before entering.

"At least he's learned to do something right."

Stas smiled, "You think so?"

Jill Edwards had put on another ten pounds since Stas had last seen her. Ten years ago, she would have been considered cute, but now she looked tired, drained, all the spark in her life gone at thirty-four. No wonder she wanted to get out, go to work. Four kids in suburbia had to be a killer. She gave Stas a peck on the cheek and extended her hand to Marlowe.

"We haven't met. I'm Jill."

Marlowe took the proffered hand, awkwardly handing Stas the twelve-pack. "I'm Chris Marlowe. Nice to meet you, Jill."

"Sid's outside doing the meat. I think the others are in the family room. Stas, let's take those to the kitchen." She led the way.

Her sister was in the dining area folding large paper napkins. Jill paused. It was evident that both women were sisters. They had the same soft, nondescript features and large doe-like brown eyes set in an oval face, but Barbara had done something to her hair, added golden highlights that brought life to its auburn color and warmth to her smile. In contrast Jill's shoulder length tresses had turned a mousey brown, streaked now with strands of gray.

"Barbara, this is one of Sid's coworkers, Chris Marlowe. You remember Stas, Sid's partner?"

She smiled at both men. "Nice to meet you, Chris. I hope you're not as elusive as Stas." She shot a look at him. "Makes me wonder about a cop's life."

Barbara was three years younger than her sister, unmarried, and from what Stas had heard from his partner, desperately looking for a change in her social life and marital status. Both Sid and Jill seemed to think that he would make a good catch, but he ruled that out the first time they met. He noticed how Barbara was looking slimmer than she had the last time she was in town when he'd been suckered into one of his partner's infamous cookouts. But this time Barbara's trip was supposed to be permanent. She'd been downsized from a job in Fresno and was planning to make LA home.

Stas took the beer and Chopin to the kitchen, found a water glass, and poured a double. "This needs to go in the freezer," he said, handing the bottle to Jill and looking under the sink for a place to dispose of the paper bag.

When Stas returned to the family room with a Samuel Adams for Marlowe who was deep in conversation walking next to Barbara as she set the table. Barbara missed Marlowe's wink when he tasted his beer.

"What are you drinking?" Stas asked her.

"I'll have what you're having." Barbara smiled her reply and tossed her hair, releasing a scent of something heavy and persistent.

"Big mistake, babe." Laughing, Stas returned to the kitchen.

"What?" Jill looked up from tossing greens.

"I guess I'm the designated bartender." He reached for a wedge of tomato on the cutting board.

"You left them alone?" Jill asked as she put the rest of the tomatoes in the bowl before he could snag another piece.

"Is that a problem?"

"Sid thinks Marlowe's...."

"Sometimes he thinks too much." He looked over the counter. "Where's the vodka?"

"You told me to put it in the freezer."

"Well, I need to break it out again."

Without waiting for directions, he opened several cupboards looking for another glass.

Jill brushed a strand of hair from her face. "I think I need one of those, too."

He looked at her, then pulled open the door to the dishwasher. "Are these clean?"

Jill nodded. He took out two glasses, retrieved the bottle from the freezer.

"Did you wash your hands?"

"Don't worry. Vodka kills everything." He dropped several cubes into the glasses, poured about two fingers in each, then refilled his own before handing Jill hers. "Let's get this show on the road," he said more to himself than to her. He hesitated in the doorway to watch Jill's reaction.

She took a swig, frowned, and grimaced.

"Hey, take it easy. You sip it. Don't throw it back. Savor the after burn." He smiled and took Barbara her drink, then went outside to check the status of the steaks and meet Luz.

Jonson sat on a peeling green bench with his arm around his wife's shoulder. He started to rise, but was waved back by Stas.

"This is Luz, the greatest thing to happen to me in years. Honey, this is Stas Nowak, one of the best detectives in the division."

Stas extended his hand and gazed into a face that radiated warmth and love. He wanted to say something but whatever came quickly to mind sounded trite. "I'm glad to meet you, Luz," was all he could muster. He left them and walked over to the grill.

Edwards pushed chicken legs and thighs to the side and put hot dogs on for the kids. He looked up. "You talk to Barbara?"

"Marlowe's keeping her entertained."

Edwards frowned, distracted, the fire flared. "Shit, shit!" He turned too quickly, dropping the long fork onto the grill. Trying to retrieve the fork and save several hot dogs from rolling off the barbecue, he hit the plastic platter that clattered to the patio floor.

"I'll get you another one." Stas picked it up and headed to the kitchen.

Edwards nodded, wiped his hands on his apron, and gingerly rolled the errant franks to the center of the grill.

Stas paused at the door, looking back at Jonson and his new bride. They seemed caught up in the newness of their relationship, whispering and laughing at some secret, intimate joke. Luz hung on Jonson's every word. Stas recognized the way she looked at her husband. He'd seen that look recently but had dismissed it. He wasn't about to set himself up for a fall.

"I need a clean platter."

Jill handed him her glass. "And I need a refill—please." Her voice had taken on a huskiness.

"You okay? Be careful, vodka can sneak up on you."

"Doesn't seem to bother you."

"Yeah, but I've been drinking it for a long time."

She waved him off with a frown. "Spare me the history."

Stas got the bottle and poured Jill another two fingers.

She took the glass, lightly brushing her hand over his, then held up her drink. "Don't patronize me."

He poured her a little more. "You want to tell me what's going on?"

"I don't know." She took a good swallow and coughed.

He stood at the corner of the counter and watched her take another hefty swig that brought tears to her eyes. "I said sip!"

"Stas, I'm so tired of this drill. I want to do something, go to school, get a job. I feel like I'm losing my mind." Her voice was almost pleading. "I know there's something missing."

"It'll be all...." He caught a hint of anger rising to the surface, giving color to her neck. "I know, don't patronize. You need to talk to Sid."

"Do you?"

Stas shook his head. "Then get some counseling."

"Did you?"

"No."

"Okay, I won't go there, but how did this party happen? I thought just you were coming over for dinner."

"Is that what Sid told you?"

"Yes, to see Barbara."

"So he was trying to hook me up?"

"Is there something wrong with that, with Barbara?"

"No, Barbara's great, but I wouldn't have been coming to dinner. I'm just not interested in a relationship...." he paused, "with Barbara."

Jill sipped her drink. "I understand."

"I don't think you do. My needs are different."

"Yeah, it all boils down to the man's needs." She turned back to the sink.

Stas left the kitchen. He had nothing to offer. His marriage had been over before it had begun, and his track record with women since then was not stellar. But there was Dina. He returned to the patio, handed Sid the platter, and watched him stack on the chicken and hot dogs before starting on the steaks. "Make mine rare."

"You know that's not good for you."

"Rare, Sid."

Luz and Barbara put platters and bowls of food on the table while Jill fixed food for the kids and called them. They bounded in grabbing plates with one hand and shoveling food with the other. As quickly as they came, they scattered to another part of the house, shouting at each other, dropping chips and salad greens in their wake.

Sid closed the sliding glass patio doors and stood at the head of the table. "C'mon, let's eat." He turned towards Barbara. "Why don't you sit over here next to Stas? You guys haven't visited."

"That's okay. I'm sitting next to Chris. He's been telling me about the rodeo. I've never met a rodeo rider before. I can talk to Stas anytime."

"Rodeo? For God's sake, he's a cop, like the rest of us." Edwards's voice cracked. He sat and waited for the others to seat themselves. "Let's join hands in prayer." He grabbed his wife's hand and bowed his head. "Heavenly Father, bless this food and this gathering. Keep us out of harms'..."

Jill cut him off. "Amen"

There was an awkward silence as plates were heaped. Everyone settled into the food, mumbling between bites. When they did reach a point where they were getting full, the dinner conversation drifted from one safe topic to another before coming to rest on the dead.

"The woman you found in the dumpster was actually frozen? Luz had speared a tomato wedge and held it in midair. How? Was she stuffed in a freezer?"

"We don't know yet," Stas said.

Edwards looked up from his plate. "I don't think that's suitable dinner table conversation."

No one paid him any attention.

Barbara turned to Chris. "Do you think she was frozen alive?" She shuddered, shaking her head in disbelief.

"No, she died of an overdose of heroin," Jonson added.

"Is that all you guys can do is talk shop?" Jill's words were slurred. "I don't want to hear any more about a dead woman. You won't want my dessert."

Jonson grimaced. "It's not something frozen is it?"

"With ladyfingers?" Barbara chimed in, laughing.

"You been drinking?" Edwards hissed at his wife, his sharp tone almost muffled by a mouth full of salad greens..

Jill smiled defiantly. "Stas fixed me up."

"Well, lay off that stuff." He looked at his partner.

"This is all so fascinating. Finding women frozen in a dumpster and the rodeo." Barbara leaned toward Marlowe. "Do you really ride those bucking..."

"Broncos." Marlowe added.

"The only thing he rides is a Crown Vic," Edwards muttered.

"Man, what the shit do you know?" Marlowe nodded towards Barbara and Luz. "Excuse my French. Sid, you ever been on a horse or to a rodeo? So shut your sorry... mouth until you have."

Once again the table fell silent while Jill excused herself, disappeared into the kitchen, then returned with a frozen, lemony dessert that had started to ooze off the serving dish. She caught a drop with her finger and licked it sensuously before putting the plate down on the table that dribbled yellow fluff onto the pink table cloth. The ladies each took a small portion, and the men passed.

Stas got up, went to the kitchen, and returned with his glass refreshed.

"Man, how much of that stuff can you put away?" Marlowe asked.

"I don't keep track."

"Maybe you should, you're driving." Marlowe turned to Barbara. "Once upon a time I could keep up, but...."

"But you're not Polish." Stas rose. "And I need to get back to LA."

Edwards glanced at his watch. "It's only seven-thirty."

Stas polished off his drink. "You know, the traffic."

Edwards glared at his partner. "It's Saturday. There's no traffic."

"There's always traffic." Stas had his keys out. "Good steaks, Sid. Just like I like'em."

"Yeah, half raw," Edwards responded.

Marlowe got up and pulled out Barbara's chair. "We got to hit the road, too."

Edwards looked at Jill, who had nodded off, then back to his sister-in-law. "Barbara, what's up?"

"Chris's giving me a lift to LA so you won't have to take me so early in the morning." Barbara put her hand on Marlowe's arm. "I'll get my things."

A chill settled at the table, draining all color from Edwards's face. He glared at his sister-in-law. "But you don't even know Chris."

Barbara smiled. "If he's one of LAPD's finest, what's not to know. He'll drive slowly. I can learn a lot on the drive back." She left the room.

Edwards looked at his wife again.

She was now awake and aware but did not look at her husband. Instead, she reached for her dessert, ran her finger along the edge of the plate, and licked her finger. "Would anyone like to take something home. We have plenty." Jill's voice droned as she moved to the kitchen.

"I'll help you clear-up." Luz grabbed her plate and glass then followed.

"Take the rest of your vodka with you," Edwards looked at his partner.

"It's empty" Jill said.

"You mean you drank a whole fifth?"

"I had help." Stas moved toward the kitchen and shouted. "Thanks, Jill."

"Where's your sister-in-law staying in LA?" Jonson asked.

Edwards spoke into his plate. "One of those extended stay places in Glendale. We'd tried to get her to stay here, but she said it was too inconvenient going back and forth on the train." He looked up at Stas. "Can't you take her, it's on your way?"

Stas had put on his jacket. "I'm not going home."

ELEVEN

On Monday, the team began in earnest to sift through the evidence. Jonson busied himself with the new murder book for the Jane Doe found in the Hollywood dumpster. Even though they hadn't ID'd her, they had taken the case over from Hollywood Division since the circumstances of the two murdered women were almost identical. Having two similar murders within a week of each other could indicate a serial killer loose again in LA, and Raymond Lenox, cousin to the Judge and prominent attorney with ties to City Hall, was bringing pressure to bear to quickly find the killer of Cynthia Lenox.

Stas laid out the photos taken at both crime scenes. The common denominator in each was the dumpster plus the uncanny resemblance of the two women from the artist's drawings, Cynthia's picture, and the crime scene photo of the second victim. Even with deterioration of each death, the women could have been sisters. They had the same facial bone structure, same hair coloring, beyond that, they both were wearing similar housedresses, had the same neat abdominal incisions, indicating both had had C-sections. These similarities could not be ignored.

Were they dealing with some deranged psychopath who got his kicks delivering the babies of his kidnap victims. If so, where were the babies? Also, Jane Doe hadn't been left to rot for four days in her Hollywood dumpster. If Carroll saw an SUV leave the crime scene shortly before he found the body, then the killer might have had her in his vehicle.

If only Carroll's memory could be trusted. Stas suspected he used meth. He seemed a little too agitated, yet a little too self-controlled, making sure he didn't say the wrong thing.

Carroll was too thin, too hyper, as if he needed to be moving, dancing, walking. Hadn't he said he'd been dancing most of the night at some club? Then his deferring to Edwards when he answered a question, insisting on having Edwards's card, putting his hand on the detective's sleeve, assuring him that he would call if he remembered anything important..

Then in the squad room, a call came at 3:34 p.m. for Edwards.

Jonson held the phone out for the detective and pursed his lips. "It's Carroll."

Edwards looked puzzled and waved the phone away.

"Hold a minute, I'll see if I can find Detective Edwards." Jonson put his hand over the receiver for a second and looked up to the ceiling. "He stepped out for a minute. I'll give him the message."

Stas watched the charade from his desk. "What was that all about?"

"It's that wit, Carroll. First he wanted to talk to Sid. Says he wants to come up and see us. He remembered something about the SUV from Thursday night. He's bringing his friend. They'll be here in twenty minutes."

Stas eye-balled his partner. "Guess you'd better set it up."

There was panic in Edwards's voice. "I'm not the lead. I don't want to interview him. Where's Marlowe?"

"Carry the ball for a change. Marlowe wasn't there this morning for the briefing. You can fill him in on the charming Ms. Carroll later."

"It's not funny. What's his story anyway?" Jonson asked.

"He strikes me as a transsexual waiting, waiting..." Stas paused, "...waiting to blossom into womanhood."

Somewhere in the background someone shouted, "Bull shit!"

"We'll do it together. Jonson can observe. If they can give us anything on the SUV, it'll be our first break," Stas added. To kill the time waiting for Carroll and friend, Stas took out a blank sheet of white paper and started to do his homework, make his list. Maybe he'd give the class another shot. He printed in his neat hand. At least the nuns had taught him that. The list was short: car, house, woman, wife, children, retirement. He crossed out house and wrote condo over it, circled the car, wrote child over children, and put a question mark next to retirement. What would he do with his spare time? He added hobby, maybe fishing, drew three lines under wife, and circled children. Was he that passionate about having kids? No, but was the idea of having a wife showing signs of paranoia? Must it be a wife? Would he settle for a woman, an all-American, mainstream girl, one he could take home to meet Vlade and Helena. She didn't have to be Polish, but it would help. He could take her to Sid's boring cookouts. She and Jill could exchange recipes. They'd discuss the kids' orthodontics.

Stas felt a stab in his gut and reached for his lukewarm coffee, then printed SEX in capital letters, wondering about Jill, Barbara, and even Luz. There was another jab when he thought about Amanda. Was he on some kind of ego trip? It hadn't worked with her the first time. Why did he want to push the envelope again when he already knew what the result would be? He looked at his effort and frowned before balling the paper up and shooting it into the trash. Goal!

Edwards parked himself in the doorway and cast a furtive glance at his partner. "It's time to interview that Carroll person."

Carroll Wilson had arrived with his friend, Clayton Minor. Both were dressed to the hilt, Carroll in a mint green, skin tight t-shirt that revealed a faint swelling of the breast. The cream pants caressed every curve, yet there was the absence of a bulge at the crouch. Stas wondered if he had had any surgery already.

The detectives ushered the two men to an interview room.

Carroll paused at the door before entering. "This is my friend, Clayton. He was with me at the club the night I found the body."

Clayton was taller than both detectives and Carroll. His jeans were so tight that he looked as if he had been liquefied and poured into them, and his red shirt was cut to the waist revealing a chest as smooth as glass. Both men were clean shaven with heavily made-up eyes.

Stas reached over and shook a soft manicured hand, catching a scent of lavender that made him think of Dina. "I'm Detective Nowak." He nodded towards his partner. "This is Detective Edwards. Have a seat."

Both men sat back and crossed their legs waiting for Edwards to begin. Stas stood just inside the door. This was to be his partner's show.

Carroll reached in his handbag for a pack of gum, offered it around, before taking a stick out, unwrapping it, and popping it, with great flair, into his mouth. He looked around for a waste basket before returning the pack and wrapper to his bag. "I'm very nervous." His voice had a high falsetto pitch. "Detective Edwards, may I call you Sid?" He continued without waiting for the detective to respond. He touched Clayton on his arm. "This is my very best friend. He can verify anything I tell you."

Edwards ran his finger around the inside of his shirt collar and looked past Carroll to Stas. "You were together at a club Thursday night?

"The Bounty," Clayton confirmed.

Carroll fluttered his lashes. "You seem nervous." He chewed vigorously. "I'm the one should be nervous. Just thinking about what happened, then thinking about coming down here. Ugh. Then thinking about what to wear to mask my lack of sleep." He turned around to Stas. "You look really good in that suit. Gray becomes you, goes with your eyes."

Stas smiled. "There's nothing to be nervous about. We're just getting your statement, for the record."

Somewhat reassured, Carroll turned back to Edwards. "You know, I have that effect on some men." He had turned again to

Stas. "But I bet I don't faze you, do I?" He leaned in toward Edwards. "He's a stud. I don't particularly like studs."

Edwards coughed. "Can you tell us what you remember about last Thursday?"

Carroll reached across the table as if to touch Edwards, but stopped short. "I saw the SUV pull up to valet park when we arrived. It was big, had that Caddy symbol on the grill."

Stas chimed in. "An Escalade?"

"I guess, plus it had tinted windows." Carroll turned to Clayton. "You saw it. I think it belongs to ... oh, what's his name, dances real cool, brings his wife sometimes. Hel-lo, how much fun can that be if you're trying to, you know, score with somebody, and there's your wife looking over your shoulder."

"If it's who I think it is, she's looking over his shoulder for her own action." Clayton added.

Carroll snapped his fingers in a Z that trailed off into his lap. "Well, whatever floats your boat, a *ménage à* three...." His energy ebbed.

Stas started to correct him but paused. "What do you do for a living?"

Carroll turned, "I'm a freelance artist. You know, design, graphics. I'm even working on a line of clothing, retro-Loretta Young or maybe a line of gay-unisex."

Edwards squirmed.

Stas smiled. "Did you get the license number?"

"I wasn't paying any attention when we went in, and the bitch tried to run me over at the dumpster."

"You saw a woman driving?" Edwards asked.

Carroll stared blankly at Edwards. "I didn't see nobody. I was too busy getting my ass out of the way." He winked, "Anyway, that's just a term of endearment, honey."

"How often do you go to this club?" Stas asked.

"A couple of times a week, if we feel like dressing. If we just want to hang out in some place quiet and have a few drinks, we go to Pasadena."

"The person that you see sometimes at the Bounty, does he frequent the club in Pasadena?" Edwards asked.

Both men shook their heads.

"No, he's strictly into the Hollywood scene," Carroll said.

"Would you recognize him if you saw him again?" Stas asked.

There was an edge of excitement in Carroll's voice. "Come with us tomorrow night. I'll point him out."

Clayton chimed in. "I bet valet parking can tell you about the SUV. There're surveillance cameras all over."

Stas opened the door to leave. "I guess we have a date."

Dixie snoozed, her nose resting on her paws, the paws resting on what was left of her blanket. She heard the truck's engine, raised her head, and turned it toward the slamming door. She really didn't feel like rushing out of her house especially since she'd been left unattended for so long. A nervous construction worker had dropped her food on a paper plate in front of her house. The food slid off into the dirt. She hated trying to eat like that and growled her disapproval.

Now a deep aluminum dish was shoved in front of her. She stuck her nose in the midst of the food and inhaled, finishing the dish's contents in record time. A shallow pan of water replaced the food's container. Dixie lapped loudly, slapping water onto the surrounding ground.

Next? Dixie whined, signaling that it was time for a walk, her tail beating the ground stirring up a whorl of dust. She watched as the container of water was removed from the entrance of her house and taken to the back of the truck. Her master returned and unfastened the chain attached to a post by the dog house. A heavy leather leash was hooked into the choke chain.

"C'mon girl". He led Dixie to the truck and opened the door.

Dixie growled. This wasn't the way for the walk. She sat a few feet away from the open passenger door. Her bottom, like a lead weight, made it almost impossible for him to move her. The second growl rumbled from deep within her being. She wasn't going anywhere.

"What is it, Dixie?"

She turned and looked back to her house.

TWELVE

The Bounty was the nickname given to a popular new Hollywood club, The Mutiny on the Bounty. An enterprising decorator high on something other than a creative imagination and with very little knowledge of the geography of Gilbert and Sullivan operettas had decked out the club to look like the *H.M.S. Pinafore* moored in an English port instead of plying the exotic waters of the South Pacific. The male waiters wore striped shirts open to the waist, exposing shaved, tanned chests, a ringed nipple, and pants so tight that they had to use fanny packs to carry change and to cover any embarrassing bulges. Some of the young men even tucked Post-it notes in the pack for quickly penned invitations suggesting assignations after closing.

At the outside entrance some customers, dressed in outlandish pirates' outfits, tried to replicate anything remotely associated with the recent swashbuckling craze and the effeminate antics of Captain Jack Sparrow. They could care less if what they wore shocked or offended. Still others, dressed as if they had just stepped from the slick pages of *GQ*, were standing three deep when Stas, Edwards, Carroll, and Clayton arrived.

Edwards looked at the line. "Are we going in there?"

Stas turned. "That's the idea."

"Do we have to?"

"If we want to get a feel for possible perps, then we need to hang with them."

"I guess you did this in Vice?"

"Many times."

Edwards looked over the line. "Suppose the place gets raided?"

Stas smiled. He seemed to be in a familiar comfort zone. "The place is legit, don't worry about it."

The detectives paid for everyone's cover after showing their IDs, then immediately entered the club amid some low grumbles from a few of the customers the furthest from the entrance. Stas had called ahead and told management that they would be there on police business.

It took a few minutes for Stas to adjust to the low lights and loud music. Edwards looked uncomfortable, blinking and shifting his gaze around the room.

"Come on!" Clayton led them to a tall table with high stools close to the dance floor where some individuals danced more with themselves than with a partner. "They haven't warmed up yet."

Edwards looked at the dancers, squinting a little, as if trying to focus on the diverse characters parading around him.

Stas stood next to his stool and leaned into the table, catching the attention of Carroll and Clayton. "What are you drinking?"

"I want an apple martini," Carroll replied.

"An apple what?" Stas had to raise his voice as the music revved up.

"Martini, apple. They make good ones. Get one for Sid." Carroll touched the detective's sleeve. "They're very tame. Better get one for Clayton, too."

Stas left the table and moved through the crowd, dodging a couple of waiters balancing full trays. At the bar he raised his hand to catch the attention of the bartender. "Three apple martinis and a double vodka neat." He put a fifty on the bar and waited for the first of the drinks and his change. "Is the manager here?" Stas held out his card. "I called earlier. He should be expecting us."

The bartender nodded, took the card, and slipped it into his shirt pocket. "I'll tell him."

After Stas made two trips from the bar with their drinks, Carroll was already scanning the crowd and popping his fingers in time to the music. Stas followed his gaze.

Suddenly, Carroll jumped off his stool and pushed pass a waiter with a full tray, almost causing a spill. "Sorry!...Stel, Stel, Stella!"

He grabbed the elbow of a woman, who looked about forty. She sported a short, mannish hair style, small gold hoop earrings, no make-up. Picking up a drink at the bar, she turned and followed Carroll back to the table.

He waved his hand like a wand across the table. "This is my friend, Sid Edwards, and his partner, Detective Nowak. We call him Stas. They're cops. We're here on police business." He took a sip. "I'm a witness..." He paused and took another sip. "... to a murder." There seemed to be a sense of pride in his attitude.

Everyone at the table leaned into the center to hear and be heard over the loud music.

"Stella's a fireman, ...person, sorry," with deliberation, "... a fi-er-fighter." Carroll added.

"That's okay." Stella removed her soft, brown leather jacket and draped it across the back of an empty chair, then gave both detectives a warm smile as she looked them over.

"What station do you work out of?" Edwards asked.

"I don't. I'm an arson investigator," she paused. "In San Bernardino County."

Edwards seemed surprised. "You come all the way to LA?"

"I like to keep my private life and my public life separated by at least fifty miles if I can." She took a sip from her drink, then leaned in towards Stas. "I'm surprised you guys are here."

"It's business," Stas said.

Carroll was looking around again. "Have you seen Mona lately?" He tapped on the table and looked around nervously.

"Not recently, sometimes she goes to Santa Monica, sometimes Pasadena, especially without her husband," Stella added.

No one spoke for a while. Conversation was almost futile when the DJ pumped up the volume even more. Stas drank slowly, eyeing the crowd.

Edwards sipped and frowned. "I can't stand this sweet stuff. I don't want to get sick." He leaned toward his partner. "What do you have?"

"Vodka neat, but if...."

Edwards eased off his stool and headed for the bar. He had to push past several well-dressed men on the edge of the dance floor. Edwards stopped to watch, frowning as the dancers went through their moves, some of which verged on the obscene.

Carroll followed the detective but stopped at the fringe of the crowd and started popping his fingers again. Never missing a beat, he screamed when a rakishly thin young man bent down with the agility of an acrobat and bit his partner on the calf. The observing crowd howled. Edwards pushed his way to the bar.

After a few minutes he returned with a glass of clear liquid and climbed back onto his stool. "I got a double." He held his glass up as if to toast.

Amid shouts and screams, Clayton pointed to a makeshift plank jutting out into a section of the dance floor. A small group rushed to gather around the plank making it difficult for Stas to see what was holding everyone's interest.

After a minute the music stopped, and the crowd parted. Some returned to their tables revealing the point of interest: a young man in black boxer briefs kept time to nothing, swaying his hips, and snapping his fingers in midair as he stood alone at the end of the plank. Dollar bills stuck out from the waistband of his shorts, forming a green, leafy fringe around his middle. Several men walked over to the lone dancer and took a look into his briefs, then tucked additional bills into his waistband as the young Adonis kept pace with a phantom rhythm until the music started again and another group gathered for his show.

"What are they doing?" Edwards asked after taking a sip of his vodka.

"Checking to see what he's packing." Clayton responded nonchalantly.

"What, a gun?" Edwards asked.

"Not hardly. They're sizing up his family jewels." Carroll grabbed his crotch. "You want to go see?"

Edwards took a gulp from his drink, coughed as his eyes watered, and turned to his partner. "We didn't come here for that. Let's talk to the parking cashier."

Stas grabbed Carroll's arm. "C'mon."

The three moved to the exit where the bouncer, who towered over them by at least five inches, stamped the backs of their hands.

"What's this?" Edward turned his hand over.

"So you can get back in," the gravelly-voiced attendant replied.

At the cashier's cage, a young woman with pink spiked hair counted money behind her metal grill. She looked up when Stas flashed his badge.

"We do something wrong?"

"No. We need some information and to see your video surveillance tapes."

She nodded, still counting her money. They waited until she bagged the cash, then called the manager, who met Edwards and Stas at the entrance.

"Adam Pugh." He did not offer his hand but moved down the hall. "I have the tapes ready for you."

He left a strong citrus scent in his wake as they followed him to an office decorated to resemble Hollywood's version of a captain's cabin on a pirate ship. Pugh pointed to a small TV, VCR and a stack of tapes on his pristine desk. "The equipment is a little dated, but it still works." After turning everything on, he stood aside as Stas slid in the top video cassette.

He turned to Edwards. "This doesn't need both of us. Go back and keep an eye on Carroll and Stella."

"Why Stella?"

"Don't you find her interesting?" Stas asked.

"Should I? Is she gay too?"

"I'd make book on it."

Edwards left Stas scrutinizing the comings and goings of patrons at the main entrance. He found nothing and ejected the first tape and inserted another labeled "Parking Lot". Before he started, Pugh paused by the door.

"What're you drinking?"

Stas looked up slowly flexing his shoulders. "Vodka, neat, no Russian stuff, please."

"Gotcha." Pugh closed the door behind him and returned in less than ten minutes, placing the drink cradled in two black napkins decorated with a white skull and cross bones on the desk next to the TV.

"Thanks." Stas took a gulp and turned back to viewing the tape. He wasn't sure just what he was looking for but felt whatever it was, it would instinctively register when he saw it.

Pugh leaned over the detective's shoulder. "Find anything?"

"Not yet." Then he felt a quick surge of adrenaline. There on the screen were two black Cadillac Escalades pulling in next to each other. The video was dark and grainy, and the screen went black when he tried to pause the picture. "Shit!" He pushed play then rewound to get the willowy images moving backwards to their vehicles. He hit play again. There were three people, a blond woman and two men. He paused the tape and looked around for Pugh, but the manager had slipped out. Stas took another gulp from his watered vodka and went back into the club to get Carroll. Although his gut was talking to him, telling him he had found the right people, he needed someone who could ID the owners of the Escalades.

He found Edwards alone at their table, swaying in rhythm with the loud music, drinking from a fresh glass with a piece of lime, two cherries, and an olive.

Stas placed a hand on his partner's shoulder. "Where's Carroll?"

103

His partner turned after fishing the olive out of his glass. "What?"

"Carroll, where is he?"

Edwards popped the olive in his mouth and pointed to the dance floor. "Out there."

Stas shook his head before wading out into the crowd of sweating, moving bodies. He tried to avoid couples dancing together, stepping instead between those who were not making bodily contact with their partners. He located Carroll alone yet moving to the music near the now vacant plank. "I need you for a minute." He walked off the floor without looking back, relieved to get out of colliding colognes, deodorants, and funk that bombarded his olfactory sense.

Carroll, dodging dancers, followed him to Pugh's office. "Nice!" as he closed the door shutting out the noise.

Stas leaned over the desk. "I want you to look at something." He pushed the play button on the VCR. "Shit." The counter was stuck on triple zero. He had to mentally gage, pushing the rewind button and holding it down for several seconds before hitting play again. This took several minutes. When he found the desired place, he straightened, and made room for Carroll, who drew closer to the detective in order to get a better view of the images on the small screen.

Stas immediately sensed an uptick in Carroll's body language when he edged even closer to the TV. "You recognize anyone?"

He pointed to the dusty screen. "That's Paul, Ryan, and that's his wife, Mona." There was an intake of breath as if the woman moving toward the entrance on the grainy thirteen inch screen had paused to caress some secret part of Carroll, awakening long dormant feeling that only a woman could arouse.

Stas looked at Carroll. A flush had feathered up his neck to give a pinkish glow to his ears. "Are you okay?"

"Maybe too many apple martinis."

"Some women have a way of doing that to you." Stas turned back to the screen. "And the SUVs?"

"They all have them." Carroll regained his composure and stayed until they finished the tape.

Stas popped in another one that covered the night after the body was found. There was no red SUV, only a red sports car that wheeled into the lot and left just as quickly when the parking attendant indicated that the lot was full.

Stas looked over at Carroll who seemed lost in a trance. "How well do you know Mona?"

"Not well enough." Carroll cleared his throat.

"But I thought...." He ejected the last tape and returned it to its case.

"I bet you meet women who make you feel that way all the time," Carroll said.

"Yeah," Stas turned off the equipment, "but not as often as you might think."

"Well, I guess a man can change his mind about the operation if he meets the right woman."

THIRTEEN

They left The Bounty just before it closed. Even the light fog rolling in from Santa Monica could not dampen their good spirits. Stas wasn't sure what he had found, but it made him feel that the night hadn't been a total waste.

Edwards tried to sing. "Doggy, dog, I'm chasing the cat."

Carroll hooked his arm into the detective's and laughed. "That's not the way the song goes."

"Shut-up, Sid. You're too drunk to sing. You should have stuck with the martinis. How many vodkas did you have?" Stas thought back. This was the first time that he and his partner had ever been to a bar.

"I don't know. I kept asking the bartender to put stuff in them. I like the olives."

"You have to watch vodka. It's sneaky. You'll get us stopped for disorderly conduct." Stas laughed. He had even enjoyed his partner's company and thought about taking him to the Second Set one night, then quickly changed his mind.

Earlier when they arrived at The Bounty, the valet parking was full, so they had found a satellite lot several blocks away. There was no attendant, only a large metal box with a series of slots that corresponded with numbered spaces. A driver would slip in five bucks, park, and go on his way. Carroll and Clayton had parked next to each other; Edwards was two spaces over. Stas, as usual, parked the farthest away, under a lone bright light.

"See, Sid, you need to loosen up more often. You know you had a good time. I love this detective work. Maybe I'll join the LAPD." Carroll squeezed Edward's arm.

The detective visibly tensed with the touch even though he seemed to have warmed somewhat after drinking a couple of apple martinis and several vodkas. "Join the Sheriffs'. I hear they're a lot more fun."

Stas hadn't felt the effects of his drinks. The vodkas he'd been nursing during the night had been watered down with too much ice and not enough alcohol but then, he shouldn't complain, the last couple of drinks had been on the house. He took his keys out and unlocked the driver's door with the remote as he approached his car.

Carroll stopped at his car. "My feet hurt!" He kicked off his shoes and popped his trunk to throw them in when a black Toyota King Cab pulled along the curb and stopped, leaving the motor running.

Clayton stood by his door, shielding his eyes from the brightness of the headlights combined with the bank of lights mounted on the top of the SUV.

"What the fu..." Carroll's nascent expletive turned into a shrill scream.

Two young men, dressed in jeans, monkey boots, and loosely hanging Air Force jackets, jumped to the curb. One wielded a golf club, the other a baseball bat. The lower halves of their faces were covered with black and white bandanas. Their shaved heads were as smooth as billiard balls.

"Shit, oh, shit," Clayton screamed again and tried to get into his car.

Edwards heard the screams and moved towards the trunk of Clayton's car. His second reaction was to reach for a weapon he didn't have. In that split second, the base of the golf club caught him on the shoulder, knocking him down. "Hey, hey, what...?"

Swish, he ducked the second time as the baseball bat hit the back fender of the car.

The attack happened so fast, that no one heard Stas approach. He didn't speak but slipped two shells filled with hard rubber pellets into his ten gauge shotgun and racked the pump.

The motion rang out like a death knell, then he fired. The blast was deafening, and acrid smoke, mingled with the fog shrouded the parking lot.

The man wielding the golf club, the one poised to swing at Carroll, was blown back into the other assailant, knocking them both to the ground. One coughed, felt his chest, and ran his trembling fingers over his head.

Stas ejected the smoking shells and held two more in his right hand, ready to insert. No one moved. The scene was like an eerie tableau. The interior of the Toyota was still, only the engine rumbled low in its sinister idle.

Stas's voice was cold and clear, made loud enough to penetrate the engine's noise so that no one could mistake his menacing intent. "I'm dropping in two more. This time the load is stainless steel buck shot. At this range, I can blow your fucking heads off."

The brief silence from the young men magnified the sound of the two cartridges being dropped into the chamber, the pump being pulled back, singing a new song as the thin red beam, piercing the late night fog, hovered on the forehead of the assailant who had regained his feet. He pulled his accomplice from the pavement and shoved him towards the SUV. The back passenger door opened, a hand reached out and pulled the stunned man into the rear of the vehicle. The other man climbed in and closed the door. The rack of lights on top went dark as the SUV peeled away from the curb.

It was over in a flash. Carroll still stood frozen by the open door of his car, tears dragging flakes of black mascara down his cheeks. Clayton dropped his jacket and ran shoeless to an angle of the lot to vomit in the darkness. The sound of his retching was the only noise to punctuate the still night air. Edwards flexed his shoulder as he struggled to get up.

Stas disappeared. When he returned, the shotgun was not with him. "Are you all right?"

"Where did you get that thing?" Edwards walked toward his partner.

"It's my birthday present. Davis modified it for me and brought it by yesterday."

Carroll, visibly shaken, sniffed. "Are the cops coming?"

"I didn't call it in."

Edwards rubbed his shoulder. "Why not?"

"For one, they bailed. Did you get a license number or a description? Two, you want to explain what you were doing at The Bounty with Carroll?"

"You were there, too."

"Yeah, but I was working, and I don't smell half as bad as you do. Plus, I don't feel like doing the report." Stas looked at his watch. "Do you?"

Carroll approached. "I'm sure as hell glad you had that cannon." He turned to Edwards. "Here, you dropped your wallet."

Clayton had retrieved his shoes and leaned against the car to slip them on. "Let's go to Dante's. I need a drink. There's no way I'll get to sleep after this...." he paused at his door, "without a little help."

Carroll locked his car. "Yeah, well, a drink won't hardly calm my shattered nerves."

"Haven't you had enough excitement for one night?" Stas asked.

Carroll waved him off and jumped into the passenger seat of Clayton's car. The black Mazda revved up and peeled out of the parking lot, before turning on the headlights.

"I wonder if they're running on something besides apple martinis and a few skinheads looking for a little excitement." Stas shook his head. "God, I hate those bastards."

"They're no worse than any of the other gangs," Edwards muttered as he moved to his car.

Stas was too tired to argue. "You going to be okay driving home?" he asked. "If you want, you can follow me and crash on the sofa."

"Okay, I got to call Jill first." He walked to his car, looked under it, then went through his pockets. "I lost my phone."

Stas handed him his cell. "Here, use mine. You may have left it at The Bounty. Get it tomorrow."

Edwards phoned his wife. "I told Jill that I was spending the night with you. If I drive home now, I'll just have to turn around and come back."

Edwards followed Stas home, parked in a space for guests and followed him up the stairs. Although he had picked Stas up many times, this was the first time he had ever been inside his apartment. He stood in the middle of the floor looking around the somewhat spartan surroundings. "No clutter. Man, no crunching toys underfoot." Edwards sat and untied his shoes, placing them near the coffee table.

Stas stood in the doorway of the bedroom, hanging up his suit. He'd already put on LAPD sweat pants. "You want a drink?" He caught Edwards' look of disapproval. "I do have coffee. There may even be some tea."

"That's okay, if I drink coffee, I won't sleep. Caffeine keeps me up."

"Whatever." Stas went back into the bedroom and returned with a pillow and blanket. "Sofa's all yours." He looked at his watch. "I'll see you in a couple of hours. There're extra towels on the sink."

After going to the bathroom, Edwards looked around the bedroom, and picked up the single photo in a carved wooden frame. It was a picture of Stas in dress blues at his graduation from the Police Academy. His partner was already in bed.

"Good night, Sid."

Edwards replaced the photo on the chest of drawers as Stas turned out the light. "Good night."

In the living room he stripped to his boxers, arranged the blanket on the sofa, fluffed the pillow, and surveyed, for the first time, his partner's apartment. He sat on the edge of the black leather sofa and looked at the wall unit facing him. All of the components looked expensive, but that was it: no frills, no little knickknacks like those that covered almost every surface in his family room. The only art was some mountains in six sepia photos on the wall opposite Stas's reading chair.

Edwards turned off the table lamp and settled under the blanket. He rearranged the pillow releasing, as if by magic, its secret, hidden in the depth of soft down. He didn't recognize the scent as it escaped to caress his head and toy with him, but it wasn't his partner's expensive cologne, and it certainly didn't smell like any of the cheap aftershaves he wore. He twitched his nose and buried it in the pillow trying to envision the woman who wore that intoxicating perfume. Well, now he had proof that someone had shared Stas's bed. He'd find out who she was. After all, he was a detective.

FOURTEEN

Stas finished his paper work and left a report for Edwards to complete before cleaning off his desk and dialing Dina. She picked up on the first ring, and if she wasn't anticipating his call, she gave no sign of it.

"Hello."

The warmth in her voice always lifted his spirits and, even at his desk, fanned feelings of desire.

"Doing anything tomorrow evening?"

"No," she paused, "why?"

"I thought I'd take you out for your birthday."

"I'm impressed. You know the date."

"I saw it on your license."

"Do I get flowers?"

"Don't push it, babe."

"Where are we going?"

"It's a surprise. Wear something red. You look good in that color."

The next day he left work in the early afternoon and drove to the Garment District to pick up a new charcoal gray suit he'd had tailored at Jimmy Wong's.

At home, he showered, shaved, and dressed. A light gray shirt with white French cuffs and collar was also new. He decided to wear a pair of light colored amber and gold cuff links that he'd bought in Gdansk. The tie was an old favorite, gray and gold with flecks of red. He slipped a small box wrapped in silver tissue from his trip to Chicago into his pocket and went to the garage.

He had planned a quiet evening, away from inquisitive eyes and prying questions. They had never had a real date, never dressed up, and gone out for dinner. He tried to take a mental assessment of their relationship that seemed to exist in a sort of limbo with no boundaries, no defining moments. His thoughts alternated between rationalization and repression. He realized that feelings of any kind for anyone would have to be dealt with, but not tonight. Still there was the tension of being discovered, but tonight, he didn't give a damn. He arrived at her apartment precisely at 7:15 p.m. He had made dinner reservations for 8:30 at the Mirage, an intimate inn in Ojai that promised an extraordinary dining experience and privacy. Stas checked his watch when Dina opened the door.

She straightened his tie and backed off. "You look delicious, but then you always do, in or out of that new suit."

He grinned slyly. "I think you just want an excuse to talk dirty to a cop."

"Is that against the law?"

At the elevator, he pushed the down button. "Only if you solicit, so watch it, babe."

"And if I'm only teasing?"

"I cuff you to the bed and exact my punishment."

"Promises, promises." She shook out a soft, cream-colored pashmina shawl and draped it over her shoulders.

As he helped her, he caught a whiff of her perfume, a scent uniquely Dina's. He looked her over in the elevator. She was modestly dressed in a black wool jersey suit that clung to all the right places. The creamy high silk collar and turned back matching cuffs accented her olive complexion. "You look great, babe, but I thought you were going to wear red?"

"I did." Dina smiled and looked straight ahead.

Before pulling out of the garage, he slipped a Marvin Gaye's disk in the car's CD player. The sensual words of "Sexual Healing" stirred his desire. A break in traffic on the 101 allowed him a quick glance over at Dina. She shifted her weight in the seat to tug at her skirt that had risen above her knees. He felt the urge to touch her silky thigh but pushed the button on the CD player instead replacing Gaye's suggestive lyrics with the relieving strains of a Chopin Polonaise that filled the car's interior. Another quick look at Dina's legs diverted his attention from the road as an SUV abruptly cut into his lane. He slowed and let a curse morph into an easy smile. *I guess I'd better pay attention to my driving if we plan to make it to dinner.*

The Mirage of Ojai was tucked amidst subtle lighting and towering, graceful palms that lined the drive. The air at the entrance was perfumed by pots of night blooming jasmine. The valet attendant waited for Stas to help Dina out of the car before getting behind the wheel.

She bent and sniffed. "Don't they smell wonderful?"

"What?"

"The flowers."

"They're okay." He took her arm as the door was opened for them to enter.

"You can't tell me you don't like good-smelling things."

"On a woman, on you. That's different."

The interior of the Mirage was decorated with wonderful pieces of art and fabrics that hinted of the North African desert. Dina seemed impressed and stood apart as Stas walked to the podium to check his reservations.

The maître d' who approached wore a black tux, but the waiters wore sand colored shirts cut like *galabiyahs*. "Your booth is ready, Mr. Nowak."

Strains of soft classical music floated up from speakers hidden among muted lights and silken foliage.

Stas tried to place the host's accent as they followed him to the entrance of the dining room. It sounded more Slavic than Moroccan. Dina edged closer, cleared her throat, then touched

114

the detective's sleeve. He felt the tension and looked to her side.

A tall well-dressed man in his early fifties stared in their direction. "Good seeing you, Dina." He jingled his key ring as if accenting his greeting.

Stas knew the look, felt his adrenaline ratchet up, felt the fine hairs rise on the back of his neck. "Dina?"

The man turned toward Stas, offering his hand. "Jason Goode." His hand was left suspended in midair.

"Hello, Jason." Dina's voice cracked with veiled strain. "It's been a long time." She turned to her companion. "This is Stas Nowak."

Before Jason could respond, a young woman, about twenty, came out of the ladies' lounge and joined him, linking her arm in his, then looking Dina over.

"Darling, can we have one more of those rummy drinks before we leave?"

Stas grabbed Dina's arm and moved her in silence to their booth. Once seated, Dina kept her eyes on the host as he draped the oversized napkin in her lap and handed her a menu.

"Can I get you a cocktail?"

"Just water," mumbled Dina, "with lemon, please."

"Bring me a double vodka, neat."

"Do you want that on the rocks?" the waiter asked.

"No!"

The waiter turned as Stas leaned closer to Dina. He tried to control his anger. "Who is he?"

"An old friend." She turned to the menu.

"And not a relative?"

Dina looked at him, a little unsettled. "No."

"The last name, just a coincidence, a john?"

She bit her lip and stared at the menu. "Must you always play the detective?"

Before he could question her again, the waiter placed a standing silver ice bucket containing a bottle draped in a white linen napkin next to Stas.

"What's this?" His voice was granite as he stared at the unsolicited offering.

"Champagne."

"I didn't...."

The waiter turned toward the lounge. "It's from the gentleman you were talking to...."

Before the waiter could finish, Stas rose, almost overturning the ice bucket.

Jason Goode was holding a jacket for his young woman when Stas approached.

With his anger smoldering just below the surface, he pulled Goode aside. "I don't care where you see her. Don't ever speak to Dina again."

Jason jerked loose from Stas's grip and straightened his cuffs.

"You don't know her anymore," Stas added.

Defiance crept into Jason's tone. "Are you her...." He looked the detective over.

Unconsciously, Stas had assumed a stance, one familiar on the street. His gray eyes narrowed. His lips tightened. "You don't want this, trust me."

Jason tried to respond in kind but found himself breathing hard. Content he had made his point, Stas wheeled and walked away. When he got back to the table, the waiter was standing, ready to take their orders. He moved aside when Stas brushed by the ice bucket again and sat down.

The waiter recited the evening's specials and paused. "Have you decided?"

"I'm not very hungry." Dina closed the menu. "I'll have a salad, the one with duck."

"I understand. The chef will make you something light. I'm sure you'll enjoy it." He turned to Stas.

"Another double."

They sat in awkward silence waiting for Dina's salad.The waiter returned with the drink. "Would you like to see the wine list."

"Not unless she wants wine."

The salad arrived, beautifully presented. The waiter fussed with placing it in front of Dina before leaving. She slowly picked at the greens and tasted some of the marinated duck before pushing the plate aside.

The waiter reappeared, looking disappointed at Dina's barely touched salad. "Can I get you something else? Would you like to see the dessert tray?"

"No, I think we're finished." Stas drained his glass, rose, and left Dina to maneuver herself out of the booth and tug at her skirt while he went to pay the check.

In the car, Stas rolled his window down and let the cold air blow in on the exposed side of his face. Dina tried to wrap herself in her shawl to ward off the chilly night air. They rode in silence. Finally, she closed her eyes to his dark mood, only to open them when she heard a gate go up. They had driven into his underground garage.

Dina straightened and looked out the window. "Aren't you taking me home?"

"Later." He got out of the car and walked towards the elevator pushing the up button.

He hadn't waited for her and didn't turn when he heard the staccato click of her heels on the concrete. When the elevator came, she entered it, but he made no effort to join her, and she made no effort to hold the closing door. He waited for a few seconds, then turned and took the stairs, two at a time.

They both arrived at his apartment at the same time. Angrily, he fumbled with his keys, finally unlocking the door and switching on his desk lamp before heading for the kitchen. Stas returned with his bottle of Chopin and two glasses. He poured and left one for Dina in the middle of the coffee table. She ignored his gesture and watched him take a long drink then flop on the sofa. He threw his suit jacket over to his recliner and, with some effort, kicked off his shoes.

Finally, he raised his face to glare at the still-standing Dina. "Now, are you going to tell me who he is?"

"I told you, he was an old friend."

"You're a bad liar. Who is he, Dina?"

"Who was he?"

Stas shifted his weight on the sofa, wanting to grab and bring her down to his level. "Who was he, then?"

Her voice was almost a whisper. "He brought me here."

"What, your ride?"

Dina slowly shook her head. He could feel pain through the liquor, but he wasn't sure whose.

Stas continued. "Your what, your husband, your lover? Who the hell is he?" He drained his glass. "All that shit you told me before was a pack of lies." He could see moisture in her eyes. "Hold the flood for Noah and tell me the goddamn truth."

Dina sat on the edge of the coffee table. He straightened and moved closer to meet her eyes. She flinched, staring into unsympathetic pools of gray ice.

She bit her lip. "He's nothing to me. He was my mother's friend in Arizona. He told her he had modeling contacts in Hollywood. So he brought me here, introduced me around to some agencies, but even with head shots and clothes, there was nothing for me, especially with no training. Anyway, he had other plans."

"Was he your pimp?"

"It wasn't like that!"

Stas cleared the huskiness in his voice. "Then tell me how it was, Dina? Did you love him? You must have fucked him. I know the look."

Dina turned to avoid his cold glare. "What look? You saw what you want to see. He left me with Carol Monti."

Stas nodded. He knew Carol Monti, a conniving whore turned unscrupulous madam who would have had her mother turning tricks on Sunset and Vine if she thought she could make a dime. "And Jason?"

"He went back to Phoenix for three more girls. When he got back, Monti put us up in an apartment off Franklin, and we went to work. At first, it was a nightmare, but Monti was a good teacher. We were party girls, and the money was good."

"Why didn't you get out?"

"I thought I was different. I knew he'd come back for me, but I got in deeper, owing Monti for my clothes, the rent. Then I met Sybil at a party and left with her. He did come back but not for me. Instead he brought new girls and sold their contracts to Monti."

"What about yours?"

"I never knew about a contract until Sybil paid Monti off. That was the last time I saw Jason until tonight."

"How did you get the same last name?"

"It was supposed to be my professional name, as a model."

"What's your real name? And don't lie to me."

"Dionne Bonamie. My mother loved the name. Thought it was so French. I didn't want the family to ever find out where I was...," she paused, "what I did, so I used his last name."

"Have you ever been arrested?"

She shook her head. "I told you before, no."

"Where's your book?"

"My book?"

"Yeah, babe, your book?"

"I got rid of it."

He stirred.

"I sold it," she added.

Exhausted, Stas closed his eyes and laid his head back on the sofa. He heard the rustle of fabric and slowly opened his eyes. She had thrown her jacket on top of his and was stepping out of her skirt. She wore no bra, but then she never needed one. Her breasts had a perfect lift and fullness that no amount of silicone could replicate. His gaze moved to the wisp of a red thong barely caressing her hips. Dina slowly inched closer. She had his attention. He leaned up, pulled the ties, and closed his eyes again. A muffled groan escaped his lips.

Her scent hovered over the buttons of his shirt as they were undone one by one, the cuff links discarded, the shirt tails pulled out, and the belt undone. He felt her warm breath on his chest as she toyed with his nipples, felt them harden as she continued. She yanked a chest hair and looked up when Stas opened his eyes.

"Show me what you learned, babe."

He awakened to a stabbing pain in his lower back. He shivered with the cold as he tried to recall why he was on the floor. The only warmth came from Dina's body curled into his. Stas got up without waking her and managed to carry her to his bed, but it was a strain. Either he was getting too old or she was too heavy for Hollywood theatrics. Deposited under the down quilt, he pulled her back to his center. He felt her heat, touched her hair, her face, the scar on her neck, making her move closer, seeking him now in her semi-wakefulness, reaching down, drawing her hand back as if shocked by his arousal. When she opened her eyes, he closed them with his lips.

Their movements were slow, languid, desiring it to last, but it didn't. She cried out, lost in her own release. Her head fell back on the pillow. He pulled her to him. It wasn't over. Her hands caressed his back then fell to her side as he caught her up in sync with his movements. This time they climaxed together and fell exhausted to the pillows.

His right arm had gone to sleep, making it difficult to disentangle himself from Dina and covers to reach the ringing phone.

"Nowak, here."

Dina moaned at being disturbed.

"Stas? Edwards."

Stas was awake now, but the irritation was evident in his tone. "I know who it is."

"I'm leaving home now. You want me to pick you up?"

"No, Sid."

"You got company?"

Stas was annoyed. "Sid, I'll see you later."

"It's no...."

Stas hung-up and eased out of bed.

Dina buried her head in the pillow to drown out the noise from the shower. When it stopped, she unburrowed herself from the warmth of the down comforter to watch him at the closet selecting clothes. The overhead light gave her a good look at his toned body, well-defined muscles, slim hips, tight butt, strong thighs and calves defined from many years of playing soccer. She eased to the edge of the bed, wanting to touch that one visible flaw that marred that seemingly perfect body, a smooth triangle that contrasted with the damp sheen of the rest of his back. She leaned up on her elbows wanting to ask about the scar but said nothing.

After he dressed, he leaned over her, covering her bare shoulders. "I can send you home in a cab."

She groaned. "I'm not ready to get up."

"Then stay until I get home."

"When's that?" She asked.

"I don't know, babe. Anyway, there's coffee, juice, eggs." He gathered his gun, wallet, badge, keys, and hit the light switch. "I left your old sweats on the chair."

Dina smiled as she heard the front door close and the dead bolt engage.

When Stas returned that evening, he found Dina sitting in his alcove, reading. The scene reminiscent of her "house arrest" as she'd called it. To him, it had been the only place he felt she would be safe from whomever killed Sybil, men who wouldn't have stopped until they had Dina.

She looked up from her book, at home in Stas's old LAPD sweats, her hair in a ponytail, her face scrubbed clean.

He went to the bedroom, put away his gun, and changed into jeans and a polo shirt. "You eat?"

She nodded. "An omelet." She waved the book. "I'm almost finished. The last book I read was here."

"What's this one?"

"The Maltese Falcon. I saw the movie but never read the book. I love Bogart." She smiled. "You remind me of him, ... a little."

Stas stood over her. "How's that?"

"He was so intense."

"He was acting, babe."

"I know, but...."

He pulled her up, tossing the book into the chair. He nuzzled her temple, her hairline, fingered the scar at her neck, kissed her ear, then whispered. "What do you want to eat?"

"Something wickedly sinful."

"Hot fudge sundae?"

Dina smiled. "With pizza for appetizer."

Stas released her. "Get your shoes. We'll go down to Whole Foods, make one stop."

She returned with her heels in one hand and a silver box in the other. "This was by the chair. It must have fallen out of your jacket pocket."

He didn't take it. "It's for you. Happy Birthday!"

The shoes were dropped to the floor while Dina concentrated on the tiny ribbon. Once it was untied, she slowly raised the silver lid. Nestled in the confines of white tissue was a black and white enamel panda with tiny diamond eyes attached to a gold chain.

"It's beautiful. I still have the little stuffed one you gave me two years ago." She touched the scar at her neck. "Where did you get it."

"Chicago."

She looked up at him as he handed her his leather jacket. "So you were thinking about me."

Dina made a funky fashion statement in Stas's large leather jacket over sweat pants and four-inch heels.

He pushed the cart while she questioned him on what he needed.

"Your cupboards are almost bare."

Amanda almost jumped when she saw them from her vantage spot in the produce section. At first she just stared, watching, uncertain if it really was Stas. She'd remembered him in a suit, but here he was in jeans and a long-sleeved Polo. Who was the woman moving so easily by his side, looking foolish in a jacket that was much too big for her and those ridiculous heels and large hoop earrings? She looked like a gypsy. She talked. He listened as she put an item in the cart, and he would reach in, look at it, and put it back in the basket or back on the shelf. Their last stop was at the take-out counter where he waited for a pizza while the woman, looking like she'd just stepped from a tanning bed, went down another aisle and returned with a carton of ice cream and a can of whipped cream.

Amanda blushed thinking about what they would do with the cream. She'd heard stories at work and wondered if Stas was into kink. Maybe that was what he had needed that night at her place. She stood transfixed among the Gala and Delicious apples. Should she just go over and introduce herself? Toss a casual "hello" at them, introduce herself to the interloper. Remind him of class, but she didn't move until she saw them pass through the cashier's line laughing as the woman patted him again.

Dina set the coffee table with the pizza box, napkins, and some designer beers. They ate their pizza sitting on the floor. After eating, she settled in his arms as they watched Heat.

Halfway through the movie, Stas cleared the table, brought coffee and a huge, hot fudge sundae. "I made the sauce from scratch." He set the concoction in front of her and watched from the vantage point of his corner of the sofa.

"I'm impressed." Dina dug into the ice cream, playing with the whipped cream, making little mounds of it before slowly licking the spoon clean and repeating the process.

He watched as she seductively toyed with chocolate and ice cream, reducing the sundae to a swirl of brown and white in the bottom of the bowl.

"Sorry, I didn't have one of those fancy dishes or some cherries." He pulled her up from the floor to sit on his lap, then took the spoon and dropped it back in the bowl.

"I'm stuffed."

Stas licked the residue of chocolate and cream from her lips. "But I haven't had my dessert."

FIFTEEN

Stas and Edwards were assigned to the second victim's postmortem. Edwards called as Stas was about to get dressed, said he wasn't going to be able to make it. There was noise in the background. Stas stood naked by the phone, ripping the plastic cleaner's bag off his brown suit. "Which kid is sick this time?"

"David's got a really bad ear infection."

"Why can't Jill take care of him?"

"I have to take him to the doctor. Jill's got to take care of the other kids." There was a long pause. "Stas, you there?"

"Yeah, I'm here, but I gotta go. The Men on Mission wait for no man." Stas tried to laugh but hung up. There was nothing funny. He knew how much his partner hated autopsies, said they made him deathly ill. Stas wondered who was really sick.

The brown suit was special, worn only to postmortems. It stayed it a plastic bag, came out for that one purpose, then went into the bag to go back to the cleaners. There was a ritual for the trip to Mission Street: Vicks in the nose, Vaseline Intensive Care lotion all over the body, leave-in conditioner in the hair. Detectives devised an assortment of remedies to reduce that particular odor of death that was so pervasive that it clung to every fiber of clothes, every inch of skin, and every strand of hair.

The phone rang as Stas was about to leave.

"Stas? Marlowe. I'm going with you. Sid's got a sick kid."

"Yeah, anything to avoid a cut. I'll see you there."

Marlowe had signed-in and was already putting on protective gear, when Stas joined him as he bent to slip on green booties over well-worn tennis shoes.

"Where are your boots?"

"In the van. I save these for the cuts, like your ugly brown suit." Marlowe nodded at Stas as he slipped on the green gown.

The autopsies were never routine. The odor, discoloration, skin slippage, and brutality of dissecting what had once been a beautiful young woman was almost enough to make both seasoned detectives sick. They watched stone faced and glum while Dr. Wu walked them through each incision, each organ removal and weighing and explained every step as if he were narrating some macabre opera, reading the translated libretto that streamed above the stage. Wu accented his performance with some "oohs, and ahs" and several "This is interesting." The only interjection missing was the "Bravo!" at the end of his stellar performance.

Stas wanted to interrupt, ask questions, but he remained silent, almost stoic, until Wu removed his face visor, gown, peeled of his stainless steel mesh gloves, and joined Marlowe and Stas in the hall. The detectives had disposed of their gowns, face masks, and booties but still breathed through their mouths and waited to hear the verdict.

"We still have to examine the tissue samples, but I'd say she's been dead four or five years. She'd been pregnant and had a C-section."

Marlowe scratched his head. "So you think the body's been kept in a freezer?"

"Yes."

"Was freezing the cause of death?" Marlowe asked.

"Probably the same as the Lenox woman, an overdose of heroin. There was a needle puncture in her neck." Wu looked tired and anxious to leave.

"Doc, but you didn't answer the question. Did the heroin kill her or did she freeze to death?" Stas asked.

"I can't tell you that until we get the tox screen back. The victim didn't seem like an addict, so any substantial dosage would have been lethal. Maybe they used the heroin to knock her out, but it proved fatal. Listen detectives, I've got to go." Wu turned and walked down the hall.

Marlowe and Stas watched the ME disappear, then they headed down the hallway in the opposite direction.

"Where the hell is my sister-in-law?" Edwards bumped Marlowe's back.

The detective turned slowly, a steaming mug in his left hand, and gave Edwards a little shove. "Back off!" His words flowed calmly as if the energy used to raise his voice would cause his hot coffee to erupt onto Edwards.

He moved, letting Marlowe pass.

"You trying to keep two women out there in Simi Valley?" The words were spoken with contempt. "You'd think with all those chaps, you'd have your hands full." Marlowe sat and sipped, turning papers on his desk, ignoring Edwards.

"Jill's worried." Edwards finally said.

"Jill's worried? She knows where Barbara's staying." Marlowe looked up slowly. "You got a problem with that?"

"It's just that she's supposed to be looking for a job and...." he walked slowly towards his desk.

"Barbara found a job. They had an opening at Pasadena PD." A smirk stole over his usually calm demeanor. "She starts Monday. Don't you have some paper work to do?"

"Where's Stas?" Edwards asked.

"Not sure, but if I were you, I'd leave your partner alone. It wasn't a pretty cut, and you were supposed to be there."

"My kid was sick this morning."

"Like I said, your partner's in a shitty mood." Marlowe turned back to his coffee. "You not even mildly curious what we found out?"

"I'll read the report!"

"I bet you will." Marlowe continued. "She was frozen, just like the other one."

"Did she OD?"

"That too, then they popped her in a freezer for five years. Like I said,... wasn't a pretty cut."

Edwards stood, his hands in his pocket. "So does anyone know where Stas went?"

"He may have gone home to change." Jonson chimed in. "You know how he hates to wear those clothes."

"Then again, he might have gone over to his new woman," Marlowe added.

Edwards turned, looking confused. "Who, the teacher?"

SIXTEEN

What was left of the lasagna had remained in the pan too long. Jill had tried to keep it warm for Sid. Now it was dry and crusty. She scraped the leftovers onto a plate and ran hot water in the sink, squeezing extra detergent into the pan, releasing tiny yellow bubbles that smelled of lemon zest. She swished the water with both hands, building frothy suds when the phone rang. "Damn." She caught it on the fifth ring, after wiping wet hands on her jeans. "Hello?"

The voice was soft, dripping honey, breathless in its request. "May I speak to Detective Edwards?"

Jill stiffened, caught off guard. "He's not here. Is this urgent?"

"No!"

"Then can I take a message?"

"Yes, have him call Carroll."

"Is there a number?"

"He knows it."

Click.

Jill turned the slim-line receiver over to look at the display on the caller ID. It was her husband's cell number. There was a flutter of heartbeats. Had something happened to Sid? She dialed his number.

"You've reached Sid Edwards. Leave your name and number, and I'll return your call as soon as possible." His message was followed by various instructions.

Jill slammed the phone down onto its cradle. It missed, releasing a loud dial tone. She righted it and returned to the sink, the suds now flat; her fears quickly turned to anger. Once again she wiped her hands on her jeans, leaving wet stripes down her thighs. Opening the freezer, she dug out a small mayonnaise jar, half-filled with a frosty liquid, what was left of a pint of vodka she'd purchased at the market. Whether he liked it or not, Sid just might end up with two vodka loving partners.

She sipped from the jar and looked at her handy work. There laid out on the table were two ties. One was a nice brown-and-white-striped polyester she'd purchased at Target while buying school clothes for the kids. It had been a gift for Sid. She didn't need to worry about putting it in the wash, and it looked nice with his brown suit. There was another tie, silk, with a label that read "dry clean only." She had found it neatly folded in the pocket of a new sports jacket. When she first saw the jacket, she wondered if he'd been shopping with Stas, then shook her head. He couldn't afford the places where his partner bought his clothes. She raised the jacket to her nose to smell for any hint of another woman's perfume. Nothing but Old Spice.

She'd sent the kids to the boys' room with overladen bowls of ice cream and chocolate chip cookies to watch a movie as she waited for her husband. David had helped her dish up rocky road for herself, but the ice cream was melting into a frothy mess as she nursed the last of her vodka. Sid had thrown out Stas's empty bottle, glad to rid his house of what he called his partner's poison. Did her husband think that she was incapable of buying her own?

Jill cocked her head when she heard the loud, straining crank of the garage door. Her stomach churned as she waited for the sound of the door's laborious closing, and for Sid to come through from the kitchen.

"Jill!"

"You son of a bitch!" She flung the words at him in a spray of venomous spit.

"What? What's wrong with you?" He stepped back a few feet.

She wanted to sound calm, but the cutting words came out, fast and furious. "I heard stories from other wives. I never thought it would happen to me." Her pale face had turned hot and blotchy from her anger and the alcohol. "Your, your bitch called here, here! This is my house, and you give some, some whore your phone, that's why you have an office. Let her call you there."

Edwards backed off even further. "What are you talking about? Who called?"

"Carol!"

"Carol?" Edwards tried to laugh it off. "He's a wit."

"A what?"

"A witness. He's a witness in a murder case."

"Bullshit! It was a woman."

"No, no, honest he's a guy. He's a homo..., he's gay."

"You lying bastard. Why does he have your phone?"

"I thought I told you. I lost it. He must have found it."

"Why use your phone? Why didn't he say he had it?"

"I don't know. Maybe he remembered something or wanted to tell me about the phone so I could get it back."

"Why didn't you report it?"

"I don't know. I thought it'd turn up, then I got busy. I guess I forgot."

"I can't believe you! How can you be without a phone?" She tried to laugh. "Well, do you remember this? She pointed to the silk tie. "Is this a gift from your damn witness?"

"It, ..., was ... when I went to that club with Stas."

"You got this from Stas?" She picked up the tie. "Looks like something he would wear. Why didn't you give it back?"

"I forgot."

"Can't you remember anything? You got dementia?" Jill took a drink from her jar and put the tie in a bag she took from under the sink. "Here, give it back." Her anger had abated somewhat as she threw him the bag. "I want you to think about this, because I've been giving it a lot of thought. I'm here all the time with the kids. You're gone all day. Lately, you're even out at night. Doing what? Working a case? Hell, you can tell me anything. Next, I guess it'll be on some fucking stake-out."

"Jill!"

She ignored him and kept talking. "Sometimes I don't know when you'll be home. I want out of suburbia. I want a job and a decent car and some new clothes. Barbara said..."

"Oh, I get it. You've been talking to your sister. You know, she's shacking with Marlowe?"

"At least he treats her with respect. He has a lady who cleans, and if she doesn't feel like cooking, they go out." Jill was almost screaming again. "I'm sick of being stuck,... of being stuck, while you screw around with your funny witnesses."

"Hey, quiet down! The kids'll hear you."

"So what! I don't give a shit if they hear." She wanted to hit him.

Edwards tried to touch Jill, but left his hands suspended in the air, inches away from her shoulders. "So this is about cooking and cleaning? You're my wife, for God's sake. That's what you're supposed to do. Barbara's gone off the deep end living with him. People will talk."

"What people? She hardly knows anyone. Anyway, she doesn't care what people say, she's happy. Would you rather have her living with your maladjusted partner, 'cause he's the right color? And if he's a drunk?"

"I never said that."

"Dammit, you did. Would you rather have my sister living with a drunk?"

"I swear, I never said that."

"You're full of shit. I can't believe anything you say. Oh, hell, forget it."

Edwards picked up Jill's jar and smelled it, then ran his tongue around the rim. He put the jar on the counter and left the room.

SEVENTEEN

It seemed that when it rained it poured. Everything made Edwards late the morning after Carroll's call. Jill made no breakfast, nor had she taken his white shirt out of dryer, leaving it wrinkled beyond recognition as a dress shirt. The traffic had been unusually heavy, putting him in an even fouler mood. He'd gotten off the freeway at the wrong exit, stopped at a Star Bucks wanna-be, picked up a coffee that spilled, leaving an ugly wet mark on his lap. When he arrived at work, he stopped in the first floor men's room and tried to adjust the hand dryer to dry the spot over his crotch. The effort made the stain look worse. Plus, he had to leave his jacket on to hide the condition of the shirt. Finally, to top everything off, his back was killing him from spending a restless night on the lumpy sofa in the family room.

Stas greeted his partner with a broad smile as he drank his coffee. "Looks like you had a rough night."

"I slept on the couch."

"You piss off Jill? I thought you had a spare room?"

"Since Barbara's playing house with Marlowe, Jill gave it to Dave."

"You should've slept with him."

"I didn't want him asking questions. It was bad enough with her screaming, losing her mind 'cause Carroll called the house yesterday."

"You give him your home number?"

Edwards shook his head and reached to massage the small of his back. "He found my phone."

"Or lifted it. I take it, you didn't cancel your service?"

"Not yet."

"Man, do it, call Carroll, or get another phone." Stas watched his partner try to reach around to find another spot to rub. "Why don't you get a massage? I know this lady."

"I'm in enough trouble."

"She's legit, but...." Stas picked up a file. "We got this from the lab. Some of the fibers taken from Cynthia Lenox's dress came from an army issue blanket circa World War II. The hairs on it are from a dog like a German shepherd. My guess, she was wrapped in the dog's blanket, then rolled her out of it, and into the dumpster."

"What about the blanket?" Edwards asked.

"I think we can forget tracing it. They probably used it to wrap the second victim too." He lifted another sheet from the file. "The tox report came back, an overdose of heroin. I bet we'll get the same report and trace evidence on our second Jane Doe, who now has a name, Elizabeth Bolton. We ID'd her from her prints, and she's local. We got an address from her last driver's license issued six years ago. Now we have an idea how long she's been missing. So we're checking out her last known address this afternoon."

Before lunch, Edwards, to replace his ruined trousers, bought some black cotton pants at a dingy little shop on Main Street. Stas stayed in the car parked in a red zone. After lunch they located the small apartment complex in an area of narrow streets that bordered Eagle Rock and Glendale. They had dodged pot holes and repair crews working on the streets, but they couldn't dodge the steam and stench of the hot tar that permeated the air.

The manager's apartment was on the first floor. The door was opened after several loud knocks as per the instructions taped above the broken bell: "Knock Loud."

"We ain't got no vacancies," a man shouted through the partially opened door that almost slammed before the detectives could produce their IDs.

"Los Angeles Police Department. May we have a word with you?" Edwards shouted back.

The door was opened tentatively by a man who looked like a refugee from the *Twilight Zone*. His hair was swept up on the sides of his head into mixed gray wings. His V-neck t-shirt had been white a decade ago but now sported spots and splotches in beiges and browns, with yellowed circles fanning out from the armpits. He stepped aside to allow the detectives into his inferno. The wall heater was turned up to the max, and an enormous black-and-white TV on a metal stand blared forth the afternoon's broadcasts in front of a worn floral-patterned sofa.

"This is Detective Edwards. I'm Detective Nowak."

"I'm Joe. Find a seat." He flopped down on the sofa.

Stas grabbed a chair from the dining area and looked from Joe to the TV. "Can you turn it down?"

Joe fiddled with a fat knob on the TV until the volume diminished.

"We're looking into the disappearance of one of your former tenants, Elizabeth Bolton," Stas said.

"Wow, that was a while back. You guys working cold cases like on TV?"

Stas nodded as Edwards pulled up another chair.

"Were you living here then?" Edwards asked.

"I've been here fifteen years. Lived upstairs in a two bedroom. Been manager for ten. Moved down here when my wife died. That girl, Elizabeth, didn't live here that long. Just left all of a sudden."

"What happened to her belongings?" Stas asked.

"She lived with this guy, Scott. I don't know what he did with her things."

"Does Scott have a last name?" Stas had his notebook and pen out.

Joe's attention had been drawn briefly to the muted TV. "Wilson."

"Does he still live here?" Stas asked.

Joe pointed up. "Number 8"

"You know what time he gets home?" Edwards stood.

"Lazy bastard don't work. Says he's an artist. But I have my doubts."

Edwards returned his chair to the dining area. "Why?"

"Lights bad in all the apartments. Always thought painters needed lots of natural light."

"Well," Stas rose, "we'll pay him a visit."

Joe walked them to the door. "I wish he'd disappear, then I could get some reliable tenants who pay on time."

Outside, Stas wiped his brow with his handkerchief. Edwards blotted his forehead with his jacket sleeve.

They took the stairs to the second landing, found number 8, and knocked. A young man in his late twenties opened the door. His 5 foot 10 inch frame, turning to bulky fat, effectively blocked the view into the apartment.

"Mr. Scott Wilson?" Edwards asked.

"Yeah?"

This time Edwards presented his ID. "I'm Detective Edwards. This is my partner, Detective Nowak."

There was movement behind Scott. Stas's height gave him an advantage, allowing him to catch a fleeting glimpse of pale, naked flesh disappearing from view.

"What do you want?"

"We need to ask you a few questions about Elizabeth Bolton," Stas said.

"Liz, God, I haven't seen her in years." Scott seemed genuinely moved.

"That's what we want to talk to you about," Edwards added.

"Come in. I was working. I'm an artist." He stepped back into the room to admit the detectives.

Stas took a quick look around the cluttered living room. The naked flesh had miraculously vanished.

Scott moved newspapers from one chair and gathered up clothes from another, dropping green briefs and leaving a green bra dangling from the bundle in his arms. He turned in circles before spilling the things behind an easel that held a painting of a nude's body beginning to take shape. The figure on the canvas was draped on a sofa, her hand partially covering the red hair of her pubic area, and one leg was bent in a provocative pose. The paint looked dry. Stas's gaze followed the other leg as it vanished into the whiteness of the canvas. Moving further into the room, he looked up to several bad oils hanging over the sofa.

The detectives finally sat in the proffered chairs and faced Scott as he folded a velvet throw and pushed it into the corner of the sofa before sitting.

Stas thought it odd that as a painter, Scott could keep his clothes looking cleaner than Joe's.

"I don't know how I can help you. I haven't seen Liz in around six years."

"Has anyone contacted you during that period?" Stas asked.

"No."

"What about her family?"

"She grew up in St. Louis. I think she was adopted. They didn't get along, so she came out here to get away from them and the cold. I don't know if they stayed in touch."

Stas sat poised with his notebook. "When did you meet?"

"Eight, nine years ago. At first, we weren't that serious, but later, we even talked about getting married, then she disappeared. I thought she got cold feet."

"You didn't find that suspicious?" Edwards asked.

"No. You know women." He looked from Edwards to Stas. "I had to get on with my life. Can you tell me what this is about?"

"We're investigating the murder of a young woman we believe might be Elizabeth. We're trying to trace her last movements." Stas watched for Scott's reaction.

"Wow! I can't believe this, but it's been years...."

"What type of work was Elizabeth doing when you last saw her?" Stas asked.

"The usual, waiting tables, but she wanted to model. Even took classes from some place she saw in an ad."

Stas looked at the painting over the sofa. "Did she pose for you?"

Scott turned around. "Yeah, I did two of her. This wasn't that good, but the one I sold was awesome. That was some of my best work. I was at Art Center then. My prof said I really had potential. I sell a few things now and then, mostly landscapes especially for those hotel art sales. Keeps the wolf from the door."

"Mind if I take a closer look?" Stas rose without waiting for an answer and got close to examine the painting. "Was the other painting a nude."

"No, a portrait. I'm working on my nudes, want to improve my technique."

As Scott started to explain, the guest closet door opened and a young woman with flaming red hair stuck her head out. "Can you hand me my clothes? I got to go home."

"Sorry." Scott gathered up the bundle behind the easel and handed them to the girl, pushing the door closed.

"Hey! Wait!" The muted voice came through. "Leave the door cracked. The light's out."

Scott stood by the door. "Is that all?"

Edwards rose and handed him a card. "Give us a call if you think of anything."

Scott looked at the card, puzzled. "Like what?"

"For one, what happened to Elizabeth's personal effects?" Stas added.

"She didn't have much. I kept a few pieces of furniture, got rid of her clothes. There's a box with some of her things around here."

"We need the address and phone number of her family in St. Louis." Stas handed him a card. "Look through your things. Since you're the only one here who knew her, we want you to come down and identify the body."

"Body? I don't know if I can do that."

"Sorry, I'm afraid you'll have to. We'll call you later for a time." Edwards said.

The closet door opened, and the girl who stepped out rivaled one of Titian's red haired beauties. She glared at Scott. "You douche bag! You owe me!" She stormed by the detectives who followed her out of the apartment.

Back in the car, Stas and Edwards finished their notes.

"So much for technique. I think that guy does more screwing than painting. You think she was a model?" Edwards asked.

"I guess those are the perks, especially if you can snare a beauty like that one, but I bet she makes him pay." Stas said. "I wonder if Cindi and Elizabeth knew each other. They were about the same age, and they resembled each other."

"How are we going to get anywhere with this? There's nothing to go on."

Stas smiled. "Be patient. Something will turn up. We need to see if the owners of B & T Construction have materialized."

EIGHTEEN

After the cops and his model left, Scott went to the bedroom closet, pushed aside clothes, and rummaged in the back, finally dragging out a large blue plastic box. He remembered buying it at Target and lugging it home soon after Liz left and hadn't returned. Her stuff had been scattered all over the place, but he finally packed what had been visible of Liz's things when he met Lori, a young waitress at Wiggles. While wolfing down a quarter pound double cheese burger with bacon, he told her she had a smile like Mona Lisa.

"Who's that?" She smacked her gum as she stood poised watching catsup dribble down his chin.

"A famous lady."

"Am I supposed to be impressed?" She handed him several napkins from a dispenser.

"I'm a painter, an artist." He opened his jacket so she could see the paint splotches on his once white t-shirt. "I'd like to capture your smile on canvas."

"What's that?" She laughed. "Only kidding. I don't have to take my clothes off do I?"

"Not for a portrait. Come up to my place when you get off. I'll show you a picture of Mona Lisa and some of my paintings."

She rearranged a curl at her temple. "I'm off at ten."

"I'll wait for you."

She shook her head. "My boss don't like guys hanging around."

"Then I'll be back."

At 10:15 he found a parking space at the curb and reached over to open the door when Lori came out ten minutes later.

She had changed into a skirt, tight sweater, and ratty, black heels. When they got to his place, he brought out a massive book of Italian Renaissance art and paged through until he found Da Vinci's masterpiece. Lori was not impressed with Mona Lisa or her smile staring back at her.

"I don't look like that. God, she's ugly."

Scott closed the big book and went to the kitchen for a couple of beers while Lori checked out two paintings hanging over the sofa and several stacked against the wall.

"These are great." She took a swig from her beer and belched.

He moved in and gently wiped the foam mustache from her upper lip. "I'd like to paint you."

It didn't take much to get Lori into bed, especially after he promised to paint her nude, but the magic spell was broken, and the portrait promise forgotten when she found an earring next to the one she'd dropped on the floor during their sexual gymnastics.

When he looked over the side of the bed, he would have loved to have painted Lori's nude figure stretched out on the rust colored carpet as she fished under the bed and found other treasures left by Liz.

When she emerged with a dusty purple thong, she broke into a string of obscenities. "You bastard. You're sick, you fucking son-of-a-bitch. Do you collect these?" She flung the underwear in the air, hitting Scott in his forehead. "Well, you won't collect mine."

Lori rummaged in the heap of hastily discarded clothes until she found her white cotton briefs and bra. She had stormed out half-dressed still spewing profanities that faded with the angry staccato click of her heels on the concrete stairs.

The next morning Scott moved furniture, got on his hands and knees, collecting anything that had belonged to Liz, and packed them away.

Now he carried the almost forgotten box into the living room and set it on the coffee table. Scott was having a hard time. Earlier when he had thought Liz had dumped him, he was angry, didn't give a damn about her. Now he cried, mourning her death. He hadn't been through her things since he had packed them away. Maybe he should just give everything to the cops. He removed the top and put it on the floor.

Wiping away tears, he pulled out six head shots from a manila envelope. As he held up the first photo, a small, white paper floated to the floor. Scott remembered; Quint Ross had taken the pictures. Liz was pretty, in an ethereal sort of way. Her features were refined, her complexion pale, her eyes a delicate blue, but she was not beautiful. She had a lovely figure, but she was not the woman that the public was dying to see on a runway or in a fashion magazine.

Liz had posed for Scott's first portrait when he attended Art Center in Pasadena. Her blonde hair framed her face, a face that prompted someone at the college's art show to pay top dollar for his painting. He wondered where it was hanging now. It was the sale of the painting that had given Liz the idea to become a model. He tried to explain that it was his talent and not her looks that gave the portrait any value. Maybe they had both been wrong. In the years since his first big sale, no one else had come beating down his door for his work, and even now, he continued to struggle.

He picked up the receipt. If Quint was still around, maybe the cops could talk to him. The rest of the box contained a few books, romance fiction. There were a few bills that had never been paid and an ad for a photo-op in Las Vegas: Nu-faces was doing a talent search for young models wanting to break into the business. He remembered telling her it was probably a scam, especially since she had to borrow money from him to pay her entrance fees and air fare. They had argued. She left a week later.

Scott looked at one of the business cards at the end of the coffee table and reached for the cordless phone. He almost missed the tentative knock at the door. When he opened it, a pretty brunette stood eye level with the artist. His attention quickly shifted from her face to her 44 DDs that bubbled from her tight tank top.

"Hey!" Scott held the door open.

"Nadine. You remember me?"

"I'd never forget a face like yours." He waved the phone toward a seat.

"I'm sorry. Were you talking to someone?"

"No, no." He sat the phone back on the coffee table. "It can wait. I'll call'em tomorrow."

NINETEEN

Stas called Dina and told her he would see her later. He pulled into The Second Set parking lot and cursed the light drizzle as the raindrops beaded on the freshly polished surface of his car. He had just had it detailed at a new place in Burbank recommended by his neighbor, who had recently moved into the building and seemed more into his wheels than Stas ever was. He engaged the car's alarm, tapping it twice. The Mercedes beeped back.

The Second Set was one of those quiet hangouts for detectives who needed a place to unwind before going home. Even some of the older, more seasoned crime reporters were known to frequent the bar for bits of info or news that they might turn into the next day's headlines.

Patrons usually avoided the dime-sized dance floor in the rear of the club but would gather around the small stage when a jazz combo played on the weekends. Most of the detectives avoided the place then, unless they were really lonely and hoped to pick up a sassy number looking for a one night stand with one of LA's finest.

Stas remembered a tale that had circulated around the divisions about a statuesque badge bunny who had a Glock tattooed on her right hip, its barrel angled toward her landing strip. She even had notches inked in blue on the grip for each sexual conquest. Rumor had it that she wanted to include badge numbers but didn't have enough room. Even a few young, inexperienced rookies had fallen for her come-on line, "Want to see my Glock?" But no one ever complained.

At the bar, Troy dusted some fancy bottles on the mirrored display behind him before giving his attention to Stas. "The usual?"

Troy and his twin brother were bar-tending legends, famous for their bottle and shaker antics for the weekends when there was a late night show with fancy glasses and bottles passing in midair between them. Troy would fill several glasses on the bar and set them aflame amid applause for his flamboyant finale. They saved their best show for Saturday nights when their younger and cuter audience was more appreciative and less cynical than the cops who wanted their booze served without a dog and pony show.

Troy placed a double vodka in front of the detective. As Stas took a sip, he was aware of a presence sliding onto the stool next to him. Without turning, he looked into the mirror backing the bar and recognized Ralph Townsend.

"Hey, Stas."

"Ralph. What's up?"

"Been looking around for you, even drove over to your place late one night. No one was home."

"Maybe I just didn't answer the door."

"You with your lady?"

"Don't have time for that kind of commitment."

"Yeah, hear you guys been busy."

Stas sipped his drink and continued to watch the reporter in the mirror.

"You any closer to finding Judge Lenox daughter's killer?"

"We're working on it."

"Sounds like one of your Captain's sound bites. Translated, 'We haven't a damn clue'." Townsend turned on his stool to observe the detective. "Now, I hear you got another one, same MO."

"Who told you that?" Stas asked.

"I have my sources."

"Not at RHD."

"No, they're not as particular at the coroners."

"Techs?'

"I'm not giving up my informants." Ralph reached for the glass that magically appeared before him. "By the way, what do you think happened to the kids? You got another serial killer on your hands?"

"With two murders?" The detective moved around on his stool. "You know, two female homicides do not a serial killer make."

"I hear rumors here and there. Bet you a double Scotch you'll get another one."

"Don't hold your breath, anyway rumors and techs won't win you a Pulitzer."

"True, true." He turned to look at Stas. "By the way, how's Dina?" Townsend asked.

Stas's straightened. "She's good."

"You still seeing her?"

"We run into each other now and then."

"Well, if it's not a regular thing, how about giving me her number?"

Stas felt a knot tighten in the pit of his stomach and drained his glass as he slid off the stool. "I told you before, smokers need not apply."

Townsend finished his Scotch, reached for a pack of cigarettes in his jacket pocket, and placed them next to his empty glass.

Troy stopped in front of Townsend, picked up the pack of Marlboros, and wiped the bar. "You want a refill?"

Townsend shook-out a cigarette. "I'm going out for a smoke. I'll be back." He slid off his stool and watched the detective walk to a vacant booth. "But she's okay with a lush?" he called to Stas.

But before the reporter could move away from the bar, a young woman in a short leather shirt and thigh-high black boots climbed onto the stool that Stas had just vacated. She brushed shoulder length brown hair off her face and gazed warmly at Townsend. "You a cop?"

"You looking for one?"

"Yeah." She ran her tongue over full, seductive lips and took a sip from the drink she'd brought with her.

"I'm a crime reporter."

"You mean you write about cops and murders?" She turned towards Townsend. "I'm impressed. You know many cops?"

"A few."

"Are there any here?" She slowly surveyed the room before turning her attention back to the reporter.

Townsend climbed back on his stool, put his cigarettes back in his pocket, and nodded towards Stas. "There's one over there."

She looked past the reporter and smiled. "Can you introduce me."

"Not tonight, but give me your name and number, and I'll see what I can do."

Stas had settled into the fake leather banquette as several other cops that he vaguely recognized from Hollywood Division entered and headed for the bar. *It's going to be a long week.*

Five minutes later Marlowe swept in shaking rain from his Stetson. He looked over at the bar, but moved to the booth when he saw Stas. "What's Townsend up to?"

"His usual, being a pain in the ass trying to get a story or pick up a girl. If you talk to him, better watch what you say or you'll be quoted in the *Times* tomorrow morning commenting on our serial killer."

"What serial killer?" Marlowe asked.

"Townsend's idea. I denied, but that never stopped him before. He has his sources, some better than ours."

"Speaking of pains, Edwards isn't coming by is he?"

"He never does. Why?"

"He bugs the hell out of Barbara, even went over to Pasadena PD to check if she had a job." Marlowe looked around for the barmaid.

"He could've called." Stas gave her a high sign when she turned from the well with a tray of drinks.

"Tell me about your new woman?"

Stas smiled slyly. "She's just a friend."

"Yeah, well, your partner thinks you're having regular orgies, said you came to the crime scene the other morning wearing the same threads you left work in. You hadn't been home?"

"Edwards talks too much." Stas frowned and drained his glass.

"He's your partner. He's looking out for your well-being, although you look like somebody's taking care of that angle."

Stas rose. "What're you drinking?"

"You buying?" He didn't wait for a response. "A double Scotch on the rocks with a Sam Adams chaser."

Stas went to the bar and ordered, his mind still on his *well-being*, which caused his smile to broaden.

The young woman sitting next to Townsend craned around his back to get a better look at the detective. She poked a finger in the reporter's side. "You gonna introduce me."

"Not now. Let's wait 'til he's alone." Townsend smiled at himself in the mirror as he placed a folded piece of paper in his jacket pocket.

Stas walked back, put two drinks on the table, and slid back into the booth. "Relationships can be strange."

"Is that it?"

"Is what it?"

"Strange relationships. Man, don't you want more out of this damn life, you know, a new woman, maybe even marriage, like Jonson?"

Stas wiped the wet ring left by his glass with a napkin. "I don't think about it. Once was enough for me." He turned to his drink.

"Well, look at Jonson. He seems happy, and it's his third time." He picked up his beer and took a few gulps to chase the Scotch. "This is new for Barbara, sorta like a defiance thing."

"Dating a black man?" Stas asked. "Checking out the myth."

Marlowe looked into his drink. "Very funny, but you wait, first the questions, then hints about marriage or moving in. You remember the drill."

Stas's gray eyes turned icy as he considered. "That's not an option... for any woman."

Marlowe finished his drink, grabbed his Stetson, and eased from the seat. He nodded towards the door just as Edwards stepped in and looked around. "Now I know I got to go, anyway Barbara's making dinner. Does yours cook?"

"Stop digging."

"Well, I guess if I had a new woman, food would be the least of my concerns."

"But you got a new woman," Stas added.

Marlowe finished his Scotch. "It's not the same."

Edwards took Marlowe's place, dragging a garment bag after him. "Hey, Chris."

"Sid." Marlowe nodded and carefully arranged his hat on his head. "See ya." He saluted Townsend on his way out.

"I was hoping you'd still be here," Edwards said.

"What's that?" Stas moved to the edge of the booth ready to make his escape.

Edwards smiled. "My new jacket." He started to unzip the bag.

"Why didn't you keep it in the car?"

"I can't take it home with me. She'll kill me."

"So why'd you buy it?"

Edwards ignored the question and continued unzipping. "Can you keep it 'til..."

Stacy, the bar maid, smelling strongly of tobacco, stopped at the table. "What're you drinking?"

Edwards looked at Stas.

"Give him a vodka and orange juice."

"Not a Shirley Temple?" She laughed as she walked to the well.

"Bitch!" Edwards said *sotto voce*.

"Be careful, she might spit in your drink."

Edwards stared in disbelief.

"Just kidding." Stas laughed. "Where'd you get the jacket?"

"Carroll took me to the Garment District."

"You and Carroll?"

"He goes to this men's outlet."

"I'm afraid to look."

Edwards slid the bag over, revealing a herringbone design sport coat. "It goes with the tie."

"What tie?"

The drink arrived, overfilled and dripping onto the table. Stacy made no effort to wipe the spill as she stood next to the table.

Stas looked up. "Put it on my tab." He turned back to his partner. "And you buy the jacket first, then the tie."

"I didn't buy it. Carroll gave me a real silk tie. I wore it the other night to the club."

"I didn't notice."

"I wanted to get a shirt, but if you don't take'em for me...."

"You'd better leave'em in your locker at work."

Townsend walked over to the booth. "Tell, Dina hello for me." He reached in his pocket for his cigarettes and turned for the exit.

Puzzled, Edwards looked from the departing Townsend to Stas. "Dina, Dina, who's Dina?"

TWENTY

B ut Stas didn't go to Dina's after leaving The Second Set. It was late, so he went home to face the solitude of his apartment. The chill seemed to magnify his frustration, especially with the case. The next morning the phone rang as he finished shaving. He caught it on the third ring and recognized the caller.

"What's up, Sid?"

"Don't go in. They want us out to the Hollywood Hills."

"Why isn't Hollywood taking the call?" He wiped his damp face with a towel and instinctively knew why before his partner answered.

"They found another girl."

"In a dumpster?"

"No, in some brush. I'm on my way."

"See ya out front." Stas hung up and went to the closet, passing over suits and jackets before selecting a pair of old navy slacks, a blue denim shirt, and a well-worn gray jacket. A body in the woods after the recent rain would be a messy call. He put the shoe trees back in his black lace-ups and took out a pair of old Doc Martens that had seen better days but were good for mucking around in wet underbrush.

Stas was waiting outside when Edwards pulled to the curb. "Who found this one?" he asked getting into the passenger side of the Crown Vic.

"Some guy taking his dog for an early morning crap." Edwards glanced into the empty street before pulling out.

"What makes Hollywood think this one should be ours?"

"Young, blonde, similar dress...."

"C-section?" Stas asked.

"No one said. I guess we'll find out when we get there."

"Hmm, no dumpster this time. Maybe our perps getting lazy... or careless." Stas straightened his Mickey Mouse tie.

"We can only hope."

Two black-and-whites blocked off the street leading to the crime scene while two uniforms set-up police barricades. Another patrol car blocked access to the street at the other end. The Coroner's van had parked on the shoulder, its back doors yawning open. The SID team waited patiently on the sidelines. One tech smoked; the photographer talked with a uniform officer as they drank steaming coffee since nothing could be done until the Coroner's team took the body and released the scene.

Edwards parked the Crown Vic on a slight incline and almost lost his balance getting out of the car. Stas waited, wanting to take in everything. He looked toward the police barricade and saw Townsend, a cigarette dangling from his lips. The reporter was with several other news men, one with a Pearl recorder, the others with notebooks as they talked to one of the officers. *How does he get here so fast?*

Stas slowly got out of the car, keeping his eyes on the group on the other side of the crime tape. When Townsend saw the detective, he fanned smoke in a wave and held up three fingers. Stas slightly nodded, then turned back to the crime scene. It wasn't difficult for him to imagine the headlines in the next day's edition screaming for action against a nascent serial killer endangering the young women of the city. He wondered if the paper would also detail the whiteness and blondness of the victims.

The surrounding area was a far cry from the first two dump sites. There were no sidewalks, curbs, street lights, or nearby houses. Brush, thick in areas, grew along the roadway and continued down a slight slope. The ground was still soggy from the previous night's rain.

After signing-in with the uniformed officer at the barricade, Stas took his time moving around the periphery of the crime scene. He dodged several muddy puddles but was caught by water still dripping from the trees when he moved under low hanging branches. He ran his fingers through damp hair and with his handkerchief wiped a rivulet of water that ran down his cheek.

Edwards, who seemed to be taking a boyish delight stirring up the sodden leaves, releasing a misty odor of decay, finally joined his partner. They were close enough to watch the Coroner's tech check the head, neck, arms, and torso of the deceased. Still, from where they stood, they could detect no trauma to the body.

The dead woman looked like a character from a Grimm's fairy tale who had wandered into the woods and fallen into a deep, peaceful sleep. The tech continued to check the lower limbs for bruising in the inner thighs. The body, dressed in the now-familiar floral print, looked in perfect condition. Stas looked around, strangely aware of the awkward silence. The tech turned the body. The detectives strained but could see no lividity on the back. She continued, making a small incision to take the body's temperature. The thermometer was inserted, withdrawn, read, reinserted, withdrawn, then read again.

Stas watched the tech walk away from the victim and back to the van absentmindedly holding the thermometer extended to her side.

"You through?" Detective John Rice from Hollywood Division asked her.

"In a minute." She returned to the corpse and unceremoniously took the temperature again with another thermometer. After withdrawing it, she frowned and walked back to the van.

Stas watched her talk to the other tech, then point back to the wooded area. Together they returned to the corpse, hesitated for a moment before bagging the hands, then prepared to remove the body from the crime scene. It was going to be awkward getting the gurney up the slope, but they managed.

Stas joined the techs at the road side as they prepared to leave the scene. "What's wrong?"

The female tech glared at him. "Who said anything's wrong?" She avoided the detective's gaze. "But if you think so, I guess you'd better make the cut."

As the Coroner Investigators pulled off, the SID team started to work in earnest. They went about their meticulous search for clues, but it seemed that the body had been brought to the site and dumped. They recovered the blanket, an old army-issue wool khaki with a corner missing.

Detective Rice stood next to Stas. "We think the body was wrapped in the blanket and rolled down from the street. Bastards didn't even have to get their feet wet."

Stas nodded in agreement. "So the blanket caught on that broken tree stump?"

"Yeah, and she kept rolling, stopped over there." Rice pointed to a patch of low cropped scrub.

Stas walked over to his partner. "There's something wrong with this one, and the tech's not talking. Wouldn't even make a guess about how long she's been dead."

Edwards brushed water from his thinning hair. "So, what does that mean?"

"We'll find out at the autopsy."

Edwards grimaced. "Maybe this one's different. Might not be connected to the others after all. I bet Hollywood just wants to hand it off to us 'cause they're too busy or too lazy."

"No, I don't think so. There're too many similarities. Did you see the blanket?"

"Yeah, but she hadn't had a C-section."

"Maybe this one gave birth naturally." Stas knew his partner was already thinking of an excuse so that he wouldn't have to attend the postmortem. "Don't wear your new jacket unless you want to take the smell of death home with you."

Edwards walked back to the car, his shoulders slumped in an attitude of defeat. He found Townsend, who had gotten past the police line, waiting for him.

When Stas got back the car, the reporter stood by the Crown Vic lighting up.

"I guess I'll see you guys around." The reporter stubbed out his cigarette and moved away from the car.

"What was that all about?" Stas asked when he settled in the passenger's seat.

"He just wanted to know what we found."

"He knows damn well what we found. What did you tell him?"

"That it was another young woman."

"Well, you'll have to explain to the Captain why a 'Serial Killer' headline is the first thing he'll see with his coffee tomorrow morning." Stas put on his shades. "Then there's the Chief... and Crum."

TWENTY-ONE

W hen they got back to Parker Center, Stas found a message from Scott Wilson that he read to Edwards. "Wilson is coming in this afternoon. He found some of Liz's things."

Edwards looked up from the new murder book for the latest Jane Doe. "I hope he can shed some light on her death."

"What we need is something to shed some light on her disappearance. After the cut, we'll know how she died."

Stas called Scott back and set an appointment for 2 o'clock.

Scott arrived on time. Stas had wished for a few minutes before the interview to let his food settle. They had gone to Monkee's for Chinese and were stuffed. To make matters worse, Edwards had spilled plum sauce on his new silk tie and tried to rub out the stain with a paper towel and cold water. The more he rubbed, the more little flecks of white fibers stuck to the tie.

"Have it dry cleaned." Stas suggested.

"But Jill washes everything."

"Then you don't want Carroll to see it after Jill runs it through the machine. Not a pretty sight, especially after the dryer."

Scott was shown to Stas's desk by the division clerk. They then took him to a nearby interview room.

The artist had changed into a pair of beige chinos and a white pullover that had a paint smear on the sleeve. He carried a Ralph's paper shopping bag.

"Have a seat." Stas indicated a chair.

Scott put the shopping bag on the table.

"What do you have here?" Edwards looked in the bag.

"I found some head shots and her address book, has her folks' number."

Edwards took the photos out of the manila envelope and looked them over before passing them to his partner.

"Nice, but was she good enough for a high-powered modeling career?" Stas asked.

"I told her she wasn't, but she was hell-bent on putting together a portfolio and doing shows even if she had to pay for them. Man, nobody was going to pay her. She had a good face but not the body." He reached in his pocket and pulled out the faded advertisement. "I found this. I think it's where she went."

Stas unfolded the paper and flattened it on the table. It was an ad for a models' workshop in Las Vegas. "This was a while back." He looked up, trying to read Scott.

"But that's the last time I saw her, honest. I wasn't sure where she went, but if she didn't go there,...." There was a catch in Scott's voice.

Edwards looked at the ad. "Was this reported when you made the missing person's report?'

Scott shook his head. "I didn't see it then. She just told me about it. Like I said, I just found it in her stuff."

"Where did she have the head shots made?" Stas asked, turning the photo over, looking at a stamped impression on the back that had faded almost beyond recognition. "I can barely make out some initials and Hollywood."

"I'm sorry, that's all I have."

After Scott left, Edwards went through the address book looking for the parents' contact information. Stas took a break, went into the hallway, and called Dina.

"I can't see you tonight, babe." He sensed the disappointment in her silence. "We have another body, so I might be working late."

"What about tomorrow?" she asked.

"I don't know. I'll call if it's not too late."

"It's never too late."

Feeling a little guilty, Stas closed his phone. If he finished early enough, he'd attend Amanda's class, turn in his homework, and check her out one last time. There had to be something there. He felt it on the plane, but he just couldn't put his finger on it.

Edwards worked the phone for over an hour but had no luck reaching Liz's parents. Even after going through the initial paper work, he found nothing that indicated they had been contacted when the missing person's report had been filed. Either the parents didn't know or care about their adopted daughter's disappearance.

Edwards left his phone to stand over his partner's desk. "I can't get anyone at either of these numbers. The area codes have changed, then one of the numbers has been disconnected, or they tell me I can't dial the number from this area code. What does that mean? It's like no one cares." He didn't wait for a comment.

Stas knew all too well about a family not caring. He leaned back in his chair. He hadn't spoken to Vlade or Helena since he returned from Chicago, and no one had bothered to call him. Still, he couldn't bring himself to return to his parents' house. To visit would require more than a couple of drinks, and since reconnecting with Dina, he hadn't felt the need to bring out that chilled bottle of Chopin as often. Being with her took the edge off a lot of things. "Send a fax to St. Louis PD. See if they can locate the family from the info in the address book."

Edwards returned to his desk to type the fax request. "Didn't it strike you how much this last vic, resembled the other two?"

"Maybe we have a collector," Stas mused. "How's your kid?"

"He's feeling better."

"Good, 'cause you're up for the next post."

Color drained from Edwards's face and neck. "When?"

"I'm not sure but soon. Maybe tomorrow morning."
"You're really curious about this one?"
"Damn right."

TWENTY-TWO

Mona shielded her eyes from the early morning light streaming into the bright kitchen. It took a couple of seconds for her to realize it was Frank, sitting on a wrought iron stool at the island counter, sipping a steaming cup of coffee.

He looked up. "You look hung-over."

"Shut the fuck up!" Mona grabbed a small bottle of designer orange juice from the fridge and gulped it down. She paid little attention to her loosely hanging robe that fell open revealing a pair of hip-hugging briefs or the liquid that dribbled down her chin and onto her bare chest.

"What are you doing here?"

"Picking up some things for Ryan." Frank did not turn to look at her but continued to drink his coffee.

Mona walked around the back of his stool before spying the large black Tumi bag at his feet. She toed it with her bare foot. "What is this?"

"My, you're full of questions so early in the morning and before your run. I'm surprised the blood is pumping through your veins yet." He looked at the bag. "Ryan's going to Germany. He needed some clothes."

She edged the bag closer to Frank not bothering to close her robe. "You packed this for him?"

"Yeah, is there a problem?."

"Why didn't he call me? Why didn't he come home and do it himself?"

"We were told you were busy last night." He continued to sip his coffee, still looking straight ahead while Mona still stood behind him.

"You came by here last night?"

"No, I called. Lupe said you were out for the evening."

"But you came back this morning. I'm surprised Lupe heard you at the door."

"She wasn't up when I got here."

"How did you...?"

Frank patted a key ring next to his coffee mug. "He gave me the key. I saw the car in the drive and figured you were still busy."

She came around to face him. "It was just Stella. She didn't feel like driving home."

"I still figured you were busy."

"You bastard!"

"You'd think after last night, you'd have a better attitude in the morning, but...oh, well...."

Mona tapped her long nails on the counter. "When is he leaving?"

"This evening."

"Why?

"Why, what?"

"Why is he going to Germany?"

"He's seeing a guy about a brewery."

"Brewery? What brewery?"

"He wants a micro-brewery. This guy does them."

"He's lost his frigging mind. Where is he going to put it?"

"At the cold storage facility."

"But the condos are going there. He sold that land."

"He canceled the deal."

"He can't. What happened to the money, the condos?"

"Be honest, would you live down there in a condo?"

"No! But a lot of yuppies would. Anyway, I've already picked out my condo. I'm,...we're waiting for the deal to close."

Mona threw her hands in the air. "Damn it all to hell. Damn him."

"You can forget that condo in Hawaii. It just ain't happening, baby. You want a condo, buy it with your own money."

She glared at Frank before turning and mumbling. "He'll be sorry, after all...." The rest of her words were lost as she headed through the door.

TWENTY-THREE

Not wanting Amanda to have access to his cell or office numbers, in case she had caller ID, Stas called her from a pay phone at Sam's.

She rushed to pick-up. "Hello."

"Amanda? This is Stas."

"How are you?"

"Good. Listen, I've been really busy, but I'm going to try to make it to class tonight."

"You promise?"

He could hear the excitement in her voice. "No promises, but I'm seriously going to try." He hung up, listened, waiting for the sound of the coins dropping, then fished a finger in the return slot and smiled. It was empty, but some boyhood habits die hard.

When Stas left work, he had enough time to grab a hot pastrami at Billie's Deli and wolf it down on the drive home. He showered, changed, then left the apartment.

At precisely 7:00 p.m. he took his seat by the back door in Amanda's class. She started on-time by passing out several handouts on journaling. Some students straggled in late and joined him in the back of the room. Jeans, shorts, t-shirts and flip-flops seemed to be the uniform of the day, making him feel overdressed even in slacks and a Polo shirt. He felt out of place and sure as hell didn't have any interest in keeping a damned journal. That was too much like writing crime reports. He looked at the large clock high on the front wall and wished for a drink. Coming back to school had been a bad idea.

Amanda started to drone on about discovering one's self and one's passion. *God, what am I doing here?* He took out his list and read it over when he heard his name.

"Mr. Nowak, what is your passion?" Her voice was soft and sweet.

He blinked, brought back from some brief distraction. "What?"

"Your passion?" Amanda repeated the question.

"The truth," Stas said.

A couple of the younger students laughed. An older man nodded.

"Isn't that a little idealistic? I would think you would want money, power, a great marriage, love...." Amanda cocked her head.

"Is that the sum of our desires?" Stas answered, trying to keep his cynicism under control. "I don't know." He ran his hand through his hair.

The young woman to his left, who had spent most of the class time texting, blurted out. "What do you do that makes truth more important than money?"

He tried to see her face, but it was obscured by a hooded sweatshirt.

"Or women?" a young male student interrupted.

Stas had no response and remained silent during the rest of the class discussion. His thoughts wandered. The more he watched Amanda, the more he thought of his ex-wife, Joy, and how that part of his life had gone down. He stifled a yawn, having second thoughts about even staying in the class after the break, but he stuck it out and waited until the class had emptied before going to the front.

"Here, I'll take that." Stas reached for her briefcase.

"You know where I live, and the coffee offer still stands."

"Let's go to Cafe Bliss. I need a stronger jolt of caffeine," he said.

"Funny, you always seem so calm. You look like you take good care of your body, at least what I've seen of it."

Stas wasn't about to get suckered into taking her home again. She would have to settle for a cup of coffee and not have another opportunity to finger her way over the roadmap of his body. They agreed to take separate cars and met at the cafe.

"You were awfully quiet in class tonight," Amanda said.

He held the door for her. "I don't like being put on the spot."

Once the waitress had seated them at a table and taken their orders, they sat in awkward silence until their coffees arrived.

"It doesn't keep you up?" she asked holding her cup to her lips.

"I keep odd hours. The caffeine helps." He sipped his coffee, avoiding her gaze.

"I thought you seemed distracted tonight."

"Yeah, I guess those young people think it's all about money and sex."

"Maybe you're not being realistic. If you did your homework, I bet a house and a woman were on it. I can't imagine sex not being included in that scenario."

"If the truth be known, they don't necessarily go together." Stas drained his cup as the waitress, standing at his elbow, refilled it.

Amanda sipped slowly. "This is delicious. You forget how good it can be." She seemed a little uneasy.

"Maybe you should get rid of the instant."

"I could if you promise...."

"Amanda!" The voice called from two tables away.

A woman who looked to be in her mid-thirties walked over, a black canvas tote visibly laden with papers hung awkwardly from her arm, a black jacket draped over her shoulders.

"Tanya, what are you doing here?"

Stas sensed a tone of annoyance in Amanda's question.

"I let'em go early. I have so many papers that I'll never catch up. I came here   to get some coffee and knock some of them out before I go home." Tanya stared at Stas.

He stood and offered his hand. "Stas Nowak."

"Tanya, this is *my* friend." Amanda addressed Stas. "Tanya is a coworker."

"Won't you join us?" Stas asked.

Tanya struggled, untangling her jacket sleeves from the tot bag's handles. He reached to assist as she eased into a chair.

"We were just leaving." Amanda rose.

Tanya regrouped, rose, and reached for her jacket. Stas held it for her, then carried her bag.

"I'll see you, Amanda." She turned to Stas. "Maybe I'll see you around."

"Maybe." Stas smiled warmly and followed the two women to the front. He fished some bills out of his pocket and placed them on the cashier's counter along with the check.

The three walked to Amanda's car. Tanya hesitated before pushing the disengage button on her car alarm. Lights blinked three cars away.

Stas had carried Tanya's bag from the cafe. "Let me help you to your car."

Amanda grabbed his jacket sleeve. "She'll be all right."

"That's okay." Tanya took her bag and headed to her car. Within minutes she was out of the lot and into traffic.

"Where're you parked?" Amanda asked.

He pointed with his ignition key to the Mercedes a few spaces away.

"I still don't know that much about you," she added.

"There's not much to know." He started to move under the light but stopped and brushed a dried leaf from her hair. *Let's get this over with.*

She looked up into gray eyes that cooly held her gaze until she turned away. "Are you married?"

"I'm divorced." He shifted his weight.

"I didn't mean to pry."

"It's all right. It was a while ago."

"Since you're single, what do you do for fun?"

His smile faded. "Drink, a little too much. I'm trying to cut back. I run, play a little racquetball when I can find a partner, fish when I have the time. Play my horn. Soccer, sometimes a pick-up game for older guys. Mostly, I watch. Why the smile?"

"Was I smiling? Maybe I was thinking of some new hobbies."

He shifted his weight again. "Amanda, I've got to run. I'll give you a call." He opened the door to her Saturn.

"When?" She looked up at him before settling in her seat and fastening her seat belt.

"Soon." He closed the door and stepped aside to let her back out of the space. He sighed in relief when she drove out of the lot.

TWENTY-FOUR

It was 11:15 p. m. when Stas got home. He grabbed two suits, four shirts, underwear, socks, ties, an extra pair of shoes, and put them in a garment bag. At midnight he knocked on Dina's door.

"Am I too late?" he smiled.

"For you, never." Dina pointed to his bag? "What's this?"

"Clothes. Edwards gets suspicious when I wear the same suit two days in a row."

"Mustn't destroy your image." She held the door open.

He sniffed. "Do I smell popcorn?"

"Yes, and I rented a mystery."

"For a quiet evening alone? Like I don't get enough at work."

"No, I was expecting someone."

He hesitated in the doorway as she tugged at the bag.

"Just kidding." Dina laughed pulling him into the apartment.

He draped his jacket over the Queen Anne chair and removed his shoes, placing them neatly next to the sofa.

Dina returned with a large bowl of fresh popcorn, its steaming fragrance doing aerial assault with the scent of lemon grass from the burning candle in the middle of the coffee table.

"What are we drinking?" he asked.

"I just brewed a new herbal concoction. It's supposed to relieve stress and tension."

"Babe, you know what does it for me."

"I thought you're cutting back?"

"I wasn't talking about Maestro Chopin."

Dina left and returned with two steaming mugs.

Stas took the tea but didn't drink. "This'll make me sleepy."

"I'll wake you for the good parts." She settled in next to him, hugging the large bowl of popcorn, and hit the remote to begin the DVD.

Between nods Stas tried to remember when he'd last spent an evening eating popcorn and falling asleep watching a movie.

"You missed the best part."

"I know the Hollywood ending, but it doesn't happen like that in real life, babe. They make it look too easy. The audience rarely sees what cops go through. Folks don't know what goes on before and after the chases and shoot-outs."

"But some movies do a pretty...."

He stood. "They don't show shit: the stress, bad relationships, suicides."

"Do they get the same things as vets?"

"You mean PTSD?"

"What's that?"

"Post-traumatic stress disorder."

Dina bit her lip. "Like nightmares?"

"Worse!"

"Have you ever had it?"

"I don't know." He started to undo his shirt and move toward the bedroom.

Dina picked up the empty popcorn bowl. "Who would?"

"My supervisor, the psych, a partner, a wife."

"Would I?"

"It depends."

"On...." Dina's response was lost as she disappeared into the kitchen.

The cell alarm played a quick, short tune. Stas reached over, turned it off, and looked at the time. Dina still slept, her arm thrown over his shoulder. He slide from her side, easing her back onto the pillow.

Stas took a quick shower and read the label on the herbal wash. "Lemon grass, seaweed, and orange." She was spoiling him: the gels, scented candles on the ledge, big thick towels, even his favorite after shave, but the throwaway razors had to go. He had to remember to bring his own toilet kit next time.

When he stepped out of the bathroom, Dina was sitting on the foot of the bed, her silk robe drawn around her body. She watched intently as he dressed.

"Are you ever going to tell me about that scar on your back?" she asked.

He slipped on his shirt, obscuring her view of his torso. "Maybe, one of these days."

"What's that on your face?"

Stas touched a piece of tissue sticking to his chin. "I cut myself. I need a real razor."

"No coffee this morning?"

"Marlowe and I are going to a cut." He read her puzzled look, "an autopsy. We'll grab something afterward."

"Who's Marlowe?"

"One of the guys in the unit."

"And Edwards, isn't that your partner? Where's he?"

"Home. His kid's sick."

Marlowe and Stas stood in the hallway talking to a haggard-looking Dr. George Jackson after the postmortem on Jessica Wright. She had been identified the evening before by her fingerprints.

Dr. Jackson removed his mask and handed it to a tech before turning to the detectives. "I read the reports on your other two vics. The cause of death was similar only this one hadn't been dead as long as the other two.

Marlowe frowned. "Well, how long's that doc?"

"It's hard to tell at this time. We have more tests to run, then..."

Stas interrupted. "The tech seemed to have trouble taking the temp at the crime site. What was that all about?"

"She was still frozen."

"Shit!" Marlowe almost fell over as he tried to drag the green bootie from his tennis shoe. Finally, he straightened and faced the ME. "And she hadn't had a baby?"

"Impossible. She had twisted tubes and undeveloped ovaries and uterus. No way for sperm to fertilize an egg. Sorry guys, no baby from this one. I'll send the report over asap."

Stas waited until Jackson had gone back into the autopsy room. "Don't hold your breath."

"So if she didn't have a kid, what's the motive for this one?"

As the investigation on Jessica Wright's death got underway, the detectives learned she had been born and raised in the West Covina area of Los Angeles County. Although her parents were deceased, she had a younger sister, Abigail Ridge, living in Azusa. She was meeting Jonson at the Coroners to identify her sister's body. In the preliminary interview, Ms. Ridge told the detective that Jessica had disappeared in Las Vegas when she attended a modeling workshop.

Las Vegas Police later faxed over a copy of the missing person's report which indicated that Jessica Wright's husband lived in Phoenix, Arizona. Her MP profile listed her as twenty-five when she went missing. She'd been married for three years. A grainy black-and-white photo accompanied the report.

Jonson passed it over to Stas. "I can't believe how fast Las Vegas responded. You think they get money from that *CSI* show?"

"Could be," Stas responded. He examined the picture. "Another pretty blonde. Let's call her husband and get this interview over with."

Jonson made the call. The husband had been notified by LAPD and was anxious to meet with the LA detectives the next day. The captain authorized the trip for Marlowe and Stas.

Early the next morning, Stas drove downtown and found Marlowe waiting behind the wheel of the car they would use, another Crown Vic. They stopped in Covina where Stas would have settled for coffee, but Marlowe had steak and eggs with home fries, and covered everything with a runny mound of catsup.

Their waitress put one hand on her hip as if the gesture alone would relieve her fatigue. She handed Stas his coffee with the other hand.

"You eat like this every morning?" Stas asked.

Marlowe drained his orange juice. "Hell, no. This is light. I usually add a stack of jacks and even grits if I stop at Roscoe's or Denny's."

Stas nodded but had to turn away from what looked like carnage on the other detective's plate. He turned his attention back to their waitress as she cleared the table next to them. She reminded him of Joy, and he wondered what his ex looked like now. It had been ten years since the divorce. There had been an outburst of vitriolic language from her and a seething anger from him that he somehow had managed to suppress. After the final papers were signed, he went back to his room at the Extended Stay Hotel off the 134 Freeway in Glendale with a bottle of chilled Chopin. He shook off the image of a forty year old Joy, wondered why thoughts of her kept surfacing. He ran his fingers through his hair and finished his coffee.

"How's Barbara?" Stas asked as Marlowe mopped his plate clean with his last wedge of toast.

"I don't know. I mean, she's fine, but I think she wants some kind of commitment." Marlowe finished his coffee and rose, grabbing his Stetson from the chair next to him.

"You shouldn't have moved her in."

"Yeah, I know. It was supposed to be until she got a job and an apartment, but things got a little intense."

"Yeah." Stas paid the check, and they headed for the car.

Back on the road, Marlowe dived into a tirade about his two previous wives. "I married Laura right after the Academy.

Man, she was fine. Tight butt, nice rack, strong legs, loud mouth, liked to talk dirty not just during sex but all the time. I thought it was fun at first, then it got old and embarrassing. She liked the club scene. I was so busy keeping my nose clean, working on a promotion, I didn't have time to deal until she took up with my ex-partner. Finally, I had to cut her loose, and it cost me."

Stas eased his seat back and adjusted the visor to keep the sun out of his face. He started to reach for his sunglasses but left them in his jacket pocket.

Marlowe continued talking. "Man, you've been married. What was your old lady like?"

"Like all the rest, I guess."

"C'mon man, I'm not Edwards. She must have done something to keep you bouncing around like you do. I see how women react to you. They want a piece of the action, but you don't let them get too close. Did she cheat on you?"

"That's past history. I really don't feel like talking about her."

"Yeah, you do, we all do. And we got a long ride ahead of us. So 'fess up. What was she doing?"

Stas tried to adjust the seat. "I never caught her cheating, if I had, I would've grabbed my stuff and bailed. I don't know what's worse, her stepping out or her indifference." He fell silent again.

Marlowe took his eyes off the road for a split second and looked over to Stas. "So what *did* she do?"

"Nothing!" Stas lapsed back into silence.

Marlowe adjusted the radio, playing with the search button. Soft rock came through loud and clear until they hit Fontana when static interrupted the music. "Shit!" He turned the radio off. "So do you always give your partner the silent treatment?"

Stas straightened in his seat and looked out the window. "Where are we?"

"San Bernardino. So you going to talk to me, man?"

"Talk about what?"

"The case, sports, sex, women, marriage, money, music, guns."

"In that order?" Stas asked.

"You think that's enough to get us to Phoenix." Marlowe moved to the far left lane and pushed the Crown Vic to 70. "So how's your new woman?"

"I don't have a new woman."

"Well, what is she?"

"Just a friend." Stas turned and smiled.

"Bullshit!"

"One down. What's next? Sports?"

"You like football?" Marlowe asked.

"It's okay. I watch if there's nothing better to do." Stas looked over, saw Marlowe frown, and felt the car accelerate. "I played soccer even in college."

"Yeah, but it'll never take here."

"I think it will when the kids playing now grow up, and we get a couple more big name European has-beens."

"Think we'll get a decent raise this year?"

"I doubt it. Chief wants to put more men on the street. I wouldn't count on anything over cost of living. Did we just skip sex?"

"Stas, I hate giving up my money. They didn't care what you do as long as you bring home the green. I put my life on the line every day. They're like counting machines. Not enough bling, then they want a divorce. Giving up half the house was bad enough, but for the first one, the judge ordered spousal support. She took the money and ran off to Detroit, then came back with a kid. Had the nerve to stand up in court, 'You know judge, ex-sex is the best sex.' He didn't buy it. She'd been gone too long. Really frosted my balls."

"Couldn't have been too frozen, you bit again."

"It was stupid. I started banging a wit. She got pregnant, so I did the right thing. No sooner did I get Laura out of one pocket then I had Jewel in the other. Damn, she was a piece of work. After little Chris was born, she shut me out. You got a kid?"

"No."

"Then why did she marry you?"

"She had visions of me being some hotshot lawyer. When I signed up for the Academy, that was the beginning of the end. So what are you doing about Barbara?"

"I like hanging with her. She's really intelligent and... fun. Did Edwards tell you Pasadena PD gave her a job? It's kinda exciting. At least she'll begin to understand police work, and I won't have to explain everything."

"So how serious is this?" Stas asked.

"Who knows. It's confusing. I don't want to deal with Edwards and his hang-ups."

"I look at Jonson and keep thinking, maybe I want what he has, but I look at Jill and Sid." Stas shook his head. "I don't want to chance it. How long will it last with Jonson and Luz? And when it's over, will they stay together because it's convenient?"

Marlowe glanced over. "So what do you want?"

"I'm not sure."

"Sure about what?

"I don't know."

"I sure as hell hope you never get arrested. You'd drive'em crazy at the interview."

Stas settled back in his seat, put on his sunglasses, and closed his eyes an hour out of Phoenix. Marlowe drove in silence, no further conversation on wives, women, sports, and money. Stas phoned Larry Wright when they reached the city limits to reconfirm the appointment and let him know they were in the city. Wright said he had the day off and would be home but indicated that he didn't want the cops dredging up painful memories.

They found the house, a modest ranch, in a middle class neighborhood of other modest homes. Stas put his shades in his pocket and blinked at the intense desert sunlight. The house had no lawn but was landscaped with scrubby desert plants and rocks, lots of rocks of varying sizes. When they rang the bell, they heard children screaming inside the house.

The front door was opened by a short, thin woman in her early thirties carrying a toddler sucking on a pacifier. Another child sucked away on his thumb and clung tightly to the hem of his mother's dress. He tried to retreat behind her leg as she opened the door for the detectives. "Are you the police from LA?"

Marlowe showed his ID. "I'm Detective Marlowe. This is Detective Nowak. Is Mr. Wright in?"

"I'm his wife. He's in the back." Her head nodded toward a family room off the living room. "I think he wants to talk to you out there. Come in."

She struggled to put one child down and pick up the other, led the detectives across a messy living room, into an equally untidy family room scattered with toys, then through sliding glass doors to a covered patio with overhanging crimson bougainvillea. The backyard with its straggly desert plants, fake volcanic rocks, and an old redwood play set seemed devoid of life.

Larry Wright was a sour looking young man whose once lean torso was showing signs of midsection fat. Sitting on a long bench at a redwood picnic table, he blinked and put down his bottle of beer when the detectives stepped onto the covered patio.

"I'm Detective Nowak, and this is Detective Marlowe. We spoke about an hour ago."

"Yeah, you made good time." Wright extended his hand. "Larry Wright." He looked at Marlowe. "Your first name Philip?"

Marlowe smiled. "No, it's Chris."

Both men sat without invitation on the bench facing Wright.

"Is this really necessary? I've gotten on with my life."

"We met your wife at the door," Stas said, ignoring Wright's comment.

"Nancy. We have two little ones. That's why I wanted to talk to you out here because she doesn't need to hear any gory details. I got a divorce for desertion."

Stas took out his notebook and pen. "You thought she left you? You weren't concerned with foul play?"

"I didn't know what to think. The police in Vegas acted like she took off. Her clothes and all her stuff were gone, and when I got the postcard saying she didn't want to be married any more, the cops were glad to get rid of me."

"Yet you filed a missing person's report." Stas quickly wrote in his notebook.

"Isn't that what you're supposed to do?"

"You still have the card?" Marlowe asked.

Wright pointed to a large plastic bag in the middle of the table. "Everything's there. It's hard to believe three years of marriage can fit in a grocery bag."

"Did you have any children with Jessica?" Stas asked.

"Children! That was one of our problems. We tried, took tests, took temperatures, shots, and pills. Nothing. Wasn't me." Wright looked toward the house.

"Did you think about adopting?" Marlowe asked.

"She said no." Wright reached in the bag and took out a manila envelope. He handed two black-and-white head shots to Stas. "She saw this model reality TV show and decided on a modeling career, even won a local beauty contest. That did it! She was off to the races. Modeling became her baby."

Stas looked at the pictures. "Do you know where she had these made?"

Wright shook his head. "Some were made here, but they didn't suit her. She got involved with some agency in LA, flew up there, and had more made. Everything cost an arm and a leg. Money we didn't have." He pulled out more papers and laid them on the table. "This is it: photos, contracts, letters, receipts, especially for that ring I bought her." He took a long brown envelope from the pile, attached to it was a colored photo of a beautiful marquise-cut diamond big enough to choke the proverbial horse and a copy of a receipt for seven thousand dollars.

Stas looked around the exterior of the house and yard. Nothing he saw indicated that Wright could afford anything like a platinum-set diamond the size of the one in the photo. "May I ask where you got the money for the ring? Was it a loan?"

"Ha! That's a joke." Wright's eyes began to water. "It was from my mother's insurance when she died. I bought it. Stupid, but I was in love."

Both detectives looked at each other.

"Did she have the ring in her possession when she went to Las Vegas?" Marlowe asked.

"She never took it off, except to clean it."

Marlowe looked at another folded paper sticking out of the same envelope. "Could she have pawned the ring or sold it?"

"Not without me or the insurance company knowing. The diamond was engraved with a number. I guess some crook could sell it to another crook but not to a jeweler, not if a buyer wanted to have it insured."

"Have you filed a claim for the ring?" Marlowe asked.

"I tried, thought they were going to laugh at me. They said she probably took off. I didn't know she was dead."

Stas looked at the photo of the ring again. "What do you think a ring like this would cost today?"

"With inflation, I've been told twenty, maybe twenty-five thousand."

Stas stood and put the papers back in the bag. "Can we take these with us."

"Take it, keep it. I only care about one thing."

Marlowe stood and handed Stas the head shots. "What's that?"

"The ring, I want it back. If you find out who killed her, get my ring back. I do the books for a finance company, but we are barely in the black from month to month. Do you have any idea what we could do with that kind of money?"

Stas wanted to say, "not much" but took an official looking paper from his pocket instead and filled it out. "This is a receipt for the bag. We'll get it back to you when our investigation is over."

"No, I don't want any of it. My wife will be happy to get this stuff out of the house."

"We'll keep in touch," Stas said.

"Don't, unless you find the ring." Wright made no movement to show them out but turned back to his lukewarm beer and his bleak garden.

When the detectives walked through the family room, they saw a frazzled Mrs. Wright feeding two toddlers in two high chairs in the kitchen.

Marlowe shouted, "We can show ourselves out!"

"Thanks." She waved a dripping spoon then turned back to two open mouths.

"At least he's not shooting blanks." Marlowe closed the door behind them. "You think they're twins?"

"Could be." Stas put the bag in the car's trunk. "Do you want me to drive back?"

"No, the car's not bad on the road. Jonson always drives in the city."

Stas put on his sunglasses. "I'm starved. Let's eat."

Before getting on the freeway, they found a restaurant, the Silver Spur, just before the on-ramp. When they entered, Stas glanced toward the bar.

A hostess in jean skirt, fringed shirt, and white cowboy boots, looked down at Marlowe's hand-tooled ones and gave the detectives a warm, "Howdy! This way, please." She handed them oversized menus when they sat down. "Would you like anything from the bar?"

"I'll have a vodka double, neat with a water back," Stas ordered.

Marlowe looked up from his menu. "Bring me a Samuel Adams."

Both men ordered food and waited for their drinks in silence.

"What do you think?" Marlowe finally spoke.

"About Wright? Seems in a rut. Maybe he didn't deserve a beautiful wife."

"Yeah, and maybe that beautiful wife didn't deserve a three carat diamond either." Marlowe toyed with his knife. "Do you think the husband's coming to the funeral?"

"I doubt it. You heard him. He's not moving unless there's a ring in the deal." Stas ordered another double when his first drink arrived.

"Man, you're a phenomenon. What are you trying to do, drown in that stuff?"

"I never had a problem."

"That's what they all say. Go to an AA meeting sometime."

Stas ignored Marlowe and dug into the steak and baked potato platter placed before him.

"Damn, no wonder Edwards is so fucked-up. Do you treat him like this all the time? You ever talk to him?" Marlowe sipped from his beer, then cut into his T-bone.

"Do you believe we're a product of our past?" The vodka was starting to warm Stas.

"What *are* you talking about? We can't afford to live in the past. If the psych tells you that, he shoveling bullshit." Marlowe stopped for a moment to chew. "Look at me. I made it okay, and sometimes growing up was a nightmare. My old man beat the hell out of me when I was a kid, but I've never touched Chris Jr. I used to go to my mom when he had a few too many, so he could take whatever was going wrong with him out on me, usually got me another beating. But at least he wouldn't touch her. Afterwards he'd go to bed. She'd make cocoa. I'd drink it, sit, watch her sew. I've never used excessive force on suspects, never shot anyone, and never made my own clothes. So much for living out my past. You?"

Stas finished his first drink and downed his water. "Don't ask". After polishing off his steak and a jumbo baked potato, he pushed his plate away and started on his second drink. The double vodka seemed to loosen his tongue. He pushed his chair back and wished for a cigarette. "My old man got out a lot, said he was going to union meetings. I still remember how he smelled when he came in late, didn't smell like booze or smoke to me. They had separate rooms by then. One night, I was out in the garage. He'd been drinking, but he wasn't drunk. There was something different. I caught my first scent of a woman on him. I found it intoxicating. See, I went to a boys' school. Nobody there smelled like that, and my old lady sure as hell didn't. The girls from St. Joan's were a joke, trying to be sexy and seductive." Stas looked into his glass as if conjuring images from the past. "I was eighteen when I got my first taste of what my old man was into, and I liked it." He finished his drink, feeling a heaviness that weighted him down mentally rather than physically.

"And are you still enjoying the experience?"

Stas gray eyes clouded, but he didn't answer. The discussion was over. He slept on the drive back to LA.

Stas called Dina when they got back to the city. "Have you eaten?"

"No, are you going to feed me?"

"How about pizza?"

"Sounds good, could you bring some beer...," she paused, "and ice cream."

"Some combination."

Dina opened the apartment door when he knocked. She took the pizza box as Stas followed her to the kitchen with a black plastic bag, putting it on the counter.

He ran his hands over her hips. "Do you ever eat?"

"I think I've been doing pretty good since you've been coming over."

His hands lingered, but she pulled away to reach for plates in the cupboard. "I like my women with a little meat on their hips," he said.

"How many of us are there?" She laughed. "You want cold pizza?"

They carried their food and beers to the living room coffee table. He folded his tie and placed it in his pocket before hanging his jacket in the closet. Stas sat on the floor while they ate and watched an episode of *Law and Order*.

After eating, he settled between Dina's legs with no intention of watching another formula police drama. "I wish we could wrap a case, go to trial, and execute in sixty minutes including commercials."

She tousled his hair. "Things kinda slow?"

"That's an understatement." He rubbed her exposed calf and inched up to her knee. "Babe, I didn't come over to discuss my case."

"Fine, then let me relax you."

He nodded as she gently massaged his scalp. When his head drooped forward in a doze, she yanked a handful of hair, pulling his head back.

Stas's eyes popped open. "What?"

"Your head's all over the place."

"I'm beat, babe."

She released his hair. "Then go to bed."

Dina stood brushing her hair in the doorway of her bathroom. She looked over at the still sleeping Stas. He'd thrown the covers off his shoulders once again revealing the rectangular scar on his left shoulder. She'd been dying to ask, since she'd first seen it, wanting to know how he'd gotten the mark. And the temptation to touch it was almost too much as she walked over to the nightstand and placed a key next to his cell phone. She finished dressing and left for an early morning meeting at

the agency, wondering if his possession of the key would unlock more than her apartment door.

TWENTY-FIVE

Jonson got right to it. "So, do we have anything more to tie all this together?" Stas straightened. After a good night's sleep, he felt rested, relaxed, ready to dig into the investigation with renewed vigor. Once again everything was neatly laid out on the table in three columns, each headed by a photo of one of the three victims.

"Cynthia Lenox disappeared first, returning from a trip to Las Vegas where she attended some wanna-be models conference. The conference or whatever it was seems to be a common factor."

"Plus, the three vics looked alike," Edwards added.

Stas nodded and continued. "We can assume the Lenox woman left Vegas since her car was found in Baker. However, anyone could have abducted her and left the car out in the desert to throw off the police, especially since Cindy's family was well-connected."

"You think the kidnappers knew about her family?" Jonson interrupted. "There was never a ransom demand. Maybe the abductor didn't know about Judge Lenox."

"Or found out about him and killed her," Marlowe interjected.

"If she's been dead for seven years, then she got pregnant right after her disappearance, or," Stas paused, "she was already expecting."

The other detectives nodded, following his reasoning. Seeing that they were following him, he pointed to the second row and continued. "Elizabeth Sloan, who went missing a year later at another models' conference in Vegas, just vanished. She didn't have a car. Her boyfriend, Scott Wilson, said she flew over, yet there was no record of a car rental or a hotel stay. She bought a round-trip ticket on Southwest Airlines but didn't take the return flight back to Burbank. The coroner indicated that she'd been dead five or six years. If her disappearance follows Cynthia's pattern, then she might have had a child nine or ten months after her abduction. That would mean there may be two kids out there a year or so apart."

Stas waited while Marlowe examined Elizabeth's photo. When he replaced the picture, Stas continued. "Lastly, we have Jessica Wright who had a fight with her husband about a modeling career. He lost, and she took off for Vegas wearing a three carat diamond ring worth about twenty thousand. She was never heard from again, and the ring never surfaced."

Jonson stood over Stas's desk and picked up Jessica's photo. "Damn, she looks just like the other two. I wonder if they were kept together?"

"Except there's no indication that she had a baby," Stas said. "As a matter of fact, she couldn't."

"What do you mean?" Edwards asked.

"She was barren. Her husband said they had tried, saw doctors, the whole nine yards and nothing," Marlowe added.

"It's possible the women were kidnapped and used as surrogate mothers. When the babies were born, the women were of no further use so they were killed." Stas took Jessica's picture from Jonson and put it back at the head of her column, then straightened the evidence. "I don't think the women were kept together. What would be the point? If you kept, let's say Cynthia, why not just impregnate her again instead of getting a new victim?"

"Why didn't they get rid of the bodies when they killed them?" Edwards asked.

Stas looked at his partner. "Think about it. It's like a cold case, excuse the pun. We've had plenty of bodies over the years. Go down to the Coroners, check out the Crypt. I bet they have fifty, sixty unclaimed bodies at any given time. We could have identified them then and launched a full scale investigation, but years later, would we have put our resources into these women to this extent if one hadn't been Judge Lenox's daughter?"

Edwards shook his head. "I still don't understand. Why freeze them?"

"Dammit, to throw everybody off, to throw any meaningful investigation off for years." Stas went for coffee and wished he had something stronger to put in it.

"The two things connecting the three women are their resemblance and modeling. The women look like sisters, and each one went to a modeling conference in Las Vegas," Marlowe continued. "There's another thing connecting Cyndi and Jennifer. They had babies. If we find the kids, I bet they look like siblings."

Edwards moved closer to the desk and examined the pictures. "So what's the motive?"

"Maybe having a baby that looked a certain way." Stas was back with fresh coffee.

"You sure about that? Why not adopt or just have a baby like normal people do?" Edwards asked.

Marlowe threw his hands up and walked away. "I can't believe you, man. Do you do this on purpose to aggravate us? My God! You're a detective, act like one."

Stas sipped his coffee. "We're probably looking for someone who can't have kids, didn't want to adopt, didn't want to bother with a surrogate, and wanted their kids to look a certain way. Wanted people to believe the kids were hers."

"So it's this last vic, the one who couldn't have a baby that's our problem. Could there be another factor in her abduction and murder?" Jonson asked.

"Only that she was dumped still frozen solid," Marlowe said.

"I think...." Stas stopped mid-sentence and went to the new murder book. Very little had been placed in it. The autopsy report was still in the folder. "The ring was the key. How long did they keep her when she didn't get pregnant? And you're right, why a new woman each time, and are there any more frozen bodies?"

The detectives glanced from one to the other, but no one spoke.

Stas looked at Edwards. "How long does it take to get someone pregnant?"

"Why ask me? I'm not the only one with kids."

"Yeah, but you're the one with the most practice." Marlowe smiled. "What you got, five?"

"We never had any problems." Edwards turned to his partner. "You and Jonson been married. Didn't you ever want kids?"

"Never mind." Stas grabbed the phone and punched several buttons. "This is Detective Nowak at RHD. Give me a call back when you get this. It's about the Wright autopsy report." He hung up the phone and read the report again.

"What's up?" Marlowe asked.

Stas handed him a page from the file. "Jessica's ring finger is missing. Jackson didn't say anything about that during the cut."

Jonson picked up the report. "Did you see anything at the site?"

He shook his head slowly, trying to envision the body at the crime scene. "I'm trying to remember." He paused. "Her hands were bagged. The tech didn't seem to notice anything odd. But then, she was caught up in taking the temperature." His cup slipped from his hand spilling coffee on the edge of his desk as it fell to the floor. Stas's voice deepened betraying his rage. "The bastards cut off her finger for the fucking ring."

TWENTY-SIX

The construction crew at the site where the first body was found had been questioned, but the owners had remained off the radar for far too long. After reviewing the three deaths, the detectives decided it was time to revisit the area and interviewees again. As if on cue, the secretary, Miss Molly Wilder of B & T Construction, telephoned and left a message that her boss had returned.

There were six cold storage businesses located in the vicinity of the first body drop. Two were owned by Paul Lundstrom. Two were closed and one was on the market with several large signs announcing "FOR SALE" "WILL BUILD TO SUIT. The last building on the list was still functioning but in a limited capacity. Marlowe and Jonson left before lunch to check it out. They theorized that warehouses and storage facilities were good places to keep a person concealed from prying eyes for an indefinite time.

When Edwards returned Miss Wilder's call, she told him that Paul Lundstrom was in the office and should be there for the better part of the day.

"She sounded really excited. Bet she thinks we're like *CSI*." Edwards smiled.

"What time, Sid?" Stas looked annoyed.

"When we get there. I told her we were leaving now."

"We'll grab something to eat when we finish. I know a place in Little Tokyo 'cause I gotta double back to Hollywood to check-out a photographer."

Edwards frowned. "I hope it's not raw fish. I hate raw fish."

"Sushi!   It's called sushi, Sid, and they do have cooked stuff."

"This guy in Hollywood, is he the one who did Jennifer's head shots?"

Stas nodded.

"How did you find him?"

"I have my sources."

"Marlowe said he does pictures for porno web sites."   Edwards frowned.

"That's the one."

The main office of the B & T Construction Company was located in a small industrial strip mall on the border of Vernon and Los Angeles.   Edwards eased the Crown Vic into an empty parking space in front of the entrance.

The receptionist was photo copying in a corner when they entered.   She looked like a young combo-goth-neo-hippy.   Her jet black hair was slightly spiked with pink tips.   There was a small silver ring in one nostril, five or six earrings in each ear, and a ring in her left arching eyebrow.   Stas wondered what her boss looked like.   She wore mid-calf, wide-legged yoga pants, a green Indian embroidered t-shirt, and black Birkenstocks without socks.

The detectives showed their IDs.

She held out her hand. "Hi, I'm Molly Wilder. Just call me Molly."   At first she spoke in a whisper as if keeping their presence her secret.   "He tried to sneak out a little while ago when I told him he had an appointment.   You're lucky we don't have a back door."   Her diction was clear and sweet, with a slight lisp.

Stas smiled when he glimpsed her pieced tongue.   Despite the body adornment, he liked her.   She beckoned them down a short hallway paneled in fake wood.   There were three closed door.   As they passed the first door, the second door opened.   Paul Lundstrom was about to make his getaway but drew back in surprise.   He was a man of casual good looks with neatly trimmed blonde hair and deep-set blue eyes that matched the blue of his Oxford shirt. He wore no tie.

"These detectives are your appointment." Molly stepped aside, letting them enter the office. When Lundstrom returned to his desk, she raised the pieced eyebrow and winked at Stas as she closed the door.

Lundstrom's office was long and narrow with a large desk at one end and a conference table at the other. The walls were filled with pictures of anglers posing with their spectacular deep sea catches. A mounted silver-blue marlin hung behind the desk. Chairs were in disarray near the table and against the wall. Lundstrom stood behind his desk and checked the detectives' IDs.

"I'm Detective Nowak. This is my partner, Detective Edwards."

"Pull up some chairs." Lundstrom sat again. "I heard about that unfortunate young woman that they found in the dumpster, but I don't know how I can help you. I've been in Cabo fishing for a couple of weeks."

"You really get around. We heard you were in Hawaii," Edwards said.

"I took a little detour." Lundstrom smiled. "The lure of the lure."

"I understand the appeal, but the police aren't interested in a time frame, yet. We just have some questions about the body found at your construction site." Stas took out his notebook, pen, and paged through before disentangling a chair.

"I really wish I could help your investigation, but like I said....."

"Yeah, I know...." Stas eyed the Marlin, "You *were* fishing, but our questions are more about the property where the body was found. Who put up the perimeter fence, and who maintains it?"

"We've rented the fence for the duration of the construction. If there's a problem, they send someone to fix it."

"Who?" Edwards asked.

"Harpers' Industrial Fencing."

"Who supplies the locks?

"We do! I mean, I don't personally. The foreman takes care of that plus giving out the keys." Lundstrom pulled a ring of keys from his pocket and looked through them, then laid them on the desk. "Let's see, I'm supposed to have one. Ryan, Mr. Talbott, has another one, but we don't use them. I'd have to ask my secretary where mine is."

"So there could be a loose key floating around?" Stas took notes.

"Mr. Lundstrom, you seem to take all of this very nonchalantly," Edwards said. "A woman's body has been found on your premises."

Lundstrom seemed unfazed. "Was she actually killed there? I thought that's what you were investigating, how she got in the dumpster?"

"That's what we want to know. We'd like to visit the site again, talk to your foreman," Stas said.

"No problem." Lundstrom reached for the phone and made a quick call, speaking in muffled tones.

Stas occupied himself with examining the fishing photos visible from where he sat. The subjects were the same four men, posing in different positions.

Molly knocked, then stuck her head through the door. "Mona is here."

Lundstrom seemed relieved as he rose. "I'm sorry, detectives, but I have another urgent appointment."

A 5 x 7 inch silver frame sat on the corner of the desk. Stas turned it so he could see two beautiful young girls smiling into the camera. "You have children, Mr. Lundstrom?"

"Yes, two." He held the door for Edwards and Stas, and walked with them down the narrow hall to the reception area.

A woman in her early thirties stood by the door, fingering her car keys. She was tall, athletic, and attractive in a tenuous way. Stas checked out her legs. They were long and muscular, a runner's legs. Her face, framed by blonde hair, was clear and

191

tanned, but the paleness of her legs did not match her overall coloring. It was her make-up that gave her that all-American, outdoors look.

Stas's gaze dropped to her hand as she impatiently tapped her tapered fingers on the edge of a metal bookcase near the door. She wore a diamond that looked vaguely familiar. Without any introduction, Paul grabbed his "appointment" by the elbow and ushered her out of the office. Neither looked back.

Stas could now put real faces to two of the trio he'd seen on the grainy video at the Bounty.

"So much for introductions," Stas said.

Edwards started for the door. "Yeah, I saw you checking out the legs."

Stas parted the mini-blinds and looked out of the window as the two got into a black Cadillac Escalade. "Is that Mrs. Lundstrom?"

Molly looked up from her desk. "There is no Mrs. Lundstrom. I take that back. There's an ex-Mrs. Lundstrom."

Stas turned back to Molly. "Somebody paid a pretty penny for the rock on her finger. I hope he got good return on his investment."

"She's his associate's wife. Yeah, somebody's reaping dividends, but I'd be at a loss to tell you who."

He smiled. He'd get back to Molly later. Secretaries always had their own slant on things. The price of a cup of herbal tea or a vegetarian dinner would be worth getting her point of view.

At the door, he turned back. "Where does Ryan Talbott have his office?"

"He's in and out. I think he still may have an office at the other building until they tear it down. He and this guy, Frank, have been moving a lot of stuff from there to storage."

"Just what does Mr. Talbott do in the business?"

Molly cocked an eyebrow. "Odd jobs, sort of the corporate handyman." She rolled the ball on her tongue as in thought. "You know, get the fencing, call demolition, check out various places or people of interest. But he usually delegates. He has enough money that he really doesn't have to do much of anything except sign the checks."

Stas got her meaning. "I may have a few more questions after we view the site. Can we go for a coffee or tea later."

"I'd like that." She handed him a business card with her number quickly scribbled on the back.

The gate stood open to the B & T construction site. Edwards parked by the foreman's trailer. The beat-up metal door was slightly ajar. He banged on the door, moving it slightly while Stas stood at a distance and looked around the hard-packed grounds. Building materials were stacked in strategic locations waiting for construction to begin. Several large metal storage units stood next to heavy equipment, but no one seemed to be working.

Avery Hilton came out of the trailer, patting his Angel's baseball cap onto sandy curls. The sleeves of his denim work shirt were rolled up to his tanned forearms.

"I'm Detective Edwards. Mr. Lundstrom called."

"Yeah, yeah, he said to expect you." Hilton looked over to Stas as he stepped down from the trailer entrance.

"That's my partner, Detective Nowak."

Stas joined them at the trailer. "Has the canvas always been there?" He swept his hand along the chain link fence.

"No, they hung it after the murder. Too many looky-loos." Hilton extended his hand to Stas. "I'm Avery Hilton, the foreman." He tried to follow the line of reference as Stas looked over the construction site. "I thought you guys were done here."

"We just want to take another look around," Edwards said.

Hilton turned back toward the trailer. "Let me know if your need any help."

Stas had already moved towards a dumpster like the one where Cynthia's body had been discovered. Building materials were piled in seven or eight locations around the site. A red metal storage unit stood amidst several stacks of prefab roof joists. He walked down a gravel path to the perimeter chain link fence that was now covered with green canvas. He called to Edwards. "Sid, walk the fence in the other direction from this point."

"What am I looking for?"

"Anything that might indicate someone could get in without using the main gate,"

"Could they have tossed the body over?" Edwards looked at the fence to test his theory.

"Yeah, but how in the hell would it land in the dumpster?"

Edwards said nothing but moved along the fence. The area smelled of pine. Stas inhaled deeply as he walked through stacks of lumber, keeping the trailer and the dumpster in sight. He paused to examine fresh looking tread marks that had escaped being obscured by the tracks of heavy duty equipment. He moved in close behind a high stack of pressed plywood partially covered by a green tarp that matched the canvas covering of the chain-link fence. There were four thick metal poles sticking into the ground. He raised the covering slightly to reveal a double chain-link gate, attached to the fencing. The lock holding the two gates together looked new but not very substantial. One like it could have been easily broken and cheaply replaced.

Stas waited for Edwards to join him at his part of the fence. "I found another entrance."

After examining the area around the gates, the two detectives walked back to the trailer. Hilton waited on the metal steps and held the door open for Stas and Edwards. The interior was furnished with a wooden table made from a discarded door, a couple of rusting filing cabinets, rolls of blue prints, and several broken and dusty folding chairs next to the table.

"Have a seat." Hilton motioned.

Edwards sat, sending motes of dust into the air.

"I'll stand." Stas moved close to the table where the foreman cleared off several rolled blue prints.

"Mr. Hilton, we found another entrance in the fence, toward the back of the property." Stas placed his hands on the edge of the table and leaned in to make his point. "Yet, when the investigating team asked, they were told that there was only one entrance." He paused. "Was the cover always there?"

"Well," Hilton's attitude became edgy. "I'm not sure when they put the cover on, but I think it was a few weeks ago."

Edwards checked his notebook. "That's the day before the body was found."

"Yeah, I remember. We had a big delivery. They had to use both gates, you know, in one, out the other." Hilton laughed.

"Why didn't you tell that to the initial investigator?" Stas asked.

"They didn't ask."

"What about the lock?"

"After the delivery, no one could find the old one, so I sent a guy out to buy a new one."

"Do you know if there was a lock on the gate before the deliveries?" Edwards asked, jotting in his notebook.

Hilton shook his head. "Should've been, but I really couldn't tell you."

Stas straightened. "Who could?"

Hilton shook his head again. "I just don't know."

"Who ordered the fence covering?" Stas asked.

Hilton looked puzzled but said nothing.

"You mean it just magically appeared out of nowhere, like the frigging body." Stas walked to the door. "What time does the night watchmen come on?"

"Who?" Hilton asked.

Edwards rose and flipped a few pages of his notebook. "Manny Torres, the guy who found the body."

"Oh, Manny. He's not here anymore."

"Since when?" Stas asked.

"He didn't come back after the accident."

"The girl in the dumpster was no accident." Stas was starting to get irritated. "Tell you what, give us his number, and we'll get out of your hair for the moment."

Edwards checked the slip of paper with Manny Torres's phone number and address handing it over to Stas who punched in the numbers. He held his cell to his ear.

"Manny Torres?"

"Jez?"

"I'm Detective Nowak. We're at B & T Construction. We'd like to speak to you briefly. We just have a few follow-up questions."

"Hokay."

Stas flicked his phone closed. "Let's go."

Manny lived near Dodger Stadium in a back house that had once been a detached garage. There were a lot of conversions in the area. They had to park the car a half-block away. Edwards engaged the Crown Vic's alarm, hitting the lock button twice so that the car beeped back.

Stas stood at the curb. "Do you actually think someone wants to steal this thing?"

"You never know. I've heard...."

"Oh, give me a break." Stas walked ahead, checking numbers on the front and sides of houses. He stopped. "This is it, in the back."

Freshly washed clothes clung to a low chain link fence. A line laden with sheets and a blanket stretched across a shared driveway. A beat-up Toyota pickup was parked at an angle to the house next to a tiny patio with two white plastic lawn chairs and a small Weber bar-b-cue. The front door was closed, but a side window was open blasting Tex-Mex music for easy two-stepping.

Stas had to bang on the door. "Mr. Torres, it's Detectives Edwards and Nowak from LAPD."

The volume was lowered, leaving just a beat, a rhythmic vibration. The door opened slowly, and Manny stepped out pulling another plastic chair after him. "Have a seat." He pointed to the two chairs on the patio.

Both detectives sat and waited for Manny to join them.

Stas took out his notebook and pen. "We're doing some follow-up work on the woman found in the dumpster. Mr. Hilton at B & T said you didn't return after discovering the body."

"I didn't discover nothing. I smelled her and called you guys. That's what they saying, even to EDD. I can't collect unemployment 'cause they lie. Say I quit, abandon my place. I got to sit home, wait for calls to repeal."

"You mean appeal," Stas interjected.

"Even I call the big boss."

"Who's that?" Edwards asked.

"Mr. Ryan."

"I thought Mr. Lundstrom was the boss." Stas flipped several pages in his notebook.

Manny smiled knowingly. "Mr. Ryan got the money. Mr. Lundstrom, the name for people to talk to."

"So did he return your call?" Edwards asked.

"Nada! I still sit, waiting."

Stas eased forward on the plastic chair. "While you were there that night, even before you found the body, did you ever see or hear anything unusual?"

"No really. Just regular noise: cops, sirens, cars passing, and the damn dog."

"What dog?" Stas asked.

"A dog coming around like somebody walk him. It bark around the fence that night."

"Did you ever see it?"

"No, but I hear it before."

"It could've been a different dog." Edwards avoided looking directly at Manny.

Manny looked puzzled. "I don't understand."

Edwards hesitated. "You don't really know since no one's seen it."

"No, I sure it was the same dog. I feel it." He rubbed his knee. "Like in the joints."

Stas flipped a couple of pages in his notebook. "When you were working at B & T, did you notice anything different, strange?"

"Yeah, no more money. Mr. Talbott don't want condos no more, want brewery. You bean down there. Who want to live there anyway?"

They had agreed to meet after Molly's yoga class. She had invited him to the class, but he declined. It was 11:15 p.m. when Stas entered a crowded tea shop on a side street in Little Tokyo. She sat at a small table in the back. He was surprised that the place was still open and doing brisk business at that late hour. Molly looked great even with all the piecing, and her workout had given her a warm afterglow.

"What can I get you?" he asked.

"You drink herbal?"

"Sometimes." He remembered some of Dina's creative brews that she passed off as tea.

"You order by numbers," she instructed. "I'll have a number Three. You better have a Seven. You look like you're a little stressed."

He went to the counter, his senses bombarded with an array of herbs held aloft by the heady steam rising from the many stainless steel tea pots lined-up and steeping on the counter. He returned with two tall mugs of strangely smelling brews, then returned for the pots. After settling into his seat, Stas inhaled, trying to identify the aromas. Then slowly sipped before getting down to business.

"What's in it?" he asked.

"Orange, bergamot, ginger, and lemon grass, I think."

"But that's what I've been using in the shower."

"It's good for that, too." Molly smiled, taking in the detective with a knowing glance over her tea. "Do you always look like this?"

Stas loosened his tie. "It's part of the dress code."

"Then why, on some of the TV shows, detectives wear jeans and t-shirts?"

"Just some young writer who hasn't done his homework."

"I know why we're here. You want the dirt on Paul." She wiggled her bottom excitedly in the chair.

"Is there dirt on him?" Stas sipped and looked coolly at Molly. "What are you dying to tell me?"

"When you work in an office, even a little one, there's always dirt, just nobody important to tell it to, and I love mysteries. Maybe I'll become a detective."

"You have to work up to that, and..." he touched his ear, "get rid of some of those,—rings and things." He could almost hear the gears grinding, decisions, sacrifice.

She rolled the silver ball on her tongue. "I'll give it some thought. Anyway, Paul's divorced. And he was the one introduced Mona to Ryan."

"Ryan?"

"Mona's husband, Ryan Talbott. He's got the money, inherited the cold storage places from his father. The old man's dead."

"What's Ryan like."

"He's either gay or metro-sexual. I'm still trying to figure which one, and he does drugs but not a lot. Anyway there's always somebody around with'em or who can get'em."

"What about his wife?"

"You saw her. She's a special piece of work." Molly rolled her tongue like she had something distasteful in her mouth. "He doesn't notice or seem to care what's going on with Paul and Mona."

"You think they're having an affair?"

"You'd have to be stupid or blind or both not to notice. That's why his wife left him." There was a twinkle in her eyes.

"And I heard that Ryan's father setup a million dollar trust for Mona when the first grandchild was born. And Paul follows the green."

"Why was the old man so generous?"

"His old secretary said Mona looked like his late wife. But no one looks like Ryan."

"What's that supposed to mean?"

"You're the detective, you figure it out. Paul's the stud. His wife had all kinds of problems getting pregnant. They finally ended up using a clinic. He made regular deposits."

"Deposits?"

Molly smiled, revealing the silver ball in the center of her tongue. "You know, the sperm-bank. I even sent payments to the place."

"I don't understand?"

Molly returned to her tea. "... for his freezer space."

"I don't think it works that way."

"Yeah, it does. You can check."

"I will. Do you think Mrs. Talbott used Paul's services? Maybe I should rephrase that."

"It doesn't matter either way, but I wouldn't be surprised."

Stas slowly sipped his tea, then looked in the mug to see how much was left. "Did the sperm bank work?"

"Something did. He had some appointments, then boom!" Molly held up two fingers as she sipped her tea.

"Twins?"

She shook her head and drained her mug. "No, two girls."

"So two trips to the bank or to someone else."

"Well, none of it would surprise me," she smiled.

"Whose Frank?" Stas pushed his mug to the side.

Molly's smile faded. "He's another strange one. I don't know what his story is. I'm not even sure who he really works for, but Ryan, Mr. Talbott, uses him a lot. Now he's doing stuff for Mr. Lundstrom. He's sorta on call, like a doctor, and when they're not working together, they're running together."

"Who's the they?"

"All of them, except the ex-wife."

"Does that include Mona?"

Molly nodded and finished her tea.

"Do you ever party with'em?"

"Are you crazy? I might look a little weird, but they're really freaky, I mean like even swapping."

"You're kidding me, right?"

"Well, I don't know for sure, but I have my suspicions. Doesn't a good detective have to be suspicious?"

He poured Molly more tea. "Was that Mrs. Talbot's Escalade?"

Molly nodded. "They all have them. It's hard to tell who's driving what."

"Three black Escalades?"

"Four. Frank has one too. They're like a matched set. You should see them driving in and lining up like four amigos." She clicked her fingers as if playing imaginary castanets.

"Does anyone have a red one?" Stas asked.

Molly paused, looked at the ceiling. "I don't ever remember seeing red."

TWENTY-SEVEN

Amanda abandoned two pounds of Gala apples, a bag of peeled carrots, and two stalks of celery in her shopping carts when she spotted Stas at the take-out section. After he'd opened to her, she was certain there was no woman in his life. Just seeing him gave her that warm feeling that radiated from her pelvis. She hurried out of the market and surveyed the west side of the parking lot where she'd seen him park before. The black Mercedes was there straddling two spaces. Her car was one row over. She could watch and easily pull out to follow when he left.

Her "stake-out" made her feel like someone in the middle of a crime drama. The rush intensified when she saw Stas unlock his car and get in. She'd write about this. Her heart raced. *Don't forget any detail.* Her hand shook as she started her car and followed, allowing several cars between his and hers. She had no problem on the freeway until they exited and merged into Los Feliz. Traffic in Hollywood was so heavy that she almost lost him when a large SUV cut in front of her, blocking her line of vision. Then she saw him again when he missed a light, and several cars made left turns narrowing the space between them.

Amanda was proud of herself. She has never driven so aggressively, but the stakes had never been so high. She wasn't going to stop until she knew everything she could about Stas Nowak. She slowed when he put his right turn signal on and pulled into the parking garage of a smart-looking apartment building. She passed but saw nothing through the metal gate. After circling the block twice and getting the address. She thought about parking and checking the tenant directory, but fear gripped her. She just couldn't muster the nerve to go back. Suppose he saw her from his window or went out again and saw her lurking in the street?

When she got back on the freeway to Pasadena, a plan started to germinate. By the time she got home, it had burst forth, full blown like some love goddess rising from the sea. She laughed to herself at the fitting metaphor. Venus must have inspired her. Now she knew how to find out what she wanted to know about Stas Nowak.

Amanda spent the next morning calling private investigators. After an hour of searching the Yellow Pages, the internet, and calling, she had spoken to only three live voices. She left a fake name and her phone number with five other agencies. Well, hiring a private detective these days was certainly more complicated and less romantic than the process in the movies. At one place the secretary told her they only handled insurance fraud cases, another worked with the courts and bail bondsmen who served papers, and the third was way too expensive for her pocketbook. I'm not giving up.

She made a cup of coffee, thought of Stas, and vowed to get some fancy ground coffee, but that would mean another expense, a new coffee maker. Well, she'd see how much she had left after paying for a private eye. She liked the ring of that. Her last call was to Walter Ruland, an investigator in Monrovia. His clear, deep voice, like a radio announcer, reassured her even more. He told her that he was a retired police detective who now worked on small cases. He specialized in spouse surveillance, a dignified term for following your husband or wife to see what they were up to.

Amanda withdrew half of her life savings from B of A and stopped at the Pasadena Jewelry Mart. The sales clerk showed her a very nice diamond solitaire engagement ring.

"This is one of our finest selections for the price."

"My fiancé got shipped to Iraq." Amanda laughed. "Can you believe it. He proposed over the internet. He just sent me the money and told me what kind of ring he liked."

"He's got great taste."

Amanda slipped the ring on and flexed her fingers, letting the light hit the diamond at various angles to catch the sparkle. "It's beautiful. I'll send him a picture. He'll be so excited."

"It's a perfect fit. Notice the clarity ...."

But Amanda wasn't listening. "I'll take it. I have an appointment." Amanda felt positive that this was the ring Stas would buy for her.

They met in a coffee shop on Myrtle in Old Town Monrovia. He was sitting at a table nursing a cup of coffee. Amanda felt a low when she checked out the man's ill-fitting jacket that exposed the frayed white cuffs of his shirt. There was at least one good point, his graying hair was perfectly styled. But there was another down tick as she joined him. His complexion, marred by blotchy spots had spidery red veins crisscrossing his nose.

Extending her hand, Amanda approached the table. "Mr. Ruland?"

He returned his cup to its saucer. "Miss Smith?"

"Yes, Anna."

"Have a seat." He rose. "Let me get you a coffee. You like a Danish?"

"Just coffee, black, would be great." Amanda took a seat and waited for the private investigator to return.

Mr. Walt Ruland told her that he worked out of his home to cut down on overhead. He had quoted her a price she could afford: $50 an hour with a ten hour minimum, plus expenses. He didn't accept personal checks, which was okay with Amanda. She'd gotten a cashier's check for $750, and used the name Anna Smith as the payor.

Ruland returned with a steaming mug and placed it in front of her. "You can call me Walt." He reached for the check and examined it before putting it in his jacket pocket. "You want to tell me about your boyfriend."

"Well, he usually goes home about six or seven." She wiped tiny beads of perspiration from her nose with a folded tissue. "I'm so embarrassed, but everything just happened so fast, and I just don't know enough about him to marry him. I've only known him a little more than a month. Don't get me wrong, he's sweet, loving," she flashed the ring, "and generous. And I do love him so."

"I think you're being smart. If more woman checked out their men before marrying, there wouldn't be as much heartache and divorce." Ruland took out a notebook and started taking notes.

Amanda dabbed her forehead. "He drives a black Mercedes, like a sports car."

"You have the license number?" Ruland asked.

"I forgot. I didn't want him seeing me checking on him, but you can't miss it."

"No, no, you're right. What about photos?"

She shook her head.

"Can you describe him?"

"He's nice looking, but not pretty, not a Hollywood type. Dark hair, brown, dark brown." She paused to recall a mental picture. "His eyes are gray, and he's taller than you."

"What? Six feet?"

"I think so, and... he dresses well."

"Sounds like a real winner. Where does he work?"

"I don't know the name, but it's in Glendale, an investment firm. Try his place..." she handed him a folded slip of paper, "this evening. If you don't see him, then wait for my call. He shops at a certain market."

"Will do."

"Do you think you can find him, in uh, ten hours?"

"I can't guarantee you results on so little info, but I'm good."

Walter Ruland promised a report as soon as he made contact and found out just what Mr. Nowak was up to.

Ruland consulted his Thomas Guide and swung by the address that Amanda had given him. He parked across the street from the entrance. The space was tight, but he could see the front of the building and the garage gate. He checked the parking sign posted on the light standard. It was after six. He had plenty of time.

"This is KGET, 641.5 on your dial. Time for our seven o'clock news' update."

The P.I. had been waiting thirty minutes. He lowered the volume, lit a cigarette, and looked out his window. A black Mercedes, fitting Amanda's description, pulled out of the underground garage. Ruland pinched off the cigarette, put it in the cup holder, and started the car. *Wow, how lucky can you get?*

He had made a mental note to get the license number and call his friend at DMV, but things were moving too fast. Tailing Stas was slow and easy even with moderately heavy street traffic. There was a woman in the passenger's seat, her head turned in animated conversation. *So the boyfriend had a girlfriend.* Ruland followed the Mercedes to the Pacifico Building.

The driver of the Mercedes double parked, and the woman, dressed in a short red leather skirt, matching jacket, and high heels, jumped out and ran into the building. An SUV pulled out of a space about four cars behind the Mercedes. Ruland quickly parked, losing sight of Stas's car for a second. By the time he had cranked his wheels to the curb, the first woman returned with another woman, an Asian, even hotter than the first.

He saw the driver lean toward the passenger's window obviously talking to the Asian woman who hesitated and walked away from the car. She was grabbed by the first woman and shoved back into the car as they both squeezed into the passenger's seat. The car eased into traffic, drove back to Vine to Warren, made a left and drove to Highland, making another left.

The Mercedes slowed and entered the small parking lot of a dingy two story brick and stucco building that sported peeling paint and a torn, half-retracted faded awning.

When Ruland saw the trio get out of the Mercedes, and the women, after tugging on shirts, followed the man through a side door. He cruised past, circled the block, and found a parking space directly across the street. He kept his eye on the building as he got out of the car and fed the parking meter.

Feeling assured that he had some time, Ruland crossed the street and looked into the display window that faced the street. Peering through the dirty glass, he saw a faded display of male and female head shots. He remembered seeing a report on television about web sites where call girls advertised. So they were taking pictures. He went back to his car, got in, and watched, finally lighting a cigarette and turning on the radio.

At first, he missed the two women when they exited the building. If they had driven off immediately, he would have lost them, but they stood and seemed to argue. The man had not joined them. The Asian woman pointed to the other woman and swung her hand in the direction of the door. The other woman slapped, then pushed the Asian into the wall. Ruland couldn't see the rest of the fight because the man emerged from the building, blocking his view. When he moved, it was to shove the Asian woman back into the store. The man and other woman talked. He made a call on his cell before returning in his car, leaving the woman standing at the entrance of the photography studio. Well, it didn't take a genius to figure out the man's business with the two women. *Investment banker, yeah, right!* Miss Smith was in for a big surprise.

Ruland had to make a quick U-turn when the Mercedes exited the parking lot and turned right. Several cars honked when he cut off a van and quickly accelerated to keep his query in sight. Leaning forward on the steering wheel, he strained to see the Mercedes in a heavy surge of traffic. He saw the car execute a quick lane change, then slow, and swing into the narrow parking lot of a liquor store.

Nowak parked near the front entrance. There wasn't enough time to follow behind the Mercedes. The P.I. continued and circled the block so that on his return, he could maneuver into the lot. The car was still there. Ruland awkwardly turned the car around and backed into the shadows of a vine-covered wall at the rear of the lot. He cut his lights so he could see Nowak when he exited. Fumbling under his seat, he felt for his Beretta. He didn't like traveling unarmed in any part of LA, especially at night. But then, he rarely had any reason to come to LA. Most of his business took him to Pasadena but rarely further than Glendale. He would have to tell Miss Smith that if she had more work for him, LA was out, or it would cost her a lot more. He patted his jacket pocket where he had slipped the check, found his cigarette pack, and nervously shook one out. He lit up and held it between his legs, looking up every second or so to make sure Nowak wasn't on the move.

The smell got his attention before he was aware of flames. Ruland jerked the cigarette up, dropping ash on his pant leg, "Shit!" giving it a quick brush, then realized there was a fire behind his car. *No, no, there's fire on the car!* He jumped, banging his knee on the steering wheel and dropping the cigarette which fell to the floor and burned into the mat. He swung open the door and got out.

"Shit! Shit!" The trunk was on fire, but there was nothing around to put out the low bluish-yellow flames that covered the entire surface. Removing his polyester jacket, he slapped the already dying fire with it and fell backwards when the cloth caught, smoldering, melting the contact fabric, and emitting a caustic smell.

Before Ruland could return to the fire's source, he lost his balance when an unseen force slammed him into the liquor store's back metal security door. A scream pieced the silence as he felt a rush of blood to his face and tried to mentally shake-off confusion, dizziness. His assailant pulled him upright and swung him around again, this time shoving him into the back driver's side door. Ruland looked up. He had come face to face with Stas Nowak who held him with one hand in an iron grip at his throat and reached with his other hand inside the private investigator's hip pocket for his wallet. All Ruland could do was concentrate on controlling his bodily functions. He felt an overwhelming urge to pee.

"Why the hell are you following me?" The demanding voice was hard, cold.

"A job..., a job." Ruland coughed and sucked in air when the detective loosened his hold and let him drop limply to the concrete.

Stas pulled Ruland's ID and private investigator's license from the wallet, then dumped the rest of the cards on the driver's seat. Reaching under the seat, he found the automatic.

Fear gripped Ruland. "Please don't hurt me. I was a cop."

"Where? Mayberry?" Stas made a sound like a laugh that brought little comfort to the PI. He released the clip, ejected the bullets, and dropped them into his pocket, then tossed the gun and the clip onto the floor behind the passenger's seat. He turned his attention back to the ID and read it by the dome light. "Who hired you?"

Breathless, Ruland remained on the ground. "A woman, I don't think she used her real name."

"What is her name?"

"Smith." He patted his shirt then panicked. The check was in the burned jacket, heaped near the rear of the car.

"What did she look like?" Stas asked.

"Pretty, light hair, blue eyes, nervous."

Stas nudged him with his foot. "Why?"

"Why is she nervous?" Ruland tried to get up.

Stas pushed him back to the pavement. "Why did she hire you?

"She needed to know more about her future husband. Flashed a ring. Thought you were cheating on her."

Stas laughed and released the pressure of his foot. "Get up!" When Ruland regained his feet, the detective pushed him against the car. "I don't ever want to see you in my rear view mirror again. I don't ever want to see your face again. Stay in Monrovia. Tell Miss Smith or whatever her name is that you can't continue the job. It's too dangerous." He sidestepped the PI's car door, walked back to the Mercedes, and backed out of the narrow lot.

Ruland waited several minutes, leaning against the car, still trying to regulate his breathing, then edged around to the front passenger side of his car to relieve himself. Finally, he wiped his runny nose on his shirt sleeve, kicked his ruined jacket to the wall, then rushed to grab it. The check, a little wrinkled, was still intact. He looked at the trunk lid trying to survey the damage. Finally, he got into the car and drove back to Monrovia.

At home, Ruland got a coke from the fridge. He wanted a beer but didn't want alcohol clouding his mind when he told Miss Smith about his night of investigation and his encounter with Nowak. He sat in his fake leather lounger and stared at the blank screen of his TV. After gulping the coke, he reached for the phone, and dialed the number from the white slip of paper. The phone rang twice, then a moment of silence on the other end.

"Miss Smith?"

"Yes?" The word was drawn out. Amanda's voice seemed anxious. "Who is this?"

"Walt Ruland."

Amanda's voice perked up. "You're fast."

"Well, yes, but that has its drawbacks. I'm sorry I can't continue with this assignment." Ruland tried to sound professional.

"Did you get the information I paid for?"

"Miss Smith, I think you should forget this man."

"Why? Is he married?"

"I don't think so, but that's not the point. He's very dangerous. I've seen his type when I did police work."

Her voice rose half an octave. "Dangerous, dangerous, how?"

"Miss, you don't want to find out. Just forget him. Cut your losses and get on with your life."

"Do you want more money? Is that what this is about?"

Ruland sighed. "Listen, you can have your retainer less my expenses. The man's crazy. He set my car on fire. I could have died out there tonight."

Amanda voice peaked with desperation. "Keep the retainer. I'll pay you more. How much do you want?"

"Lady, I don't want anything from you. The man carries a gun."

There was a pause. "It's a lie." She screamed. "I don't believe you."

"All right. He's a pimp."

"A what?"

"He traffics in women, prostitutes."

Silence.

"Didn't you hear me. He's a pimp." Now it was Ruland's turn to shout.

The line went dead.

After her conversation with Walt Ruland, Amanda threw herself on the bed and cried, wetting the new bedspread she'd just bought to show off when Stas came again. Later she avoided the bathroom, not wanting to see the puffy, swollen face, the red eyes, the splotchy complexion. *Damn men! Damn him!*

Ruland's revelation sent her into a cleaning frenzy, finishing after midnight. Exhausted, she finally slept. The next morning she twisted the solitaire engagement ring off her finger, put it to soak in jewelry cleaner, and scrubbed her hands until they were almost raw. She cleaned and polished the ring, admiring its brilliance. She was tempted to call Tracy, tell her that the man of her dreams was a pimp, that he hustled women. What was she going to do? Her teacher friends at Glendale Community

College, especially the women, had been given very few details about her new lover, yet they knew she was engaged. How was she to fix that lie? Tears spilled down her cheeks again.

Well, maybe that was his game, to catch her at a weak moment, make her want him and need him sexually so that she would willingly become part of his.... What did they call it? She'd forgotten, but he would make her his whore.

She reached for the phone, then put it back. Amanda didn't call Tracy, didn't confess her deceit, or was it his deceit? She put the ring back on her finger and climbed onto bed. Before long, another plan started to take root in her mind. She'd make him sorry for trying to seduce her. She'd make him pay.

TWENTY-EIGHT

S tas had met Dina at her place at 7:30. He couldn't understand all the mystery about the photographer, except he was supposed to be good. The Hansen Agency used him for its models though they would never grace fashion runways or the pages of a legitimate magazine. Now they were meeting Dar Ling. He wasn't sure of her status in the agency since Sybil's death. The Asian beauty had made a play for him the first time he went with Dina to check out the agency's crashed computer. Dar Ling was hot but not his type. There was an underlying venerability in all that sexual heat. He preferred keeping his distance from her fiery dysfunction.

Stas pulled into a narrow parking space, leaving the back end of the Mercedes' sticking out in traffic. He quickly checked his rearview mirror for any cruising boys in blue. Dina jumped out of the car and dashed through the double-door entrance of the Pacifica Building. He leaned towards the passenger window and watched Dina disappear. Her heels were too high, her leather skirt was short, too short for his liking but the long legs made him appreciate rising hemlines as he got out of the car and waited on the sidewalk. Frowning, he wondered where she was going dressed like ...., then dismissed the thought as both women emerged through the door.

Out of breath, Dina asked. "You remember Dar Ling?"

"How could I forget."

Dar Ling looked the car over. "Nice!"

He held the door. "Get in!"

"Where?"

"Just get in," he shouted. "You'll fit." Stas, oblivious to the horns of the passing traffic that skirted the car, was anxious to leave.

Dar Ling got in first. "And if we get a ticket?"

"Don't worry about it."

Dina squeezed onto the other half of the seat."

"Where to?" he asked.

"On Wilton, near Lemongrove, turn left." Dar Ling instructed.

Stas pulled out into traffic, checking his rear view mirror from time to time.

Dar Ling reached for the button on the car stereo. "Can I get something else?"

"You don't like Chopin?"

"Classical music numbs my senses."

He pushed the FM button.

"... is KROC A at 106.7 on your FM dial. The time is 7:47 as we head into the evening traffic report...." Soft rock floated through the Bose speaker system.

Stas turned the volume down when they pulled into a parking lot next to a dingy, stucco and brick building.

"We'll be late." Dar Ling climbed out of the car after Dina.

Stas looked after them. "We?"

"I'm going to a meeting." Dina looked back.

"Actually, it's a... launching party for our new Asian market." Dar Ling tugged her short skirt and flung her long silken tresses over her shoulder before opening the dirty glass door.

He followed them inside without comment.

Neil Luman Photos occupied the building on the south side of the parking lot. The dingy window facing the street was decorated with faded head shots. Inside, the front of the shop looked as if very little business was conducted there. Dusty cameras and photo equipment were locked behind sliding glass doors in wall-hanging cabinets.

Dar Ling tapped her fingers on the counter and smiled at the young male clerk. "Where's Neil?

He pointed to a door in the back wall. "The dark room."

Stas joined Dar Ling. "Ask him to come out. It's important."

The clerk stared at Stas. "He's kinda busy."

"It *is* important." Stas didn't want to pull rank, threaten any shutdown action if Neil Luman was doing anything illegal.

The clerk blinked, then slowly moved to the back door, and knocked. "You got some customers getting anxious. You need to come out."

The young man went back to his counter giving his attention to Dar Ling. Dina walked around the room and checked the many fading head shots lining two of the walls.

The back door opened. Neil Luman, in his forties, brushed his dark thinning hair back further . "Hey, Dar."

Dar Ling touched his sleeve. "You know Dina. She's taking over since Sybil died."

"I remember." Neil turned his gaze to the detective."

"This is Dina's friend, Stas."

Neil moved around the counter to join his clerk. "What's up?"

Stas showed pictures of Cindi and Jennifer, then the death photo of Jessica Wright. "I need some info on these women if you took their head shots."

The photographer looked at the images and handed them back. "You a cop?"

"Yes." Stas turned the pictures over. "I think this is your stamp."

Neil reached for the pictures again. "Little faded."

"I know, but you can make it out, can't you?" It was a question that carried with it the weight of an unvoiced threat tempered with a plea for cooperation.

"What happened?" Neil asked.

"They were murdered, two left in a dumpster, another thrown in the Hollywood Hills."

Neil seemed fascinated with Jessica Wright's death photo. "Wow! I never took anything like this."

Stas took the picture back and slipped it with the other two into his pocket. "Yeah, death's a bitch."

Neil looked from Dar Ling to Dina. "So what do you want from me?"

"Dar Ling tells me you took pictures of the women who worked at Hansen's, but you were also taking head shots for other agencies?"

"I stopped doing head shots of real models a few years ago."

"So what's this, a front?" Stas asked.

Neil smiled. "I do photography for web sites. Nothing illegal, and the money's better. "

"I really could care less. I just want to check out your old shots."

"Help yourself. What's left's in those boxes." He pointed to a dusty table in a corner near the front windows. Brown cartons filled the space beneath the table.

Dar Ling looked at her watch as she stood in the open door. "Hey, I'm late."

Dina moved outside. A thud and scream were simultaneous and loud enough to stop both men in their tracks. When Stas rushed to the outside, he found Dar Ling sprawled on the narrow walk next to the building. A red splotch was swelling on her face just below her left eye.

Dina stood over her. "You bitch!"

Stas pushed her against the wall and reached down for Dar Ling, who, once regaining her feet reached with menacing scarlet talons for Dina's face, but her attempt was weak and misdirected. He pushed her roughly back into the shop.

"Let me go!" She tried to pull her arm out of his grasp.

Neil had not moved. "I guess I don't need to call the police. This happens all the time. I've witnessed more cat fights out there. Let her go. They kinda lose their venom after a while."

Stas hauled Dar Ling to the counter. "Call this one a cab and keep her 'til it gets here."

"I can't go to a party looking like this." She touched the discolored area of her face and looked for a mirror.

"I don't give a damn where you go after you get your cab," Stas ordered.

"What are you going to do about Dina?"

"Don't worry about it." Stas opened the door.

Dar Ling shouted at his back. "Oh, I know, now you take her home for her big reward."

Outside, Stas pulled Dina to him. "Are you okay?"

She pushed him away. He grabbed her back and lifted her chin to look into her eyes.

"What was that all about?" he asked.

"Just call me a taxi if you're not taking me home."

He raised his hands in defeat.

"Are you leaving?"

"I've got some business to take care of." He looked over his shoulder to the street. "Just wait here. Neil is keeping her under wraps." He nodded towards the door. "I'll see you later, babe."

Stas called Dina a taxi from his cell, then looked across the street before getting into his car and slowly pulling out into traffic, keeping his eye on his rearview mirror. He put on his left turn signal and carefully maneuvered into the left turn lane. From there he turned, then circled another block and making several more turns. He was looking for an old haunt he had frequented in the area when he worked Vice. He vaguely remembered that it had a dark, narrow parking lot.

It took about seven minutes in moderate traffic to get to Cody's Liquors and Spirits. Stas parked in the handicapped space closest to the entrance and went inside. Jim Cody, the owner, was behind the counter reading a racing form.

"Long time no see. What can I get you, Nowak?"

"A can of lighter fluid, a book of matches, and unlock the back door." The detective tossed a few bills on the counter and waited for Cody to lead the way with his ring of jangling keys to the back.

For the time it took to unlock the back door and security gate, Stas thought they could have broken into Fort Knox. He hoped his prey would be there as he stepped into a garbage strewn concrete slab and recoiled from the stench of urine and vomit. "You need to clean this place up. And get some lights."

"You going to report me, old buddy?"

"Not me, but somebody else might."

"You coming back in this way?" Cody asked.

"Nope. After I finish my little business, I'm leaving from outside." He spoke quietly to the figure silhouetted in the partially opened door. "You didn't see or smell anything."

"Just don't burn me down."

Stas waited until he heard the heavy metal security door close and the chains and locks engage before moving to the rear of the dark lot. He crouched behind the lone car parked there, opened the can of lighter fluid, and poured the contents on the trunk. He then threw a lit match on the liquid, creating a swoosh that quickly engulfed the back of the car in a bluish-yellow flame. Stas stood back in the shadows and waited.

After scaring the hell out of Ruland, then listening to his story, Stas left him in the parking lot trying to save his jacket and access the damage to his car. He put the Mercedes in gear, pushed the CD button, and let the sound system adjust to the street noise and his laugh. At first Stas felt flattered that a woman would spend good money to have him followed when all she had to do was ask if she wanted to know more about him. But then, there were certain things he knew he wouldn't tell her. *The nerve. Who did she think she was?* Soon anger crept into his psyche overriding the humor of Amanda's actions. He could feel acid rising to his throat, but the only thing he had for relief was the sound of Marvin Gaye. He pushed another button and listened to "Mercy, Mercy" as he drove back to Neil's.

TWENTY-NINE

Stas got back to Neil's studio an hour before it officially closed. From what went on in the back, setting-up web-sites for people in the sex trades, the detective doubted they ever had regular hours for their lucrative operation.

Neil came out wiping his hands on a paper towel. "I've been in the darkroom. Listen, Dar Ling called back, said you worked vice. I don't want any trouble."

"If I still worked vice, maybe I'd be all over you and Dar Ling, too, but I could care less what you do in the back as long as all of the bodies are breathing, and they're not minors." Stas took the pictures out again. "I need to check your old photos to see if you did any of these women. Let me rephrase that, to see if you photographed them."

"I don't do commercial shots anymore, and if I did, I may not have them anymore. We recycle the paper."

"These were taken maybe seven, eight years ago. Those pictures in your windows weren't recycled."

"We couldn't reuse that paper. Anyway, I've been too busy to take'em down."

"What's in the boxes in the front?"

"Old head shots for the trash. Again, too busy."

"... to throw out?"

Neil nodded. "Help yourself, they may be old enough. Pull up a chair." He turned towards the back. "I've got work to do."

Stas took off his jacket, rolled up his sleeves, and settled on the floor. There were seven boxes of photos. It took him an hour to get through the first two boxes. He was interrupted twice by two statuesque beauties. One, who made him think she was auditioning for "the Queen of the Amazons," had to be at least six-foot four. Her hair, an expensive weave, made Diana Ross's mane look skimpy.

She checked-out the detective. "You the new assistant? It's about time he got a real man in here."

Neil locked the outside door. "He's a cop, Bev. He ain't interested in your sorry ass. Come on, woman."

Bev picked several curls, winked at Stas, and went to the back studio.

The photographer came out later to let the Amazon out. Stas realized she had been replaced when a pair of shapely legs drew his attention away from his third box. He looked up to a young woman sporting a short purple and white cheerleader's skirt and a Harvard sweat shirt. He didn't have to strain his imagination to guess what was underneath.

He looked up at Neil after she swished pass. "She'd better be legal."

"Are you carding now?" she asked.

"Back off, she's twenty-nine. Come on, woman. I want to get outta here before dawn." Neil pushed her ahead of him.

The cheerleader must have been Stas's good luck charm. Within twenty minutes of her going into the rear, he found a sheet of composite shoots of Jennifer and two head shots plus a sheet of poses of Jessica Wright, the third victim. He set them aside, flexed his back muscles, and smiled, wishing for Dina's nimble fingers.

He stretched and looked at his watch. If he could finish the next box, he'd stop by her place for a drink and a serious talk about Jason Goode. *I'll give it another half hour.* He was on his fifth box when he pulled a photo of a familiar face. It was Mona Talbott from B & T construction. There were three sheets of her photos. Stas put them aside with the others, dusted off his dirty hands, and headed for the back.

The door was unlocked, but there was no one in the dark room. A large digital printer almost blocked access to another door that was partially open. When he stuck his head through, he could feel the heat generated by the lamps and spots. Neil's back was to the door as he photographed Miss Cheerleader posing in her pleated skirt, saddle shoes, and pompoms. Her hair was done up in two pony tails on either side of her head. Her bare breast, firm and perky, the nipples rouged and erect, were the focal point of the shoot. She smiled coquettishly into the camera.

Click, click, click! Poses changed from innocent to provocative. Neil said nothing, but continued to click away. The model seemed to know the drill.

Stas watched for several minutes. The cheerleader licked her lips and seductively zeroed in on her new audience. The raw sex generated by the erotic posing was starting to get to him. It was time to get out.

"Listen," Stas called back, "don't do anything with those boxes until I talk with you tomorrow."

Neil turned from his work.

The cheerleader changed her pose before the detective could escape. "Oh, don't leave now. We're just gettin' warmed up."

Stas thought he heard the faint whisper of the skirt's zipper. He was tempted to look back, but all he could muster was, "I'm out of here."

THIRTY

Amanda, angry, hurt, and disappointed, wanted to slam something. Stas Nowak had betrayed her. She had desired him, wanted him to be a part of her life, of her future. But then, had he actually lied to her. There were questions she should have asked. What he did for a living for starters, instead of being seduced by the cut of his clothes, his beautiful car, his cool demeanor. Then there was the expensive watch. She'd seen one like it, with its fancy price tag, in one of her many magazines. Hadn't she checked out the things that mattered, the things that told her he had money, that he was a good catch?

She had been seduced by how he looked at her, how he blocked out other people, other distractions when she was with him. How often had that been?

But would he have told her the truth if she had asked? "By the way, Amanda, I run a string of whores. Would you like to join my girls?"

Well, wasn't not telling her anything as good as lying? She opened the dishwasher, took out a cloudy glass, put it back, then poured in more detergent and set the machine for pots and pans. She stood with her palms down on the counter, letting the vibration of the machine and the swishing of the water calm her.

Later Amanda sat at her dining table and sipped some tea. What had Ruland called him? "A pimp!" And the detective had seen him manhandling his girls. Coughing, she almost choked.

In the bathroom, she ran a glass of water, took a container of pills from the cabinet, popped two into her mouth, and returned the bottle to the cabinet. In the living room, she rearranged her *Cosmopolitans*, fluffed the sofa pillows, and adjusted the blinds. Returning to the magazines, she flipped through the pages of one, looking at nubile young models who didn't look a day over seventeen exhorting the readership on the forty-five ways to please your man in bed or extolling the same young women in the fifty surefire ways to achieve multiple orgasms.

Staring from the glossy pages were women with bodies that Amanda knew she could never achieve. She flung the magazine across the room, then went to pick it up, smoothing the cover, and taking it with her to the bathroom where she stripped and stood on the scale. She'd lost ten pounds since she met Stas on the plane. *I bet he doesn't like skinny women.*

She touched herself and imagined Stas stripping to join her in the shower, wondering what it would be like to have him make love to her under a cascade of water. She closed her eyes, losing herself to a myriad of sensations. The shrill ring of the phone jolted Amanda back to reality. Shivering, she ran to answer it.

"Amanda, what're you doing?"

"Tanya! I was thinking about you." She played with the diamond ring on her finger. "You saw my ring?"

"It's gorgeous. When's the date?"

"We haven't decided yet. I'm beginning to have second thoughts. He's become so possessive since we got engaged."

"Girl, watch that. If he's doing that before you get married, imagine what he'll be like after the wedding," Tanya offered.

"He's getting a little rough, too."

"He hit you?"

"No, it's just in bed. I said I didn't want sex, but.... You remember that night you met him."

"Yeah, I remember, at the coffee shop."

"He had wanted an espresso. We went to my place afterwards. He almost raped me."

"Oh, my God! You need to do something."

"That's just what I'm going to do."

THIRTY-ONE

Stas wearily reached into his coat pocket, pulled out his cell, and speed-dialed the familiar number. After Dina's quiet hello, he opened with, "Babe, I'm sorry about last night. And I don't think I'll make it tonight. Going back to Neil's." Stas sounded tired.

"I understand." Dina's respond seemed heavy with disappointment.

"Are you okay?" He was concerned.

"Where are you now?"

"Home, putting on jeans. That place is filthy, but I still need to finish the last few boxes."

"Do you want company?"

There was a pause. "Sounds like a winner. I'll pick you up in forty-five minutes."

Dina hung up the kitchen phone and finished her few dinner dishes before changing into sweats. She might as well keep an eye on Neil's late evening clients, keep them from getting any ideas about Stas.

Later at Neil's, Dina sat cross-legged on the floor with a dirty brown cardboard box on one side and a pile of dusty head shots on her other side. She took her time scrutinizing each picture.

Stas stopped. "You're not working for the FBI, babe. Just look at the photos and the women. If you think you got a match, check the back for the date and the agency's name. I'll take care of the rest." He had taped the deceased women's pictures on the rim of the table.

Dina looked up at the photos and back to her pile. "You never told me what happened when you left here yesterday."

"What makes you think something happened?" He didn't look up.

"I'm not stupid. I've seen you go into detective mode before."

Stas avoided her gaze. "Some hick PI was following us."

"Are you sure?"

"I think I know when someone has me in his crosshairs."

"But why?"

"A woman hired him to keep tabs on me."

Dina straightened, dropping several photos to the floor. "Oh! What woman?"

He rummaged noisily in the bottom of the box. "I met her on the plane from Chicago."

"Really?" She inched closer. "You're telling me a woman you met on a plane, a total stranger, pays someone to follow you?" Her question gave fire to her eyes. "Stas, you're talking to me. You can't bullshit me. Either she wanted something from you, or got something from you and wanted more. Which is it?"

"Hey, back off a little. We got together one night."

"Got together? Hooked up?" She paused. "How? Did you sleep with her?"

"What? Hell no! We had coffee, and I left."

"Why?"

"Why, what?" He knew what she wanted as he threw some photos in the box avoiding Dina's stare. "She didn't turn me on."

Dina moved back to her box. "When did you see her last?"

"A while back when I went to her class. She teaches at Glendale College."

"I can't believe this. You, going back to school. What does she teach?"

He half smiled. "A class about discovering your passion in life."

"Hell, I can give her a blow by blow description of your passion and mine."

"Anyway, it's over."

Dina frowned. "I wouldn't count on it." She spoke to the head shots.

They worked in awkward silence for another hour.

Stas found another sheet of head shots of Jessica Wright and several sheets of provocative poses of Mona Talbott. On the back was an address and phone number plus a notation to bill the Gaines Agency.

Neil came out of the back at 12:17 p.m. and unlocked the front door. "I have a couple of clients coming in. You almost finished?"

Stas stood and untaped the pictures he had attached to the table. "We're through." He held up the poses he'd taken from the box. "I'd like these for a while."

"Keep'em. I'm tossing the rest."

"Do you still do business with the Gaines Agency?" The detective asked.

"Gaines? Oh, Eileen Gaines. She's still around somewhere. I heard she sold the business, and it folded. I hope she got her money out."

"You have a number?"

"Maybe. Let me check my Rolodex." Neil went around the counter and rummaged through several drawers.

The door opened and a shapely redhead entered wearing a red string bikini beneath a clear plastic raincoat and bright red vinyl boots. "Hey, Neil." She looked pass Dina, who was still on the floor returning pictures to boxes, and eyed Stas as he slipped into his leather jacket. "Is he a new prop?"

"Not in this life." Dina waved her hand at Stas for him to pull her up.

Once on her feet, he grabbed his large envelope, and waited for Gaines's information.

Neil scribbled a number on the back of a business card and handed it to Stas.

"Thanks for the help."

Neil nodded and grabbed the arm of his new client. "Please keep your vice friends away from here. I'd appreciate it."

The redhead shouted over her shoulder. "Hey, you in vice? I know some guys in vice."

Neil slapped her butt, his hand sticking briefly to the plastic as they entered the studio in the rear.

"I bet that's not all she knows." Dina moved to the door.

Stas wasn't smiling. "Let's get out of here."

THIRTY-TWO

Eileen Gaines's apartment was located in a pink stucco complex near Fairfax and Santa Monica. The Division secretary made an appointment for 1:30 p.m. and left the address and directions on Edwards's desk. The detectives left Parker Center at noon and stopped for an early lunch at Saul's Deli on Fairfax. Their sandwiches, piled high with lean, juicy corn beef and served with smoky green kosher dills were famous.

Driving over to Hollywood, Stas's mouth had watered when he described one of his favorite lunches to his partner. Edwards seemed unimpressed by the menu, ordered a ham on white, and requested sweet pickles. The waitress looked at him like he'd lost a few marbles in the La Brea Tar Pits, took their order, and never returned.

A busboy delivered their sandwiches and left the check. After eating, Stas picked up the bill, looked it over, then fished two fives from his pocket, leaving them on the table for a tip.

Edwards picked up the money and dropped them back on the table. "Did you mean to leave that much?"

Stas nodded and walked to the cashier to pay their bill.

They arrived at the Sunset Plaza Apartments at 1:30 sharp but finding a parking space took another ten minutes. They were buzzed in and took the elevator to the third floor. A young man, tanned and lean, with dark, heavy eyebrows that gave him the look of a gothic model answered the door.

"We're with the Los Angeles Police Department. We have an appointment with Mrs. Gaines."

The young man nodded, then disappeared into the back. A few minutes later Eileen Gaines emerged. She was a large woman, big boned, and tall, wearing a housedress.

Stas was struck by its design. It was a floral print, similar to the dresses worn by the deceased women. The garment was short, revealing fat knees and even fatter legs. Her feet and ankles though swollen were squeezed awkwardly into well-worn flip-flops. She walked to the window and opened several vertical blinds.

"This is Detective Nowak. I'm Detective Edwards." Both men presented their IDs.

Gaines ignored them and moved to a large recliner. "Won't you have a seat."

Both men sat on the sofa. When Edwards took out his notebook, Stas removed head shots from a large manila envelope.

He passed them over to Gaines. "Do you recognize these women?"

Gaines squinted as she looked at Elizabeth Sloane's, Mona Talbott's ,and Jessica Wright's head shots, then shook her head and started to hand them back.

Stas noticed indentations on her nose. "Could you put on your glasses and take a closer look? These were taken a few years back."

She reluctantly reached into her pocket, took out a pair of wire-rimmed glasses, and examined the photos again. She studied Mona Talbott's and nodded. "I remember her."

Both men leaned closer.

"She came to my modeling classes. Had the look but no talent, no moves."

"Did you have any special programs, like workshops for aspiring models, say in Las Vegas?" Stas asked.

"I never ran anything there. I basically worked with young women who wanted to be models. We conducted classes: make-up, posture, proper clothes, runway presence. I evaluated them after they finished the classes and sent them on various photo shoots or modeling job. Some made it. You know, did some local work. I got a commission for any jobs I sent girls on, but I had only two women who made it to the big time."

"Did Mrs. Talbott take any of your workshops?" Edwards asked.

"She may have. There were so many girls. It's been a while. You can't expect me to remember them all?"

"But there must've been a reason that you remembered her?" Stas took the picture back and put it in the envelope.

"Well, yes. I couldn't forget a girl who had an agency bought for her." Gaines smiled.

Both detectives looked at each other.

"I don't understand. You mean you sold her your agency?" Edwards asked.

"Not to her. She couldn't buy anything or run it for that matter. What did she know? Do you have any idea how many girls I've had photographed?"

Stas wanted to make a stab at it but held the thought. Somehow he couldn't imagine Gaines running anything with top ranked models. "Who bought your business?"

"Mr. Talbott." Her smile morphed into a smirk.

"The father or the son?" Edwards asked.

"The old man. That girl wrapped that old fart around her finger." She shook her head. "Would you believe, I even made a play for him. He wouldn't give me the time of day, bastard."

Stas moved to the edge of the sofa. "So a young woman, without experience was able to run a modeling agency?"

"Talbott kept on a few of the girls who ran the office for me plus some of the instructors. I didn't care. He made me an offer I couldn't refuse."

"So could she have continued with the agency after you sold it?" Stas wasn't giving up on Mona Talbott.

"I'm certain she did. That was the whole point."

Stas looked puzzled. "What point?"

"Paying me more than the agency was worth."

"I don't understand," Edwards said.

"Mr. Talbott wanted it for her. You could tell he wasn't into it for the return on his money. I know because I could barely keep my head above water. Maybe they started the Vegas program after I sold."

Stas rose. "Must be nice to have a father-in-law who can buy you a business, especially one where you can do anything you want with it."

"He was quite smitten with Mona. He came across as someone who would do anything for her and her look. It was like an obsession."

Stas handed Eileen Gaines his card. "Thanks for your help. If you think of anything else, please give us a call. By the way, I'm curious. Where did you get your dress?"

"Oh, this thing. It's old but very comfortable. I had them made by the gross. All the girls in my program received one. They used them when they did their hair and make-up. Saved a lot of clothes and encouraged a uniform neatness."

"When did you sell the agency?" Stas asked.

"About nine years ago. Whatever I had left went with the new owners."

Edwards started to close his notebook but paused. "What did you mean about that look?"

Gaines struggled out of her chair. "That kind of pale, air-brushed blonde look, like the old Breck girls, but that look's been out for years."

"Umm, Breck girl?" He closed his notebook and followed Stas out into the hallway. "What's a Breck girl?"

When Edwards and Stas returned to the squad room at RHD, Jonson waved a paper.

"Hey, Edwards, you just got a blip on your radar screen Your honey is back."

Edwards grimaced as he snatched the paper and read the message. "Call Carroll, remembered something very important." He handed the note to Stas. "He wants me to call."

Stas looked at the slip. "Then do it, could be important."

Edwards and Stas met Carroll at a popular coffee shop on Santa Monica near Fairfax. Carroll, looking somber and pale, sat at an outside table. His usual exuberance seemed toned down, but he managed a smile and a wave when he saw the detectives.

Edwards stood back, looking over the scene, as if he could do the interview on his feet in record time.

Carroll reached out and touched his sleeve. "C'mon Sid, you're not still mad?"

"You stole my phone."

"That piece of junk? I thought you'd be pissed 'cause I talked to your wife. Was she frosted, thinking you had another woman? I'm sorry. It was a cheap shot. I was high."

Stas pulled out a chair. "Sid, take a seat and hear him out."

"Look," Carroll ran his hand down his black crew-neck sweater and black jeans. "I'm getting clean. I just got signed up for rehab."

Edwards reached over to an empty chair but did not pull it up to the table when he sat. "What?"

Carroll looked disappointed. "What?" He stared at Edwards. "No, 'You're looking better. Hope you're giving up your thieving ways and staying out of dumpsters.'" Carroll turned to Stas. "You're looking good as usual. I like the suit. Too bad your good taste doesn't rub off. I saw some of the detectives where you work. They could use major makeovers."

"Listen, I didn't drive all the way out here for small talk and insults." Edwards looked nervous.

"What's this all about?" Stas asked as he looked around for a waiter.

"Since I'm getting my head straight, lots of things are happening. I'm remembering things and dreaming things." He sipped from his large glass of orange juice. "God, I hate dreaming."

"You brought us here to tell us about your frigging dreams?" Edwards pushed his chair further back.

The waiter stood at Stas's elbow. Stas turned. "Two black coffees, please."

Carroll's voice cracked, taking on a deeper resonance. "Remember, I told you about some of the people we hang with at the club. The three we saw on the video, even Stella. You remember her? She's another piece of work. Mona and that bitch." He rubbed his hand over his eyes.

"Let's get back to your story," Stas said.

"We all flirt and talk shit but nothing's going on with us. One night, after you'd been there. It was just Mona and me talking about kids and family. It was like being on a date. Her husband was there for a change, flitting around like some damned butterfly, but he was trying to pick up this hot guy. I told you about that, right." Carroll stopped to let the waiter put the steaming mugs down.

Edwards hand shook as he reached for his, spilling coffee when he tried to drink. Stas sighed and passed some paper napkins to his partner.

Carroll moved his hand across the table towards Edwards. "I'm really sorry about the phone. I'll get you a new one, a good one. I was strung-out on meth."

"Tell us about Mona," Stas pressed on.

"Okay, okay! I was telling her that I was planning to have the operation. I was about to start the hormone treatments. But the more I looked at her, the more I wanted to sleep with her."

Edwards interrupted. "You and the ice queen?"

Stas sipped his coffee. "Let him finish."

"Ryan came back to the table, but when he sat down, her mood seemed to change."

"Change how?" Stas's interest peaked.

"It was the look she gave him, 'cause I felt her hand moving up my thigh, so I asked her to dance."

"What did her husband do?" Edwards asked.

"He watched us for a couple of numbers, then Gold went over to our table."

"Gold?"

"Malcomb Gold, his partner in crime. They run together. They may even live together. Ryan spends a lot of time at Gold's condo."

"So what happened with Mona?" Stas seemed impatient.

"She worked on my ear, my neck. She moved against me like she wanted it right there on the dance floor. We decided to leave."

"Where did you go?" Edwards pulled his chair in closer.

"Back to the table. We all sat there for a hot second and finished our drinks. Mona said she had a headache." Carroll smiled. "I never thought I'd be happy to hear that excuse. We went to Clayton's place 'cause he lives nearby."

"So you got it on with the Ice Queen?" Stas eased back in his chair, amused.

"That was my plan. We didn't even need to talk. It was like we had ESP."

"How hard was that? You both just wanted to break outta he box." Stas stifled a laugh.

"Yeah, but nothing happened. I almost whipped it to death. Nothing. We tried everything except the vacuum. Then the bitch laughed at me. I could have beat her. Then I got sick. I heard her call somebody. It sounded far off, like she was in outer space. She told him to come get her."

"Who?" Stas took his notebook and pen out and placed them by his mug.

"I think I heard her say 'Frank, come get me'."

"Why Frank, why not Ryan?" Stas asked.

"I guess Ryan was with Gold. Anyway, Frank works for them."

Edwards pushed his chair back from the table. "So you okay now?"

"Hell, no." Color started to rise in Carroll's neck . "I called Clayton to take me to emergency."

"Why?" Edwards asked.

"They drugged us."

"Who?" Stas asked.

"I don't know, her husband I guess. Thought I might get a little piece."

"Drugged you with what?" Edwards asked.

"Special K."

Edwards looked towards his partner. "The cereal?"

Stas glanced at his partner. "Ketamine, cat tranquilizer. It used to be popular at raves. Now you can get it at the clubs."

Carroll interrupted. "I've used other stuff before but not that." He looked at both detectives. "Why would I? First, I'm thinking I'm super-stud. My feelings were so intense. I mean, I felt that she was the love of my life. Then, when we get to Clayton's place, nothing."

"Back up a sec." Stas was taking notes. "When you were talking about kids, what did she say?"

"I told her about how I was feeling about the operation and regretting how when it's all over, I couldn't have kids. I love kids. She laughed, said I should be glad, that they were a pain, that she wouldn't have them, the stretch marks, the flabby tits." Carroll looked up. "But she's got kids. I remembered what she really said at the club."

"What was that?" Stas asked.

"She said, 'I can't have kids.'"

Edwards came to life. "They're not hers?"

Carroll continued. "Then she looked across the dance floor at Ryan. He was dancing with some cute guy. She just laughed and said something about him not having enough sperm to make a decent donation. It wasn't the kind of thing you say like you're joking. She was telling the truth."

"Where was he making donations?" Finally engaged, Edwards pulled his chair closer and looked at his partner.

"I guess we'll have to find out." Stas rose and picked up the check.

They made the ride back to Parker Center in silence. Stas put on his shades and reclined his seat, not to nap but to think.

At his desk, Stas called Dina. "Hey, babe. I'll see you later. I'll pick up Chinese."

"Can you get some ice cream?"

"Whatever your heart desires, babe."

Edwards stood by his desk listening to the one-sided conversation. "You not going home?"

Stas neatly rearranged two file folders on his desk, lining them parallel with the left edge. He wiped the rest of the desk's clean surface with a paper towel before looking over to his partner. "Eventually."

Dina took empty dishes and cartons to the kitchen and returned with what was becoming an evening ritual, a bowl of popcorn and a pot of herbal tea, the vapors perfuming the air as she poured two fresh cups. She placed everything on the coffee table and joined Stas on the floor.

"Isn't this a kinda strange combination, popcorn and tea?" he asked.

"Would you rather wash it down with some vodka?" She started to rise, but he pulled her back down.

"What's on TV?"

"Your favorite, *CSI*." She laughed as she reached for the remote and handed it to him.

"Not tonight, not any night." He surfed the channels before settling with a movie on Star.

Later Dina settled between his legs while he massaged her neck, letting her head roll back on his chest.

"What was she like?" she asked.

"Who?"

"Your ex?"

"What brought this on?" His whole body seemed to tense.

She felt it and turned to face him. "Just wanting to know more about you. Don't lock me out."

"Was I doing that?"

"You always do. Let me in?"

"Where Dina?" He laid back.

"In that dark place you keep shut to everyone." She moved away, giving him space.

"Then maybe you don't need to go there."

"I've never heard you use the word love. Not even when...."

He looked at her with gray eyes that tried to understand what she wanted.

"Didn't anyone in your family ever tell you they loved you: Helena, your sister,.... your mother?" She touched his thigh.

"Did your mother tell you she loved you?" Stas asked.

"No, she told my brother all the time, but that was all right 'cause my father loved me and told me. Something in me died when he left. I never forgave her for running him away." She stood. "As a child, did you forgive Helena for not loving you?"

"I never gave it any thought."

"And do you give any thought to your feelings about me?"

Stas closed his eyes for a second then opened them to look at Dina. "I've given lots of consideration to my feelings...."

"And?"

He looked away as if in pain.

"I can't be your lover one moment and your whore the next, especially one you hide in the closet." She stood and faced him, her hand on her hip.

A noise caught in his throat. He looked down, not sure where it came from.

"What?" She asked.

"Nothing! But you're right, babe."

238

Stas left Dina's and drove to the Second Set.   He parked in his usual space near the rear of the lot just as Marlowe pulled up and opened the door to his SUV.

"You coming or going?" The detective threw his Stetson on his car seat and smiled. "We got to stop meeting like this. People will talk."

"Go to hell, Marlowe." Stas engaged the alarm on the Mercedes.

"I'm not even sure I like you either. At least Jonson talks to me when we travel."

"You think I give a shit." Stas frowned. "I never trusted black cowboys anyway."

They entered the bar together and headed for a booth in the back, taking it before the new bar maid, Viv, could finish wiping the table.

"Leave it." Marlowe slid across the fake leather seat.

She shifted her weight and popped her gum. "What's it going to be?"

Stas looked around. "Where's Stella? In the back?"

"Her dad died."

"I'm sorry to hear that, but give me a Samuel Adams," Marlowe ordered, then nodded at Stas. "He drinks vodka."

"Make it two doubles on the rocks."

Viv moved to the well and gave the order to Troy.

"What brought you out tonight?" Marlowe asked.

"A little disagreement—over not enough popcorn or too many questions. It doesn't matter now. How's Barbara?"

"She's spending the night in Simi Valley. One of the kid's birthday. I wasn't invited."

"You're lucky."

The drinks arrived. Stas's first double was gulped down.

"Was it that bad?" Marlowe took a drink of his Samuel Adams.

"It's always bad when they ask questions. I hate being interrogated, especially about my past and by women."

"It goes with the territory. I bet you ask her questions and get answers, or you take your toys and go home."

Stas sucked on some ice. "I know enough."

"Yeah, but you don't tell her enough. You're not the pillow talk type. No moans and groans from Stas Nowak."

"Speaking of sex," Stas added.

"Was I talking about that?"

"We're paying Mrs. Talbott a visit tomorrow. Her father-in-law bought her a modeling agency about the time the Lenox woman disappeared, so she could have set up the shows in Vegas."

"Why you changing the subject? You need to go back to your woman, tell her you sorry, and make some mind-blowing love. That's the best when you make-up."

Stas started on his second drink.

Marlowe took another swig from his beer. "And leave that stuff alone. You keep this up, you're going to turn into an alcoholic."

"Are you finished, Abby?" Stas asked.

"Okay, okay. So tell me why would someone go through so much trouble to kidnap the vic?"

"She needed someone who looked like her. Someone who could have a baby that looked like her." Stas pushed his glass aside.

"Why didn't she have her own?"

"She told Carroll she couldn't."

"You believe that?"

"Yeah, I do, especially if we find out where her husband made his donations."

Marlowe gave Stas a wicked smile. "What?"

"Supposedly he deposited sperm at a fertility clinic."

"Hell, that's no fun."

THIRTY-THREE

Stas stood in the hall outside of the Division's clerk's office talking to Maxwell Paige from Vice who still wore his hair long and sported the beginnings of a beard. He layered his shirts over well-worn jeans and beat-up monkey boots. Over the years the two cops had maintained a distant friendship even after Stas's transfer downtown.

"Really pissed me off when I saw Dar Ling at Gorman's retirement party. It surprised me that Smitty would bring her." Paige gestured. "At the bar she said she knew a cop from Vice and dropped your name. My second surprise, 'cause she looked kinda young. Did you know Dar Ling when you were in Vice?"

"No, I met her when Sybil Hansen died, a long story. Smitty should've known better." Stas added.

"He thought it was funny, but Gorman wasn't laughing. Plus, they were both high. Panacik asked them to leave. There were wives there, for god's sake."

Edwards stood by the door, hesitant to intrude.

Stas motioned for him to join them. "Max, this is my partner, Sid Edwards." Both men shook hands.

"Maxwell Paige, Vice, I use to work with Stas. You're lucky. I know guys would sell their first born to partner with him."

Edwards smiled weakly. "He can have my first born any time."

Paige slapped Stas on the back. "Got to go."

"See you around." He turned to Edwards. "You ready?"

"What time is our appointment?"

"Didn't make one."

"Suppose no one's home."

"We'll worry about that when we get there. I want to see her when she hasn't had time to prepare for our interview, anticipate our questions." Stas punched the down button on the elevator.

The Talbott home was located up a winding road that led into the Hollywood Hills. The day was clear for a change.

"Wow!" Edwards lowered his window and leaned out to take in the magnificent view before pressing the button over the intercom in the wall near the gate.

"Hel-lo," Lupe's voice floated through the speaker.

"Good afternoon. We're here to see Mr. Talbott," Edwards announced.

"He no here." There was a hollow click, then silence.

Stas reached over and killed the engine. "Call back. Tell her we're from Los Angeles Police, and want to see Mrs. Talbott."

"Suppose she's not here?"

Stas straightened and looked over the dash through the wrought iron gates to the paved drive. "She's here, and she has company."

Edwards pushed the button over the intercom again.

"Hel-lo."

"This is the Los Angeles Police. We'd like to see Mrs. Talbott."

There was a metallic clank as the gates disengaged and slowly swung inward. Edwards drove in and parked near the house. "Okay, what are we looking for?"

"Besides her responses, watch her body language, her inflection, anything, no matter how insignificant."

"I'm not too good at that kind of thing." Edwards had his ID ready as he headed for the wooden and glass entrance that framed the petite Lupe.

Stas took his time getting out of the car, giving his attention to a red sports car parked in front of one of the four closed garage doors. The car resembled the one he had seen on the surveillance video at The Bounty. Walking back towards the entrance, he stopped at the well-attended flower beds ablaze with colors, then bent to smell a lavender rose in full bloom. He'd never seen one that color, and its fragrance was intoxicating. His partner and Lupe stood waiting for him in the open doorway. At the door he handed Lupe his card. "I'm Detective Nowak."

Lupe blushed and put the card in her smock pocket.

"Is Mrs. Talbott in?" Edwards asked following Lupe into the living room.

"She in kitchen with her friend."

In the ornate entry hall, Stas caught a glimpse of himself in a gilt floor-to-ceiling mirror, straightened his tie, and checked his cuffs. When he stepped down into the spacious living room, he was struck by its order. Everything was immaculate. The white and gold colors were accented with pieces of sparkling crystal. The furnishings were sparse, but located in strategic places around the room so that one did not notice their massiveness. Large, expensive oriental rugs, situated around the room on highly polished hardwood floors, provided splashes of color.

Lupe pointed to overstuffed white chairs that flanked the equally overstuffed ten-foot sofa. Stas looked around the room for a more appropriate seating arrangement and saw none. *Hmmm, divide and conquer.*

Edwards eased himself into one of the chairs, sinking into its cloudy softness.

Stas remained standing, surveying the rest of the room. "You take care of all of this?" he asked Lupe.

She nodded. "Lots of work, and now we got dog." Her eyes moved in the direction of a large, floor-to-ceiling window that overlooked a vast, well-tended garden.

He walked over to the window and strained to take in everything. There was a patio furnished with expensive outdoor furniture to the right of the window and a terraced garden leading to a pool beyond that. By getting up close to the window, he could make out a metal post anchoring part of a chain-link fence, perhaps enclosing a dog run. When he turned to inquire, Lupe had disappeared.

Mona Talbott dressed in designer, velour black sweats entered with Stella who was heading for the foyer. Mona stopped abruptly when she saw her visitors. "Who are you?"

Stella interrupted. "LAPD."

Mona tried to soften her annoyance when she turned to Stella. "You know them?"

"We've met."

Stas presented his ID. "I'm Detective Nowak," pointing to his partner as he struggled out of his chair. "This is Detective Edwards."

"I never got your last name, Stella?" Stas asked.

"Majors."

Mona's displeasure started to surface. "Well, so much for this little reunion of public servants, why are you here?"

"We're investigating a series of homicides and have a few questions to ask, especially since one of the bodies was found at a site owned by your husband."

"Sold by my husband," Mona coldly interjected.

Stella touched Mona's arm. "I'll catch you later."

"You have to go now?"

"Yeah, I think I'd better. I'll let myself out."

Stas moved to the sofa, perched on the edge of a cushion and watched the parting scenario unfold. Edwards had his hand in a crystal bowl of chocolate bonbons, unwrapped one, and popped it into his mouth as he waited for Mona to sit and answer their questions.

"Okay!" Mona turned her attention to the detectives, looked at the seating arrangement, and brought a white empire chair to make a triangle. "But I really don't see how I can help."

Stas took out his notebook. Mona took a cigarette from a square crystal box on the end table and looked at Edwards, who had just stuffed another chocolate into his mouth and wrapping papers into his jacket pocket.

"You like those?" She smiled at Edwards. "They're imported."

Stas picked up a sphere-shaped lighter and flicked a strong flame to the tip of her cigarette.

Caught in the cold glare of Stas's steel gray eyes, Mona mouthed a "Thanks," and sucked smoke into her lungs, then coughed before smashing the butt into a crystal ash tray. She looked with watering eyes into Stas's. "I told you, my husband sold the property."

"Really?" Stas flipped several pages. "It's our understanding that your husband is in a partnership with the developer, Paul Lundstrom."

"Yes, yes, but he's only a silent partner. He put up some money."

"Silent or not, his name's on the deed. Did the money come from the sale of other property?" Stas asked.

"I really don't know, but I think the whole project was a little stupid. He was offered good money for that property by a microbrewery. Have you been down there on Mission? Who in his right mind would want a condo down there?"

Edwards made an effort to pull himself to the front of his chair and speak but broke out into a fit of coughing. "Wat...ter...."

Stas rose and looked towards the kitchen. "He needs some water."

Mona nodded and pointed in his line of vision but didn't move. "Lupe'll give him a drink."

He continued to the kitchen, noting that the white and gold had given way to cream, stainless steel, and pink marble. He looked around before moving to the sink.

"Lupe!"

"Down here."

He looked around the island and found her on her knees wiping up the floor. "Why don't you use a mop?"

"Miss Mona don't like, says it's messy."

"Screw Miss Mona. Do you always do it her way?"

"When she here."

"Good for you! Sorry to bother you, but I need some water. My partner choked on the candy."

"It's old, for show."

"Like the cigarettes?"

Lupe smiled as she started to get up. Stas gave her his hand. "Where's the dog?"

She pointed through the window over the sink to a long dog run enclosed with six-foot high chain link, then poured a glass of water from a bottle she took from the pantry.

"Thanks, Lupe." He took the glass. "We may need to talk later."

Edwards made a rapid recovery after drinking the water, then took his notebook out, flipped pages, holding his pen poised. "You're a model right?"

"Yes, when I was younger, before I had my family."

"So you don't model anymore?" Stas looked her over. "You've kept yourself in great shape."

"I work at it."

"How long ago did you quit?" Edwards looked up from his notebook.

"Seven, eight years ago."

Edwards flipped a few more pages. "What happened to your modeling agency?"

Mona started to reach for another cigarette but rearranged the dish instead. "What agency?"

"The one your father-in-law bought," Stas added.

"If my father-in-law bought it, how did it get to be mine?" She smiled.

"Because he deeded it to you right after he bought it," Edwards said.

"That? It wasn't viable. Do you have any idea how many agencies there are in this area? Unless you're scamming your women or you're big time, you can't make any money," Mona added.

Stas looked at Mona, but she would not meet his gaze. "Were you in it for the money or to advance your own career?"

"Neither, my family came first."

Stas looked toward the garden. "Mrs. Talbott, you have a dog?"

"Yes."

"I'd like to see him."

"He's at the groomers." Mona rose. "Now if you don't have any more questions, I have an appointment."

"We'll let you know if there's anything else." Edwards returned his notebook to his pocket.

"I'm sure you'd rather talk to my husband."

Waiting for Edwards to struggle out of his chair, Stas stood and walked over to the fireplace, an elaborately carved work in marble and granite. He looked down to the antique andirons and thought, what great murder weapons, then took in the painting of a beautiful blonde looking down on him. "That's a striking portrait over the mantel." He noted the hair, the eyes, there even seemed to be an attitude in her half-smile that seemed to be copied by Mona.

"That's my late mother-in-law. She died several years before I met my husband. My poor father-in-law was devoted to her."

"And to you?" He walked to the entry hall. "I see a resemblance."

"Funny, I never noticed."

At the car, Stas looked back at the house while Edwards moved around to the driver's side. Lupe stood at the entrance, watching the two detectives, until Mona came and slammed the door.

"Well, what do you think about Stella?" Edwards asked.

"What do *you* think?"

Edwards cleared his throat. "That they're lovers?"

Stas nodded.

"But she's married. Look at all the stuff." Edwards paused. It's just hard for me to deal with. She's got a good husband. Why would she want a woman?"

"We don't know what he's doing. Look where they all hangout. What did Carroll say? Anyway, we still need to come back with a search warrant."

"Why?" Edwards asked. "Do we have probable cause?"

"Did you see the rock on her finger?"

"No, I wasn't paying attention to her hand."

"Sometimes I can't believe you, Sid. When you do an interview in someone's house or office, what do you look at?"

"Well, I look at the face. Look at the eyes, try to see if they're lying."

"So now you're a walking lie detector. Sid, you got to be more observant. I'd say that ring was at least three-four carats. It looks like the picture Wright gave us."

"Wouldn't Jill love me to go into more debt to get her something like that?"

"That's not my point. The third woman disappeared wearing a diamond worth at least seven grand then, think what it's worth now."

"Wow, you saw all that? Amazing."

Stas walked around to the driver's side of the Crown Vic. "Give me the keys."

"What?" Edwards tightly fingered the key ring.

"The keys." He held out his hand. "I'm driving."

"Why?"

"I want to check out something."

"But I can drive."

"I don't feel like giving directions. Just get in."

"Where're we going."

"You'll see," Stas said.

They drove slowly down the winding road before merging into heavy traffic at the bottom of the hill. There was no conversation as they took the Hollywood Freeway east, exiting at

Hope, turning left on First. Stas continued through Little Tokyo over the First Street Bridge, then took a right onto Mission.

They found the third property of B & T Construction off Mission near the Fourth Street Bridge. Whatever buildings that had once occupied the site had been razed.

"Mona was right. Would you buy a condo in this wasteland?" Stas asked.

Edwards looked out the window and grimaced. The street was strewn with newspapers, wrapping papers, sheets of computer paper, and plastic bottles of all shapes and sizes. "There's not a patch of green anywhere." He sniffed. "My God, what's that awful smell?"

"Diesel!"

"And the noise?" Edwards asked.

"The train yard, it's on the other side, next to the river."

"Yeah! I knew that."

The empty lot was fenced like the first crime scene with green canvas covering the section of the chain link that faced the street.

Stas pulled into a narrow service street that ran between B & T Construction and Potter Warehouse. He parked half on what was once a sidewalk to allow room for another vehicle. Even in broad daylight everything was shut down.

Edwards waited in the car while his partner walked along the perimeter of the fence. There wasn't much to see. A gaping hole in the ground where the old, deep foundation had been, plus stacks of tarp covered building materials. A beat-up gray metal trailer stood sentinel.

Stas waited. "I can't see behind the trailer."

Edwards took his time getting out of the car and catching up to his partner. They walked along the fence until Stas stopped, lining-up with the rear of the trailer.

"You know we need a warrant. Go over that fence, and we're in trouble. See the sign?" Edwards warned.

"What does it say?" Stas asked.

Edwards read: "WARNING—NO TRESPASSING. PRIVATE PROPERTY. MONITORED BY ON SITE GUARDS AND ALARM SYSTEM. VIOLATORS WILL BE PROSECUTED. There's a phone number."

"You planning to call."

"Suppose somebody comes."

"Any sign of a guard?" Stas craned to see beyond the trailer then turned back. "There's a dog house. That's probably the alarm system."

"You're not going over are you?"

"No, Sid. I know we need a warrant."

"Great! Now throw me the keys." Edwards headed back to the Crown Vic. "Nobody's going to give you a warrant for this. What do you want anyway?"

"A match."

Edwards frowned. "A match for what?"

"The dog hairs on the blanket and the dresses of the deceased." Stas sighed.

"And if the hair matches?"

"We'd go checkout the Talbott's dog."

"You think it's the same dog?"

Stas hung back, drawing a mental picture of the lay out of the site before getting in the car and exercising a perfect U-turn. "I'd make book on it."

After grabbing several slices of pizza from Whole Foods, Stas went home, changed into black jeans, black crew neck sweater, a pair of old, black running shoes, and leather jacket. He ate standing in the kitchen and washed his food down with four fingers of vodka. It took thirty minutes to drive from Glendale to Little Tokyo and another fifteen to find a suitable parking place. He fingered the small flashlight in his jacket pocket hoping it would be adequate to examine whatever was behind the trailer.

The narrow street was dark and deserted on the south side of the fence that surrounded the B & T site. There was no sign of the "Posted Guard". Stas retraced his earlier steps, checked the perimeter that merged into darkened shadows where pavement gave way to broken asphalt and potholes. Finding a sag in the chain-link, he got an easy foothold and lifted himself over, hitting the ground on the other side.

His light traced the block foundation of the trailer. Stas moved behind the outbuilding, and there in the narrow illumination was a large, wooden dog house. It smelled of stale dog and dried feces. Swinging an arc of light close to the ground, he jumped when he saw the head of a black and white dog resting on strangely disfigured paws, which on a closer look at the canine turned out to be parts torn from a dirty, stuffed animal with half its kapok guts trailing into the soil.

He stepped to the opening of the dog house, slipped on latex gloves, and bent down to sweep with his fingers clumps of matted dog hair into a plastic bag.

Stas sensed the black-and-white cruiser before he saw it slowly make a U-turn in front of the site. He flicked off his light, glad he hadn't brought the more powerful mag-light, eased into the shadows of the trailer, and waited. Concealed behind the metal wall, he listened for noise from the street but was distracted by the noise of movement of freight cars below in the nearby train yards. When all was quiet and clear, he peeled off the gloves and jammed them in his jean pockets before going back over the fence. His landing the second time was awkward causing him to slip and fell, slightly bruising his thigh and knee.

"Damn! Damn!" Stas tried to straightened his leg as a sharp pain shot from his groin to his calf. He eased his left foot down and walked back and forth a few feet, shifting his weight to find a less painful position before returning the several blocks to his car.

Caught in the bright beam of a cruiser's spot, Stas turned, blinded by the intense light.

"You okay, fellow?" The uniform in the passenger seat started to get out of the car.

Stas shielded his eyes but did not respond, keeping his hands high and in sight.

"How about some I.D.?"

Slowly reaching in a pocket, Stas silently flashed his shield.

The uniformed officer relaxed his stance. "Are you all right, detective? You need anything?"

"I fell, hurt my leg." Stas pointed. "That's my car down the street."

"You want a ride?"

"I can make it. Thanks anyway."

But Stas didn't go home. He went to Dina's, left his shoes and socks, then dropped his jeans in the middle of her bathroom to examine a swollen purple bruise that extended from his left thigh to his knee.

Where the hell is Dina? He needed something for pain and checked the medicine cabinet. *Nothing, no aspirin, nothing!*

Limping to the kitchen, he opened cabinets, finding labelled tins and jars of assorted herbs but no magic bullet for his pain. Well, there was always one solution. The good Doctor Chopin in the freezer was known to cure a multitude of ailments.

He settled on the sofa and grabbed the remote. The vodka eased the pain while the drone of late night TV lulled him into a fitful doze. He didn't hear the key in the door or see Dina's embarrassed look as she held the door for Vance, Raven's nephew, struggling with a heavy file box.

"Stas!"

His eyes opened, but he didn't move. "Dina!"

Vance dropped the box and backed toward the still open door not waiting for an introduction or an explanation. "I need to go."

Dina closed the door and turned the dead-bolt. "What the hell is going on? Where are your pants?"

Stas looked down to his black boxer briefs but made no effort to move. "In the bathroom."

"What are they doing there?"

"That's where I took'em off."

"Why? Since when did you start dropping your pants and, and go parading around in your shorts."

"Since I needed to see my leg."

She followed his gaze to his swollen and bruised thigh. "My God, what happened?"

"I fell."

"Doing what?"

"Doing stupid." His voice faded. "I fell jumping over a fence."

Dina moved to touch the bruised flesh, but Stas grimaced.

"Why didn't you call paramedics, go to emergency?"

"It's okay." He shifted his weight and reached for his glass. "I'll be okay."

She shook her head. "Well, that means you were someplace you shouldn't have been? Cops!" She reached for his glass. "You don't need this."

"Hell, I don't." He tried to get up but fell back onto the sofa. "Why don't you have some fucking pain-killers?"

"Drink some tea."

"Tea? For pain? I didn't see anything in there for pain."

"Is that what your mother did, give you liquor when you were hurt?"

"She caused more than she relieved."

"And what did your wife do?" Dina asked.

"Give it a rest, babe."

"Dammit, why can't I ask? You know everything about me. What do I know about you besides the cop part?" She headed for the kitchen. "I'd learn more watching *The Shield*."

"What are you doing?" He rose slowly to follow.

"I'm making you tea."

"That's it?"

"It'll relax you."

"I don't need to relax." His tone was sharp.

Dina ignored him, filled the kettle, and put it on the stove. "Why can't we have a conversation about you, about your past?"

"I don't live in my past."

She turned on him. "Then I don't know what you live for, certainly not the future. Why is everything so secret?" The kettle whistled. Dina poured steaming water into a blue tea pot.

Stas moved from the wall he was holding up and looked on the sink for his glass. "Babe, why are you doing this to me. I'm dead tired and..."

"Drink this, it'll ease the pain."

He smelled the concoction and coughed. "What's in it?"

"Don't worry about it." She followed him to the living room, then to the bedroom. "You know I never ask about your women, but I've heard."

"Then let that satisfy your curiosity and keep my ex out of it."

"Why? She didn't satisfy you. Did any of them?"

"Is this some voodoo shit?" He took a sip. "I heard you can poison...."

Dina interrupted. "More cop talk. Your one track mind. If I had a potion, it wouldn't be to ease pain in your leg. And you didn't answer my question."

He sat on the bed. "I need some rest."

"Don't go to sleep on me, Stas Nowak." She kneeled next to him and took his half empty teacup, putting it on the nightstand. "Come on, tell me."

"Tell you what? What do you need from me?" He fell across the bed and closed his eyes.

"Feelings, caring,..." She paused and looked at him. "...love."

He groaned.

Dina shifted her weight. "There must be something, someone you cared about." Her voice faded.

"My job—and a good..." the words were lost in a throaty snort, then a loud snore.

She sighed and rose from the bed pulling the quilt over his sleeping body.

THIRTY-FOUR

Early the next morning Stas awoke still in his briefs and tucked in Dina's bed. He located the rest of his clothes and dressed. Her side of the bed was empty. As he passed through the living room, he found her wrapped in the mauve throw sound asleep on the sofa. He left the apartment without waking her. Back at his place, he re-examined his leg under the bright light in his bathroom. There was still some bruising on his thigh, but the soreness was almost gone. Maybe Dina's brew had worked miracles. After changing he called Molly on her cell.

"Hello. It's Detective Nowak. How are you?"

"I'm great! What's up?"

"I know it's early, but I was wondering if we could have a talk. I still have a few more questions."

"This morning's good. No one comes in early. Why don't you come by around eight-thirty?"

Stas got to the building before Molly, parked, and waited ten minutes. She arrived in an old bright chartreuse VW Bug with red flames painted on the wheel-wells and pulled in next to him. She climbed out of her car and walked to the Mercedes.

"Nice wheels. I bet it's really a chick magnet. I just knew that big, bulky Ford wasn't yours."

"The Crown Vic belongs to the Department."

At the office Molly pulled out a large ring of keys, unlocked the door, then turned off the alarm system.

"I don't know why we have this ritual every day. We don't keep any money."

"Probably for insurance. Some rival might want to steal the plans."

Molly laughed. "I don't see why. I doubt if they'll ever build anything where they found that poor girl. Now Ryan has another grand idea for the property." She opened the blinds and dropped her oversized handbag next to her desk.

Stas wondered what she carried in it. He imagined a .45 the way the purse sounded when it landed.

"Molly, people are funny, they'll build or buy anywhere as long as the price is right. But tell me something. What do you know about Frank? What's his last name?"

"Stack."

"Where is he from originally?"

"I'm not sure, the Midwest, I think. He was already working here when I came, but I can check the file." She bent over and pulled out the bottom drawer of a gray file cabinet next to her desk.

Her green jersey top rose up her back revealing the head of a dragon, its emerald eyes staring up her spine, the multi-colored wings expanded to caress her waist, its tail disappearing into her yoga pants. Stas smiled, imagining where it ended. Good, old Molly. She sure had a way of brightening one's day.

"While you're in there, can I con you out of Mrs. Lundstrom's phone number?

"What?" Molly stood, holding an empty folder in her hand. "There's nothing in here."

"Where do you keep the W-2's?" he asked.

She moved back to her desk and took out a large business folder from the bottom drawer and found Frank's paper work.

Stas jotted down Frank's social security number in his notebook. "Do you have Mrs. Lundstrom's number?" he asked again.

Molly flipped through the rolodex on her desk and handed him a card. He added the ex-wife's info to his notes.

"You've been a sweetheart. I owe you another one."

"Well, you can write a fantastic reference letter for me when I apply."

He was at the door. "Apply?"

"LAPD, of course."

Stas touched his ear.

"Yeah, I know," Molly laughed, "but I'll make a helleva cop."

Dina opened her apartment door to the smell of coffee, but she hadn't made any before leaving for the agency. She dropped her purse on the dining area table and went to the kitchen. The carafe in the machine was half full and still warm. Retracing her steps, she went to her bedroom. The shower was running, the bathroom door was ajar, and men's clothes were neatly laid out on the bed. A watch, wallet, and holstered gun were on the night stand.

She waited until the water stopped before venturing into the steamy bathroom and handing a towel to a dripping Stas.

"Why aren't you working today?" she asked.

"I'm at lunch."

"Yeah, naked and wet in my bathroom? This is getting to be a habit, but...." she ran her eyes over his damp frame.

"I needed to clear my head."

Dina turned back to the bedroom. "What, by taking off your clothes?"

Stas followed her and started to dress. "I didn't have any coffee or tea at my place."

"That's no excuse. There's a Starbucks on nearly every block."

He sat in the chair to put one his socks and shoes. "But no Peets. Sorry, I guess I should've called. Edwards and I have an interview later."

"How's your leg?"

"Better. Guess your tea does work."

"You coming by later?"

"I don't know. I have paper work to finish up. My lieutenant's been breathing down my neck."

"You afraid I'll give you the third degree?"

"Is that what you called it last night? I thought you were just being nosy." He stood and gave Dina a peck on the cheek and slipped on his jacket. "I'm a big boy, babe."

"What about your partner?"

"Believe it or not, he's really good at reports."

"Then I hope his typing skills makes his wife happy."

The two detectives pulled into Mrs. Lundstrom's driveway at 3:05 p.m. Edwards jumped out of the driver's side eager to escape an overheated car with a broken AC while Stas buttoned his collar, arranged his tie, and put on his jacket.

"Lock the car!" Edwards shouted back.

Stas's hand was poised on the LOCK switch. "Do you think someone wants to steal this piece...."

Edwards wiped perspiration from his brow as he poised to ring the bell, his ID in hand. His partner moved to peer under the front of the Crown Vic where a stream of green coolant dripped from the radiator to the driveway.

Should've parked on the street. Stas knew how particular some people were about their driveways. Sue the city for damage to their pavement in a hot minute. He moved towards the two car garage. Its door stood open. A soccer ball had rolled behind the rear right tire of a red Cadillac Escalade. He looked further into the garage. There were several orange cones, a small, portable goal half folded against a workbench, a pair of roller blades had been thrown on top. A baseball bat and mitt were mixed with tools on the other end of the bench which seemed more suited as a catch-all for more boys' toys than a serious place for a man who fiddled around the house or yard.

"Stas!" Edwards called from the front porch.

Mrs. Lundstrom stood in baggy sweats and flip-flops holding the door for the detectives.

Stas couldn't help staring in confusion. Was she the mother of the two girls whose pictures he'd seen in Lundstrom's office? He held out his ID. "Stas Nowak."

She closed the door behind them and led the way into the living room. "Have a seat," pointing to a red sofa and plaid chairs that made the room seem even warmer. "Christie." She sat on one of the chairs. "Just call me Christie."

Edwards perched on the edge of the sofa, his notebook and pen out.

"What is this all about?" she asked.

"We're investigating the murder of a young woman found in a dumpster on some property owned by your husband," Edwards said.

She hunched her shoulders. "I'm sorry. I don't know anything about any murder or girl. My husband and I have been divorced for two years, but if he's got some property I don't know about...."

Stas let his partner take the lead while he checked out their surroundings.

Edwards flipped several pages. "Well, the woman's death took place about seven years ago. Although we just found the body, it's what we call a cold case, so you and your husband were still together."

"I don't understand. What does that have to do with me?"

Edwards looked at his partner.

"Mrs. Lundstrom, I know it's been a while, but do you think you may have ever seen this woman?" Stas took a small photo from his jacket pocket and handed it to Christie.

She shook her head. "I never went to the office, and Paul never brought anyone home. As a matter of fact, that's probably why we're not together now. My ex spent more time with his boss's wife and with his fishing buddies than he did at home or with me."

"Do you mean Mrs. Talbott?" Stas asked.

Christie nodded. "I've never figured that arrangement out. Paul even introduced them. They had a whirlwind romance. Then my ex proposed to me. Naturally, I said yes."

"Naturally?" Stas added.

"We had dated off and on. He was a good catch. I just knew I'd take his mind off Mona, but they still ran together, the club scene, dinners, like they were single and dating."

"Did they take you?" Edwards looked up.

"Are you kidding? They never even invited me."

"I see that you have a red Escalade. Do you drive much in the city at night?" Stas asked.

"Rarely, I'm home most evenings unless it's something with the kids."

"Do you ever loan it to your ex?"

"Oh, since he bought it for me, he thinks he can borrow it whenever his is in the shop."

"Has he borrowed it lately?" Stas asked, feeling a slight adrenaline surge.

"He used it a couple of times last month. I'm not sure when. You'd better ask him." She looked at her watch and stood. "You know, I'm sorry, I've got to do my car pool."

Stas rose. "I see your girls play soccer. I play a pick-up game sometimes. It's great how young women have taken to the sport."

"Oh, I don't have girls. I wish. I'd trade X-men and Little League for Barbies any time." She reached over to the desk in the corner and showed them two photos in a hinged wooden frame of two blonde boys in gold and blue soccer jerseys.

"We saw a photo of two girls in Mr. Lundstrom's office. We thought...." Stas studied the picture.

"He's their godfather. Their Ryan's kids."

"Ryan and Mona's?" Edwards asked.

She led the way to the door, picked up her purse, keys, and held the door for the detectives. "Yeah, right!"

They watched her as she pulled around them and into the street before they got into the Crown Vic.

261

"You think they could find anything in the SUV?" Stas waited for Edwards to start the car before putting his jacket on the backseat, and lowering the window.

"Unless we find some way to tie it to the homicides besides Carroll's shaky description." Stas took his shades from his pocket. "You need to have them service the air-conditioner or get another car."

"I don't like driving other cars."

"And I don't like riding in an oven."

"Won't we need a warrant?" Edwards looked over to his partner.

"What?" Stas slipped on his shades.

"The red SUV."

"I guess we'll have to work on that, along with finding out more about the Talbott girls. I just felt in my gut that the girls were,... they kinda look like Lundstrom."

"Well, you were wrong for a change! How does that feel Mr. I'd-Make-Book-On-It?"

THIRTY-FIVE

There was a loud scream followed by "Shit! Shit! Lupe! Did you track shit in the house?" Mona stepped gingerly around several loose piles of dog feces.

Lupe stood in the open doorway off the patio, holding tennis shoes wet from cleaning. "I, I ..." She shook her head. "Mr. Frank bring in the dog. I step in mess. I jus' wash my shoes."

"I'm sorry, but you need to clean this up, too. And spray something. It smells like dog shit. It smells worse than dog shit. It's awful." Mona gagged, then spit in the sink leaving the water running.

Lupe looked at her boss with loathing and walked in her bare feet to turn off the water.

Mona took the backstairs to the second floor play room. Toys filled a corner, books were scattered on several tables and the floor. A large 45 inch plasma TV took up most of one wall. Frank and the girls were stretched out on a long sofa eating popcorn and watching the Disney channel.

"Girls, it's time for bed," Mona called from the door.

No one moved.

"Frank, the girls need to take their baths."

Still, no one moved, although Heather turned to look pleadingly at her mother.

"Where's Lupe?" Frank asked.

"In the kitchen, cleaning up after your damn dog. I told you it wasn't going to work." She started to leave the room. "You know what you can do?"

"What?"

"Run the girls' bath."

263

She left the room amidst high-pitched squeals as the girls dragged him to their bathroom.

Frank later joined Mona in her bedroom. She was dressed for the evening and sat at her dressing table applying the last of her make-up. He wiped his hands and arms on a towel. She watched him in her mirror. He slowly rolled down his shirt sleeves, covering a tattoo on his left arm.

"I didn't know you were ex-marine.?"

"I'm not."

"Then why the tattoo?"

"You just noticing?" He paused. "My fantasy. I would have joined if...."

"Aren't you a little old for fantasies?"

"We're never too old for fantasies. You're still living one."

Mona started to apply her lipstick. "I don't have any."

Frank looked around the room, his eyes stopping at her bed. "Bullshit, what do you call this?"

"What?"

"A bed you don't share with your husband, the big Hollywood house, Motherhood? I take that back. It's not a fantasy. It's all a joke."

THIRTY-SIX

The phone rang. "Hello?" Stas answered to heavy staccato breathing. "Hello?" He repeated louder, impatience mounting. Finally, there was a low bass voice on the other end. "Stas?"

"Vlade? What's wrong?"

"It's your mother." Another pause.

"What happened?"

"She fell. The paramedics took her to the hospital."

"How long ago?"

"Two days."

"And you're just calling me?"

"I wasn't sure how serious it was."

"So what's wrong?"

"Not over the phone."

"Then I'll be over."

"Was that Dina?" Edwards asked.

Stas looked over at his partner as he closed his phone. "That was my old man."

"Is everything okay?"

"I don't know. I'm going to see."

Forty-five minutes later, Stas pulled into the driveway of his parents' bungalow. The house stood apart from the others of similar design on the street only because it had no flowers, no trees, and no shrubs. The grass was an anemic green with brown patches, and now, if Helena was going to be confined to the hospital for any length of time, Vlade had more of an excuse not to even water or even mow the sorry excuse for a lawn.

The house desperately needed a paint job, plus drawn blinds at the front windows added to the overall exterior drabness of the place. Stas stepped over a pile of yellowed flyers and opened the front door to the living room's cold dankness, as if Helena had been gone for years instead of days, but then when had she ever brought color or warmth to anything. He certainly had never been on the receiving end of any affection from her.

Once in the house, he realized how nothing in it ever changed. If he had been blind, he could have easily found his way through the room and around the house. Furniture had been in the same spots since his childhood. The few upholstered pieces had been rearranged for the anniversary party a few months before, only to be quickly put back as if the celebration had been a figment of everyone's imagination.

A light shone from the back of the house, laying down a shaft of brightness through the slightly ajar door to the kitchen. The elder Nowak, in a dark terry robe, stood at the stove, his bare feet stuffed in a pair of hard leather slippers, a gift purchased from a street vendor in Zakopane on Stas's last visit to Poland.

There were two heavy iron skillets on the stove. The larger one sizzled with the fat of kielbasas browning with onions and green peppers. The aroma of the succulent sausages rose on the steam, caressing the nostrils, and enticing the taste buds.

"You eat already?" Vlade asked.

"I'm not hungry," Stas lied. In the car he had heard the grumble in his gut but ignored it. Now the hunger pangs were back demanding satisfaction. He moved to the stove and lifted the lid to the back skillet. More steam escaped. The aroma of fried potatoes mingled with the smell of spices triggered an audible growl from Stas's stomach.

"Get two plates." Vlade ordered, turning off the burners. "Beers in the fridge."

Hanging his jacket on the back of a kitchen chair, Stas got plates, knives, and forks, then sat down when Vlade brought the steaming skillets to the table sitting them down on thick, homemade hot pads. It was like old times. Kielbasa and potatoes with onions and green peppers had always been Vlade's specialty, usually cooked on the nights Helena went to bunko.

His father sat down after getting an opener and two Stellas from the fridge. "You hungry now?"

Stas didn't answer but heaped his plate. He planned to make-up for his missed lunch. They ate and drank in silence. The old man hadn't lost his culinary touch. The food vanished. Vlade pushed his empty plate aside and let out a loud belch of satisfaction, then pulled a pack of cigarettes and matches from his robe pocket and offered the pack to his son.

Stas pushed them back. "I quit."

Vlade lit his. "You getting virtuous in your middle age? My God, you're forty!" He raised his half-empty second bottle of beer. "Happy Birthday!"

Stas ignored the toast. "What's with Helena?" He was in no hurry to discuss her predicament but knew it was inevitable.

"She had a stroke."

"When?"

"They think sometime Saturday." Vlade blew smoke away from the table.

"So why did you wait until this afternoon to call?"

"Mara thought I should wait 'til the tests were through."

"Who's Mara?" Stas asked.

"One of Helene's bunko buddies. She's been visiting her. A couple of the others came and took some of her stuff over to the hospital."

"Helene can't be that bad off. She seems to have enough people at her beck and call."

"You need to go see her. She keeps asking for you."

"Now I have to jump through her hoops. Well, I'm going back to work."

"Do what you need to." Vlade raked his fingers through a stock of thick, silver hair. "I called you first, then I called Anna. She's coming down this weekend. Do you want to run into her if you change your mind?" He took a long pull on his cigarette and blew smoke rings across the kitchen table.

Stas sat in his car in the Nowak driveway for nearly an hour before heading for the hospital instead of work. Although he hadn't seen Helena for over six weeks, forgetting her was not so easy. Somehow she always seemed to seep like some noxious vapor into his subconscious bringing pain that had been etched into his brain and seared into his soul.

Had it been less than two months since Vlade revealed that Helena was not his mother, that he had fathered him with Irina, Helena's younger sister? Even now, Stas could barely come to grips with that revelation, then he discovered his birth mother had been a high-priced call girl. Somehow he should have suspected. And then to find out that a daughter, his half-sister had followed in her footsteps. His very existence was like some painful joke. Now, both women were dead, and Helena, who had mentally and physically abused him since his childhood, was in the hospital and wanted to see him. What new torment did she have in store for him?

Stas turned the key in the ignition but hesitated. Looking at the house, he thought about times in his youth when he had been home with the flu and caught the heady smell of onions and sausages only to fall back on his pillow when Helena brought him watery cucumber soup. Once in the middle of the night she had caught him eating cold kielbasa by the light of the open fridge. She screamed some expletives in Polish, grabbed the sausage and tossed it in the garage can, its raised lid releasing the strong, earthy odor of wilted cabbage leaves. He sulked back to bed dreading the cabbage soup he would have to endure the next day.

Helena had tried to involve herself in every aspect of his life, even trying to teach his ex-wife, Joy, how to cook some simple Polish dishes. When the lessons failed, Helena resorted to sending care packages with Joy, having her pass by the elder Nowak's home to pick up the dishes on her way home from work. After a while, Joy stopped cooking; the care packages became less frequent, and Stas ate out more.

When he pulled into the street, he automatically headed back to work but suddenly turned toward Adventist Hospital in Glendale.

After parking, Stas sat in the first floor waiting area, watching the evening surge of visitors rush to the elevator. He lost track of time and nodded over the newspaper he'd found in the chair next to him. He wondered if the visitors were really that eager to see sick and dying family or friends, or if, like himself, he waited until the last hour hoping to reduce the time of a face to face confrontation.

Finally he approached the woman at the information desk who told him that Helena Nowak was on the third floor.

"I'm not sure of the room because Mrs. Nowak was scheduled to be moved." She gave him a yellow visitor's pass marked 'Third Floor,' but the room number was blank.

At 6:55 p.m. he headed for the elevator. A loud Bling announced his arrival on Three. Stas exited and identified himself at the nurses' station.

The nurse, whose badge read, Mrs. Semona, looked up from her clipboard and smiled. "Mrs. Nowak? She's in 314." She looked at her watch. "You don't have a lot of time. Visiting hours are over at eight."

"Thanks. I didn't plan to stay long." He turned to look at the room numbers posted on the opposite wall.

Nurse Semona pointed to his right. Stas took his time reading the names in the slots next to the doors. At Room 314, he was surprised that Helena had a private room.

When he entered, he found her propped-up in bed watching something on the overhead television. She looked pale and old. There was a droop and sag on the left side of her face. Her left hand rested limply on the white thermal blanket. With her right hand she muted the sound and turned her attention to Stas as he pulled a chair to her bed.

Her smile looked crooked. Her platinum hair was pulled back and pinned into a neat bun. "So you decided to come after all. Vlade said..."

"Yeah, I changed my mind. How are you?"

"How do I look? I can't feel much on my left side."

"They'll give you therapy. Lots of people have a full recovery." He avoided her steely stare and looked across the room to a table pushed against the wall.

She followed his gaze. "Like the flowers?"

He stared in disbelief. "I thought you didn't like those gaudy arrangements."

"I can live without them, but guess who sent them?"

"I didn't come here to play games with you, Helena."

"Why can't you be like other men?" She tried to straightened the curl to her lip.

"What's that supposed to mean?"

"Look what you do, what you see. It's turned you cold. Anna said..."

"What the fuck does she know about me?"

"Stas!"

He blinked and sat back in the chair. "When did you ever shower anyone with your love? God, ask Vlade."

"You just can't bring yourself to say it can you?"

"Say what?"

"Mother! Why can't you say mother anymore?"

"Because you're not my mother."

"I was for forty years."

Stas thought she was going to cry. "Now you're not."

"Suppose you hadn't found out?"

"But I did."

270

"Can't you give me credit for anything. You know what Irina was?"

He straightened in his chair and looked directly at Helena. "Did you know I had a sister?"

"Yes."

"Did you ever see her?"

"I saw a picture. That was all I needed to see."

Stas felt the old knot manifest itself in his gut. "Did you also know that Irina had married a cop?"

"I heard about it after she died, from our cousin in Chicago. I guess that's when she wanted you, when she married."

"Why didn't you give me back since raising me was such a...." He turned trying to find the right word from that sterile atmosphere. "Duty?"

"I did everything to keep you from turning out like your mother."

"Give her some credit. She did get her life together."

"Did she? What did she do after her husband died?"

He lied. "I don't know." He had found out what she had returned to when he graduated from high school, and she gave him his graduation gifts.

"I wanted you to be normal, to fit in. I guess I should be thankful you became a cop, if that can be called normal. Why didn't you become a lawyer?"

"Maybe I didn't want to. I like what I do."

"What? Associating with killers, whores, and drug addicts. You would have been a lot happier a lawyer. Maybe you would still be married, and I would be a grandmother by now."

"You still wouldn't have been a grandmother. It would have been Irina's grandchild." He saw his verbal blow hit its mark.

Helena face twitched. "You're right. It would have been hers, just like you were hers. Then, who knows, you may not have had a child. Joy said you had some strange needs, that's why..." She left the rest unsaid.

A vein throbbed in his neck. "You talked to her about our intimate....? She told you that?"

"No, she told Anne."

"And she told you. I can't believe I'm sitting here listening to this." The chair overturned as he jumped up.

"Don't you want to hear what Irina told me?" Helena asked.

"Not really?" He righted the chair.

She raised off the pillow. "She taught you things. She said if she couldn't have her son, she'd..."

"You're sick!" He spit the words out. "You're lying!"

"She hated me. Vlade hates me, and you.... I don't have a husband or a son."

"I never was your son. You spent all those years living a lie and caught me up in your sick shit."

She lifted her left hand with her right to the middle of the blanket. "I thought I would have the comforts of my children and grandchildren ..."

"You have Anne."

"I don't want Anne. I want you!"

"You can't have me! I'm not yours!"

She cried out. "Stas!"

"I can't give you something I don't have to give."

Her attitude seemed to warm a degree. "Before you go, look at the card by the flowers."

"Why?"

"Humor me."

He took the bait, first by looking at the tag attached to a plastic stick in the flowers. It read "Love, Joy". He reached for the card. A photo fell to the floor and stared up at him. It was a picture of Joy, still looking attractive with a child of five or six standing next to her. He picked it up and read the inscription on the back. "To grand, love Joy and Abby"

"It seems you have your grandchild without benefit of my perverted seed." He returned the card to the table next to the plant and left without looking back.

He paused in the corridor outside of Helena's room and heard the volume return to the TV.

Stas drove until he found a liquor store. He moved past the rows of bottles and waited patiently behind an older, hunched over customer.

When it was Stas's turn, the cashier glanced at the detectives' empty hands pressed on the counter. "What can I get ya?"

"A pack of cigarettes."

"What kind?"

"I don't care. I guess Marlboro's good as any."

The young man took the proffered ten, and pressed a red and white box on the counter, and slapped down a couple of singles and three quarters.

Stas seemed surprised at the change.

The clerk smiled. "Dawg, you musta quit."

"Dawg, how 'bout some matches?" Stas wasn't smiling.

A book that advertised a local bail bondsman was passed over the counter in mute indifference. Outside, Stas stood at the curb, lit a cigarette from the pack, and took a long, deep drag, the smoke burning his lungs as they filled. He coughed, exhaled a stream of smoke, then coughed again. God! How he hated the habit, that still flicker of need. He took several more quick drags then flicked the long butt into the street. Back in the car, he put the pack in the glove compartment. He wasn't quite ready to toss $7.25 in the gutter.

Stas put the key in the ignition. Twenty-two years flooded his memory like some twisted rerun as his young life played back on scratched and faded film. Had Irina used him to get back at Helena for not giving him up as a child? Had he been both sisters' pawns? Had they given any thought to how they had fucked-up his life? What would have been his future if Irina had raised him? Enough questions. He pulled into traffic. Well, he had been accused of dressing the part. Just how far removed was he now from being a pimp? He ran his fingers through his hair, frightened by the thought that he might have enjoyed it.

THIRTY-SEVEN

Slowly Dina opened her eyes to glance over at the nightstand where the luminous green dial of the clock read 3:12 a.m. She tried to shake the overwhelming feeling of apprehension and return to sleep. *Why am I so tired?* She pulled the duvet up over her head, then tossed it aside. She kept remembering that nothing had been promised, even with Stas's late night visits or their early morning love making. He didn't seem ready to be pressed into a relationship no matter how much she wanted a commitment. She turned on her side and felt for Stas. His side of the bed was empty and cold. Edging back to her side, she burrowed deeper under the down comforter and fell into a fitful sleep.

When she awoke, a muted gray dawn, its icy ribbons of light crept across the mauve carpet. She lingered, still feeling alone and anxious. She glanced at the clock. There was a meeting at 10:00 a.m. with the new manager of the boutique. Dina bit her lip. She dreaded the thought of Dar Ling flitting in, making stupid comments, wasting people's time. Her behavior was becoming more and more erratic. Dina suspected drugs. The last thing the Agency needed was cops coming around asking questions.

Finally she rose and wrapped herself in a green silk robe, drawing the belt tightly as she headed to the kitchen. On the sink, an empty Chopin bottle greeted her. It hadn't been there the night before. She retraced her steps back through the living room.

An empty old fashioned glass stood next to highly polished black shoes under the Queen Anne chair. Stas's suit jacket was

275

draped over the chair's back; trousers and shirt were neatly folded on the cushion.

His muscular frame, stretching the length of the sofa, was partially covered to the waist with the mauve chenille throw. Dina watched from the back of the chair as he moved toward wakefulness. Sensing a presence he turned and opened his eyes.

"You look awful," she said.

He swung his legs around as he slowly sat up, rearranging the throw to cover his black boxer briefs, then patted a space on the sofa for her to join him.

Dina didn't move. "What's happening?" She tried to keep her tone even, unemotional.

"I didn't feel like going home."

"Why didn't you come to bed?"

"I needed to be alone."

"Then you should have gone to your place!" Dina snapped.

"Yeah, maybe." There was a catch in his voice. "Vlade called."

"Your father? What's happened?"

"Helena's in the hospital. She, she had a stroke."

"I'm sorry."

"Don't be. She's still in top form, cracking her whip. She reminds me of that thing in *Lord of the Rings*."

"What are you talking about?" she asked, confused.

"It was the...." he shuttered "Balrog."

"What's that?"

"You don't want to know unless you like nightmares." He paused and spoke almost as an afterthought. "It's something from the mean streets of Hell."

Dina seemed to sense that he spoke from experience. She joined him on the sofa, wanting to touch, to take him in her arms and comfort, instead she pulled the robe's tie even tighter around her waist.

"Vlade said she wanted to see me," he continued.

"Did you go?"

Stas nodded. "I thought she wanted to admit...."

"What?" she interrupted.

He shook his head. "Hell, I don't know—admit that she'd been wrong all these years."

"So what did she want?"

"To play her games, to prove she can still manipulate."

"Why didn't you leave?"

"I did." He ran his fingers over the stubble on his cheeks.

She touched his thigh. "Why do you shut me out?"

"Do I?" He looked at Dina, then down to her hand. "It's not about you, babe."

"But it is.... Whatever happens.... damn I'm not stupid." She withdrew her hand. "Visiting hours at hospitals are over at eight. I went to bed at midnight." She took a deep breath and moved back. "You've been drinking. And you smell like cigarettes. Are you going to tell me what happened?"

He wiped his mouth, shifted his position, and rearranged the throw. "She hates flowers."

"Well, the acorn doesn't fall far from the tree." She tugged at a stray curl that had fallen onto her forehead. "So this is about flowers somebody sent to Helena. Stas,... that made you finish off a bottle of vodka that you hadn't touched in over a week?"

"Joy sent the flowers."

"Who is Joy?"

"My ex."

"Nice name." She tried to mask the sarcasm with a smile.

"Ironic isn't it?"

"Why should that upset you? Can't she still send flowers to someone in the hospital? She divorced you, not your..., not Helena." She stared at him, waiting.

"There was a card with a picture of her and a kid."

Dina straightened, the smile gone. "Yours?"

"No."

"Did you want it to be?"

"What kind of question is that?"

"I don't know. All I get from you are bits and pieces. Finally, I learn her name. Now she has a kid that you say isn't yours, and all this has sent you into a fucking funk. If this upset you so, why didn't you have a kid with her?"

"We wanted a kid, at least I did." He ran his fingers through his hair. "She got pregnant but lost it. Had a D and C and told me she couldn't have another baby."

"And you believed her?"

"I wanted to, but after the miscarriage or whatever she had, it didn't make any difference. I didn't want anything else, at least not with her. I didn't love her."

"So now you know she lied. Did you ever love her?" Dina paused. "Have you ever loved anyone?"

"I... I." He looked down at his hands.

"Don't you think she wanted you to tell her something."

"Who?"

"Helena."

"Tell her what?"

"That you loved her. That you forgave her."

He laughed. "You don't know her. She never loved anybody. Why should she expect love or forgiveness from me?"

"She must have loved your father."

He tried to laugh again, but snorted, as if remembering some cruel joke. "He was working in Chicago. She married him to come to this country. I never saw him touch her, kiss her. I use to think they only did it twice, and got us. There was always this great silence between them that I never understood until I got married. I mean they would talk. 'What's for dinner? Don't forget to cut the grass, or Thursday is my bunco night, don't forget to feed Stas.'" He turned his back to her but could barely reach the scar on his shoulder. "You once asked me about this. Well, call it a token of her love."

Dina ran her fingers over the scar on his left shoulder. It felt cold to her touch. "When?"

"I was fifteen, sixteen. I don't remember exactly, but I came out of the bathroom, a towel wrapped around my middle. She was in the kitchen, ironing. I got juice from the fridge, went to the sink for a glass. Vlade's *Playboy* was on the counter. I opened it to the centerfold and boom, got a hard-on. My back was to her, but somehow she saw it or sensed it, called me a perverted bastard, and hit me in the shoulder with the hot iron. I didn't see it coming. God! It burned like hell."

"Did she take you to emergency?"

"Hell, no! She just slapped some of that green sludge on it and went back to her ironing."

Dina shuttered, then rose and headed to the kitchen. "I'll make some coffee."

While she was gone, Stas went to the bathroom. When he returned, he slipped into his pants and grabbed his shirt but didn't put it on. Dina returned with two mugs, handing one to Stas.

"Is your ex in town?"

He nodded.

"Does it bother you?"

"Dina, she's the past. My life, my life with her, there was nothing. We were young. I was stupid. I'd just gotten out of the service, an officer, all spit and polish. She liked that, thought I was going to law school. The trouble started when I joined LAPD. I still had a uniform, but it was different. I was driving around in a black-and-white, a rookie. After that, she just didn't give a damn about me or my job."

She held her coffee with both hands, letting the hot liquid warm her. She needed to continue. "I've never heard you use the word love. Since Helena never told you she loved you, did she tell your sister?"

He looked at her with smoky gray eyes that seemed shrouded in a lifetime of pain. "Did your mother tell you she loved you?"

"No, but she told my brother all the time. That was all right because my father loved me and told me so. I was his princess." Dina bit her lip. "Something in me died when he left. I never forgave her for running him,... for running him away."

Stas finished his coffee and picked up his shirt. "I got to go, babe." He bent, avoiding Dina's gaze, as he put on his shoes. He patted her on the head. "Forgiveness doesn't come that easy."

As they both stood, she put down her cup, and ran the tips of her fingers over his smooth, triangular scar.

THIRTY-EIGHT

Edwards was already at his desk reading the *Times* and munching on a sugared donut when Stas arrived in the squad room and hung his jacket on the back of his desk chair. He smiled when he found the lab report centered in the middle his desk. The results confirmed that the hairs found on the clothes of the victims matched the hairs he had collected in the dog house at the construction site. He closed the folder and placed it in his top drawer.

"So what are we doing this morning?" Edwards folded the paper.

"Going back to the Talbotts."

"Why?"

"I want to see the dog."

"Don't we need a warrant?"

"I'm not gonna to search it. I just wanna look at it."

"Yeah, and pick up a stray hair or two? She didn't let you see the dog the last time. What makes you think she'll let you see it today?" Edwards brushed powdered sugar off his hands and jacket front. "You know whatever you find won't be admissible if this goes to court 'cause we didn't get a warrant'."

"I'm hoping she'll be out doing her thing. Maybe Lupe will give us a look, if not, I'll ask Mona again."

"Suppose that housekeeper girl won't let you see the dog?"

"She will." Stas spoke with confidence. "I just need a couple of hairs. You know dogs shed all over the place."

"Why are you always so cocksure about everything, especially women?"

"Is that how you see me? I'm really very quiet and shy." Stas laughed.

"Yeah. Well, tell me something, why didn't Mona fall all over herself to accommodate you."

"Maybe I'm not her type. She was too busy falling over Stella. Or didn't you notice."

"Why so much interest? The dog didn't have anything to do with the murders."

"Have you forgotten about the blanket? Weren't you listening? The hairs on the victims' clothes, the blanket, and those I took from the dog house, they all match."

Edwards rubbed his eyes, then patted his thinning hair. "I didn't get much sleep last night."

"You still on the sofa?"

"No, but I might as well be."

"What'd you do to piss Jill off this time?"

"She's just mad 'cause she still wants to go to work."

"Better let her get it out of her system if you want any peace." Stas looked over to his partner slouched down in his chair and scooped up the Crown Vic's keys next to an empty mug. "Come on."

They rode in silence from downtown until they exited the Hollywood Freeway.

"Are you going to start driving now?" Edwards asked.

"No, you can have the wheel back after this."

"Suppose there's no one home. You going over the fence here too? You know it's against policy." He looked over to his partner. "I don't want anything negative in...," his voice trailed off.

"Don't worry about it. If anything happens, plead ignorance. You do that well. As for me, it'll be just another reprimand to keep the others company."

"If you have so many, how come nothing ever happens to you?"

"You think it hasn't? I'm not going anywhere, especially not up."

"Then why keep you at RHO?" Edwards asked.

"Why? Because I'm good, not just me but the whole unit. We get results. Plus, they can keep tighter reins on me there. I loved Vice, but it didn't love me. So I guess everything works out for the best. Why do you think Moore warned us about Crum?"

"Judge Crum?"

"Yeah, that was for my benefit. We tangled before."

"I see." Edwards grunted then directed his attention to the landscape outside his window as the car slowly edged up into the Hollywood Hills.

When Stas pulled over to the side of the narrow street by the Talbotts' house, Lupe was coming out of the gate, closing it behind her. She looked tired with her arms wrapped around a large white plastic bag that seemed to weigh her down.

Stas stopped the car and opened his door, calling to her when she turned into the street. "Lupe!"

She looked at the car and blinked into the bright sunlight.

"Detective Nowak, remember?"

Lupe smiled. "Yes."

As he reached her side, he started to take her bag. She hesitated. "It's okay." He ushered her towards the car. "We were coming to see you or Mrs. Talbott. Is she home?"

"No, she out with Mr. Frank."

"Where are you going?"

"Home, I quit!"

"Somebody do something to you?"

She released the bag to Stas's arms and wiped away gathering tears.

He opened the back door of the car. "Come on, we'll give you a ride down the hill."

Lupe settled in the seat and worked with the seat belt.

Edwards turned and watched. "Did you do something wrong. Mrs. Talbott seemed like such a nice lady."

"Too much work. I clean, feed kids, take to school, but the dog,..." she shook her head. "... she's too much work."

Stas got behind the wheel and adjusted the rearview mirror so he could see Lupe. "Where is the dog?"

"Wid Mr. Frank. I told Miss Mona I tired of cleaning dog sheet, and she laugh. She said that what I get paid for." Lupe shook her head trying to fight back more tears. "I don't like cleanin' sheet."

"Who's home with the kids?" Edwards asked.

"They in school. Mr. Ryan back. He pick'em up."

Stas turned back and started the car. "So Mrs. Talbott and Frank took the dog?"

"Frank? Who's he?" Edwards interrupted still leaning over the back of his seat.

"Her friend. He work for the company." Lupe paused. "I no like him. He spend lots of time with the girls, hugging, touching. Not right. He touch Miss Mona too. He touch me once. I slap his hand."

"What company does he work for, the Talbotts or B & T Construction?" Stas asked.

"I no sure." Lupe shook her head.

"Where do you live?" Edwards faced front as they headed toward the freeway.

"Pasadena, wid my sister." She gave them the address.

Stas took Los Feliz and headed for the 5.

The detectives dropped Lupe off at her sister's place on Summit in West Pasadena.

Stas helped her with her bag when she got out of the car. "Lupe, what do you wear when you take care of the dog?"

She looked puzzled. "My clothes."

"Did the dog ever jump on you or rub against you?"

She shook her head. "I no understand."

"I'd like to get a sample of the dog's hair."

She smiled. "Like *CSI*?"

Stas laughed. "That's right, like *CSI*."

Lupe put the bag down, reached in, and pulled out a brown sweater. "This morning she jump and knock me down in the run. I get sheet on my pants."

"I don't need that sample, but let me take this for a few days?"

She handed over the sweater.

"Can I have a bag?"

"Okay." She waved good-bye to Edwards and ran into the house.

"Wait!" Stas had his notebook out and hefted Lupe's bag to the porch. "Better give me your full name and a phone number so I can get your sweater back to you."

Lupe returned with a black plastic bag and a slip of paper handing both to him.

When he got to the car, Edwards stood by the driver's side, his hand out for the keys. Stas's cell phone buzzed as he walked around to the passenger's side.

"Hello."

"Detective Nowak?"

"Yes?"

"This is Molly at B & T."

"What's up?"

"Mr. Talbott is here. He said he's not leaving until it's time to pick up the girls. So you'd better get over here if you still want to talk to him."

"Good girl, Molly. I owe you one."

"I won't forget."

"I bet." He waved Edwards back to the passenger side.

"Now *where* are we going?" Edward frowned as he got into the car.

"That was Molly at B & T. It seems the elusive Mr. Talbott has finally gone in to work."

As he drove, Stas started to miss being able to block out everything when his partner was behind the wheel. He took Fair Oaks all the way to the South Pas on-ramp of the Pasadena Freeway. He exited in Chinatown and continued on to B & T, making the trip from Pasadena in twenty minutes. There in a space marked "President" stood a shiny Black Escalade, detailed to the max. That Stas could appreciate. He parked, got out of the car, and ran his finger over the surface of the left front fender of the SUV. It came up clean.

Molly met them at the door. "He's still in there. You want me to tell him you're here?"

Stas let his partner go ahead of him. "That's okay. We always like the element of surprise."

"He's in 3."

They walked down the narrow hall. Edwards knocked at Talbott's door.

A mellow baritone voice came through the closed door. "Molly, I sure as hell hope this is important. Come in."

Edwards turned the knob and stepped into a small office filled with storage boxes and rolls of blueprints scattered on a long table near the wall. "I'm Detective Edwards from the Los Angeles Police Department. This is my partner, Detective Nowak."

Ryan Talbott rose and leaned across his desk extending a soft manicured hand to Edwards. "I'm sorry I missed you when you came before. Just move some of that stuff to the floor. Everything here's in flux. I don't even have a proper office anymore, but hopefully, that will soon change."

Edwards took an empty chair close to the desk. Stas removed a stack of folders and placed then neatly on the floor next to a rusting metal folding chair. Before sitting he looked around, checking the disorder of the office versus the perfection of Talbott: the fit of his custom made shirt, the monograms over the pocket, and the gold nugget cufflinks. *A little overdone.*

"What can I do for you gentlemen? I know you've already spoken with Paul and my wife. I don't know if I have anything more to add to what they've told you."

"Let us be the judge of that." Stas took out his notebook and pen. "We need some clarification on your properties, especially the one where we found a young woman's body."

"There isn't much to that. My father owned three large storage facilities. He died. I sold two and went in as a partner with Paul. He's the developer. We plan to build condos and lofts in the Alameda corridor. We've demolished two of the buildings on the last site and started construction."

Edwards had his notebook out and paged through. "That's the one where the first victim was found?"

"Yes, that's what I was told."

"Did you know a young woman named Cynthia Lenox?" Stas pulled a photo from his jacket pocket and handed it to Talbott.

He glanced briefly at the picture and shook his head. When he gave it back to Stas, he looked quickly past the detective to the far wall. "No, no, I've never seen her."

Stas thought he detected a slight tic and several staccato blinks. "What would be your theory for someone dumping a body at one of your secure building sites?'

Talbott looked at his watch. "I don't have a clue." He stood and removed a well-tailored jacket from the back of his chair. "You'll have to excuse me. I have to pick up my children from school. I don't want to be late."

"Mr. Talbott, is Frank Stack your employee?" Stas remained seated. Maybe the kids' pickup would have to wait a bit.

"He used to work for my father. He works for B & T now."

"What are his duties?"

"He's like a supervisor/troubleshooter. But you'll have to ask Paul or Frank."

"Does Frank have a dog?"

"What? A dog?" He looked at his watch. "I'll ask him. But I really have to go now."

Edwards stood, opened the door of the office, and followed Talbott down the hall. "We may have a few more questions for you. Are you planning to leave town again?"

Talbott slipped on his jacket and kept walking.

Stas brought up the rear. "Let us know if you have any travel plans, Mr. Talbott."

Talbott turned to look back at the detective. "Do I need to call my attorney?"

"That's up to you."

The three men walked out together. Stas watched Talbott drive off in his Escalade, then tossed the Crown Vic's keys to Edwards, but instead of getting in the car, he went back to the office.

Molly was standing by the door and stepped aside as he entered. "I thought you'd be back."

"Can I take a closer look at a picture on Talbott's wall?"

Molly grabbed a ring of keys and bounced down the hallway. "This is so exciting! Is he going to be arrested?"

"I don't think so, Molly. I just want to see something." The office door wasn't locked. Stas entered, walked over to the wall, and took down an 8 x 10 photo of four men posing on a dock with a wonderful specimen of a Marlin. "Do you know where this was taken?"

"Probably Cabo, but I'm not sure."

"I recognize Ryan and Paul. Who are the other two?"

Molly joined him. "Let's see," she lisped. "That's Frank next to Ryan, then Robert." She eased in closer and pointed. "Robert, that's Dr. Crum, then there's Paul." She grabbed Stas's arm in her excitement. "Do I win the prize?"

"Name your place, Molly. Dinner's on me." He turned back to the picture. "When was this taken?"

"A few years ago, but they go deep-sea fishing a couple times a year. There's another picture in Paul's office, but he locks up, and I don't have a key."

"That's okay." He handed the frame to Molly. "Do you have a color copier?"

"Yeah. Com'on."

Molly went to the machine by her desk, made two copies of the fishing photo, and handed them to Stas.

"You're a jewel. I'll call you." He hesitated in the doorway. "When was the last time you saw Dr. Crum?"

"It's been a while. He only comes around if they're planning a trip. They use this travel guy in Glendale near Whole Foods. I usually go over there to pick up the tickets."

"Yeah, I know the place. I'll check him out, see if they have any trips planned."

Edwards was sitting behind the wheel when Stas got in on the passenger's side. "So what was that all about? You making a date with the wit?"

"You don't have to date witnesses, just being nice can go a long way." Stas passed one of the copies to his partner. "You recognize Talbott. Well, the guy next to him is Frank, the dog owner. The other one is Robert Crum."

Edwards took a closer look. "Robert Crum? Who's he?"

"Dr. Robert Crum, Judge Crum's son, Cynthia Lenox's old boyfriend."

"Oh, yeah. I remember. So they all know each other? Well, you gonna try to talk to him?"

"I may." Stas took out his sunglasses and pushed his seat back. "You want to stop in Chinatown and get something to eat?"

"Where?"

"Mon-kees."

Edwards wheeled into the street. "Hey, ain't Crum's son off limits?"

"Well, there are *off*-limits and there are off-*limits*. We just have to choose the right one."

THIRTY-NINE

Amanda sat at her coffee table, looking through the glossy colored images in *Modern Bride*. She had dog-eared a full page ad for a creamy satin strapless gown with the bodice beaded in seed pearls. She traced the long train with a well-manicured fingertip and smiled, then nervously twisted the engagement ring until it started to create a red chafe mark on her finger.

A spiral notebook was opened to a long list of names under "Guests." Several sample wedding invitations lay next to it. There was a red X on a cream engraved packet. She had just started to cut from the magazine a picture of a tall, handsome man in a black tux and jumped when the phone rang.

"Hello." Her voice was almost as shrill as the ring.

"Amanda? What are you doing?" It was Tanya.

"Just going through my plans." She closed the notebook.

"You guys made up?"

"Yes. He's so sweet. You should see the flowers he sent me."

"Have you set a date yet?"

"We're doing that tonight. I even picked out the color for your dress."

"I hope you give me enough time to get my pennies together."

"Don't worry about that. Stas says he's paying for everything."

"See, it's good to fall out sometimes. Let them come back with flowers, begging for forgiveness."

"That's just what he did. Making up was wonderful."

"He hasn't gotten rough again has he?"

"No, but I got a diamond tennis bracelet for that." Amanda laughed. "Listen, I've got to go. He'll be over in a minute. I'll put the fabric sample in your mailbox. Let me know if you like the color."

She placed the phone in its charger and went to the bedroom. There were several bags on the bed. From one Amanda emptied a package of men's briefs and a package of T-shirts onto the bed, then tore the plastic wrap on a man's dress shirt and pulled the pins out, throwing them with the other bags and plastic into a waste basket by her night stand. She grabbed the underwear and shirt, took them to the bathroom where she dumped them into the clothes hamper.

Well, Mr. Nowak let's see how you're going to get out of this one.

Amanda smiled as she crawled into bed and embraced her body pillow. She would fantasize about Stas sharing her bed, not as he had first appeared in her dreams but now as a more aggressive lover, taking her with force. She humped her pillow and moaned his name before drifting into an erotic yet fitful sleep.

FORTY

Screeching brakes and blaring horns almost drowned out the distinctive ring of Dina's doorbell. She stopped filling a green planter with potting mix and cocked her head to listen as she moved closer to the sliding glass doors. The second time the ring came through louder, longer, and with much more urgency. Whoever it was must have leaned on the bell.

She dropped the large plastic bag and rushed to the intercom phone, catching her breath. "Yes?"

"Brent-Aire Florist, I have a delivery for Ms. Dina Goode."

"This is she. I'm on the third floor." She pushed a button on the phone and hung up.

Dina waited by her open door, wiping flecks of dirt from her hands onto her gray sweats. Down the hall the elevator door opened, and a young man in a dark green uniform emerged carrying a large bouquet of flowers in a tall crystal vase.

He looked toward the open door. "Ms. Goode?"

Dina nodded and motioned for him to enter. Her eyes were bright with disbelief. She pointed to the coffee table. "There's fine."

He placed the vase in the center of the table where the delicate blooms reflected the morning sunlight that streamed through the open patio doors. "They'll need some more water." The young man turned to leave.

"Wait! Wait a minute." She ran off to the bedroom, then returned to press a folded bill into his palm.

He took a quick glance and smiled. "Thanks!"

"Oh, they're really lovely. I've never seen anything so beautiful. Who sent them?"

He pointed to the flowers. "Lady, there's a card."

Dina slowly removed it from a miniature envelope held by a long clear forked-pick protruding from the center of the arrangement. The card read "Stars?" She looked at the delivery man, puzzled. "I don't understand."

The young man took the card and read. "Stars." He handed the card back to Dina. "You know anybody named Stars?"

Dina shook her head. "No! Maybe there's a mistake. The person I know with a similar name would never send me flowers." She frowned. "He doesn't like flowers."

He pulled an invoice from his shirt pocket. "Dina Goode, this address. Nothing else. You want me to call?"

"Could you?"

He took a cell phone from his pocket and punched in a number. "Hey, Kay. Do you know who sent the flowers to Dina Goode?" Pause "Yeah, Sterling Silver with Honors, yeah, the white ones." He held his cell to his ear for a second and looked at Dina. "It was called in, charged to Mr. S. NOWAK."

Her frown broke into a broad smile. "It's pronounced N-0-V-A-K. But that's all right. It's Stas, S-T-A-S not Stars. I know who it is."

"Well, you must have made a heck of an impression if you say he hates flowers. These ain't no cheap daisies."

Dina followed the young man to the door and locked it behind him. Returning to the sofa, she contemplated the flowers, a bouquet of a dozen long-stem delicate lavender roses, mixed with half a dozen white roses, maidenhair fern, and a spray of baby's breath. They gave off a fragrance sweeter than lavender, a scent as smooth as silk, mingled with a light, winsomeness that perfumed the whole room.

She went to the kitchen and made tea, inhaling its minty steam, then returned to sit cross-legged on the sofa to discern any hidden meaning in the flowers. Memories, both painful and pleasant, flooded her mind. How long had it been? She'd met Stas two years earlier when he'd rescued her from a vicious john bent on cutting her throat. Nothing had happened with the detective during that brief encounter, and now he was back in her life when he came to her apartment after Sybil's death. He had thrown out the flowers in her kitchen, saying they were dead. She knew they only needed fresh water. Well, these beauties more than made up for the original flower tossing.

Dina finished her tea and looked at the few leaves in the bottom of the mug, wishing she could read into them what was in store for their future. Her fingers trembled slightly as she touched the scar on her neck and laughed. Maybe this was the breakthrough.

Later, she returned to her balcony to finish the replanting of a gallon container of night blooming jasmine. Her hands were grimy, but she liked the sensuous feel of the cool earth. She had remembered the plants' fragrance and wanted one ever since their ruined dinner date in Ojai. *Damn! Damn! Jason!* She jammed the trowel into the planter.

Finished with the dirty work, she pushed her hair out of her eyes and tied up tentacles of the delicate blossoms to a white trellis, then pushed the planter against the wall next to the stationary section of the glass slider. When the double doors were open, not only would the jasmine be visible from the living room, but its delicate blooms would perfume both the interior and balcony of her apartment.

After cleaning up outside, she showered, dressed, and went to the kitchen, looking for something in the fridge for dinner. She jumped at the loud knock at the door almost dropping a container of leftover gumbo.

"Dammit" She headed for the entry. "Hold on, I'm coming."

Dina opened the door to Raven, dressed as if she had just stepped off a Parisian fashion runway, and April Frost, one of the escorts working with Raven in Paris. Both women seemed exhausted as they entered the apartment.

Dina looked beyond them into the otherwise empty hall-way. "How did you get in?"

"Some old lady with too many bags. We helped her. I was a little surprised. She seemed more worried about her ice cream melting than some black Amazon running amuck in your hall-ways, ravishing your senior men." Raven laughed at her own joke. "If she's married to one of those old guys I saw creeping down the street, maybe she'd wish I'd run amuck."

"When did you get back?" Dina moved into the living room, turning on lights.

"This morning. You know, I hate flying back to LA. It gives me jet lag for days." Raven threw her navy Armani jacket over the chair.

"Make yourself comfortable."

April remained standing, legs together. "Where's the bath-room?"

Dina pointed towards the bedroom. "Through there."

"She must have filled up half the barf bags on the flight." Raven said. "You shouldn't fly when you're pregnant."

"Is that why you're back?" Dina asked.

"That's why she's back. I'm here to finalize the Asian opera-tion."

A loud whistle caused Dina to rush back into the kitchen. Raven followed. Turning off the fire, she grabbed the kettle, and poured boiling water over a stainless steel egg filled with one of her favorite tea blends into a green China teapot. "Want some tea?"

"Not really." Raven looked around the tiny kitchen. "You got anything stronger?"

"In the freezer."

Raven opened the door and seemed unfazed by the chilled bottle of Chopin vodka facing her. "Where're the glasses?"

Dina pointed to the cabinet over the sink. Raven took out two old-fashioned glasses and held them up to the light.

"They're clean." Dina knitted her brows.

Raven poured her glass about a quarter full and hesitated at the second glass leaving it empty on the counter. "Give her tea."

Dina filled two mugs just as April came in. "You feeling better?" She was surprised at how much April had changed. Her once beautiful mane of red hair now fell limply past her shoulders. Her complexion that was usually flawlessly made-up, was now pale and sallow. Her green eyes were dull and lifeless. Dina had been told that pregnancy was supposed to do just the opposite.

Raven leaned back against the counter, sipped her drink, and looked at the bottle. "This is good, very smooth." She looked at April. "Well, when you're pregnant, as soon as you stop vomiting, you have to pee every fifteen minutes, and then there's the heartburn."

Dina looked over in surprise. "How do you know?"

Raven took a gulp of vodka and swallowed hard. "Believe me, I know."

April took a mug of tea from Dina. "The doctor said it will pass."

The conversation abruptly switched from motherhood to other engaging subjects: old lovers, new prospects, and the heartbreak of betrayals. Their voices grew louder and louder, interrupting, talking over each other. No one seemed aware of the rising decibels common to women in the excitement of a heated discussion.

"They all lie! You think they going to be there for you, and the bastards bail." Anger was rising in Raven's tone.

"Maybe some men can't make a commitment because...." April seemed to withdraw into herself after that comment.

Raven took another long swig. "Yeah, like a wife, other kids, a job...." She coughed.

"He's coming here later," April offered.

"Don't hold your breath!" Raven drained her glass and put it in the sink.

Dina looked from one to the other. "Who?"

"The father," April added.

"Sometimes you have to take what you can." Dina tried to sound positive.

"Well, I guess if it's mind-blowing sex, you'd better hold on to it, 'cause that's about all you're going to get." Raven frowned.

No one heard the door open or close, or the rattle of plastic bags. Stas's entrance into the apartment went unnoticed.

"French men still make great lovers, but I had to get tangled-up with a married American diplomat." April patted her slightly curving belly. "Look what it got me."

"At least you don't have to straighten out the Japanese and compete with their damn dolly whore houses." Raven refilled her glass. "I think Sybil had the right idea. Get a regular lover and be done with it."

"You can say that when you're not working." April had regained some of her color and animation. "What are you doing now? Must be something special from the look of all those flowers."

Dina was at the sink, her back turned from the intrusion and its accompanying silence. Stas stopped next to Raven, who stood tall, looking down. She was a good three inches taller in her four inch heels.

"Dina, you have company," April interjected.

She turned, saw him, and reacted like a naughty five-year-old caught with her hand in the cookie jar. "Stas!"

He smiled. "Ladies, I hope I'm not intruding. Dina didn't tell me...."

Raven cut in. "She didn't tell us either, but then, she didn't know we were coming. I just popped over to discuss a couple of problems we're having."

"Popped over an ocean?" Stas smiled.

"There are organizational problems." She reached for an empty glass and pushed the Chopin his way. "Can I fix you a drink?"

"No thanks."

Raven looked past Stas to the entry. "Didn't we close the door?"

"He has a key," Dina offered.

'I'm April." She extended her hand to Stas. "Evidently," she nodded at Raven. "you know each other."

Raven made the introduction. "Stas Nowak."

There was a moment of awkward silence before he picked up a glass. "I think I will have that drink."

Raven poured and spied the two bags on the dining table. "I hope there's food in those bags. I'm starved."

"I hope you like Chinese."

Dina got plates. Stas put the Chopin back in the freezer. Raven watched him move with ease in Dina's kitchen. The table was quickly set, the food warmed in the microwave, and places taken at the table.

What little conversation there was, was punctuated by monosyllables of approval and the clicking of chopsticks.

A bouquet of garlic, ginger, and peppers perfumed the atmosphere. Dina watched April, hoping the spicy food would not upset her stomach.

"So why *are* you back?" Stas poised his chopsticks over some shrimp.

"The last time I was here, we sealed a deal for an Asian agency. The principals were satisfied. Dar Ling was set to go and take care of our interest."

Stas plucked several shrimp from the carton and dropped them on his plate. "Send her to Japan, get rid of her, but I wouldn't have her running anything. I don't know. It could be dangerous. I've been hearing things about Dar Ling, and they're not good."

April looked from Stas to Raven and back to the detective. She opened her mouth to speak but caught a slight head shake from Dina.

"She can't go now even if I could get rid of her. She's using. I can send Sindy. Four months ago, I could have sent April."

Raven shook her head. "I've got to do something about Dar Ling."

Stas finished an egg roll and caught a loose piece of cabbage with his finger, popping it into his mouth. "She could be arrested and sent to rehab as part of her sentencing. That could get her out of your hair for a while."

"What?" Raven tried to stifle her surprise.

"You heard me. You know who to call. Max is still around."

Raven rose. "I need a smoke."

"Not in here." Dina pointed to the slightly opened glass doors to the balcony.

"Stas, you want to join me?"

He held up his finger to decline.

"Com'on. We can talk." Raven looked at the flowers on the coffee table as she moved toward the balcony. "Damn, it smells like a fucking wake in here."

"How would you know?" Dina asked, irritated.

"In East St. Louis, my dad and uncle ran the local funeral home. They thought I was going to join'em, keep the business in the family. They even enrolled me in mortuary college just before I graduated from high school." She frowned. "I'd seen enough dead guys by the time I was eighteen to last me a lifetime. Although for some guys, life isn't much of an improvement."

Stas rose and followed her to the balcony.

"Who is he?" April zeroed in on Dina.

"A friend."

"With a key?"

Dina started to clear the table.

Outside, Stas took Raven's silver lighter and lit her cigarette. She took a long drag and blew a whirl of smoke over the railing.

She turned back to him after dumping ashes into the planter. "I'm surprised."

"At what?"

"That you came back. I told her you wouldn't. You made a liar out of me."

"Probably not the first time. Anyway, I like Dina." The words seemed spoken without emotion.

"I guess so. It's a win-win situation for you." Raven blew smoke in his direction.

He fanned the air. "How's that?"

"She's physically out of the business, so I guess she's yours exclusively."

"Seems like that's good for her, too."

"Dina deserves better."

"She can kick me to the curb whenever she wants to."

"And give up the best sex she ever had." Raven laughed.

"She told you that?" Stas looked back into the apartment.

"No, she doesn't have to. I'm not blind. You can tell when a woman's having her needs met on a regular basis, and you're looking pretty good yourself."

"She needs to get out of the business altogether. She can still be charged with pandering."

"Suppose we liquidate?"

"Meaning?"

"Get rid of everything: sell it, give it away. I don't care. I'm not coming back here. Would that be good enough for you?" Raven stubbed her butt out in the bag of planting mix.

Stas didn't respond but followed her back into the apartment.

She paused at the entrance. "You know, I wish we'd met ten years ago, we could have been great business partners."

"I had a job."

"Yeah, but ten, twelve years ago you would've left. We would have made it worth your while." Raven put cigarettes and lighter back into her bag.

Stas stood looking through the living room to Dina as she moved to the kitchen. "Babe, I've got to go."

April turned in her seat and followed the detective's line of vision. "Won't Dina be disappointed?"

"It won't be the first time." He started for the door but turned back. "By the way, did any of you ladies ever model?"

Raven stifled a laugh.

"I mean, seriously," he added.

"There were a few. I even did a spread—I mean, a shoot for a motorcycle ad. I never saw it in print though." Raven returned to her chair. "Hope it sold a lot of bikes."

Dina stood in the doorway of the kitchen, wiping her hands on a dish towel. "I did a lingerie show at the Beverly Hilton once, sort of a faux Victoria Secret for some new women's store."

Stas's eyed her intently, as if imagining her in one of his favorites. "What happened?"

"Nothing, we went home after the show." Dina struck a modeling pose.

He turned back to Raven. "Did you use an agency?"

"We were an agency." She smiled.

"I'm serious," Stas said.

"A few of the girls used a woman, think she had a name like dog food." Dina straightened.

"Gaines?" he said.

"That's it. Do you know her?"

Stas nodded.

"She was legit, but I heard she started to specialize," Raven said.

"In what?"

Raven shook her head and reached for her purse. "Boy toys or toy dogs, I don't remember. That was a while ago."

Stas started for the door. Dina joined him.

"Thanks for the roses. What brought that on?"

"A moment of weakness. I smelled them and thought of you. " He kissed her on the cheek as he opened the door.

She wanted to grab him back. "I thought you didn't like flowers."

"I still don't, but these.... I'll call you." He pulled the door closed.

"What was that all about?" April asked before Dina could escape back to the kitchen. "Why the questions about modeling? Is he looking for girls?"

"Not the way you think. Stas's a cop." Raven took her cigarettes and lighter out of her bag and returned to the balcony.

"Oh, shit!" April quickly rose and headed to the bathroom.

Stas checked his watch after leaving Dina's and headed for the Second Set, partly to prove to himself that evenings at her place weren't becoming a habit, that he could return to his old *modus operandi* without any problem.

He should have recognized the signs from the partially empty parking lot. Inside it was even worse. A few couples occupied some of the back booths, their heads bent in deep conversations. The DJ's station was abandoned, his CD player covered in black as if in mourning.

The bar was almost empty giving Stas his choice of stools. He settled on a middle one where he could see the comings and goings of everyone in the place. "Where's Jim?" he asked, nodding toward the DJ's area next to the stamp-sized dance floor.

Roy looked unsmiling toward the back. "His mother's sick. He had to go out of town. We didn't have time for a replacement. What can I get you?"

If Troy had been there tending bar, he wouldn't have asked Stas. A vodka neat would have appeared automatically. "Give me a Chopin over ice."

It arrived without fanfare or comment. Stas slowly nursed his drink and thought about Dina's visitors. Even though Raven was operating the business out of Paris, it was evident that he had been the subject of Raven and Dina's conversations. He wondered how much Raven had told her about his days in Vice or how much Dina had told her about their current involvement.

He took a hard swallow and almost choked, getting more ice than vodka. Looking into the mirror behind the bar, he recognized Ralph Townsend's signature corduroy jacket sliding onto the stool next to him.

"What's up, Nowak? Dina kick you out?"

"You wish." Stas folded and unfolded his damp black napkin.

"But you'll let me know when she does, right?"

Stas sucked on a piece of ice. "How many times must I tell you, smokers need not apply?"

Townsend leaned over to get the bartender's attention. "Give me a Scotch on the rocks." He turned towards the detective as the drink was placed on a napkin. "Which one is that?" Townsend's pointed to the bartender as he moved to the other end of the bar.

"Roy," Stas responded.

"Yeah, the silent one, a man can stay home if he wanted the silent treatment."

"You got somebody at home these days?" Stas asked.

Townsend shook his head and took out a pack of cigarettes. "Just a figure of speech. You can't do much with that." He toyed with the box. "You still laying off?"

Stas nodded and sipped his drink.

"You slowing down on the booze too?" He looked at Stas's half-empty glass. "Usually when you give up one thing, you got something else to take its place."

"Hey, Roy, how much you paying the reporter-turned philosopher here?"

Townsend smiled. "I like giving advice especially to cops like you."

"Why is that?" Stas asked.

"One, you're not talking, especially about the three sisters. If I didn't have a couple of techs over on Mission, I'd starve to death."

"What sisters?"

As if on cue, a burst of loud feminine laughter flooded through the front door. Both men turned on their stools. Three women entered, their voices pitched too high from too much alcohol. They looked toward the bar before sliding into a booth. Leslie, the new barmaid, didn't make any sudden move from where she stood at the well.

"See, it's an ill wind that blows us no good." Townsend smiled at the new arrivals.

"Orange County wives testing LA waters." Roy smiled as he wiped the spot in front of the reporter.

Stas turned back to his drink. He could observe everything through the mirror.

"Why don't you take an interest?" Townsend continued.

"Why should I?"

The reporter seemed torn between the women being served by Leslie and picking Stas's brain. "Did you know that Judge Crum claimed the Lenox's body?"

"He's her godfather." Stas crunched on more ice. "It was in all the papers."

Townsend frowned. "You did know that she was engaged to Crum's son?"

"Yeah, I heard something like that." Stas drained his glass.

"Do you think the kid was his."

"What kid?"

"The autopsy report said she had a C-section." Townsend turned when a loud ripple of laughter came from the women in the second booth.

"Makes you wonder." Stas laid some bills on the bar and slid off his stool. "Why don't you try your theory out on some Orange County wives? Have you seen the show, or did it get canned?"

As Stas reached the door, one of the ladies, a brunette of dubious original anatomical parts called out to him. "Why are you leaving so soon?"

He smiled and nodded towards Townsend. "My friend at the bar would love to join you ladies and tell you some of his most gruesome stories. He's a crime reporter for the *Times*. He knows things even the cops don't."

FORTY-ONE

The next morning, Stas woke wondering how Townsend had dealt with his sudden popularity. No doubt with practiced skill. Occupational hazard, he supposed. He picked up his cell, punched in numbers, then held it to his ear and waited.

"Hello." The voice on the other end responded with a slight lisp. "This is B &T Construction. May I help you?"

"Detective Nowak. Can you talk?"

"Oh, hi. I'm alone. What's up?"

"I need another favor."

"Wow, they're starting to add up."

"Can you give me the name of the sperm bank that Mr. Talbott used?"

"Give me a minute." There was a pause.

Stas looked at his watch.

"Detective?"

"I'm still here, Molly."

"It's been a while, but the last check I wrote went to Cyber Neo-genetics."

"Where's that?" Stas asked.

"They're in Burbank at 589 Fernando Road, 818-876-xxxx. I'm not sure they're still there, 'cause I vaguely remember a brochure announcing an expansion. So you'd better call."

"Thanks, Molly, I'll be in touch." He ended the call and punched in the number he'd written on his notepad.

"Ramon Cortes, Consultant, how can I help you?"

"This is Detective Nowak with Los Angeles Police Department. We're looking for Cyber Neo-genetics and were given this number."

"This is an investment company. We've been here for over a year. Well, for sixteen months to be exact, and we've had this number all that time."

Stas thanked Mr. Cortes and hung up before dialing 411. The Cyber Neo-genetics Company was now located in Thousand Oaks. He called the new number and spoke with a woman with a high-pitched voice, who gave him the new address and verified that they were, indeed, a sperm back open for business. He hoped she heard his title and didn't think he was interested in their services.

Edwards dropped a dingy folder on his desk and hung his jacket on the back of his chair. "She makes me sick."

"Who?" Stas asked. "What are you talking about?"

"Susan Shaw, down in Forensics. She always wants to know why you don't come down to get stuff."

"You tell her I'm busy?"

Edwards held up the folder. "Look what she put it in. You know, I get tired of being treated like an errand boy."

"I'll go down next time."

"Anyway, all the dresses came from the same fabric and die lot. Plus, there were blanket fibers and matching dog hairs on all three."

"I could have told you that. Get your jacket. We're going to Thousand Oaks."

"Why?" Edwards put the folder in his drawer.

Stas stood, put the piece of paper in the pocket, then slipped on his jacket. "I want to check on the number of deposits and withdrawals made by Lundstrom and Talbott,"

"Withdrawals?"

"Sperm!"

"Whose?"

"That's what we're going to find out."

Edwards presented his ID to the receptionist who sat behind a stainless steel and glass counter affixing address labels to manila envelopes. She was in her mid-thirties with a blotched complexion and limp brown hair. She looked past the proffered credentials into the detective's face and frowned.

"How can I help you, officer?" Her voice was hoarse. She cleared her throat, coughing up phlegm, and spitting into a tissue.

Stas had not approached the counter but walked around the waiting room admiring the tasteful yet clinical decor. There were several wall-displayed photos of happy results: beaming, beautiful babies, some alone, others lovingly held by smiling mothers. A grouping of a gray leather sofa and matching easy chairs were placed along another wall. An array of magazines devoted to family life and parenting were displayed on several metal and smoky glass end tables. He wondered what kind of magazines he'd find in the room where the donors made their deposits.

The receptionist leaned over her counter and shouted at Stas. "Sir, Sir, who are you?"

Edwards turned slightly. "Detective Nowak, he's with me. We'd like to see the director. We called earlier."

Without a word she disappeared. Both men waited in silence. After a few minutes, a door opened, and the receptionist stuck her head out. "The Director will see you." She held the door open to allow the detectives to enter, then pointed to another open door.

The sign on the desk read "Mr. Perkins." He stood when Stas and Edwards entered and presented their IDs.

"I'm Detective Nowak. This is Detective Edwards."

"I'm Ray Perkins. Have a seat." He indicated two gray leather chairs identical to the ones in the reception area. "What can I do for you?"

"We're investigating a case that may involve one or more of your client-donors." Stas removed his notebook and pen from his inside jacket pocket and paged through. "Mr. Ryan Talbott and Mr. Paul Lundstrom."

"Do you know when these gentlemen used our services?"

"We think eight years ago, could have been nine years, though," Stas said.

"I'm sorry. We have no records of these gentlemen."

Edwards eased forward. "But you haven't even checked."

"I don't need to check. We can't divulge any information about clients' deposits or withdrawals." Perkins started to rise.

Stas closed his notebook. "We didn't think it was going to be easy, but you can cooperate with us now or we can subpoena your records. This involves a triple homicide."

Perkins dropped back into his seat. His eyelids fluttered as he tapped the tips of his fingers on the glass desk top. Both detectives sat silently, giving the Director time to reconsider.

His fingers slowed their tapping. "Well," he paused. "I guess it all depends on what you want to know."

"Basically, when both men made deposits and withdrawals?" Stas asked.

Perkins rose and walked around the desk. "Come with me. There's nothing in this computer." He patted the ultra-slim monitor. "It's just for show." He led the detectives from his office, down a wide carpeted corridor to a set of double doors where he punched a code into a key pad to his right. "Everything past this point is highly secured and temperature controlled." There was a metallic click. Perkins held one door open, allowing the detectives to enter. "Come this way."

The overhead lights were not as bright in this area, and it was at least ten degrees cooler. They stopped outside another heavy door with a glass window reinforced with mesh wiring.

"I'm going to get one of the techs to access the data though I must insist that you limit your search to the individuals that you indicated and only deposits and withdrawals in that specific time frame. If you want more information, I'm afraid you will have to get a subpoena." His tone was clipped and to the point.

Stas knew there would be no room to maneuver the tech to disclose more information if she was anything like her boss.

Perkins left the detectives waiting in the hall while he went for a tech.

"It's unnatural," Edwards said.

"What's so unnatural about it?" Stas asked.

"Going into a room and jerking off. Why would a guy put himself through that?"

"I can't believe you. Guys do it all the time."

"I don't mean that. I mean in a place like this."

"They do it to impregnate a woman. Have a kid. Think about it. Now science makes it easier. If you keep at it, the only down side—a cramp in your hand." Stas laughed.

"You're a pervert." Edwards shook his right hand as if it had gone to sleep. "I still think it's unnatural."

"You mean you never..."

The conversation was cut short when the Director returned with a young woman. "This is Maureen."

The tech stood about five feet and sported a mop of unruly light brown hair piled atop her head that added several inches to her height. Her unbuttoned white lab coat barely covered a green turtleneck sweater and a black skirt that fell to her knees. Stas's gaze lingered a few seconds longer than usual. Her legs were beautifully shaped and as white as fine bone china.

"I'm Detective Nowak."

She gave Stas a quick smile.

Edwards stepped closer and offered his hand. "I'm Detective Edwards."

Maureen offered several limp fingers that Edwards touched lightly then withdrew. She touched Edwards's arm, moving him aside and punched in a code that unlocked the door to a room containing several computers and flat panel monitors.

"It seems a lot like overkill. All this technology just to have a kid," Edwards said.

"We have to maintain not only our freezers, but lots of sensitive data as well. Do you officers have children?"

"No." Stas pulled a chair next to the computer. "Get a chair, Sid."

Edwards stood over Maureen. "I have four."

She looked up at him and smiled. "Well, you certainly don't need our services. What's your time frame?"

Stas looked in his notebook. "We need to go back at least nine years."

"That's a while ago. Let's hope we have all the data in the system"

"And if not?" Stas asked.

"Some of the old files haven't been updated in the computers." Her fingers played the keys like a piano virtuoso. "And the names?"

"Ryan Talbott and Paul Lundstrom."

Maureen worked in silence for several minutes. There was a blur of names, numbers, and what looked like dates. When she looked up, Stas noted green eyes flecked with gold.

"Which Ryan Talbott do you want, junior or senior?"

Edwards coughed and cleared his throat. He looked from the tech to his partner. "You mean both men made deposits?"

"Yes, first Mr. Talbott junior, then a month later, Mr. Talbott, the old man, which is a little unusual, since donors can't be too old."

"How old is too old?" Stas asked.

"Thirty-five, although I've known them to take men as old as forty."

Edwards flexed his hands. "All this makes my hands feel weak."

Stas looked unsmiling at the computer. "When were the withdrawals made?"

"The younger Talbott never made any. The old man made two within a month of each other."

"That's it?" Edwards asked.

"I'm afraid so. Their contracts were terminated after six months."

"Terminated, what do you mean?" Edwards looked puzzled. "Had they made babies?"

Maureen turned towards Edwards. "We don't do that here. We're just a collection and storage facility."

"And the eggs?" The detective seemed to have a difficult time masking his discomfort.

"They're collected at the clinic. That's where they're fertilized and implanted."

"What clinic did they use?" Stas asked.

"You'll have to ask Mr. Perkins." She started to push away from the computer.

Stas leaned in. "What about Lundstrom?"

Maureen turned back to the computer. "He came about the same time as Mr. Talbott, but they didn't come in together. He made deposits and withdrawals over a four year period. He ended his contract three years ago." She touched a couple of keys, and the screen went black. "I'll take you back to Mr. Perkins. If you want more specific information, you'll have to ask him."

The detectives walked out and waited in the hallway as the tech shut down her operation and secured the door.

Perkins met them outside his office. "I spoke to my superior. If you need any more specifics, I'm afraid you will have to get that subpoena." He handed both men a brochure. "For general information." He walked them back to the reception area.

"Thanks." Stas said. Outside he took his sunglasses from his jacket pocket and walked to the car.

The afternoon sun felt warm as they opened the doors to let some of the heat out of the car. "What am I supposed to do with this?" Edwards grimaced at the brochure but held it up to shade his eyes from the sun. He removed his jacket and put it on the back seat of the Crown Vic before getting behind the wheel. "Places like this give me the creeps." He fumbled trying to insert the key in the ignition. "Pretty soon women won't need men,... so unnatural."

"Yeah, it wasn't what nature intended, but some people will do just about anything for a baby, even murder."

"So you think that's what this is all about, babies?"

"I'd make book on it." Stas settled back in his seat and closed his eyes behind his shades.

Molly looked up from her desk and broke into a broad grin when Edwards and Stas entered B & T Construction.

"Is that Mr. Talbott's SUV in the parking lot?" Stas paused lightly touching Molly's shoulder as Edwards barged ahead into the narrow hallway.

She turned in her chair and looked after the detective. "He's in his office."

Stas followed his partner as Molly rose to watch them knock on Talbott's door.

"I thought I told you not to disturb me," Talbott shouted as the door opened.

"We needed to ask you a few more questions and thought we'd drop in since we were in the neighborhood." Edwards didn't wait for an invitation but pulled up a chair and sat down.

Stas stood in the doorway. "Mr. Talbott, nine years ago you bought a modeling agency and conducted a scam, luring young women to Vegas for a bogus workshop. One of those aspiring models disappeared and turned up in a dumpster on a construction site that you own."

"Owned. It's not my property. It belongs to B & T Construction." Talbott blinked.

Edwards took out his notebook and paged through. "Mr. Lundstrom told us that you are his partner."

"I'm his silent partner. He runs everything, and I had nothing to do with the modeling agency. That was my father's fiasco."

Stas moved into the room, unfolded a metal chair, and dusted if off with his handkerchief before sitting down. "Fiasco?"

312

"You need to understand my father's obsession with my wife. You should have seen him when he first met her. He kept going on about how much she looked like my mother. I really didn't see it. Granted she had the coloring and the hair, but..."

Stas interrupted. "And your mother is deceased?"

Ryan nodded. "She passed away when I was twelve. He never got over it. But when he met Mona, it gave him a new lease on life. He was seduced by what he called her ethereal beauty. He claimed my mother had it and thought he could recapture it in my wife."

"Recapture it?" Stas looked puzzled. "Sounds a little strange for your father to take that kind of interest in Mona. How do you go about doing something like that?"

Ryan frowned as if to dismiss his feelings. "It really didn't matter. It made him happy, and I could finally do what I wanted."

"How long after you met your wife before you were married?" Edwards asked.

"Three, four months. We all drove over to Vegas and did it."

"Did it? It doesn't sound like you were too enthused about marriage." Now Edwards looked puzzled.

"I really wasn't into the whole matrimony thing. To tell you the truth, I married to keep the old man off my case."

"Since he was single, why didn't he marry her?" Stas asked.

"Their relationship was platonic but satisfying for him since he could still feel loyal to my mother. He gave Mona a million dollar trust fund when our daughter was born and added another million at the birth of the second."

"And your father's involvement with your wife...." Stas didn't get to finish.

"He was never involved with her. He was old enough to be her father, for God's sake." Talbott's neck flushed.

"Then would you say that you and your wife had a normal married life?" Stas moved closer to the desk to observe Talbott's body language.

"Not exactly, we've been having problems." He ran his finger around his shirt collar. "You know, this is embarrassing. Why do you cops have to know about, ugh, my intimate life?"

"You forget, we're investigating a series of murders. We gather information. Sometimes embarrassing questions are asked." Stas relaxed. "Did you work with a fertility clinic in the conception of your first child?"

"Do I have to answer these questions? Don't I need my attorney present?"

Edwards straightened. "You can answer our questions here, sorta off the record, or we can go downtown, and you can bring your lawyer."

Talbott fussed with his shirt cuff. "I don't have anything to hide. We just couldn't manage to conceive."

"Was there some medical reason?" Stas asked.

"Inclination, interest." Talbott squirmed.

"Yours or hers."

"I guess it was mine, so I went to a sperm bank."

"To make a deposit or withdrawal?" Edwards looked amused.

"We ended up using donor sperm."

Stas shifted his weight in the hard chair. His butt was getting numb. "Did you know the donor?"

"They're kept anonymous. We listed traits. I guess that's what they were called, what the donor had to have, intelligent, blonde, blue eyes, tall."

"Could your wife have known the donor?" Stas asked.

The color rose higher in Talbott's face. "I told you they're kept anonymous. I didn't want to know. Why would she?"

Stas decided to go all the way. "Did you know that your business partner used the same sperm bank?"

Talbott seemed unfazed. "He recommended it. They used it because his wife was having a hard time conceiving."

"Did you know that your father also made a deposit?" Stas asked.

Talbott's jaw dropped. "What?"

"And a withdrawal." Edwards added.

Back in the squad room, Stas looked at his partner in a short sleeved, dingy shirt that he knew had once been white. Edwards hung his jacket on the back of his desk chair and sat down preparing to write a report. Stas was also fascinated by his partner's sports coat that he had been wearing for a week.

"You gonna present this to the Captain?" Edwards asked.

"Why not?"

"Maybe you'd better tell me again what you think you got."

Stas grabbed his mug and went to the coffee machine, leaving Edwards leaning over his keyboard. After filling his cup, he put it on the Cryno-tech brochure. "We got motive: babies and money. Old man Talbott gave Mona that trust when she had the grandchildren. Who knows what else he gave her. Oh, yeah, let's not forgot the ring. The old man was probably obsessed with having a kid carry on his name. I bet anything the first kid was his. That's why he gave Mona that trust."

Edwards shook his head. "I don't know. Who fathered the second child?"

"Lundstrom!" Stas took a sip of coffee. "He's blonde, blue eyes. You saw the photo of his kids. They all look like each other."

"This is too much like incest. Suppose the kids hook up later. Damn! They could all be related." Edwards toyed with his mouse.

"Well, we'll find out whose kid is whose when we get some DNA results."

Edwards turned to his partner. "And just how are we going to do that? How are we getting back in the house without a warrant?"

"We'll get one."

"You must be dreaming. You're going to need more than your hunches. That's not evidence." Edwards turned back to his computer. "I'm tired. I got to finish and go home."

"The Captain said he wasn't going to Crum for a warrant. He told me to just find a judge who's not too picky and have him sign it." Stas walked back to his desk, speaking over his shoulder. "And that's just what I'm going to do."

"Good luck! What you going do, catch a judge poking his law clerks in chambers?" Edwards asked.

"There are other places to catch them with their pants down."

Edwards continued typing while Stas went back to the murder book. Neither detectives noticed Jonson's entrance until he handed Stas a slip of white paper.

"This guy, Guzman, called you earlier. Said 'things were set'."

Edwards looked over. "What's that all about?"

"Guzman works for the insurance company." He glanced at the paper and reached for the phone.

Edwards didn't wait for an answer but grabbed his jacket and left. Stas waited on hold. Hopefully, Guzman had some good news. Anything would be helpful since the investigation was going so slowly. Stas knew they'd better tie things together pretty soon, or with the weight of one of the victims being a judge's daughter or not, the case would go into the cold file and freeze the girls over once again.

Marlowe came in looking like he was in pain. He tossed a file on Stas's desk and tried to stifle a moan. "This is for you. What did you do to get it back so fast?"

Stas look a quick look at the report. "They matched the dog hairs with those found on the house dresses of the three vics." He broke into a broad smile. "Plus, they're the same hairs from the blanket and the doghouse."

Marlowe looked over his shoulder, his obvious pain mixed with surprise. "What doghouse?" He moved in closer to get a better view of the report. "This is the first time I've heard of a frigging doghouse."

Stas glanced up at the suffering detective. "What's the matter with you?"

"I just left the dentist. They started a damn root canal. I hate dentists, but I hate getting my ass chewed out even worse. Tell me what you gathered was legit, that what's on this report isn't gonna...."

Stas interrupted. "Listen, you know they found dog hairs on the vics. There were even a few hairs from a younger dog, a puppy, but the same dog. So it's been in the picture for a while. Now the dog is older."

Marlowe frowned. "I don't want to hear any doggy stories, just tell me where you got the other hairs?"

"From the nanny, off her sweater."

"In her house?"

Stas held up his finger. "The hairs from the doghouse also match."

Marlowe straightened. "Did you get a warrant?"

"No!"

"Man, you know damn well we can't use it."

"But it's an argument."

"For what?"

"To get a warrant!"

"Predicated on what?"

"The dog hairs."

"Shit, are you crazy—do you actually think I'm going to Moore and have him ask Crum or some other judge to give us a warrant to check-out a dog house that you illegally took hairs from." He shook his head in disbelief.

"The hairs came from another dog house. I need to check out the Talbott's house for a match."

"You want inside the house. That changes the scope. Forget it! I'm not even tiptoeing past the Captain's office. Unless you got a judge in your pocket, you better forget it."

"Babe, I need you to find me a judge." Stas stood in the kitchen entrance undoing his tie and collar bottom.

Dina turned from a pot she'd been stirring and replaced the lid. "A judge? What do you want fixing?"

"I need a warrant." He took a deep breath, inhaling the aroma of garlic and other spices he couldn't readily identify.

She moved to the sink and threw a box in the trash underneath before turning back to him. "How do you normally get one?"

"This is special. I can't go through regular channels. C'mon, I know there's some bad boy judge who doesn't want his game spoiled. I think I even recognized some names from Sybil's database."

"Why don't you check your little strip or dick ..."

"Disk, babe."

"Well, whatever you call it."

"I gave'em to you, remember?"

Dina fanned him with a wooden spoon as she moved back to the stove. "I don't believe you didn't keep something for your files."

He pulled her to him and kissed her, tasting her lips. "What's on the menu?"

"Gumbo!"

"You know how to make gumbo?"

"Yes, with a little help from Mr. Zatarain."

"When I was in Vice, my partner took me to Bells."

"You mean Harold and Belles?"

"Yeah, the one on Jefferson."

Dina turned from his arms to stir the pot and reduce the heat after tasting her spoon.

"Don't I get a taste?"

"You just had one." She put the spoon in the slot. "I'll call Sindy. I think there's something tomorrow night at the Clairmore."

She left him standing at the stove folding his tie and staring at the pot. When she returned, Stas had his Chopin out and was pouring a drink.

"You want one?" He indicated a second glass.

She ignored his offer. "You tasted." Dina looked from him and his bottle to the spoon slot on the stove.

"What?" A sly grin met the rim of the glass.

"Don't try to act innocent. You've been around too many crooks—anyway the spoon's been moved and," she wiped the corner of his mouth with her finger, "you left some."

He took a sip and held his glass up to her in a mock salute. "Caught in the act."

"You're in luck. The party's tonight. If you want to call it that."

"Yeah, I know."

"Your buddy Dar Ling's there. Don't wait too late or you'll catch him bare."

"That's the best way, makes for a quick signature."

"You know the Clairmore?"

"From Vice, the best whortel in town."

Dina didn't react.

Stas took his glass and went into the bedroom, flicking on the nightstand light. He opened his phone, scrolling through a list of numbers before calling.

"Coop? Stas Nowak."

The voice on the other end cleared his throat. "What's up?"

"Man, I need a favor."

There was a brief silence on the other end, then, "What kind?"

"A warrant." Stas looked up, distracted by Dina standing in the doorway. "Where are you?"

"Not home. Where are you?"

"Ditto." He looked at his watch. "Can you get away a little later tonight?"

There was background talking, a high-pitched female voice. "Yeah, but it'll cost you."

"How much?" Stas asked.

"Two fifths of Chivas Regal?"

"Kinda steep." Dina joined him on the bed. He inhaled, smelling unfamiliar scents and heard his stomach growl. "Okay, you got it."

"Tonight!"

"I said you got it. Call me when you have the paper work in hand."

Dina touched his lips and jumped off the bed, just avoiding his grasp.

He sighed and gave Coop the particulars and a place to meet.

Dina paused in the doorway. "Are you staying?"

He shook his head. "But I will eat. I found an ADA to get the warrant."

After finishing his gumbo, he called his partner. Edwards refused to drive back into the city especially since the act of obtaining the warrant sounded suspect. Stas called Marlowe's cell. He was relaxing, having a drink at the Second Set waiting for Barbara who was working late.

"Okay, man, I'll go with you 'cause I'm curious. I want to see how you're going to pull this one off," Marlowe said, a slight slur in his speech.

"Are you drunk?" Stas asked.

"I'm working on it. Dammit, didn't I tell you my mouth hurt?"

"Well, slow down."

"You *did* get an ADA?" Marlowe asked.

"Bill Cooper said he'd do it, so have Troy give you some black coffee."

"Pick me up, and this better not take all night." There was a pause. "Do you read me?"

"Loud and clear. I'm on my way."

Dina stood at the door. He slipped on his jacket and worked the tie under his collar.

"Here." She handed him a plastic card. "You must go through the garage. This is for the gate. She tucked a piece of paper into his jacket pocket. "This is the code for the elevator.

If the elevator is locked, use this." She gave him a shiny brass key on a narrow, red satin ribbon."

He swung it before her eyes as if to hypnotize.

"Stop! If you want to play games...!"

Stas looked at the key again. "What else does this unlock?"

"Nothing else. Listen, I called security and told them you were coming, so they won't bother you if they see you on the surveillance monitor. There shouldn't be any problem as long as you get in and out quickly."

"Babe, you know that's not my MO," he laughed, "but I'll do my best."

"He's in Suite 1041."

Stas paused in the hallway. "What's his name?"

Dina stood inside the doorway. "The Honorable Delman Black."

Stas wasn't smiling. "Shit, I know him."

FORTY-TWO

It was sprinkling when Stas pulled into the Second Set lot. He parked and hurried toward the entrance, passing two scantily clad young women in their mid-twenties. Their skirts were short; their midriffs bare, and their attitudes a little sullen as they tried to get the top up on their red Miata.

Stas slowed. One lady switched from tugging at the canvas top to tugging at a skirt that barely covered a black thong. He wondered if she was advertising, shopping, or both.

"Can you give us a hand?" Her smile had morphed into something resembling a painful grimace. The dampness was straightening her hairdo, flattening her bangs into her eyes.

"I'm working, ladies, but...." He stopped, got out of his car, and gave the front frame of the top a forceful pull. As he reached up, he exposed, for a second, the Glock.

The woman on the other side of the car saw the gun. "This a cop bar?" She stopped chewing her gum long enough to follow his movements as he parked and moved to the entrance of the Second Set where he met Marlowe at the entrance of the club.

"You ready? Why didn't you come out?" Stas asked.

Marlowe stuck his hand out to feel for rain. "'Cause it's raining, and this is a new hat." He swept his hand over the nicely turned brim on his Stetson before putting it on.

"I thought those things were waterproof. You never see cowboys dodging the rain, protecting their hats."

"Yeah, I bet they never paid what I did for this one."

Both men fell into a deliberate stride.

"Thanks," the girls spoke in unison watching both detectives walk to the Mercedes.

"Who are the ladies?" Marlowe checked them as they passed the car.

"Potential badge bunnies searching for a hole.""

"Shouldn't it be the other way around?" Marlowe stopped at the car. "We need to pick up anything?"

"I got it." He pointed to a bag behind his seat. "Get in!"

Marlowe folded his frame into the passenger seat of the Mercedes. "You sure Coop is going to meet us?"

"He owes me."

"If I collected on everybody who owes me, I could call the shots from my desk and never go out on the street. Our arrest record would be close to ninety-five percent without any help from the DA's office."

"Well, I never give up on them and that 'milk of human kindness'." Stas started the car.

"Who said that?" Marlowe asked.

"The Captain, think he borrowed it from Will Shakespeare."

Marlowe looked out the window. "Where we going?"

"The Clairmore."

Marlowe looked over at the speedometer as Stas sped through rain slick streets. "Who hooked you up, Vice?"

"Not really." Stas ran a yellow light just turning red.

"You know the girl he's with?"

"Sorta."

"Is that going to be a problem?"

"Not if we're cool and fast. All he has to do is sign, and we're out of there."

"Getting out is one thing, but how are we getting in."

Stas patted his jacket pocket. "I got the key."

"When do you plan to serve it?"

"Bright and early in the morning."

"All this because of a damn dog!"

A block from the Clairmore, Stas did a wide U turn in front of a Starbucks', cut the engine, and waited for Assistant D.A.

William Cooper who watched from a window. When he recognized the Mercedes, he exited the popular coffee shop carrying a tall paper cup of steaming coffee.

"You're not turning me into some damn pretzel. We'll go in my car." He turned and led the way to a black Lexus parked down the street. You pull in when I pull out.

Marlowe slid into the back seat behind Coop and arranged his hat on the seat next to him. "You been waiting long?"

"Long enough to get a coffee and check things out."

"Coop, a man forever on the prowl." Stas fastened his seat belt as Copper got underway.

"When we get to the hotel, you'd better stand back in the shadows dressed like that," Marlowe said.

Cooper, wearing black jeans and a black crew neck sweater, looked at the detective through his rear view mirror. I got a jacket and shirt in the trunk."

The Clairmore was located on a side street off Sunset on the western edge of Hollywood. It had undergone many changes since its heyday during the '30's and '40's. Now it was a combination of offices, condos, and residential suites/mini-hotel that occupied the top three floors with security that was both ample and discreet.

Coop slowly rolled down the drive to the subterranean parking structure. Stas handed him the plastic keycard that the ADA slid into the black slot. There was a loud metallic clank, as the gate rolled up. They parked in a space near a door marked "Stairs." The three men got out of the car. Cooper popped his trunk and changed into a white shirt and dark suit jacket. Once changed, he led the way.

"I'm not putting on a tie. We're not going to his courtroom." He tried the handle. "Locked."

Stas walked to the elevator and turned the brass key in a slot above the up button. They waited for what seemed like an eternity in the dimly lit garage.

"How'd you get all this shit?" Marlowe asked. "Don't tell me, somebody owed you."

Stas didn't answer as the brown metal doors opened revealing an interior of walnut paneling and beveled floor-to-ceiling mirrors. Like three studs on a cock walk, they examined their reflections before turning to face the closing doors. Stas punched 10 on the panel.

He ran his fingers through his hair, smoothing it as best he could. He felt stubble on his chin. "Maybe I should've gone home, shaved, and changed." Stas spoke more to his reflection in the mirror than to his companions.

"You should keep a razor at her place." Marlowe did not turn to see any reaction. If he had, he would have seen the icy glare that matched Stas's cold, gray eyes.

They rode up in silence. When they reached the tenth floor, they stepped out into a quiet corridor decorated in subdued purple with accents of olive and gold. Their shoes sank into deep, plush carpet that complimented the colors on the walls. They watched the numbers as they moved slowly down the hallway finally stopping at suite 1041.

Marlowe moved in closer and tried to whisper. "How are we going to do this?"

"Coop is going to ask him to sign the warrant. If he asks any questions, we'll answer." Stas spoke *sotto voce*.

Cooper took the warrant from his inside jacket pocket. "Let's pray he's not in the middle of something."

"Better yet, let's pray he is and wants to hurry back to it. We'll thank him and get the hell out of here." Stas stood poised to ring the tiny gilded button located next to the door frame.

"Suppose he asks us how we knew he was here?" Marlowe asked.

"Then I'll make up some outrageous lie. If you were up here getting it on with someone whose only job is to make your fantasy a reality, would you want to stand around jawing with us? I don't think so." Stas pressed the buzzer and stood aside.

Cooper was left standing in front of the viewer.

After a minute, a husky voice from the other side of the door asked. "Who is it?"

The ADA cleared his throat in an effort to alleviate any nervousness in his voice. "It's William Cooper from the DA's office. We have a warrant for your signature. It's, ugh, urgent."

"Shit! Who's with you?" The judge coughed.

"Detectives Marlowe and Nowak," Cooper added.

There was a female laugh from the other side as the dead bolt disengaged, and the door opened slightly. The security chain remained engaged. "Show me some ID." A hairy hand reached through the space.

Cooper and Stas held their IDs at what they thought would be eye level. The door closed enough to let the Judge remove the chain, then it opened about a foot, revealing a short, robust man with a chest of silvery mane. No one dared look past the chest to what was beyond.

"Give me the fucking warrant."

"Yes, sir." Cooper handed it over along with his uncapped black and gold Mont Blanc pen.

The judge snatched everything, almost dropping the pen, and signed the warrant against the inside wall. When he returned the paper work and pen to Cooper, he squinted at Stas. "Don't I know you? You used to work Vice." He kept his eyes on the detective.

"Yes, sir." Stas moved farther into the hallway. "Thank you, sir. Have a good night."

The door slammed. "Goddamn Vice. Got informants everywhere... always have ways of finding you."

They heard the chain being replaced.

"Come on to bed, baby," a purring voice invited.

Even in its most seductive mode, Stas recognized Dar Ling's voice.

Marlowe had started down the corridor then turned. "Man, you got some balls."

Stas smiled. "Enough to get this puppy signed."

By the time the three men reached the elevator, they were having a difficult time keeping it together. Once in the elevator, a roar of laughter broke out. By the time they reached the garage, they were almost bent over in tears.

"Have a good night, sir," Cooper parroted.

"Damn right! I had to let him know it wasn't personal," Stas said.

In the car, Marlowe moved his hat over so he wouldn't sit on it. "Let me buy you guys a drink. See if those damsels in distress are still at the bar and looking for some of LA's finest."

"I can't. I got to get some sleep. We need to serve this," Stas patted his jacket pocket. "First thing in the morning."

FORTY-THREE

Jonson and Edwards both drove their assigned Crown Vics to the Talbott estate. The four detectives were met by two black-and-whites outside the gate.

"What are we looking for, specifically?" Jonson asked as they huddled together waiting for directions.

"Anything that might prove that someone here had contact with any of the victims. I want hair, everybody's hair, any evidence of drug usage, especially heroin. Also look for dog hair, pieces of a dog blanket, make-up smocks, modeling photos, head shots, postcards from tourist sites, especially Europe. If you're not sure, ask me." Stas ran his fingers through his hair and tried to think if he had forgotten anything.

"Postcards?" Marlowe questioned, his hand poised at the buzzer on the intercom.

"Someone sent Cyndi's grandmother postcards over a period of seven years. Some of them were postmarked from cities on the East Coast. There was even one from Paris," Stas said.

Marlowe pressed the bell.

The voice that came through was definitely not Hispanic or American. "Whoever you be, we not buying no-ting, we does not want a ting."

"Lady, we're from LAPD. We're here to serve a warrant," the detective added.

"LA who?" The voice had a musical lilt to it.

"Los Angeles Police Department, ma'am." Jonson moved next to the intercom and raised his voice. "We're here to serve a warrant."

Marlowe looked at his partner. "She's not deaf. She's West Indian."

"Police? There be no-body at home."

"Listen, miss, you're here. Open the gate. You want to obstruct justice?" Marlowe seemed to get irritated.

The voice now came back with a pitch of excitement. "I do not obstruct no-ting, but ...."

"Open the gate!" Marlowe and Jonson shouted in unison.

The iron gate swung slowly inward. A tall black woman with almond shaped brown eyes, a smooth complexion the color of cafe au lait, and short black hair done up neatly in twists stood with her hands on her hips. She smiled slowly and sized up Marlowe.

He was the first one at the entrance. "You the new housekeeper?" he asked.

"Yes. Now let me see someting that tell me who you are." She didn't move until IDs had been produced and checked. "So what you goin' to do?"

"We're going to search the place. What's your name?" Marlowe asked.

"Dahlia."

"Like the Black Dahlia?" Jonson put away his ID and strained to get a better look pass the entry into the living room. "Where are the Talbotts?"

"Missus took the girls to school, then she runs." Dahlia turned to go back into the house, leaving the double doors open for the last uniformed cop to close.

"Dahlia!" Stas called as she headed toward the kitchen. "Where did you get your dress?"

She looked down at the fading print. "She don't furnish no uniform, and I ain't mucking 'round in the house in me good clothes. There be a whole bunch in a closet downstairs. So I use this one, thought they might be like uniforms."

"Has Mrs. Talbott seen you in it."

"No, I found them after she leave."

"When we finish, can you show one of us this closet?" Stas asked.

"No problem." Dahlia continued on to the kitchen while the detectives, almost in unison, slipped on their latex gloves.

Stas called after her again. "Dahlia, where's the dog?"

"Oh, I set her straight right off. I don't clean up for no animals. Her friend come take her away."

"A man?"

"Yes, and he a little too *fa-mil-liar* around here to suit me." She didn't expand but went on to the kitchen.

"Since I don't know what the hell you're really looking for, I'll take downstairs. Jonson, check the basement." Marlowe turned to the uniformed cops. "Check the dog run. Get some hair samples from the run and don't step in any dog shit. See if there's a blanket or a piece of one. Stas, since you and Edwards have been here before, you guys do the upstairs."

Edwards made a stop at the coffee table and helped himself to chocolates, unwrapping the little gold foil and jamming two into his mouth before slipping a handful into his jacket pocket.

"Come on, Edwards." Stas headed for the wide staircase. "Stop stuffing your face." He didn't wait for his partner. Before he reached the landing, he looked up. There was a long iron table topped with a gleaming slab of white Carrara marble. A gorgeous arrangement of flowers stood in the center. Stas recognized roses and lilies, but the rest of the foliage was unfamiliar, and the brilliant colors and scents were almost overwhelming to his senses. Remembering what he had paid for Dina's flowers, he wondered how much a display like that cost and why someone would spend the money to only have the flowers die in a couple of days.

Above the floral array was another painting of the late Mrs. Talbott wearing a gown that shimmered as it caught some unseen light. Stas moved closer, drawn to the woman, yet repelled by the floral scents doing battle with each other. The heady essence seemed to engulf the woman like an aura. Her undraped arms seemed longer than normal. The visible bone structure was unusually delicate, and her stance projected a refinement that Stas had rarely seem. The full length painting reminded him of those he had seen in Polish museums when he was there on vacation five years earlier.

He realized that such women not only existed, but there were also women who tried to emulate the look found in those portraits: copying the hair style, make-up, jewels, and expensive clothes. He stepped back and gave the painting a long look, then briefly contrasted the late Mrs. Talbott with the earthy reality of women like Dina. He spun around on the landing, almost colliding with his partner coming up the stairs.

"Take a look at that." Stas pointed to the painting.

Edwards looked briefly but didn't stop. Instead, he popped another chocolate into his mouth. "Looks like the one in the living room." A brown web had collected in the corner of his mouth.

"Wipe your mouth." Stas called back taking the rest of the stairs two at a time. At the top he stopped at the open gilded railing that overlooked a part of the living room, then moved on to the first child's room where Edwards waited.

Stas pulled several small evidence bags from his jacket pocket. "For hair samples."

Edwards took one of the proffered bags. "Are you sure we're not going beyond the scope of the warrant?"

"This is a cold case. We're not going to find blood spatters or fingerprints, so we have to include everything that might be relevant. That includes hair samples. I want to find out who the children's father is."

"Well, I don't know." Edwards hesitated, then moved into the connecting bathroom between the two bedrooms.

"Just get the samples, Sid."

"Do you want the toothbrushes?"

"Hair should do it." Stas left his partner bagging strands of hair pulled from hair brushes. "Make sure you don't mix the hair." He watched his partner for a few minutes, then moved down the hall to the master suite.

The room was large with white walls and high ceilings framed by deep crown molding. The furniture was a cold antique white, and white plantation shutters were open emitting streams of sunlight yet did nothing to warm the atmosphere of the room. There was little evidence of a couple sharing what should have been an intimate space. This was Mona's domain.

The bed seemed massive with white silken covers thrown half over its foot. Clothes were strewn about. A fifty-inch plasma TV hung over a triple dresser and faced the bed. Stas found the remote near one of the many pillows piled against the headboard. He stood by the night stand and turned on the TV, curious to see what channel Mona watched at night or in the early morning. Three briefly clad, shapely young woman were still going through their exercise routines on the large screen. He switched off the set and moved across the room.

He kicked a white lacy bra out of his way, disentangling his shoe from the straps. At her desk, his attention was drawn to an oil portrait, in a style almost identical to the one hanging over the mantel. There was something about the lighting and brush strokes that looked familiar. Moving the desk back from the wall and getting closer for a look at the signature, he saw stylized initials, SB, in the right hand corner. Moving back, and concentrating on the subject, he was positive it was Elizabeth Bolton. Scott Biggars had told the detectives that he had done some paintings of his girlfriend. This must have been the one he said he sold.

Stas wished for a magnifying glass, wanting to examine every detail. It was uncanny how much Elizabeth looked like Mona. Now he had a connection between Scott, Liz, and Mona. They were going to have to pay Scott another visit.

Standing on the desk chair, he was able to remove the painting from its hook. After pushing the faux Louis XIV chair back to its precise place, he sat and started going through the three drawers. The middle one yielded only jumbo paper clips, a business envelope with an assortment of rubber bands, a few loose birthday and get-well cards, plus, loose 33-cent and 20-

cent postage stamps. There were seven blank postcards from New York, Milan, Paris, New Orleans before Katrina, Chicago, San Francisco, and London in the back of the bottom drawer. The cards were blank: no message, no addressee, no stamps.

The top right hand drawer held a hodgepodge of local business cards and appointment cards. He held out one of interest, a Beverly Hills colorist. So Mona's blonde tresses were not necessarily the ones Mother Nature had given her. He dropped the card along with the postcards into a bag and slipped it in his pocket, then looked through the dresser, lifting sports bras and lacy underwear, yet nothing gave off any aura of sensuality. He imagined Dina and her array of sexy lingerie. *Better hold that thought 'til later.* He found nothing else of interest.

The walk-in closet was the size of some track homes' bedrooms. Mona's wardrobe was dichromatic with the whites hanging on one side, the blacks on another. He moved them along the rod, going through the pockets and handbags. The shoes hung in canvas pocketed slots. Again Stas came up empty with anything else of interest.

The counter in the bathroom contained an array of jars and bottles of various crèmes and sprays. Before going through the drawers, he bagged some strands of blonde hair from a brush left on the counter. The first drawer held make-up, an assortment of brushes, and unused sponge triangles. Another deep drawer of feminine products made him wonder if she was barren or sterile by choice. He found no birth control pills or condoms in any of the cabinets. There was a bottle of Astro-glide but no sign of sex toys. He was surprised to find a short smock in the same pattern of the ones worn by the dead women hanging on a hook behind the bathroom door.

Stas returned to the bedroom, picked up the painting, and headed for the staircase.

Edwards and Jonson were standing in the doorway of another room.

"You'd better come take a look," Edwards said.

Stas followed his partner into a large walk-in closet that he would have died for. He touched the wood that lined the walls and ceiling. Cedar. The drawers of the built-in dresser were constructed of the same material. "What is this?"

Jonson ran his fingers nimbly over the dresser top. "Never seen anything like it, but I bet it cost a fortune."

Stas inhaled deeply picking up a subtle hint of cedar.

Edwards pushed back several suits and pulled out a black suit bag. Blackwood's in large gold letters was printed across the upper quarter of the zippered bag. "There're a couple more. You want us to bring them?"

Stas looked around catching a glimpse of a glossy black bag near the neatly racked shoes. He paused for a second, distracted by the professional shine and the cedar tree in each shoe, then reached for the black bag. It was identical to the one he'd gotten from Blackwood's. There was a black gift card attached to the handles that read: 'Happy Birthday, dear'

"What's that?" Jonson moved in closer.

Stas showed him the card and the contents of the bag. Two shirts were still wrapped in black and gold tissue. "We'll take these. If she bought these, there's our connection to the store and maybe the dumpster out back."

"Couldn't Ryan have shopped at Blackwood's?" Edwards looked in the bag.

"He could, but I don't think he's writing notes to himself and calling himself, 'dear'" Stas caught a whiff of citrus and bay rum. He looked from Jonson to Edwards. "What's that smell?'

Jonson brushed his nose. "Your partner went sampling."

"Find *anything* else interesting?" Stas asked.

"You've seen it. Clothes, shoes, and more clothes. Found a box where he keeps his stash, but nothing's in it, just a few stems. I don't think he sleeps here much. Everything's in order: no dust, clothes picked up, bed made, dry toothbrush, clean electric razor. The towels looked like they haven't been used."

Jonson pulled off his latex gloves and stuffed them in his pocket. "Oh, yeah, there's a safe behind a print."

"Another woman?" Stas asked.

"No, a really nice picture of Miles Davis with his horn. Otherwise, no porn, straight or gay, no condoms. Like I said, I don't think he spends much time here, plus he seems to travel a lot." Jonson held out a brown 5 x 10 accordion document case. "He keeps his travel docs and receipts in this."

"Take that too." Stas handed the black bag to Jonson. "We can check where he's been going for the last six or seven years."

"It shouldn't be too hard. He's been using the same travel agent over in Glendale." Jonson was about to hand the pouch to Stas but saw him pick up the painting. "Mrs. Talbott?"

Stas held it up for Jonson to get a better look. "I'm pretty sure it's one of the vics. They all look so much alike, but I think that's the primary connection."

"Mrs. Talbott's lucky. Someone could have kidnapped her." Jonson suggested.

"I don't think so...." Stas left the rest unsaid, as if that thought was interrupted by another. "Did you see any photos or paintings of the girls?"

"That is strange. There's nothing, not even a school picture, but their rooms are decorated with feathered masks and beads. Seems somebody's been to New Orleans." Jonson headed for the stairs.

"I hope before Katrina," Stas said. "I guess we're finished up here." Downstairs they found Marlowe in the entry hall talking with Dahlia.

"She vex me you know, and now she call. She comin', and she hoppin' mad."

Stas rested the painting against the hall console and looked at Marlowe's Trader Joe's bag.

"It's one of the dresses. There's a box of 'em downstairs. I just took one."

One of the uniformed officers had gone. Edwards had walked back into the living room to help himself to more chocolates. Stas started to fill out a receipt for the painting when one of the front double doors that had been left ajar flew open.

Mona almost sprinted into the house coming face to face with Stas. Her makeup had been sweated away leaving a face pinched and reddened with anger. He stood tall, his pen poised. The other detectives stood at a distance waiting for the confrontation.

"Why are you here?" Mona screamed.

"Serving a warrant," Stas replied.

"A what?" She looked at the other officers.

"We're here serving a search warrant." He smiled.

"What right? Why?"

Stas moved closer, challenging, getting in her face.

She backed off and looked down at the painting. "Why are you taking this?"

"It's evidence in a murder investigation. I've written you a receipt." He held out the completed form.

"I don't want your fucking receipt." Her lip quivered as she snatched the paper, crumbled it into a ball, and threw it back at Stas. It bounced off his chest and fell to the floor.

She grabbed for the painting. He clamped down on her wrist, restraining her. With her free hand, she lashed out, her red talons poised to rake across his face. Anticipating her move, he parried, gripping the other wrist. Her eyes blinked in startled realization, even as she strained to pull away, he held her in an iron grip. She looked into his cold, gray eyes, then he smiled, slightly, almost daring her to try another maneuver.

She pulled hard, trying to free her hands. Mona raised her foot, aiming her knee at his groin. Stas twisted her half around keeping her off balance and her nails out of his face. She tried to resist but gave in when Stas called to the uniform officer in the doorway.

"Cuff her and don't forget to Mirandize her."

She jerked again as if Stas had instructed the officer to brutalize her in some new diabolical way. "Why are you doing this to me? You bastards." Spittle sprayed with her expletive but missed the cop.

"For assault, Mrs. Talbott." Stas released her after the cuffs had been secured.

Her muscles relaxed as she allowed herself to be led away.

Edwards watched Mona Talbott's departure from his vantage point in the entry hall. "You did that on purpose."

"Did what, Sid?" There was a trace of sarcasm in his tone.

"You, you made her mad, that's why she kicked you. You know it won't stick."

"It'll stick long enough for my purpose."

Marlowe moved towards the door left open by the departing policeman and Mrs. Talbott. "Dahlia will stay here with the kids after school."

"Where's the husband?" Stas asked.

"She hasn't seen him for two days. She'll call him and tell him what's going on. She doesn't want to stay the night if she can help it."

Later, after Mona Talbott had been booked, she was taken to an interview room where Stas and Edwards waited with her.

Mona eased herself into one of the hard wooden chairs and seemed to draw herself inwards as she kept her eyes on the door. She didn't have to wait long. It swung open with a flourish.

"Detectives, have you lost your collective minds or is this still another example of police incompetence?"

Edwards recoiled. "Who are you?"

A business card appeared as if magically drawn from his well-tailored suit sleeve. "Boston Satler. Do you desire to continue in this line of work at this unhallowed institution, or do you want to join some of your overzealous colleagues on the street or in prison?"

"We're investigating a murder," Edwards offered.

Stas remained silent since his partner seemed to want to take the lead.

"I'm well aware that three women have been brutally murdered, and I'm sorry, but all you have is a carton of make-up smocks that Mrs. Talbott obtained from the previous owner of their modeling agency. Why don't you haul Mrs. Gaines in and twist her poor wrists? You are all a bunch of sadists." Sadler took a breath. "And what do you hope to do with her painting?"

Stas finally spoke. "It was a portrait of the second victim." His cold tone implied he would not be bullied, especially by some slick Eastern lawyer named Boston.

Sadler turned. "Purely coincidence. If you arrested everyone who had a picture of some murder victim, you wouldn't have room in jail for the real criminals."

Edwards nodded in agreement.

"So if that's all you have, I think I can take Mrs. Talbott home. After all, she's a mother with young children. I shall note all of this when I file my complaint. I had hoped with the new Chief, that the Los Angeles police was finally shedding its warrior cop mentality. You can't brutalize a woman and expect to get away with it."

A sound of anger started deep in Stas's throat but materialized as a cough. "But there's the question of assault."

"You provoked her!" Another card flashed as if by magic. "When I spoke with..." he looked at the card, Detective Edwards in the corridor, "he said that my client reacted when you provoked her."

Stas looked from Sadler to his partner. "I've never been called a warrior or a rogue in my career, and I resent it. Plus, Detective Edwards wouldn't know provocation if it bit him in the..." He rose and left the room.

FORTY-FOUR

It was late when Stas left downtown. Even with the encounter with Mona Talbott and her attorney, he felt buoyed. He had gone back to the property room and, after presenting ID, filled out the paper work to check-out her belongings. He already had the fake diamond ring in a coin envelope and quickly made the exchange with an exact replica of Mona's ring provided by the insurance company. If she ever noticed the switch, she couldn't complain without implicating herself in at least one murder.

Mark Guzman, the adjustor, and Al Swain, gem expert, at the Fountain Insurance Company, had first met with Stas when he inquired about the diamond ring and the insurance. They had discussed the ring's recovery.

When Guzman left the detective and Swain alone in a small conference room, it was Swain who broached the subject of finding who really had the ring. It was as if he could read Stas's mind.

"What do you do if you find someone in possession of the ring but there's no evidence of how the ring came into their possession? There must be other means of recovery."

Stas stared blankly at Swain. "I don't understand?"

"I'll be candid with you. We insure lots of jewelry worth a great deal more than we paid out to Mr. Wright. But whether a loss is big or small, they all add up. I have something to show you." Swain took two ring boxes, one black and one blue from his pocket and raised the lids. The rings were exquisite.

Stas had never seen anything so beautiful, except on Mona's finger.

"Detective, can you tell me which ring is worth thirty grand?" Swain paused and pushed both boxes toward Stas. "And which one is fake?"

Stas looked long and hard. "I don't have a clue?"

"And neither does the wearer. I think you know where the real ring is. I know police procedure, and I know you can't just take the ring from the person who has it, but if there is any way during your investigation you could make a switch. I could give you an exact copy. No one could tell the difference with his naked eye. Well, frankly, I could care less, because if a jeweler did examine the fake, all he would discover is that the owner had good taste in buying paste."

"Well, I don't know. I need to think about this, ask my Captain." Stas lied. He wasn't going to ask anyone. If he decided to make the switch, it would be on him. After all, cops lied and played tricks all the time. He reasoned that cops had to always be one step ahead of the criminal element.

Before the switch, Stas looked at the fake from every imagined angle but could see nothing to indicate it wasn't the real thing. It shone brilliantly. After the switch he waited to hear from Mr. Swain who had authenticated the stone by its almost invisible numbers engraved on the diamond. The ring was indeed Jessica Wright's. The detectives now had an important piece of evidence. Yet possession of the ring did not prove that Mona had committed the three homicides. And how was Stas going to explain to the Captain how he obtained a ring to make the exchange in the first place. He had to step gingerly, for he was in deep departmental shit.

Well, an evening with Dina always took the edge off whatever he was doing. He was starting to enjoy quiet evenings in front of the TV. His concern now was the DNA from the Talbott girls. Stas was anxious to see if the senior Talbott had fathered the oldest girl. Well, I'll worry about all that later.

He went home shaved, showered, and changed. On his way to Hollywood, he picked up some Chinese. When he unlocked the door to her apartment, he was aware of a new scent perfuming the air. There were several candles burning on the far end of the dining table and a large one burning on the coffee table.

"Dina?" He took his bag of take-out to the kitchen and looked at the clock on the stove. It was 11:37 p.m.

When he turned, she was standing in the doorway of the kitchen, a long purple silk nightgown clinging to some of the damp surfaces of her skin that she had missed drying. Her scent seemed suspended like an aura as she moved into the kitchen. It always awakened his own senses, at times magnifying one hunger, diminishing another. He felt a quickening pulse, a surge of warmth.

She looked into the bag. "I'd given up on you."

He ignored the food, drawing close enough to smell her damp hair and run his hand slowly over her hip.

She pushed the bag aside but left his hand to roam over her waist and up to her breasts. "Aren't you going to eat?"

"Maybe later."

Stas sat on the side of the bed in his boxer briefs stuffing his neatly folded socks into his shoes.

"You're in a good mood tonight." Dina knelt behind him, kneading his bare shoulders. "Not so tense."

"Things are starting to come together on the case. We just might break it pretty soon." He leaned over and placed his shoes on the floor and slipped off his briefs. "I've been thinking about you all day." He swung around onto the bed, bringing her to him and easing the gown off.

She looked down at his nude body and smiled. "You went around like this all day?"

A low throaty moan was punctuated by a ring that seemed to come from some place in another sphere. Another moan, a ring, a cry of desperation as Dina clutched Stas's shoulders to force him to continue as she neared her peak. But all movement ceased when he reached for the phone on the third ring. He collapsed and rolled off Dina as a deep baritone voice completed its message.

"It was good seeing you, Dina. Maybe we'll run into each other sometime. I'm going to be in the area for a while. Thank Dar Ling for giving me your number. She really is a dear. Ciao!"

"Don't, don't turn on the light." There was anger, hurt, frustration in her voice.

Stas rose and collected his clothes from the chair and went into the bathroom, leaving the door ajar. Switching on the light, he dressed. "How did he get this number?"

Dina threw a towel to the floor and pulled the covers over her nakedness. "You heard him, from Dar Ling, I guess. She told me he called the agency the night we went to Neil's."

"And you didn't tell me?"

"I didn't think he'd call. He knew I was with you. I wasn't interested."

Stas stood in the doorway of the bathroom, the light creating a backlight to his frame. "Dina, change your number."

"I was going to...."

"Why didn't you."

She sighed. "I called, but.... Why must I always be the one to make the changes."

"Because that's the way it has to be."

"By whose decree, LAPD?"

"By mine!" He switched the light off and stood in the darkness at the foot of the bed.

"Why, so I can be your part-time whore, sometime girlfriend. Stas, you can't have it your way all the time."

He moved to the night stand and fumbled in the dark for his keys and wallet. He picked up his shoes and socks and carried them to the living room where he sat to put them on. When he finished, he grabbed his jacket and closed, as gently as possible, the door to the apartment.

Dina rolled to her side and buried her head in her pillow but did not cry. "Fuck you, Stas Nowak!"

FORTY-FIVE

There was no Chopin in the freezer. There was no Chopin under the sink. Stas stood in the middle of the kitchen trying to think where he had put the extra bottle. His mind was a blank. He returned to the car and got the pack of Marlboros from his glove compartment. There were no matches so he lit the cigarette from the burner on the stove almost singeing his eyebrows in the process. He inhaled, slowly drawing the smoke into his lungs. What he needed was a drink. Then he remembered putting two fifths in the back of his closet.

He flicked what was left of his smoke into the sink, grabbed a glass, and headed for his bedroom. The room was cold. The bed would be even colder, and he knew from experience that the vodka, no matter how much he consumed, could not provide the physical solace that Dina's soft, warm body could. Still he took the bottle to bed with him, filling the glass on the night stand before stripping and getting under the down comforter. He took his time and sipped, replaying what had unfolded at Dina's and wondering if she would call. His last thought, as he drifted into a dreamless sleep was, should I?

The next morning Stas awoke early and realized it was Saturday. Marlowe was having his monthly poker party. This was the first time that he and Edwards had been invited. Stas went back to bed and slept until 12:15 p.m. When he got up, he glanced at his answering machine. There was no red light blinking.

After tidying the apartment, he took two suits and five shirts to the cleaners, got a haircut, then went to the bank. He checked his machine again when he returned home, nothing. He doubted Dina would call, so he dressed and bagged the two bottles of Chopin. One was three-quarters full; the other hadn't been opened. Marlowe said to bring your own. If the poker didn't distract him, the vodka should ease him slowly into a state of oblivion.

Amanda stalked Whole Foods almost everyday looking for Stas. The hope of sighting him had become an obsession. She parked by Barnes and Noble then walked over to the market on the lookout for his black Mercedes. She started when she saw him get out of his car near the entrance. He usually parked at the northwest side of the lot. Amanda had to rush to pick up a few items, enough that she could have managed on a bus to Pasadena.

Dodging behind displays of vitamins and face creams, she watched his movements. He selected several bottles of wine before heading for the takeout counter, where he ordered. Stas seemed in a hurry, checking his watch while they heated then boxed several slices of pizza. While he waited, she took her cart to check-out, looking over her shoulder, keeping him in sight.

She carried her bag outside, took her phone out of her pocket, and waited, but there he was.

Her bag tipped over. "Stas! What a surprise! You've missed class."

"Hello, Amanda." His greeting was cold as he headed to his car.

She picked up her bag and followed, double stepping to keep up with his long strides. "Stas!" She called after him.

He turned. The car beeped.

She still held her phone out. "Can you do me a really big favor, just this once. My car's in the shop and my ride...."

"Get in!" He put his bag behind his seat, ignoring his hunger and the pizza.

He didn't come around to open the door. She climbed into the front seat, glad her bag was light resting there on her lap.

"You know where I live?"

"Not really." He eased the car out into the northbound traffic on Glendale Boulevard.

"On Euclid, in Pasadena. You remember?"

"Give me directions when we get on the freeway."

"We've missed you in class." Amanda tried to turn towards Stas.

"I've been busy, plus I really couldn't get into writing about my inner whatever." He pushed a button on the car stereo filling the interior with the sound of strings and oboe.

Distracted by the music, she was finding it impossible to think out her next move.

He exited the freeway at Orange Grove, made a right, then a left on Del Mar.

He does remember, she thought.

"What's the number?"

She told him. He maneuvered into a narrow space about ten feet from her walkway. Amanda struggled with opening the door and locked herself in instead. Stas came around and opened it, taking her bag while she climbed out.

"Here, I'll get it."

She smiled and walked ahead of him. At the cottage, as if on cue, Amanda tripped, falling across the first of three steps. He didn't see her hand move into a bed of orange, pink, and white begonias for a piece of glass. But her scream brought him to her side.

"You okay?"

"I cut my hand." She reached for him getting blood on his shirt front.

He didn't seem to notice. "Where's your key?" Stas picked up her purse, opened it, and rummaged inside, then took out his handkerchief from his pocket to wrap her bleeding hand.

She indicated a key on a large key ring, and he unlocked the door.

"You got a first aid kit?"

"In the bathroom." She led the way and nodded to the medicine cabinet.

Stas took her hand and held it under the faucet, gently washing it, then opening the kit, he started to unwind gauze and looked around. "Scissors?"

Amanda lowered the lid on the toilet and collapsed on it. "In the kitchen."

"You gonna be all right?"

"I just felt a little faint."

He went to the kitchen, grabbed scissors from the cutlery block, and returned to the bathroom. He found Amanda leaning over the basin and more blood seeping through the loose gauge. He cut new gauze and tape, affixing several strips to the sink's edge. Amanda reached for him as she tried to stand.

"Damn!" He tried to steady her, easing her back to sit. "Do you want me to call the paramedics, take you over to Huntington?"

"No, no. I'm starting to feel much better." She gave him a smile. "See."

He returned the gauze and tape to the box, putting it back on the shelf in the medicine cabinet. "The bleeding's almost stopped. I think you'll be okay. Stay put for a while. You don't want to pass out." He took the scissors. "I'll put your groceries in the kitchen and let myself out."

"Stas, thanks so much."

"No problem. It's really just a surface cut. Glad I was able to help."

She nodded. "You'll never know how much."

After hearing the front door close, Amanda got up and took a white undershirt and Fruit-of-the-Loom briefs from the clothes hamper, placing them in the sink. She reached beside the toilet, retrieving Stas's handkerchief, wet it, and blotted blood on the two pieces of underwear.

She spent the next hour banging into the door jam and hitting herself. The most damage was done by a cast-iron pot. With it, she hit her left arm and the left side of her face and lip. By evening she was black and blue in what she thought were the right places. She then smashed a small lamp she'd bought at Goodwill, cleaned up some of the debris, then dialed Tanya.

"Hello."

"This, this is Amanda." She broke into weak sobs.

"Amanda! What's wrong?"

"Can you come over? Stas went crazy, smashed my stuff." She paused. "He beat me."

"Oh, my God! I'll be right over!"

Amanda hung up, unlocked the front door, and got into bed.

Marlowe lived off Los Flores in Altadena. It was an older established neighborhood with large gnarled oaks that, in places, hung over the road, forming a canopy of joining branches. There were no sidewalks so Stas parked next to a large bush that extended several feet into the street. He recognized Smart's van and Jonson's SUV parked closer to their host's house.

Stas was late. After being side-tracked by Amanda, he'd driven back to Glendale to change. He didn't see Edwards' car, unless Jill had taken it for the ladies' night out.

Too lazy to lock his gun in the trunk, he shoved it under the driver's seat, and grabbed a Whole Foods bag from the passenger seat. Engaging the car's alarm, he looked towards Marlowe's house. The porch light was off, but it seemed every light in the house was on.

The front door was open, so he went in without knocking and put the wine he'd purchased for his partner along with the new Chopin on a card table in the living room and took the open bottle with him to the dining room where the guys had taken their seats.

John Smart was dragging one of the side chairs out of his way so that he could maneuver his motorized wheelchair to the table. Smart was ex-LAPD who had caught a .45 slug in his spine and was paralyzed from the waist down. Since going on disability, he had outfitted a large van with everything but a round satin bed and a mirror on the ceiling. After the shooting five years ago, his wife had left him, but that didn't seem to deter him from making it with the ladies. It was even rumored that Smart had a three year old love child. Despite his handicap he stayed fit and could be the life of any party or bar.

Jonson sat next to Smart. Stas took the seat next to him, putting his bottle underneath. Marlowe, a green visor shading his eyes and a stained chef's apron covering his front, stood in the doorway between the dining room and the kitchen wiping his hands on a napkin. "Glad you could finally make it, Nowak. Ribs and chicken in the kitchen. Barbara made potato salad. Luz brought some kind of bean salad."

"Three beans." Jonson stacked white, blue, and red chips on the green felt table covering, then looked up at Stas. "You got to buy your chips from the bank."

Stas pulled three, crisp hundred dollar bills from his wallet. "Who's the bank?"

"I am." Edwards walked out of the kitchen with a bottle of Sam Adams in his hand. He sat opposite his partner.

"I thought you weren't coming." Stas handed him the money.

"I changed my mind." He started to count chips from a box on the side board.

Jonson laughed. "You mean Jill changed your mind."

Stas slid his chips over and started to make neat stacks. "Where are the ladies?"

"Out!" Jonson replied.

"We don't know where." Edwards added. He didn't seem pleased with the prospect that his wife might have a good time with the girls.

When Marlowe passed Stas a glass after he motioned for one, he poured about four fingers from his bottle and put it back under his seat. The game finally got underway. The host briefly reviewed the game rules since Stas and Edwards were new to Marlowe's poker nights.

"The dealer bottom passes to the left. The little blind is five dollars. The big blind is ten," Marlowe explained.

"What's the difference?" Edwards asked.

"A blind is the same as the ante, but you pay it in two steps, that's all," Smart said. He was the first to get the deal. The blinds were placed in the center of the table, and he dealt everyone two cards face down.

Edwards peered at his cards then fingered his chips. Marlowe folded. Stas threw his two cards in and sipped from his drink. Jonson loudly toyed with his chips as he dropped them on top of each other, spilling some over onto the table.

"Jonson!" Smart was ready to deal the flop.

"What?"

"Stop playing with the damn chips. It's annoying."

"You nervous?" Jonson asked Edwards as he kept peering at his hole cards.

"Yeah!" Edwards threw in his cards.

Jonson pulled in the ante and rearranged his chips.

The play went on for several hours. Jonson had the early lead. Edwards was second and looked over at his partner, seeming to enjoy having more chips than Stas.

"I need to take a piss and have a smoke." Smart rolled away from the table.

"In that order?" Marlowe asked. "The bathroom's down the hall. Take your cigarette to the porch, Barbara will have a fit if she smells smoke in the house. We just had the drapes cleaned."

"You're starting to sound whipped." Stas reached down to the floor, leaned over, and emptied the bottle in his glass. "There, I didn't spill a drop."

"Can you even see your cards?" Edwards asked, patting his stack that had grown largely at his partner's expense.

"I bet I can see well enough to win my money back." Stas got up and opened the Chopin on the card table, then put it under his chair with the fallen empty. "Am I the only one drinking vodka?"

"Yeah, you're the only who drinks that hard shit." Jonson looked on disapprovingly.

Smart returned to the table. Marlowe adjusted his eye shade and started to deal. As the night advanced and the deal moved around, Jonson and Edwards continued to share the chip lead. Over the next hour Stas managed to win enough to keep himself in the game. But even with the injection of two more crisp hundred dollar bills, he still continued to lose. He stood, stretched, and looked around as if trying to focus.

"You not playing anymore?" Marlowe asked.

Stas swept his hand over his meager stack. "I might as well quit."

Jonson smiled. "You can always throw your car keys in the pot."

"You been watching too many westerns." He looked at Marlowe. "What's your partner been smoking?"

"Or the watch." Edwards drummed on the table. "I've always admired that watch."

"How always?" Marlowe questioned. "Hell, she just gave it to him for his birthday."

Edwards looked around the table. "She who?"

No one responded.

"Okay, deal me in." Stas sat and slowly slid the Tag Heuer off his wrist, placing it next to the few chips he had left.

Smart on the dealer's left threw in his chip for the small blind.

Edwards smiled confidently. "Am I the big blind?" He didn't wait for an answer but threw in four chips.

"What the hell are you doing? You know how to play." Marlowe looked at the pot and its five chips. "The big blind is ten bucks."

"Why is that? We've been making the big blind whatever we want, haven't we?" Edwards looked around the table for confirmation. "You can't make up new rules in midstream."

"Are you drunk? I haven't changed a thing, but I *can* any damn time I please, Sid. It's my house. Now take your extra chips back."

Edwards took two from the center of the table while the others put in their ante. Jonson slowly dealt everyone two hole cards. Each man took a few seconds to take cautious peeks. The first round of betting fell on Marlowe who threw in a ten dollar chip, plus a five for a raise. Stas added his three five dollar chips and toyed with the five he had left. Jonson and Smart added their chips to the pile. All eyes turned to Edwards who anxiously looked at his hole cards then picked up five chips.

"Are you raising, man?" Smart asked.

Edwards dropped in two, then dropped the extras back on his stack. Jonson took the top card and placed it on the bottom of the deck.

"Why'd you do that?" Edwards asked.

Jonson looked at the deck in his hands. "Why did I do what?"

"Put the flop card under the deck?" Edwards frowned.

"Shit, pay attention. We've been doing it all night." Jonson flipped over three cards: a king of diamonds, a seven of spades, and an ace of hearts.

Smart bet another ten.

Edwards dropped a ten dollar chip on the pile, looked around the table, then laid down another chip. "I raise you ten."

Marlowe threw his twenty in and eyed Stas's last three chips. He had enough to cover the raise.

Jonson burned another card before flipping over the turn, a five of spades. Smart bet twenty. Jonson raised it to fifty. Marlowe threw in enough chips to match the raise. All eyes turned to Stas who looked at his one chip and the Tag.

Stas picked up the watch. "Here's my fifty, and I raise you two hundred." He threw it on top of the heap of chips. "This should more than cover it. That's it. I'm all in."

"Some woman gave you this?" Edwards picked up the watch and turned it over in his hand. "What's it worth?"

"Maybe a couple grand." Smart counted out his chips and let them drop on the pile.

"Sid, put *it* back." Marlowe shoved his chips to the center of the table.

Edwards laid the watch back on top and shoved his chips to the edge of the pile.

Jonson tapped his cards. "I fold." He picked up the deck, burned the top card, then dealt the river, a six of spades.

There was a surge of energy. Even Stas felt it, and reached under his chair fumbling for his bottle.

Smart counted out his chips and moved them to the center.

Marlowe carefully counted out all but two five dollar chips. "Here, I raise you ten." He pushed everything to the center.

Little attention was paid to Marlowe. All eyes turned to Stas.

Edwards jumped up. "He's out. What can he do with one chip?" He caught a dribble of spittle with the back of his hand and wiped it on his sleeve.

Jonson chimed in. "He didn't fold. I think he has enough in that watch to cover his bet."

"Can't I raise again?" Edwards asked.

"What?" Marlowe picked up the watch. "I think he did raise, the full value of the watch. Let's see..."

"Okay, okay." Edwards sat down.

"What you got?" Jonson asked.

Smart turned over his hole cards, an ace of diamonds and a six of clubs. "Two pair, ace high."

"I guess nothing." Stas stood and flipped over his king and jack. "Two pair, king high. I got nothing."

"Ha, ha, ain't good enough, pard. I got three of a kind, ace high." Edwards threw his pair of aces defiantly on the table and poised to collect the pot.

"Hey, wait!" Smart interjected. "Marlowe's not out, is he?"

A smile formed on the host's face. Later, Jonson described the smile as wicked. Smart as diabolical. Marlowe slowly turned over an eight of spades and a four of spades.

Edwards looked at the cards, then to Jonson and Marlowe. "What the hell is that?"

Stas chuckled. "If I'm not mistaken, that's the winning hand, a straight flush." He pocketed his single chip, finished his drink, walked deliberately through the living room.

Marlowe followed. "You all right, man? I'm sorry about the watch."

"I'm okay." Stas straightened.

"You shouldn't be driving. You know this is sheriff's territory. You can stretch out in the spare room." Marlowe touched Stas's sleeve, then let his hand drop and followed the detective to the door.

Stas shouted back from the edge of the porch. "Can't say it's been fun being reamed by you bastards." He had to focus to navigate the steps. "Hey, Marlowe, turn on the fucking light before I fall and break my neck."

The porch light went on long enough for him to get to the street. At the car he fumbled with the buttons on the key pad, being extra careful not to activate the alarm. *Marlowe'll love me for that.* He tried to fit the key in the ignition and missed. *Shit, glad you're not my woman. She'd be out of luck tonight.* The keys fell to the carpet. Stas groaned as he fished for them, feeling his gun instead. He let the seat back, stretched out, closed his eyes, and thought of Dina.

The vibrations of the loud bass in the passing car jarred Stas awake. The *BOOM, BOOM* of the music ceased right after it passed his car. He opened his eyes and looked out to see a low riding Honda Civic pull over into shadows across from Smart's van. He felt a surge of adrenaline that quickly overrode the vodka. Something was wrong.

Stas watched from his vantage point as three young men got out of the car. Two crossed the street and examined the van. One looked into the driver's side window, the other circled to the passenger side.

Out of the blue, a voice boomed at the man at the passenger door. "Hey, what the fuck you doing?" The racing wheelchair was at the door before the man could react.

"We jus checkin' it out, bro."

"We?" Smart looked around for the other half of the 'we' and was broad sided by a .38, knocking Smart and his chair to the ground. His keys jangled to the asphalt.

Marlowe's porch light went on. Several seconds later, the front door swung open, and he took his front steps two at a time, almost losing his balance when he landed in the walkway, his Glock drawn. "Get your ass away from the chair!" His voice was hard and cold. The gun was trained on the man picking up Smart's keys. "Spread and put your hands on your heads, now!" He took several quick steps moving around Smart, avoiding rocks, his back to the parked car in the shadows.

Stas had fumbled for his phone and punched in 911. He was quickly patched into the Sheriff's station in Altadena and was assured they were rolling asap. Reaching under the seat, he grabbed the Glock and quietly opened the door. He pushed off his shoes, then saw a third figure creep across the dark street. Even in the distant light from Marlowe's porch, Stas detected a glint of metal. He moved through the shadows until he was close enough to smell the third man's sweat.

"I should blow these motherfuckers off the planet." The third man waved his revolver at Marlowe, then at his cohort. "Get his piece. If it's a Glock, it's mine." Then he froze in his tracks.

"Or mine ready to blow your fucking brains out," Stas whispered. "You feel this?" He pushed the cold muzzle into the assailant's neck.

"Oh, fuck!" The loud expletive got everyone's attention.

"Lay'em down and step away!" Stas's message were crystal clear.

It took over an hour to process the scene and haul off the young thugs, two of whom had outstanding warrants, plus the .38 in their procession was stolen. After their car had been impounded, statements taken, and the usual cop bullshit dispensed with, the sheriffs and Smart departed, leaving Marlowe and Stas sitting in their stocking feet on the front steps.

"So where is Barbara?" Stas asked.

"She's spending the night with Jill. I'm glad she wasn't here for this." Marlowe smashed a moth, wiped his hands on his pant leg, then waited several minutes. "You want to tell me what's bothering you."

"Nothing."

"Man, I been there. You and your woman have a fight?"

Stas coughed.

"You know sometimes the best of us needs to talk to somebody. You going to tell me about it?"

"There's nothing to tell. It's just not working out."

"You have a fight?"

"It's worse than a fight." Stas held his head in his hands.

"What happened?"

"I got stupid." He looked over at Marlowe who seemed to be waiting for more.

"Yeah, like the watch. That was stupid."

"I walked out."

"Yeah, another stupid move. What did she do?"

"Nothing really." Stas stood and started down the steps.

"Then why don't you call her and apologize."

"Maybe I will." Stas paused on the walk and kicked a rock with his stockinged foot.

"If you don't, maybe you'll lose her, if you care."

"It's hard."

"It always is, losing or caring."

"Yeah, tell me about it." There was enough light from the early dawn that he was able to avoid the other rocks and debris in the street. Stas inhaled. He hadn't remembered the smell of eucalyptus the night before.

FORTY-SIX

S tas felt the knot expand in his abdomen, then rise with icy tentacles to squeeze his heart. He felt faint, a frigid wave surged to his brain. His ears rang. He must have heard wrong. "Did you say Amanda Brighten?" he asked.

"You been seeing this woman?" Moore's words were clipped and even, like reading from a training manual.

Lt. William Boyer pulled a chair over and shoved it to Stas. "Maybe you should sit."

The detective slumped into one of the Captain's infamous hard chairs. "Seeing?"

"Dating, dancing, fucking, Don't play stupid, Nowak."

"I've seen her maybe four times. They certainly weren't dates. What's this about?"

"Did you see her Saturday?" Moore asked.

Stas didn't hesitate. "I gave her a ride. She said her car was in the shop." He tried to control his breathing, get control of the pressure in his chest.

"Did you go in her house, spend time with her?"

"Why?" Stas felt icy fingers tapping his spine, chilling him throughout. "What's this about?"

"We're asking the questions, Nowak," Boyer said.

"Yes, I helped her with...." He wiped tiny beads of sweat from his brow trying to postpone the nightmare, but he knew what was coming next.

"She said you assaulted her." Boyer stared at Stas.

"Rape?" Uttering the word sent a foul taste to the back of this throat.

"No! Just that you roughed her up," Boyer added.

"I took her stuff in. She fell and cut her hand. I bandaged it and left. I couldn't have been in her house more than fifteen minutes. I never touched her."

"Why didn't you call the paramedics?" Boyer asked.

"For what? A little cut on her hand? They would have laughed me out of Pasadena."

Boyer handed the detective an open file. There were photos of Amanda, her face and arms purple with bruising.

Stas shook his head, looked down at his hands. "There wasn't a mark on her when I left except the cut on her hand. When did I do this?"

"She said that evening."

Stas jumped up, almost overturning his chair. "Impossible! I played poker at Marlowe's 'til two or three."

"Doesn't he live in Altadena?" Moore asked. "Miss Brighten lives in Pasadena. You could have done a number on her and still gone to Marlowe's."

He made a broad sweep over the pictures. "Yeah, and someone else could have assaulted her. If I'd done that...." He looked down. "My hands would have been bruised. The guys would have noticed. I couldn't hide my hands. Ask them?"

"We will." The Captain took several more drags, blew smoke towards his air purifier, before stubbing what was left of the cigarette out in a stained saucer. "Pasadena's investigating plus Internal Affairs. In the meantime, you know the drill."

"Yeah, gun, shield, ID." Stas took off his holster, wrapped it around his Glock, and laid it on the corner of the desk.

"You're on administrative leave. Stay home during work hours and don't communicate with anyone regarding anything you were working on," Boyer said.

Stas put his ID and blue and gold shield on top of his holster.

"We'll get someone to partner with Edwards while you're out," Boyer added.

"Good luck with that." Stas didn't look back when he left the Captain's office. In the squad room he grabbed his jacket from the back of his chair and headed for the men's room. He didn't stop at a urinal but pushed the door open to a stall, banging it back in his urgency to release the contents of his gut. It came up like a geyser, turning the water in the toilet bowl a greenish-brown. He heaved, bringing up more foul waste, then broke into a cold sweat, his face clammy to his touch. He could taste caffeine and bile as he pulled the door of the narrow stall shut.

Stas waited for another round of vomiting, imagining some vital organ rushing to produce more vile fluid. Leaning over the bowl, he retched again, but nothing more came. Feeling light headed he leaned back against the door tasting a nasty presence in his mouth and on his tongue. When he finally left the stall, Marlowe stood at the sink watching Stas through the mirror.

He turned, a frown of concern on his face. "You going to be okay?"

"You keep asking me that. You don't want to start mothering your detectives, do you?" Stas went to an adjoining sink, rinsed his mouth, splashed cold water on his face, and wiped it with a paper towel. "I've been suspended, pending an investigation." The words were spoken as if delivered in a vacuum. "I've never hit a woman in my life." He spit in the sink, still trying to rid his mouth of a metallic taste, and tossed the wadded towel towards the can, missed but didn't look back.

All eyes were on Marlowe when he returned to the squad room.

"Captain wants to see you," Jonson said.

Marlowe returned with a file, sat at his desk with the preliminary report. "This just doesn't sound at all like Stas."

"What doesn't sound like Stas?" Edwards sat at his partner's desk.

Marlowe read. "He beat me out of frustration—when he couldn't perform."

"What? You think he has ED? I think it's all show with him anyway." Edwards' laugh bordered on cynicism. "He couldn't get it up, and it pissed him off."

"What the hell you talking about? This just doesn't sound like him. Anyway, he's been seeing someone. You said so yourself. Why would he beat up another woman?" Marlowe questioned.

"How do we know it's another woman? You know, it all adds up, the clothes, the car, even the haircuts. He's trying to compensate for something, but that Talbott woman didn't fall under his spell, neither did Barbara." Edwards turned back to his work.

Marlowe frowned. "I thought she liked him. Weren't you trying to hook'em up?"

"No! If she'd wanted him, why'd she go after you? Anyway, I knew about the teacher. He was even taking a class from her, probably even screwing her for homework." He chuckled to himself. "The morning we found the second vic, I called his cell. He wasn't home. He was with her."

"With this Amanda Brighten?" Marlowe looked at the file.

"Yeah!"

"You sure?" Marlowe looked puzzled. "But he didn't meet her until a couple of days before he got back from his vacation. Who was he with before that?"

"Some one night stand? You ever know him to have a steady woman?"

Marlowe took his mug to the coffee machine. "Then who gave him the watch? Who's Dina?"

When Edwards came in the next morning, a man in a dark blue suit, stark white shirt, navy tie was going through Stas's desk.

Edwards smiled and introduced himself. "Sid Edwards, I was Stas Nowak's partner."

"Desmond Abbott, IAD."

"I knew Internal Affairs would finally catch-up with him. It's about time."

"You sound like you don't expect him back." Abbott closed the drawer he'd been going through. "Looks like he's not expecting to return either from the looks of his desk."

"Oh, it always looks like that."

Taylor turned his chair to face Edwards. "Your partner must talk to you about his female interest?"

"Yeah, I knew he was seeing that teacher, taking a class." Edwards set aside his mug and brushed off his desk.

"What did he tell you about their engagement? The wedding? Were you going to be the best man?"

"Nothing, he told me nothing. But that's typical." Edwards reflected. "Women like him."

"Does he ever date witnesses?"

"I don't know." Edwards fidgeted with some papers.

Marlowe entered and looked from Edwards to Abbott "Hey, Des. How's the investigating going?"

"Slow, Nowak doesn't leave much of a paper trail: messages, phone numbers, e-mail addresses."

"He's very private." Marlowe placed his Stetson on a chair next to his desk. "That's why it's hard for me to believe he hooked-up with this teacher-chick, not his style."

Abbott turned toward Marlowe. "What is his style?"

Marlowe thought for a minute. "Classy, not necessarily beautiful, but well put together. He likes legs."

"Yeah, one who could afford to buy him an expensive watch." Edwards interjected.

Later that afternoon, Marlowe planted himself heavily in his chair and sighed. "You didn't paint a nice picture of your partner to IAD or Pasadena PD for that matter."

Edwards shrugged. "Where'd you get that?"

"The Captain, he told me about their preliminary interview. I didn't know you knew so much about his personal life."

"I know enough." He gulped coffee and sloshed some on his tie. "I can put two and two together. What did the Captain tell them?"

"That he had an excellent closure record, one of the highest, that there had been a couple of incidents in the past, but since he came here, he's been very professional, easy to get along with, easy to work with." Marlowe looked over at Edwards.

"Then you should ride with him."

"I have."

Edwards made no comment but busied himself at his computer. Marlowe left the squad room and later returned with Jonson.

"Did you know that Sid thought Miss Brighten was Dina?" Marlowe voice was loud, almost caustic. "Even told Pasadena that Stas spent a few nights with her, and from the smell on his pillow, she's stayed at his place."

Jonson looked interested. "How long have they been riding together?"

"Evidently, not long enough for him to know his partner better. He's not my partner, but I know what makes him a good cop. He sure as hell saved my sorry ass, in that chilly fashion of his, seeing as he was drunk as hell. That situation could have been a fucking mess. My neighbors never knew anything went down."

Edwards seemed oblivious to the conversation between the two partners. He continued typing at his computer.

Marlowe continued. "You know, if I remember correctly," he looked over at Edwards, Stas had been your partner the longest, cut him some slack."

"I'm getting a new partner. Why should I care about that Polack? " He turned back to his computer.

Marlowe slammed his fist so hard on his desk that it overturned his mug, spending it to the floor. "Well, I do, especially when he's getting a raw deal!"

FORTY-SEVEN

Mona relaxed, her body submerged in a foamy bath of sea salts, lavender body wash, and essential oils. Her head rested on a terry covered bath pillow, her eyes covered with a blue, icy mask. She had just turned the jets off in the tub and was not ready for any intrusion when the door burst open.

"You bitch!"

She recognized Ryan's voice before she removed the mask. He was back from one of his trips or his other abode. She tossed the mask at his feet. "What do you want?" She looked up at him, not sure if his face was red with anger or the heat of the bathroom.

"You bitch!" he spewed again.

"Yes, I know, dear, but you're being redundant." Tiny purplish suds ran off her breast as she raised herself from the tub.

Ryan reached for a towel and wiped his face. "Did you think I was never going to find out?"

"Find out what?"

"About you and my father!"

"Me and your father? I never did anything with your old man." She pointed to a terry robe draped over the back of a chair, "Hand me my robe."

"Get it your damn self." He moved back as she got out of the tub. "You fucked with my father's mind and his money. He wanted the name carried on. That's all he cared about."

Mona laughed and slipped into the robe. "No, he wanted a daughter and granddaughters who looked like your mother, and I gave them to him." She pushed past him into her bed-room. "Get out of my way!"

Ryan followed and sat on the edge of the unmade bed. "We had a deal. We all got what we wanted, but you went too far. Now I've got to think, really think about the girls, if they're my sisters, I need to provide for them."

She sat at her desk, half turned to look at him. "Weren't you going to take care of them anyway?

"This makes it personal." He looked past Mona's head. "Where's the painting?"

"The police took it."

Ryan jumped up. "What do you mean? 'Took it?' Why?"

"I thought you knew it was Cynthia Lenox, but then you never come in here. We never have those little intimate conver-sations that married couples have when they wake in the morn-ing."

"You're out of here. I'm seeing my lawyers in the morning and getting the girls tested."

"Do you think that's wise?"

"I need to know?"

"Then knowing just might cost you."

"Bitch, don't try to blackmail me."

"There's enough money for all of us."

"You got the trust my father gave you. That's enough."

"Listen, you have a family, his fortune, your freedom to do what you want. So don't come in here acting innocent and in-dignant. I did what I had to do, what was necessary, so did you." She turned back to her mirror and watched Ryan.

"And Frank and that woman were necessary?" He turned in the doorway. "Well, enjoy 'cause this luxury is soon coming to an end. I've gone along with your schemes and said nothing. And forget any more money. I'm building a microbrewery, signed the contracts, already hired my brewmeister."

"What about Paul and the lofts?"

"You'd better worry about yourself and forget Paul."

Concern clouded Mona's face. "I'm going to need money for an attorney."

"Don't worry. I'll take care of any fees for the divorce. It's in the pre-nup."

"No, I need it for my assault charge against the LAPD."

"Whatever you guys did, you better take care of it yourself. I don't even want to know about it. Anyway, you have enough money."

She got up and followed him to his bedroom.

"Now, what?"

"I need to get in the safe."

Wearing the same sweats he'd slept in, Stas sat in his reading alcove with a day-old *LA Times*. The rough stubble on his face was turning into beard. At first he didn't move when the phone rang but then jumped catching it on the fifth ring.

"I was about to hang up." It was Marlowe. "Man, you all right?"

Stas started to say something smart-assed but didn't. "I'm doing okay. What's going on downtown?"

"Edwards is working with Pollitano. His partner's still in rehab."

"Yeah, I bet Brown loves the little vacation. Pollitano can be a real bitch."

"We've all been interviewed by Pasadena PD and Abbott from IAD."

"How did it go?" Stas asked.

"Fast and easy, especially since we know nothing about your personal life. You need to talk to somebody sometime."

"I'll remember that."

"Stas, by the way..."

"Yeah?"

"Never mind, I'll keep you updated."

"Thanks, man." Stas hung-up and went to the kitchen. The Chopin was on the counter. He didn't bother with a glass or ice but turned the bottle up and took a long swig which seemed to give him enough energy to go to the bedroom and hang-up clothes from the previous night at the Second Set. It had been the first time that he had ventured out for a drink since his suspension. He had taken an empty stool at the far end of the bar. Roy served him without a greeting. Stas had never in his life felt like a social outcast, but lifting his gaze to his image in the mirror, he didn't like what he saw. And to be brought to this because of an attractive woman on the plane who seemed like the ideal all-American mate. Bitch! He downed the last of his drink and turned to face Bucky Cramer, a detective from Rampart Division.

"Nowak, I've been looking for you." Cramer leaned over the bar. "Give me a Scotch on the rocks and another of whatever he's drinking." He pushed Stas to a booth.

"Okay, you found me, what's up?"

"Man, I heard. I'm really sorry."

"So you're looking for me to tell me you're sorry?"

"Hell, no. I wanted to see if you'd like to play with us."

The drinks arrived.

"I don't play much soccer any more. Besides, I heard the over-thirty-fives weren't playing anymore."

Cramer took a sip of his drink. "No, man, I mean music. Someone told me you play a mean sax."

Stas started on his drink. "Who told you that?"

"Well, do you?"

"I played with a jazz group in the Army."

"Well, I heard you can still play. We got a drummer, keyboard, bass guitar. We need a sax. We get that, and we have a group."

"I can't do that."

Anger flashed across Cramer's face. "So what can you do? Stay home and feel sorry for yourself, then.... You're not the only one. Some wit accused me of being her baby's daddy."

"Were you?"

"Hell, no, but I got one out there that they never discovered. Don't worry about it."

"Yeah, but I do."

"Well, then worry, but can you meet with us later?"

Stas downed his drink. "I doubt it." He rose.

"Hey, give me your card anyway."

"They may not be any good after all this."

Cramer pulled a notebook from his pocket. "Man, give me a number, any number."

FORTY-EIGHT

Marlowe read the names as he scrolled through the list of residents. There were several names with the first initial of D. Since he didn't have a last name, he buzzed the manager's apartment.

"We don't have no vacancies."

The voice that came through the intercom was raspy, probably a heavy smoker, maybe a drinker. Marlowe hoped she wouldn't be a flake.

"I'm Detective Marlowe, LAPD. Could I have a word with you?"

There was no response, just a loud, metallic click that unlocked the building's front door. Marlowe pushed through and entered Livia's garden of well-tended plants in the foyer. He turned right, following a white arrow that pointed to the Manager's apartment. Livia stood posed in her doorway, looking over glasses that rode low on her nose, sizing up the detective.

"You got ID?"

Marlowe handed it over. Livia looked at it, then gave it back. She shifted her weight in her red high-heeled mules and scrutinized the detective once more.

"What can I do for you?"

Marlowe hesitated, his gaze taking in the shoes, moving up the legs, then to the face. Something had been lost in the translation. With those legs she should have been drop-dead gorgeous. It was hard to tell about the figure since it was shrouded in a bright, Hawaiian-print muumuu that stopped just above well-dimpled knees.

"I'm a friend of Detective Nowak," Marlowe offered.

"Stas?" She smiled. "Com'on in."

Livia muted the blaring TV and pointed to a chair.

"You know Detective Nowak?" Marlowe asked.

"We're good friends, had dinner with him not too long ago."

Marlowe cocked his head. "Really?"

"And I told those Pasadena cops he didn't live here. I don't know where they got that."

"What else did you tell them?"

"Is he in some kind of trouble?"

"Detective Nowak,... Stas is involved in an on-going investigation."

"Honey, I may not watch that many cop shows, but that sounds like some political double talk."

"Well, back to the Pasadena Police. What did you tell them?"

"Nothing. They're detectives. Let them find out for themselves." Livia laughed, shook her head, and reached for a pack of cigarettes on the coffee table. "Is this, uh, investigation something recent?"

"I can't discuss anything on-going. I'm just doing follow-up."

She reached for a bright red BIC but didn't light up, letting the unfiltered cigarette dangle from her mouth. "Well, Detective Marlowe, since I'm just a friend and not his woman, I don't know much." She removed some loose tobacco from red lips. "And since you can't tell me anything. Maybe you should talk to somebody who knows him better." She flicked the lighter. "He helped her out of a jam a few years ago. She's up in 504."

"In this building?"

Livia lit her cigarette, fanning smoke as she escorted him to the door. "Yeah, Dina Goode in 504."

Marlowe felt her gaze burning into his back as he walked to the elevator. He pushed the up button, turned, and waved.

"Detective," she called after him, "are you married?"

He shook his head, got in, and pushed five.

When he found 504, loud music, an upbeat jazz tune came from the apartment. Marlowe knocked, got no immediate response, then knocked harder. The volume diminished.

"Who is it?"

"Detective Chris Marlowe, LAPD."

He heard a chain, then a deadbolt before the door opened to a serious face damp with perspiration. Her exotic beauty took him by surprise. The olive complexion, the crinkled curls, the hazel eyes, so this was Nowak's woman?

"Detective Marlowe, I've heard about you." Dina looked down at his boots, then back at his face. "You do rodeos. Come on in."

"Heard the music, thought you were having a party."

"Just jazzercise." She was flush from the exertion that left her complexion with a warm afterglow. She indicated he take a seat on the sofa.

Marlowe sat on the edge. He had to mentally adjust to another revelation. Stas's woman was black, well, obviously mixed with some other stuff, but that didn't matter, she was still black.

Dina still stood, a note of concern in her tone. "Has something happened to Stas?" She bit her lip. "Where is he?"

"He's probably home getting drunk."

"He doesn't get drunk."

"Right, but he probably putting it away and that worries me. I shouldn't be telling you this, but he's been suspended for assaulting a woman in Pasadena, a teacher at Glendale College."

The color seemed to drain from Dina's face.

Marlowe continued. "She told the Pasadena Police that he lived here, but your manager cleared that up. I work with Stas. He doesn't talk about his personal life much. And I've never heard of any woman, at least in the department, that he dated talk about him. I can't imagine him being rough with one."

Dina finally sat down in the Queen Anne chair and listened even more intently.

Marlowe continued. "We all know he's been seeing some-one, but he's not talking. I've read the file from Pasadena PD, and the one accusing him doesn't seem his type."

Dina straightened. "And I am?"

"I don't know. Nowak could be a loose cannon, I know that. I even think the Captain knows that, yet Stas manages to keep it all under control, but one day...."

She rose. "Can I get you a drink?"

Marlowe hesitated. "I'll have a Scotch on the rocks if you have it."

"Are you on duty?"

"No, and this is not an official visit."

She nodded without commenting.

His gaze followed her until she disappeared into the kitch-en. He got up and walked around the living room, touching flowers to see if they were real, smelling the candles, and pag-ing through the *Vogue* on the coffee table. He read the name on the mailing label: Hansen Modeling Agency.

Dina returned with a small tray holding his Scotch in a mul-tifaceted old fashioned glass and a linen cocktail napkin. She handed him his drink and placed the napkin on the table before taking her seat again.

"Detective Marlowe, why are you telling me all this?"

"Well, things just don't add up."

"So what do you want from me?"

"You were one of Sybil's girls?"

Dina seemed to bristle. "Sybil has no girls. She's dead. And why would you think I worked for Sybil?"

"To be truthful, I didn't. I just guessed. I met her a while back. I knew the kind of woman she was and the kind of girls in her service. Stas knew her. I just imagined.... He glanced at the magazine. Oh, shit, I am a detective. I do put two and two together sometimes and come up with four."

"I don't entertain clients anymore."

Marlowe nodded and sipped his drink. "No, with Stas you couldn't."

"You still haven't told me what you want?"

"I'm not sure. I guess I owe him one. I want to help."

"Maybe he doesn't want my help."

Marlowe turned the glass several times, letting the light play on the amber liquid before taking another sip. "You ever get the feeling, that as smart as he is, there are times when Stas doesn't know what he wants?"

Dina nodded. "I was so confused. At first I thought it was a race thing or me being an occupational hazard."

"I don't think being black or mixed has anything to do with it. It's the job, and it's him. Don't get me wrong, I'm as bad as the other guys. I've chased as hard as any other cop. I understand. It's just hard to have it out in the open."

"We don't have to worry about that anymore."

"Well, I don't know what kind of arrangement you had. You might be over him, but he sure as hell's not over you. That's why I know this woman is lying through her teeth."

"He told me about her. Said he saw her a few times. On the plane, in class. He took her home one night."

"You think he slept with her?"

"Does it matter? But Stas isn't rough." She folded her hands in her lap. "I still don't know what I can do. I'm not even sure I want to help."

"He's a good cop. I don't know what you think, but he doesn't deserve this. Talk to our Captain."

Dina shook her head.

Marlowe moved in closer, trying to reassure. "Tell him about your relationship with Stas, times you've spent together. You don't have to elaborate."

"But I would. I can just see him, wanting every little detail. Won't they drag up my, my..." She paused.

"Not if we play this right. You have a record, been arrested?"

"Never!"

"I didn't see your name on the bell."

"I changed it back."

"See they don't have to know what your stage-name was. We got to discredit this woman."

"And if I don't?"

Marlowe straightened. "His ass is cooked. He's sacked, loses his pension, might go to jail. It's not a pretty picture and all because...."

"She couldn't get in his pants." She rose. "Let me think about it. I'm going to make some tea. Do you want some?"

Marlowe drained his Scotch.

"I guess not." Dina went to the kitchen.

He sat on the edge of the sofa and looked the apartment over again trying to see why Stas sought out this particular woman's company. Her place was warm, relaxing, a sanctuary from the mean streets of LA. And in this setting, he was sure Stas was beginning to have his needs met. Now there was this other woman.

Dina came back with two mugs and handed one to Marlowe. "This is Stas's favorite."

"Tea?" Marlowe raised the mug to his nose and inhaled.

"Try it."

"It won't make me sick after drinking Scotch?"

"You'll be okay."

Marlowe grimaced, took a sip, and smiled. "Not bad. Tell me, where are you from?"

"Milwaukee, but this woman, what's she like?"

"I didn't interview her. I only read the transcript. She thought he assaulted her to prove his manhood, his sexual prowess."

"Don't you rape somebody to prove that?"

"She didn't accuse him of that. I wouldn't even call a few cuts and bruises an assault. But then, I've seen a hundred times worse."

Dina held her cup in both hands and smiled. "Do you believe Stas would have to beat up some woman to get sex? I'm sure you've seen how some women react to him."

"Yeah! But it seems she's kinda naive, a teacher. Maybe she took something he said or did the wrong way."

"But he's not into rough sex," Dina interjected.

"We're going to need some specifics to counter her accusation."

She glared at Marlowe. "You just said I didn't have to get into details. You guys just love this?"

"What?"

"The intimate details." Dina frowned. "I've heard how they've found peep holes and mini-cams in female cops' locker rooms."

"Hey, come back for a minute. Remember this is about Stas." He took out his notebook and paged through. "What kind of underwear does he wear."

"What does that have to do with anything?"

"Amanda had some of his shorts, white Fruit-of-the-Loom."

Dina laughed. "He wears black, Polo boxer briefs. But forget the underwear. How did he treat her?"

"She said he was rough. I told you there were bruises."

"What did the paramedics say?"

"She didn't call them. She called the police later that day."

"Do you have dates?"

"Yes. But the Captain can go over them with you if you two meet."

"I'm curious. What did she say he was like in bed?"

Marlowe closed his notebook. "She didn't."

"If she'd been with him, she would've told you some intimate details. Her proof."

"So, will you talk to the Captain."

"I don't want to go to...."

"We can arrange for a statement some place private, then he can decide about going to Pasadena PD."

"Will there be a trial?"

"Not if she drops the charges. That's what we've got to get her to do."

"And if she doesn't?"

"We have to prove she lied, so you're going to have to be very convincing."

Dina rose, took the tray to the kitchen. "Can you give me a ride to Glendale?"

"You know the address?"

"Yes." Dina grabbed a coat from the hall closet, then paused. "Wait a minute."

He looked at his watch. "No problem!"

She disappeared into the bedroom.

Marlowe double parked in front of Stas's building in Glendale. Dina joined him by the intercom system. They scrolled through the list of occupants, then punched in his code. Stas picked up on the third ring.

"Yes?" The voice sounded heavy with sleep or drink.

"It's Marlowe. I need to drop something off about the case."

"I'm in 215."

The door buzzed. Dina entered and waved. As she ran up the steps, Marlowe caught sight of a long, bare leg when her coattail flipped up. He smiled and returned to his car.

Stas moved from his desk upon hearing the timid knock at his door. *Marlowe must be losing his touch.* He opened the door to Dina standing there, the belt of her all-weather coat pulled tightly at her waist. He looked down to four inch heels and tan legs, then stepped back.

Dina still didn't move. "May I come in?"

He rubbed the stubble on his face and moved to let her enter. She paused by the closet.

"Marlowe brought me. We need to talk."

"Yeah." He closed the door but gave her no room to pass.

Reaching down to the her belt, he pulled. The coat fell open. There was a slight intake of breath as he pushed the coat from her bare shoulders, letting it fall in a heap to the floor.

He whispered hoarsely into her ear. "You can be arrested for going out like this."

"I was with a cop."

"Some say Marlowe's got x-ray vision."

He moved her backward. She reached around to feel the cold doorknob pushing into the small of her back, then moved into his arms to exchange the one intrusion for another. With one hand, she caught the elastic waist of his sweats, dragging them over his hips. She used her foot to push them to the floor. Without releasing her, he stepped out of the bundled mess and kicked them out of their way. His pulled her even closer, lifting her off the floor, letting her straddle his hips. She moaned burying her head into his shoulder as he moved into her.

Dina choked out his name. "Stas!"

How long had it been? Too long! He pushed her against the wall for greater leverage, then slowed his movements letting Dina abandon herself for the moment. She wrapped her arms around his neck, his back, pulling him even closer. Finally, she groaned into that sweet, agonized release. She panted his name in her heart-pounding exhaustion. Stas still sought release from his own pent-up emotions, and when it came, he held her balanced in his arms before easing her to the floor. Somehow during the evening, they ended up in his bed.

Dina awoke to the sound of an electric razor. She vaguely remembered the feel of his beard, and thought if that was the price she had to pay to have him back, she could live with it. Now he was shaving it off. She could hear him dressing, but she didn't want to leave the warm sanctuary of his bed, not yet. A few minutes later, she got up and went into the chilly living room after the door to the apartment slammed shut. Her shoes stood neatly on the floor by the sofa. Her coat had been hung in the hall closet. She retrieved a toothbrush from her pocket. In the bathroom Dina slipped on his terry robe after a shower. Marlowe was going to set up a meeting with the Captain.

Hopefully, her input would give them something to confront that woman and her lies, then Stas would be reinstated, and things might go back to the way they were.

She peered into the mirror. Her hair was a mess; she'd lost an earring, but she felt alive. Back in the bedroom, Dina realized she had nothing to wear. Her thoughts returned to Amanda. If she didn't tell the truth, Stas would be an ex-cop. *What did ex-cops do? Don't think about it.*

When he returned, he found Dina in his reading alcove, about twenty pages into one of Elmore Leonards' *Get Shorty*.

"Aren't you hungry?"

She looked up. "I'm okay."

"I got some bagels."

"I'll help."

"No, I'll do it. It's good to have you here. Like old times."

He returned with a tray of bagels spread with cream cheese and two steaming mugs of tea.

Dina joined him on the sofa, snuggled in his terry robe, her bare feet tucked under her. "What's this?"

"Tea, green. See I'm learning."

"Did you let it steep?"

He joined her and bit into the bagel without responding.

"Why didn't you tell me more about this woman?" she asked.

"Amanda? What's there to tell?"

"You must have made quite an impression. Did she ever see you," she moved her hands indicating his lower torso. "without your clothes?"

"No!" He looked at Dina. "It never went that far."

"Could it have?"

"She wasn't my type."

"That's what I keep hearing. Marlowe said she told the police you gave her a diamond," she paused and touched a gold chain at her neck, "all I got was a cute little panda."

"Yeah, but he came with diamond eyes and a helleva fringe benefit."

FORTY-NINE

Amanda parked in the lot behind the Pasadena Main Library on Walnut. She checked her hair and make-up in the visor mirror. Weren't first impressions important? Her appointment with the Pasadena Police was for 11:00 a.m., but since she was early, she'd gone inside the historic library and checked out a book so she could have something to read while she waited.

She looked at her watch at the check-out counter. Seventeen minutes to get to the Pasadena Police Headquarters across the street. She took her time walking the one block. Amanda touched her hair and stated her business to the information clerk.

"Someone will be with you in a few minutes." The name on the name tag read George Smith who was a volunteer and manned the information desk on the first floor.

"Thank you." She wanted to appear prim and proper, smoothing her skirt at her sides and folding her hands in her lap when she took a seat on a hard bench in the waiting area. The book, Pride and Prejudice, meant to enhance the impression, remained closed beside her.

A well-groomed detective in a dark blue suit came to escort her upstairs to an interview room. His dark brown hair was neat and short, his brown eyes seemed cold, indifferent. Amanda wanted to look away.

"Hello, I'm Detective Vega. Sorry to keep you waiting. Won't you come with me?"

Amanda grabbed her things and followed him to an inter-view room where he indicated she take a seat on one side of a wooden table.

"This interview is being recorded. When we're finished, a secretary will transcribe it, and give you a copy to sign."

She nodded and toyed with the handbag in her lap.

"I know you've been over this with the other officers, but I just need to review some points about the assault. An attack like that can be very traumatizing." He looked over at the book she'd moved to the end of the table. "Well, any kind of attack can be. I'm curious." He paged through an open file. "Why didn't you call the paramedics or police right away? We pride ourselves on our quick response." Vega looked intently at Amanda. "Why call your friend first?"

She forced a smile. "Well, I wanted a witness."

"A witness? Was she there to see the attack?"

"No, but I called her, and she rushed over. I guess I needed some moral support."

"I would think you would have wanted medical attention and the police to immediately document the incident." He flipped through some photos. "Does your friend live nearby, in the neighborhood?"

"No, she lives in Eagle Rock."

"Were you planning to have her take you to the ER?"

Amanda wrinkled her nose. "ER?"

Vega looked up. "Emergency Room. The one at the Hun-tington is close to you."

"No! I just wanted her to see what he had done."

"And she didn't advise you to call the police?"

"No, yes, I told her I would as soon as she left, and I did."

"Is Miss Tanya Phelps an EMT or a nurse?" He tapped the open file with his pen. "I'm just having a hard time under-standing why you would call her first."

"She's a good friend. We work together."

"You teach English at Glendale College?"

"Yes."

"But there's no record of Stas Nowak being enrolled in your class or even being registered at the school."

"It had already started." Amanda shifted in her chair. "I told him he didn't have to enroll at the time. He was basically checking it out."

"Does the college allow that?"

She blinked. "I don't know!"

"How many times did he 'check it out'"?

Amanda looked at the lights on the ceiling. "I'm not sure, maybe five or six times."

"That means he was in fairly regular attendance, over a month to made up his mind, yet he made no effort to enroll. Or was it already too late?"

Vega didn't wait for an answer but turned over another sheet of paper. "You told the investigating officer that Mr. Nowak was a shady character."

"Did I say that?" She folded her hands.

"You said, 'I think he's a pimp.'" Vega tried to suppress a smile. "But, in fact, Mr. Nowak is a homicide detective with the Los Angeles Police Department. Why would you think he was a pimp?"

Amanda blinked. "I didn't know. I thought... he looked, his clothes, his car..."

"Maybe he just likes nice things." Vega turned another sheet. "Detective Nowak indicated in his interview with us that he had only seen you four times: on the plane, twice in your class, and the last time when he took you home, the time of the alleged assault. That's hardly enough time for an engagement, especially if he's a pimp! Wouldn't you want to know him better?"

"Haven't you ever heard of love at first sight?" Amanda bristled.

"Yes, I suppose it happens to some people, but Detective Nowak said he never bought you a ring or authorized you to buy one for him."

"Well, he's lying!"

"Do you have a receipt because there's no record of him purchasing a ring with his credit card, unless he paid cash?" He waited for a response. None came. "Or did he give you the money?" Vega leaned closer as if he expected her to produce proof of purchase.

Amanda wiped tiny beads of perspiration from her forehead. "He, he told me to buy it, and he'd pay me back."

"Did he ever reimburse you?"

She shook her head. "May I have some water? It's a little close in here."

Vega left the room and returned a few minutes later with a styrofoam cup of tepid water and handed it to Amanda.

"Thanks! Is this going to take much longer?"

"Just a few more questions. What else besides his clothes and car led you to believe Detective Nowak was a pimp?"

She didn't answer.

"Did you use some of the money you withdrew from your saving account," Vega slid a copy of a withdrawal form across the table, "to hire a private detective?"

She ignored the form. "Why would you think that?"

"You phone records indicate calls to and from Mr. Ruland, a private detective. Did you hire him?"

"I may have asked his advice."

"Did he tell you that Detective Nowak was a pimp?"

"He did say that he looked like one, especially when he saw him with some women that looked like prostitutes."

"So you did hire him?"

Amanda ignored the question and reached for the form and read it. "How did you get this?"

"We have access to a lot of records that can assist us in an investigation. For example, there is no record of Detective Nowak withdrawing money from his savings. He did, however, make a withdrawal the day of the alleged assault but lost it in a poker game. The three police officers there will vouch for him, even testify that there were no bruises on his hands that would indicate that he'd beat you."

Amanda shook her head. "I may have hurt myself when I fell trying to avoid being hit."

"You know, wait a minute, before I forget. There's no record of him calling you from his cell or his land line. None! Also, there is no record of you ever calling him. But you did receive several calls from a pay phone near Parker Center. Why so little communication from your fiancé and all one way?"

"I guess he was busy."

"The pattern seems to indicate that he didn't want you to have his number."

"I don't see why you would think that."

"I just told you, plus many cops don't want certain people to have access to them if it's not about police business. But back to why you hired a private detective."

"Who said I hired a private detective? I just asked a few questions to determine if I wanted to."

"Mr. Ruland told us you hired him. Also Detective Nowak indicated the same thing. You put the private investigator in jeopardy. He could have been hurt or even killed. A man has to be careful running up on a cop. As a matter of fact, Mr. Ruland told us he feared for his life." Vega stared at Amanda and waited, "So, are you going to tell me?"

Amanda drained her cup. "I just wanted to find out what he did for a living."

"Why didn't you ask him?" He turned another page and continued without waiting for an answer. "We sent an officer to talk to your neighbors."

Amanda sat rigidly in her chair, her eyes focused on the door behind Vega.

"Mrs. Ruby Clarke, lives in the cottage next to yours. She remembers the day of the alleged assault. She also remembers seeing a man fitting Detective Nowak description carrying a bag of groceries into your house. She saw him leave soon afterwards."

"But she didn't see me fall."

"No, she didn't, but she saw your friend, Miss Phelps come, and later that evening, the police."

Amanda looked surprised.

"So you see, your time line doesn't quite sync with ours."

She shook her head. "I can't figure out what's wrong. I told it like I remember it."

"We did some more checking. You seem to have a pattern of, what would you call it, one-sided involvement with men." He paused for a reaction, then continued. "In the last two years you have accused two male college professors of improper behavior toward you. One quit under the shadow of possible dismissal for sexual harassment. The other one moved to San Diego after you spread rumors of a pending engagement with him."

Amanda shook her head. "I'm really not sure why he left."

Vega closed the file and stared across the table. "You know, Miss Brighten, Detective Nowak puts his life on the line for people like you and me every day. His Captain says he's a fine detective. So if you go forth with this accusation, we'll have one less good cop working for the public. But if he's done something wrong, he deserves to be off the street, maybe in jail. If he didn't, though, he'll lose his job, his pension, his reputation. And if we find out that you lied to us, he'll be perfectly in his rights to sue you for slander. As a matter of fact, we can even bring charges. If you're convicted, you could get probation or even jail time. What would that do to your teaching career?"

She took a deep breath and reached for her empty cup. "I don't know."

"You'd never teach again. Miss Brighten, we need more details of your affair with Detective Nowak. Would you be willing to describe his nude body? Tell us about any scars or tattoos, any discolorations on his body, be able to describe his genitals." He paused. "You know what I mean."

Amanda seemed to sink into herself, but she did not respond.

"Was Detective Nowak ever intimate with you?"

Amanda did not respond.

"Did Detective Nowak ever strike you?"

"I don't remember. I'm just so confused."

"Why don't you take some time to think about it?"

FIFTY

Dina stood in the doorway of Stas's bathroom watching him dress. He'd been called back work, to see Lieutenant Boyer and not the team at IAD. It was all over. He ran his hands through damp hair and realized he needed a haircut, but that would have to wait. His clothes had been selected with care the night before: nothing too new, nothing too stylish. He knotted his tie, then inspected the results in the closet mirror.

"What do you think?" Stas turned for Dina's final approval.

She smiled. "You look great!"

He pocketed his wallet and keys. "Will you be here when I get back?"

She looked down at her LAPD sweats. " Do you need me to be?"

He nodded.

"Were you anxious?" Dina asked.

"Hell, yes! My career, my whole life was on the line, and they could dispense with it in twenty minutes."

She walked over to him as he turned the deadbolt and, standing on her toes, planted a gentle kiss on his cheek.

As he started the car, his cell rang. It was Boyer. He was to meet with his union rep in the lieutenant's office to sign-off on the paper work.

When Stas arrived at the squad room, Boyer had his door open, The rep, Ted Rand, was already seated at the desk. Boyer waved Stas in and closed the door.

Boyer took a seat and broke into a broad smile as he looked at an open file on his desk file. "Detective Stas Nowak you have been exonerated. All charges have been dropped, and we are reinstating you." The lieutenant stood and reached across his desk to shake Stas' hand. "Man, I didn't believe any of this for one second."

Rand stood and shook Stas' hand. "I guess you won't be needing me. Just glad it turned out good."

"Thanks!" Stas nodded as Rand left.

Boyer retrieved a package from his bottom desk drawer and handed it to Stas. I think you'll be needing these. By the way, who's Miss Dionne Bonamie?"

Stas smiled. "A friend, a good friend."

When he got back to his apartment, the "good friend" was waiting. When she saw the broad smile on his face, she jumped into his arms. When she felt the gun in his shoulder hoister, she cried her joy. Later, in the bedroom she cried a different kind of joy.

On his first day back at work, he found his desk dusted and his computer screen cleaned which gave him the eerie feeling that maybe they hadn't expected his return. There was a 5x7 manila envelope in the center of his desk. The metal clasps broke off when he pushed them up to remove the contents. Inside were a MapQuest printout and a half sheet of yellow legal paper. The note read:

"Hey, Stas. Welcome back. Knew they couldn't keep you down or out. Bet you need some R and R after this. Remember the place I told you about in Los Gatos? It's not more than a shack, but it's clean. The caretaker lives in the back house and tends my vines. Yes, I'm making wine. Got eighty bottles last year. Let me know when you want to go up. Don't try to drink me dry. Max. "

Stas smiled and dumped the rest of the envelope's contents on the desk. A door key slid across clean surface, coming to rest near the computer monitor.

Marlowe dropped his Stetson on his desk. "Glad to have you back." Before sitting, he passed over a single sheet of white paper. "This should bring you up to speed, although you probably know more than we do."

"It's good to be back. Thanks for...."

Marlowe waved him off. "I owed you one." He reached in his pocket and took out the Tag Heuer, placing it on Stas's desk. "Didn't go with my image."

Stas slid it on his wrist and was about to speak when Marge, the Division clerk, stepped between the two detectives, waving a pink "While You Were Out" memo at Stas.

"Some guy named Clayton called yesterday. Said it was urgent."

"Why didn't you give it to Edwards?" Stas asked.

She brushed by both men. "He left on an errand, said he'd be back later. I haven't seen him since."

Stas looked at the note and reached for the phone.

He sat at his desk and dialed the first of two numbers. An answering machine came on. "I'm sorry we can't take your call. Please leave a phone number and a detailed message, and someone will get back to you as soon as possible."

"This is Detective Stas Nowak returning your call."

The line was picked up immediately. "Hello!"

"Clayton?"

There was a breathless, "Oh! Detective Nowak. Carroll's missing." There was panic in Clayton's tone.

"You sure he hasn't gone off to rehab or to have his operation?" Stas offered.

"You haven't heard?"

"Afraid not. I've been out of the office for a few days."

"He stopped his shots, says he's in love."

"Well, maybe he's off with his new boyfriend."

"You don't understand. It's a woman. He's so mixed up. I just don't know what he's thinking."

Stas straightened, trying to form a picture of where Carroll was both mentally and physically. How fucked-up was that? "Clayton, who's he been with?"

"That bitch, Mona Talbott. I went over to his place. The car was there, but a lot of his things were gone. You think he went off with her?"

"Let us check around. I'll call you if I find out anything, and you call me if anything turns up." Stas hung up.

Marlowe paused at Stas's desk.

"The old man wants to see you." Marlowe handed him a file. "He'll want to go over these while you're there. And the DNA tests came back on the girls and the Talbotts. Neither one's the father, not the old man or Ryan."

"What about Lundstrom? Did we get anything on his kids?"

"Not a thing. So we still don't know who the father is, but we do know that the two women victims were their mothers."

"What do we do about Mona and Ryan Talbott since we now have motive: for Ryan carrying on the family name, for Mona, money, and with them owning the modeling agency, opportunity?" Stas asked.

"See what the Captain thinks."

Stas grabbed the file and headed for Moore's office. When he returned an hour later, Stas looked shaken. Moore told him that even though Amanda had accepted a plea and agreed to psychological counseling, LAPD's IAD was holding on to everything, keeping an eye on him. But if Amanda ever tried to contact him, the court could issue a Restraining Order. Whatever decision the Pasadena ADA and the police made was okay with him as long as she kept her distance. *Well, so much for going back to school.* He sat and stared at the dark computer monitor for several minutes before turning it on and opening a file.

Edwards, standing by Stas's desk, brought him back to the reality of the squad room.

"Good to have you back." Edwards seemed anxious. "So what did Captain Moore say?"

Stas focused on the file that had come to life on the screen. "Forget the dog hairs."

"See, I told you." Edwards caught a glimpse of the watch on Stas's wrist. "You get another Tag?"

"Marlowe gave the old one back. Didn't match his Stetson."

Edwards glared at his partner but made no comment.

"What's that about a dog?" Marlowe asked.

Edwards finally smiled. "He went over a fence to get hairs without a warrant."

Marlowe frowned. "You did what?"

"I needed them to compare with the ones we had from the dresses."

"Did you do anything else stupid?"

"I had a visit with Dr. Crum."

Marlowe stared at Stas in disbelief. "You got some kind of death wish. You want to be out on your ass and have your woman taking care of you? Shit! I can't believe you! You haven't been back a day and...."

Edwards looked from Stas to Marlowe. Something had passed between the two detectives, something that he wasn't privy to. "What woman?"

"Don't worry about it." Both men spoke in unison.

"Okay, what happens when Judge Crum finds out you went to see his son?" Marlowe asked.

"I had a legitimate reason. He's a urologist, and I needed my prostate exam."

"My God, you'd put yourself through that just to question somebody?" Edwards grimaced.

"Not really," Stas looked at Marlowe. "We need to have an annual exam once you hit forty, right?"

Marlowe frowned. "I'm not touching that. I take it everything's working?"

Stas smiled. "I'm fine, and guess what? He had the same fishing pictures in his office as Lundstrom. I told him I thought

I knew one of the guys, met him at Modern World Travel. Then he told me something very interesting."

"What?"

"Crum and Ryan Talbott have been friends since college. They were in med-school together. Talbott dropped out after his second year and went to work for his father. Paul Lundstrom met Ryan when he did some work for the old man. The three guys started going on fishing trips, mostly Cabo, three, four times a year. Later, Paul introduced Ryan to Mona. We know the rest." Stas sat back in his chair.

Edwards returned to his desk. "So you figured it all out while you were on suspension?" He looked at his partner. "What about the girls?"

"Cynthia and Elizabeth gave birth. So I figure Ryan could have done the C-sections, later gave them overdoses of heroin, and stuck them in one of his old man's freezers." Stas's tone was cold, angry.

"Yeah, and since the women had been missing for so long, you just dump the bodies later. And what do we have? A bunch of cold cases. Who would have paid much attention if Cynthia hadn't been Judge Lenox's daughter?" Edwards got up to go for coffee. "Sure as hell, RHD wouldn't have been involved in the investigation."

Stas got a call from Molly on his cell around eleven p.m. She told him that dynamite charges were being set, and the demolition crew planned to take down the Talbott Cold Storage Facility within two days, so if the cops wanted to get in the building they'd better hurry.

"There's something funny going on," Molly continued, Ryan's lawyer's been calling all day, wanted to know if Ryan got some papers sent to the house. No one's heard from Ryan for two days. So I even called his hideaway and left messages, but he hasn't called back. He's supposed to be at the warehouse when they implode it."

"Has anyone seen Mona or any of her friends?" Stas asked.

"No, but Frank's been running around like a madman. He had a shouting match with someone on the phone in Paul's office. I couldn't hear what he was saying, but I think he was talking to Mona."

The next day, Edwards and Stas, joined by two cruisers for back-up, were assigned the Talbott's residence. Marlowe and Jonson, along with a SID team, were to check-out the storage facility.

Before they left, Boyer handed out the warrants.

Marlowe hesitated, brushing his Stetson.

"Did I miss something?" Boyer paused.

"Jonson's still at the dentist."

"You knew this earlier?" Boyer asked.

"Yeah, but knowing doesn't change anything. He'll be on his way."

Boyer looked over at Stas. "I sure hope so. You guys need to close this one ASAP. You and Edwards can get on it." He left them standing in the hall.

The drive to Hollywood in heavy traffic took almost an hour. When they exited the freeway, they heard the wail of sirens and the blast of fire engine horns.

"Shit, we'll never get past them," Stas said.

He navigated his partner through some short cuts that took them to Briarcliff, but Edwards had to slow and turn right on Taft. They were stopped at Foothill by a uniformed officer standing next to his black-and-white. Now they would be behind the engines and any other first responders.

Stas rolled down his window and flashed his ID.

The officer pointed up the hill. "There's a pretty big fire up there, just happened all of a sudden. Nobody's going up any time soon."

"It doesn't matter." Edwards turned to his partner. "I guess we're stuck here for the time being." He pulled to the side of the street and parked.

Stas got out of the car, stretched, and looked in the direction of the fire. Black clouds had started to rise above a red glow. Several television news choppers circled like vultures trying to avoid each other and the rising smoke. They would do anything to satisfy the public's morbid curiosity for gory details about mega-mansions engulfed in flames, and their super rich owners left homeless. Fine particles of ash started to drift to the street. Stas ran his hand through his hair to brush away the gray flakes that were beginning to fall like snow. As he started back to the car, he spied a smart red sports car parked on a side street that narrowly snaked up the hill. He walked over. A spidery swirl of smoke escaped through the cracked window. Inside, Stella stared ahead, nervously puffing on a half-spent cigarette.

He tapped on the window. "What are you doing up here?"

She rolled her window down further as she recognized the detective. "I'm waiting for...." Her eyes followed his as he looked into the back of the car, packed to the hilt with luggage partially covered by a jacket.

"You going on a trip?" Stas asked.

"No, I'm just waiting."

"Looks to me like somebody's doing some traveling. Why are you even here? There's a fire on the hill. You of all people should know the drill. Only emergency personnel...." He looked up the hill and back into the car. He unbuttoned his jacket and leaned in again. "Where's Mona?"

Before she could answer, Edwards was out of the Crown Vic and at the rear of the sports car. "It's the Talbott house that's on fire."

Stella started the engine.

Stas reached into the car, switched off the engine, and removed the keys. "Sid, go back to the car and get a unit over here." He stepped back to the car, put his hand on the roof, and opened the door. "Get out! Please!"

"What for?" Stella hesitated.

"I don't want to have to remove you."

She swung her legs out onto the pavement.

"I called for a black-and-white to take you to Hollywood Station and keep you on ice until the fire's out."

"You can't do that."

"Watch me." He took Stella to the car where Edwards helped her into the back seat. Stas went to the trunk of the Crown Vic, popped it, and took out his body armor.

Edwards watched as his partner fitted it over the passenger seat head rest so he could easily slip it on later. "You think we're going to need that?"

"I'm not taking any chances."

Both men got in the car, rolled up the windows, and turned on the air.

They waited in silence watching flakes of ash fall like some macabre storm from hell. After the uniformed officers finally arrived, it took another ten minutes for Stas to explain what he wanted them to do. When he finished, he wondered if they were new to the force or if they simply weren't that smart. Getting back into the car, he decided they weren't that new.

FIFTY-ONE

Despite the delay in Hollywood, Stas and Edwards were able to rendezvous with Marlowe, Jonson, and the two black-and-whites assigned to them in the vicinity of Mission and the Fourth Street Bridge. The building they sought was a three story gray brick that had been used over decades for various forms of cold storage. Its facade was posted with multiple signs: DANGER, KEEP OUT, NO TRESPASSING. A chain link fence blocked the front entrance and stretched along the length of the building that faced Mission Street; however, enough of the fence had been rolled back to allow access to the parking lot on the north side. A large Master lock hung open on the post.

The detectives drove their two cars into the asphalt area adjacent to the building. One black-and-white pulled-up next to the loading dock. The other one parked on the curb, blocking any further access to the parking lot. Once out of his Crown Vic, Marlowe unrolled the building's blue prints, spreading them on the trunk of the car. The plans indicated a business entrance plus two truck bays near a high, concrete block wall. Stas climbed on the loading dock and peered over the wall.

"What's on the other side?" Marlowe asked.

Stas jumped down. "Train yard, then the river." He got back into the car, sat in the passenger seat, reached back and slipped his bullet-proof vest over his head. Out of the car, he adjusted his holster and the side velcro tabs.

The other detectives followed suit and joined him at the side door which easily gave way under the effort of two forceful shoulders.

"Are we waiting for SID?" Edwards asked.

"They'll get here when they get here." Marlowe growled, rubbing his shoulder.

Once in the building, they took several steps to the main floor. Even though it was late afternoon, very little light filtered through open doorways that once led to offices. Evidently most of the doors, light fixtures, and anything salvageable had been removed. The detectives took out their Maglites and swept the walls and floor revealing patterns of muted footprints, along with marks left by scurrying feet of smaller inhabitants who roamed the dusty, deserted corridors at will.

Several pieces of broken furniture, along with the debris of half-eaten cardboard file boxes and animal droppings littered the floors. Birds fluttered about, disturbed by Edwards's light on the ceiling. Some flew out of broken windows when he scanned a large office with broken partitions. "Smells like shit in here."

"That's what it is." Jonson blew his nose into a handkerchief. "Bothers my sinuses."

After checking the offices, the four detectives and two uniformed officers gathered on the stairwell.

Marlowe had retrieved the building's plans and with help from his partner held them up against the wall. "Stas and Edwards, you do the lower level." He looked around to get his bearings. "Fur storage was on the other side, on this floor. Ice making and refrigeration units downstairs. Jonson and I'll do the rest of this floor. When you finish below, let's meet here unless you find something. Then we can do the next level."

Edwards moved in closer illuminating the upper portion of the plans. "Looks like more storage. What do we hope to find here? We should leave it to the techs."

Marlowe rolled up the plans and handed them to one of the uniformed officers. "You guys hold down the fort."

Edwards and Stas made their way down trash strewn steps. Stas had unholstered his gun and attached his light to it leaving his left hand free. When they descended into the lower level they were met with a pungent mingling of smells: stagnant water, mold, death, and decay.

Stas inhaled through his mouth. "Worse than the morgue."

Edwards focused his Maglite. Two bright beams illuminated a cavernous hall much larger than the corridor on the main level. The floor was damp with puddles of water that had collected under rusting and dripping pipes.

Stas stepped to the concrete floor and studied a heavy iron door at the far wall. Their roving lights revealed freshly dislodged gray plaster scattered in mounds around the hall. Large holes had been bored into strategic places in weight-bearing walls. He figured they were for the explosive charges that would soon bring down the building. Or they were already in place, just concealed from the untrained eye. "I don't like being down here if they've already set the explosives. Let's hurry-up and get the hell out of here."

"You think they placed the dynamite already?"

"I wouldn't want to make book on it."

They entered a large room festooned with streamers of cobwebs and spider-webs interwoven with remnants of broken pipes, some still dangling from broken connections in the walls and ceiling. Feeble rays of sunset from a few high windows cast a rosy hue onto pieces of sheet metal thrown aside from giant ice-making and refrigeration units.

They moved on, casting light into dark and empty spaces before entering another large room. Stas moved along the perimeter letting his light scan the far wall, before focusing his beam on a long, metal table with a cracked leather strap encircling its center. He zeroed in on its dusty, rusted surface. "Looks like the tables at the coroners."

Edwards stiffened. "You think they used it for the, the births?"

Stas coughed to stifle his growing rage. "I want those bastards!"

Edwards moved to a deep, galvanized sink against the wall. "What about prints?"

"I doubt it after all these years but put your gloves on just in case."

Edwards slipped on latex gloves before turning on a faucet. Brown water shot out with such force that it took both men to shut it off. He pulled an oblong enamel pan from several inches of water and held it up. "What do you think?" The once white surface had been eaten through in spots to black metal.

"In better days, it would be the right size for surgical instruments. Leave it for the techs."

As they moved on, Stas stood back to let Edwards force the heavy handle on a the metal and wooden door that opened into an adjoining room. They paused, repulsed by an eerie, imagined cold, before stepping into a giant freezer. Both men looked at each other, as if realizing what might have occupied this space within the last eight years.

Edwards raised his hand to his nose. "What's that smell?"

Stas sniffed the air. "I'm not sure."

"You think it's Freon or radon?"

"Freon's... odorless." Stas shrugged his shoulders. "Radon, maybe, I don't know. But there's a lot of mold in here plus whatever else we're stepping in."

Edwards focused a beam of light on the floor to ceiling lockers on the far wall. "You think that's where they kept the girls' bodies?"

Stas touched Edwards's sleeve keeping him from going any further into the room. "Let's get out of here and leave this for SID."

They backtracked and ascended the stairs to meet the others.

Even on the main level, Stas couldn't shake the chill. It was unearthly, generated by the idea that three young women had been frozen and kept in this desolate tomb.

"I'm positive they did it down there. The lab boys need to get their asses in gear." Stas joined Marlowe and Jonson as they headed to the third floor.

"What did you find?" Jonson asked on the way up.

"The place where they did the surgery and next to it, a walk-in freezer," Edwards said.

The four men moved to the third level as if weighed down by the gravity of what had been discovered on the lower level. With weapons drawn they started to check the first rooms at the head of the stairs when a blood curdling howl stopped them in their tracks. They heard a door open, followed by the sound of rushing footsteps. They cautiously moved to the end of the hall and were met with loud barks as they approached a partially opened door.

Edwards looked at his partner. "You think that's the dog?"

"Is he loose?" Marlowe stopped at the threshold.

In the room, a growl rumbled deep in the dog's chest.

Jonson slowly stuck his head through the door, aiming his weapon as he entered. "It's chained, and there's someone on a bed."

Marlowe followed his partner, his gun on the dog. "Okay, who wants to get him?"

Stas edged around the dog to the bed and ripped a wide piece of duct tape from the captive's mouth. It was Carroll who screamed, sucked in air, and exhaled. "Frank!" Another gasp for breath. "Frank...ran!"

Stas now knew what the previous sounds had been. "Son of a bitch!" He was at the door before anyone could stop him. "I'm going down," he shouted from the hall. "Get some air support on the river!" He found the back stairs and listened for movement as he slowly descended. Halfway down he heard the wrenching sound of a heavy metal door being opened. *Frank was going out the back.*

When Stas reached the lower level, he quickly realized that he was in a different part of the building. He focused his light on the far wall where a door stood open, yawning like some gigantic serpent's maw stretching to the river. Stas peered into the black void, then entered, his gun and light trained along the sides and center of the passageway. The ceiling was low. He bent and cautiously continued, slouching through a puddle of putrid water as his feet touched something soft. "Fuck!" Smells reconfirmed that there was a decomposing object right under his feet, while something wet and cold dripped onto his hair and ran down the side of his face. Tempted to rush, he maintained his pace until he felt a soft breeze warm his face, promising cleaner air. Faint light was visible at the passage's end.

When he emerged from the tunnel, he saw the LA skyline, heard the rumble of freight cars, and faced the outline of black tank cars standing in jagged rows like fat, stubby sentinels blocking his way. He stood still, then sensed movement to his left. A dark figure rolled under a tanker and disappeared for a moment in the rock bed of the tracks. When he rolled out from under the car, he stayed low, and moved south. *Frank. Gotta be Frank.*

Before advancing Stas glanced over his shoulder for his partner. No one! So much for Sid having his back. Stas moved to the first row of tankers, bent, and peered under a car, following the movements of the lone figure until it disappeared over a concrete rise and down to the LA River. There had to be a hole in the fence. Stas looked up and down the tracks for any sign of train movement before slipping under the nearest tanker.

On the other side, he stooped to repeat the maneuver with another tanker and heard a noise behind him, when he turned he saw the dog bearing down on him. Stas tried to roll under a car, but the dog broad-sided him, knocking him into a sharp piece of protruding metal. "Damn, damn...." He managed to stay on his feet, but felt a jabbing pain his thigh.

Up ahead the dog slowed and sniffed.

He's looking for Frank.

Still no sign of Edwards. Stas lost sight of the dog for a moment, but could hear the rattle of her chain being dragged along stones and concrete ties. Then he saw the German Shepherd slow until she picked up Frank's scent again. Stas passed around an end tanker and crossed the last set of track when he saw a flash of movement parallel to the fence separating the train yard from the river. The dog was running now, headed for the hole in fence. Stas was having trouble keeping up. Something had popped when he rolled under the last car. He could feel a wet, burning sensation in his left thigh but continued until he heard the painful howl of the animal echoing loudly across the concrete channel. He looked back across the train yard. Had the dog been shot?

Stas heard it before he saw it. A helicopter, drowning out other sounds, its bright stream of lights melding into the twilight as it flew over the 4th Street Bridge. Then he saw the head of the dog, his choke chain caught on a rebar that protruded from a broken concrete block. He also caught sight of a figure moving down the river bed. If he could escape through a storm drain, he'd be hell to apprehend. The helicopter hovered over the center of the river flooding Frank in its intensive light and stirring up the shallow flow of brackish water.

The figure stopped and stood, trying to brace himself against the power of the rotors that almost blew him over. He made a visible effort to remain upright, then slowly turned to retrace his steps. The helicopter lifted higher, still keeping the man in its bright lights. Had Frank heard the dog's distress? If not, had he sensed the dog's pain. Stas waited for him to climb the embankment to reach the strangling dog and release the caught loop of chain.

When Stas slipped through the gaping hole in the fence, he found Frank with the released dog nuzzling into her master's groin. He trained his Glock on Frank. "Secure the dog." He pointed to a post holding up part of the fence.

Frank stood shivering from the cold, mucky water, his trousers wet to his mid-thigh. The dog raised her head and growled at approaching footsteps on the coarse stones. Stas turned a split-second to see his partner approaching his gun pointed at the Shepherd.

"Fucking dog!" Edwards aimed and pulled the trigger. Nothing! The gun jammed.

In a split-second, the dog sprang covering the distance to Edwards knocking him to the ground. The gun flew. Frank dived across Stas's path as he sprang for the gun, the dog, or Edwards, but Stas swept Frank's legs from under him, sending him sprawling at Edwards' feet. Kicking the gun out of reach, Stas slammed Frank's head into the rocks, then turned his Glock on the dog.

"Don't shoot her." Frank tried to shout as blood oozed from his mouth and broken nose.

"Tell her to heel or sit or she's dead." Stas spit out the warning.

"Down, Dixie!"

The dog moved off Edwards and toward her master.

Stas still held his gun on Frank and the dog as he nodded for Edwards to cuff him.

Frank's hands started to shake. "I need to go back." He tried to get up, but Stas pushed him back down.

"You ain't going nowhere." The words were labored and strained. Stas's left leg was continued to hurt.

Frank struggled to rise, using his cuffed hands as leverage to push himself up. He almost made it on the second try, but Stas kicked him over.

"Dammit, stay down!"

"The girls! I know she's going to hurt them."

After cuffing Frank, Edwards seemed to have regained his composure and his gun. "What do you mean?"

Frank coughed, spitting blood. "Stella told me they were here with Dixie." Another bloody coughing fit. "Did you get the bitch?"

Stas shifted his weight, feeling his knee through the torn fabric of his trouser leg. "We got Stella but not Mona."

"Why do you care so much?" Edwards asked.

Frank ran his tongue over his teeth and spit again. "I liked the girls."

"Lupe thought you liked them a little too much, and I'm beginning to agree. Leave it to us and protective services. They'll take care of them. You got enough on your plate."

"Let their father worry about them." Edwards added.

"And who do you think that is?" Frank gave Edwards a hard glare. "It's ain't Ryan!"

" Is it Paul Lundstrom?" Stas asked.

"Nah, I was the one, gave Cindy drugs in Vegas. It was easy with her. Mona met us in Baker on the way back." Frank seemed to ease into confessing.

Stas felt sick as he started to understand Frank's role. "So what are you saying? You're one of the girl's father."

"They're both mine."

"What the hell do you mean?" Stas asked.

"I just told you. I did Cindy in Vegas. Ryan did the others, nothing, so he tried the other way. Nothing!"

"Bastard!" Stas wanted to lash out, pound Frank head into the gravel. "Did Mona kill them?"

Frank made a rising guttural sound that seemed to cause more blood to trickle from his nose. "Didn't have the guts. Got sick cutting off the ring."

Stas had to walk away as he holstered his gun. There were now enough officers present to secure the scene. Needing to lash out, Stas turned to Edwards. "You took your goddamn time backing me up."

"We had to.... I was...., the dog."

"And who am I, the fucking Lone Ranger?"

Marlowe joined the two detectives and observed Stas's limp. "You okay?"

"I'll live, but we got to go back to the house." Stas nodded toward Frank. "The others can finish with him."

Marlowe hooked his thumbs in his belt. "You need to get to the ER and let them take a look at you. Paramedics are at the loading dock."

Stas shook his head and moved toward the still tankers.

Edwards followed. "Can it wait? Why do we need to go back?"

"I was all wrong. Frank fathered the girls." Stas paused trying to find the best way over the tracks and back to the warehouse without causing his injured leg additional pain.

"We charging him with rape?" Edwards caught up with his partner.

"That and a whole list more. If he's convicted, he won't be going anywhere." Stas maneuvered with some difficulty around an end tank car and over tracks. He headed for an opening in a fence on the south side of the building where he was met with the bright lights of several cruisers and emergency vehicles.

Marlowe met him with the EMT.

"Does anyone know what's going on at the house?" Stas waved the attendant off. "Frank thought that Mona was going to kill them."

"That's crazy!" Edwards seemed to look around for support. None came.

Stas glared at Edwards. "Throw me the keys."

"You're in no condition to drive." Marlowe caught them in mid-air. "Com'on I'll drive if you promise to let them take a look at you afterwards."

Stas nodded, then took his time getting into the Crown Vic.

They were able to drive all the way to what was left of the Talbott house. The last of the fire crew was mopping up, trying to catch any flare-ups. The scene smelled of charred wood, burned metal, and rubber. The Coroner's van was still parked in the drive. Stas's felt a sinking in his gut when he got out of the car. Battalion Chief Thomas met them by the once profuse rose beds that were now trampled and flooded.

Marlowe produced ID, introduced himself and Stas as he fumbled under his vest to retrieve his. The chief waved them off.

"Who's in the van?" Stas asked pinching his nostrils, the acrid smoke burning his nasal tissue.

"Mona Talbott." Thomas turned back to glance at the house. "She didn't make it." He pulled an evidence bag out of his jacket pocket. "Seems she went back for this. It had rolled under the bed." It was a ring. "She got wedged in trying to get it. It was about two inches away."

"Was she the only fatality?" Marlowe asked.

The Chief nodded. "The husband's gone to the burn unit at Mt. Sinai."

"The girls?" Marlowe and Stas asked in unison.

"Luckily, they were with the housekeeper. She got here about fifteen minutes ago, so she's taking them back to her place tonight. You guys can sort all that out later. We have our own investigation to conduct. Whoever set it was good but not that good. Set devices in too many places in the house. Timing was off. The fire accelerated too quickly. We'll have it sorted out so you guys can file charges."

Marlowe followed the Coroner's van to Franklin where it turned left on its run to Mission Road. "Seems Frank couldn't stop talking on his way to booking."

"Yeah, he's worried about the girls."

Marlowe turned right. "It's a shame they saved Ryan from the needle."

"He'll get his day in hell." Stas's tone was cold. "He'll just have to wait awhile."

"I kinda felt sorry for Talbott, trying to please everybody," Marlowe offered.

"He should have stopped eight years ago, maybe he would've been around to have one of his own beers."

They rode in silence until they got to St. Joe's ER.

"What's with the ring?" Marlowe half turned to Stas.

"It's a long story, you can read it in the report. Well, maybe not. I'll tell you about it later after I finalize with the Captain,"

Stas managed a smile despite the returning pain. "It's ironic. The one thing she loved the most, she died trying to get back."

"I guess there's some kind of lesson there."

"Maybe."

FIFTY-TWO

Having stripped down to his black boxer briefs, Stas sat on a narrow gurney in a curtained cubicle in the ER waiting for promised meds. He neatly refolded his wrecked trousers and kevlar vest and placed them on a nearby stool. He took a closer look at the nasty purple bruise on his left thigh just above the knee. It looked awful. *Maybe Dina can work her magic again.*

Dr. Morgan pushed through the curtain and handed Stas an envelope. "Take these as directed for pain and stay off that leg for a few days. Can you manage that?"

Stas nodded.

"You drink?"

Stas looked at him questioningly.

"if you do, don't with these. I'm going to have the nurse give you a shot."

Marlowe stuck his head in the cubicle when the doctor left. "Amanda did get it wrong."

"What?"

"The shorts—said you were a Fruit of the Loom man."

"Not hardly. She never got past my belt buckle."

"Listen, I hope you don't mind, I called Dina to pick you up. I think you've had enough of your partner for one night. Also Boyer and Moore are on their way so we'd better get our stories straight, all our stories before they get here."

Stas reached for his torn pants. "My story's fine."

Marlowe closed the curtain and sat on the edge of the table. "No! It's got a few holes, and we need to plug'em."

"What's wrong?"

407

"The damn ring, for one. You didn't blink an eye when the chief told us about Mona and the ring. Why was that?"

Stas took a deep breath and started to slip his right leg into his pants. "It was the wrong ring."

"Wasn't it the ring she cut off the vic's finger? The one that you were suspicious of?"

"Well, yes and no."

"Nowak, don't play fucking games with me. I'm not Edwards." Marlowe looked at his watch. "Man, we don't have all night. We got to brief your partner if he's writing the report."

Stas looked down at his bruised leg and remembered the promised shot. "Well, I'm taking some time off, so he has to do his magic."

Marlowe edged closer. "Then tell me about the ring."

"I exchanged it."

"You did what?"

"I exchanged the real one for a fake."

"How the hell did you do that?"

"It wasn't easy, but I had a connection with the insurance company. He hooked me up with a fake. He didn't want that loss in his file. I exchanged it in the property room for the real one."

"Oh, shit!" Marlowe shook his head. "I can't believe this; don't tell me any more."

"Who has to know about the ring? Mona's not talking. It's just a piece of jewelry found near her body. We'll just keep it out of our report."

Marlowe rubbed his hand over his face. "Didn't your suspension sink in?"

"Didn't what sink in?" Edwards parted the curtain and stepped inside the cubicle.

Marlowe stood. "The importance of writing an excellent report, no holes, therefore, no questions. Do one of your numbers on it."

"Explain something to me. Why do all this to have a couple of kids?" Edwards asked.

"Family ego, money! She got money, house, and the..." Stas hesitated, when Marlowe's shook his head slightly, "bling. Plus, she got to run a modeling agency, well, run it into the ground, not to mention a rich husband who didn't give a damn what she did. And the old man, don't forget old man Talbott. He wanted grandchildren."

"But they weren't Ryan's kids," Edwards added.

"Yeah, we know that now, but with both men making donations—they had no way of knowing, and Mona wasn't telling them any different. She had a good thing going," Stas said.

"So they used Frank?" Edwards asked.

"Who did she have left that could give her the look? We don't know if Paul was willing, but good old Frank stepped up to the plate. Two took. They had no way of knowing the last vic was sterile." Stas eased his left leg into his pants. "What better place to keep the women than a boarded-up warehouse?"

Marlowe pulled back the curtain. "Yeah, maybe they'd still be there if Ryan hadn't gotten thirsty for his own brew."

"Okay, okay! Who took care of them? Why didn't workers know what was going on?"

Stas smiled. "One worker did, Frank. You and Jonson have fun wrapping-up."

"What's going to happen to Ryan?" Edwards asked.

Marlowe frowned. "Should have let him finish burning, now let's hope for the needle."

Jonson joined them, squeezing into the cubicle. "They think Mona's girlfriend set the fire. So there's probably enough to take to the ADA."

"Good! With no OIS, you and Edwards can draft the report," Marlowe added.

"Unless you want to add Sid's jammed gun," Stas interrupted.

"The Glock's a piece of crap."

"It's not the gun, Sid, it's not even you, it's your load. I told you not to use that cheap shit from the range." Stas tried to put his full weight on his left leg, then grimaced but shook off the pain.

"So everything is settled?" Marlowe glanced at Edwards. "Go write your best. Make the Captain and Boyer proud. Moore may even get a box of cigars and Boyer...."

"Gets to move permanently to the sixth floor." Jonson pulled back the curtain. "They got three cold cases solved for the price of one, and now Judge Lenox can rest in peace."

Ralph Townsend stood smoking outside St. Joe's ER. He crushed the butt when he saw Dina park the green Saab near the entrance.

"Hello, Dina," he called across the walk. "I certainly didn't expect to see you here."

He held the door and followed her into the waiting area. She avoided getting too close. His entire being reeked of stale tobacco. She looked around for Stas but was distracted by a couple of screaming children and a distraught mother holding a whimpering infant.

"Why are you here?" she asked.

"This is what I do, cover the cops." He smiled. "No pun intended."

Marlowe, who had been talking with a nurse, walked over and pulled Dina aside. He spoke in guarded whispers before returning alone to the cubicle.

"Did Stas get shot?" Townsend edged closer, filling the void left by the lead detective.

Dina jerked around. "No! I came to pick him up."

"Can I call you for a ride when my car breaks down?"

"Get serious. He was hurt. Detective Marlowe called and said they're not going to keep him. He'll just have to stay off his leg for a few days."

"Well, that shouldn't be too hard with you, uh, nursing him."

Dina was silent and tried to avoid his gaze as they stood watching the parade of late night casualties from the mean streets of LA.

Edwards was the first to move through the waiting area and stop at a vending machine. He fished in his pocket for change, his back to Stas and Marlowe as they headed for the exit.

Townsend didn't move from Dina's side when he saw a limping Stas approach. "Well, I guess he's at your mercy. If you ever get tired of him, let me know." Townsend handed her a card. "You deserve better. You deserve a Pulitzer Prize winner. The best he can do is get some damn commendation. Won't even get him a raise."

Dina dropped the card in her pocket.

"You never miss a beat do you, Townsend?" Stas said taking Dina by the arm and moving toward the exit.

"Can't afford to, not with my eye on the Prize."

The automatic doors had closed behind them leaving Marlowe still inside speaking with a shapely nurse. Edwards joined them as he blew on his steaming coffee. "Where's Stas?"

Marlowe looked around. "I think he left."

"When? How? I was going to give him a lift home."

"Dina picked him up."

"Dina? She was here? Where? I didn't see her!" Edwards almost spilled his coffee looking for her.

"She was standing over there talking with Townsend a few minutes ago."

"No, I mean I saw him with some woman. How was I supposed to know?"

Marlowe smiled. "I guess you missed out again, man."

FIFTY-THREE

Dina opened the door on the passenger side of her car. "What did the doctor say?" Teeth gritted, Stas replied. "To take a few days off. Keep the weight off my left leg." Coming around to the driver side, Dina got behind the wheel and headed out into traffic.

Easing the uncooperative limb, Stas settled into the passenger seat. "We have to take a little detour. I need to get some things from the house."

Dina looked over at Stas. "What house?"

"My folks'. Vlade left a message on my cell. Helena had a setback. They've put her in a nursing home."

"Why stop now? Can't it wait 'til later."

"Why not now? It's on the way. I'll give you directions. Anyway, it's his poker night. He won't be there."

Dina parked in front of the Nowak house and set the brake but made no effort to get out.

"C'mon, babe. This may be your only chance to see Hell House." He waited for her to join him on the sidewalk.

Taking his arm, she walked with him to the front door. Stas fumbled with his key ring until he found the right key and opened the door. Dina hesitated when cold, stale air, as if trying to escape into the night, met them at the entrance to the living room.. He took her hand and slowly led her to Helena's bedroom before switching on a light. The room was in perfect order except for a half-packed open suitcase on the made bed.

Stas went to the dresser, opened a drawer, and took out a box.

"What's that?"

"My scout medals. You know I made Eagle Scout." He handed Dina the box and turned out the light.

"We came here for these?"

"I was never allowed to have them, and I earned them. I don't want some bitch to toss them."

"Your sister would do that?"

"Now, you're learning.

When they walked through the dining room, they could see a light shining under the kitchen door. Stas moved towards it and pushed. Vlade stood by the fridge, drinking from a bottle of beer. He had on the same terry bath robe and hard Polish slippers that he'd been wearing the last time Stas saw him.

Vlade peered around the fridge door. "You been here long?"

"We just came in for my badges."

"We?" Vlade looked past his son to Dina who stood in the dark shadows of the unlit dining room.

Stas took her hand and pulled her into the glaring kitchen light.

Vlade closed the fridge door and ran his fingers through his mane of silver, unkempt hair. "Who's this?" His smile was warm, inviting, seemingly oblivious to his son's presence.

"This is Dina, Dina Goode." He turned slightly. "This is my father, Vlade Nowak."

She held out her hand. "It's nice to meet you, Mr. Nowak."

Vlade grip was strong, electric. "Call me Vlade." His gaze settled on her face. "I'm glad my son's found a real woman."

Dina moved closer to Stas as the door from the hallway swung into the kitchen, and a woman wearing only a clinging black silk slip walked in.

"Vlade, what's taking you so long?" Then she saw Stas. "You Stas?" She offered her hand. "I'm Maria."

"Yeah, I remember. You're one of Helena's bunco bud-dies?"

"I told Vlade..." she touched the arm of his bathrobe, "that I'd come over and pack up some of Helena's things for him." She then saw Dina. "Who's this?"

"Dina, Stas's friend." Vlade seemed to warm to the pres-ence of two women.

Maria stared. "You're not Polish, are you?" She turned to Vlade. "She's too dark to be Polish."

Stas grabbed Dina's arm and pushed her into the dining room. "No, she's not Polish, and we need to go."

They left Vlade and Maria standing in the middle of the kitchen.

"Bastard! He could have gotten someone else, not from her bunco!" In the car Stas shook a couple of pills from a paper packet into his mouth and leaned back before Dina started the car. "I didn't get my shot."

She looked over at Stas, his eyes closed, his jaws tight. "You have to just let it go. You can't go on judging him,... them for what they do or what they did."

His facial muscles relaxed a little. "It's not that easy. He's never stopped with the women and the closer the better. It's like he gets off on always having you guessing, thinking.... I even saw it in her eyes, the way he looked at you, almost baiting me. It only took a second." He closed his eyes.

"You got what you wanted from the house. We don't need to go back, then there'll be no one for him to play his little game with. And for what it's worth, I wasn't impressed." She put her hand on his thigh and felt him tense.

They drove the rest of the way in silence. Dina double parked in front of his building. "There's no space."

Stas felt for his keys. "Drive around the block. I'll open the gate."

Dina waited until a car behind her honked then circled the block and pulled into the garage entrance as the metallic gate swung upward. He was leaning against his Mercedes and beckoned for her to park in the space next to him. "Now what?"

He walked with her to the elevator. "I've got to change and get some directions. Then we're taking a trip."

"I can't go anywhere."

"Sure you can. Call that girl who works for you, Sindy. You don't want to miss this, having me all to yourself, flat on my back, for a couple of days in the mountains."

Dina smiled. "Hmmmm, that sounds promising. Maybe I can go, but I need to go home and pack."

"We'll get what we need on the way."

"I still need to go home unless you're taking an oath of celibacy."

Stas didn't smile.

"I need my pills. And suppose I don't like the mountains?"

"I wasn't planning to go out. I'm injured, remember? We'll make a fire and relax. The Captain told me to get some R and R."

"Whatever that is."

Stas smiled. "I'll show you. This will be just the place to sort things out. And I'll answer ten questions."

"Just ten?"

"Maybe more, I promise, scout's honor." He hoped his injury or the medication wouldn't affect his libido or his performance. He was glad to have Dina back in his life. *Am I ready for...I'm glad they didn't give me that damn shot.*